RACHEL L. SCHADE

RACHEL L. SCHADE

EMPIRE OF RUINS

CURSED EMPIRE 4

DRAGON SHADOW
PUBLISHING

Cover & map design by MoorBooks Design

ISBN: 978-1-7364856-6-8

www.rachelschadeauthor.com

OTHER BOOKS BY RACHEL L. SCHADE

Silent Kingdom Series

Silent Kingdom (Book 1)

Forsaken Kingdom (Book 2)

Broken Kingdom (Book 3)

Cursed Empire Series

Empire of Dragons (Book 1)

Empire of Traitors (Book 2)

Empire of Monsters (Book 3)

To the overcomers. May you smile through your tears. May you find freedom in love. May you be the ones to change your worlds.

PRONUNCIATION GUIDE

People

Lo'laeni (LO-lane-ee)
Nolanhou (No-LAWN-hu)
Jaliana (JAY-lee-ahn-uh)
Kovi (KOH-vee)
Ettonou (ETT-uh-new)
Caesiem (KAY-see-um)
Xalenos (Zuh-LEE-nos)
Revaed (Ruh-VAYD)
Pauni'a (PAWN-ee-uh)
O'emia (OH-em-ee-uh)
Mio'e (MEE-oh-ay)
Naina (NAYN-uh)
Karye (KAR-yay)
Ilowhe (ILL-oh-way)
Adriatus (AY-dree-at-us)
Marukio (Muh-ROO-kee-oh)
Yelaia (YUL-ay-uh)
No'haleo (No-HAY-lee-oh)
Olahni (Oh-LAWN-ee)
Ah'Koni (Ah-KOHN-ee)
Huvoki (HOO-voh-kee)
Meli (Muh-LEE)

Locations

Alrenor (Al-REN-or),
Alrenian (Al-REN-ee-uhn)
Forwyth (For-WITH),
Forwyn (For-WIN)
Teramyl (TARE-uh-mill),
Teramese (TARE-uh-meez)
Inalgoth (I-NEEL-goth)
Wenu (WEHN-ew)
Corapaxu (Core-uh-PAX-ew)

Other

Ryke (RY-kee)
Karos (Kair-OHS)
Elhani (Ell-HAN-ee)
Nesrelle (NEZ-rell)
Vylae (Vill-AY)
Kowra (KOW-ruh)
Hilvoku (Hill-VOH-ku)
Elha'tonu (ELL-ah-toh-new)

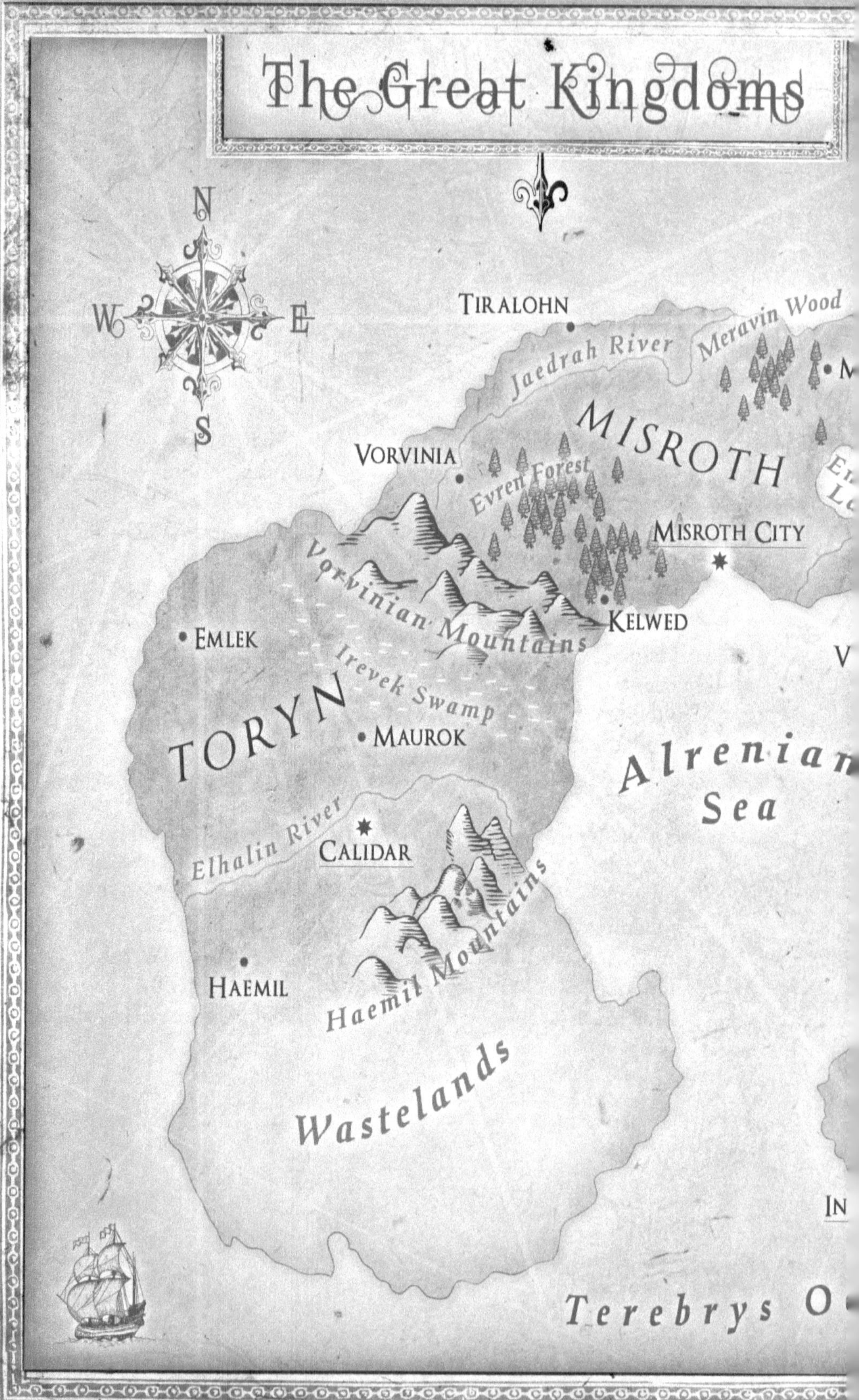

The Great Kingdoms
N
W
E
S
TIRALOHN
Jaedrah River
Meravin Wood
VORVINIA
MISROTH
Evren Forest
MISROTH CITY
Vorvinian Mountains
KELWED
EMLEK
Irevek Swamp
TORYN
MAUROK
Alrenian Sea
Elhalin River
CALIDAR
Haemit Mountains
HAEMIL
Wastelands
Terebrys O

The Lesser Kingdoms
Hült Mountains
HÜLTEN
Shüldi River
BREVINN
Brevi Mountains
Emrell River
GELON
Layvok River
Brema Wood
Wild Lands
Great Sea
ALRENOR
LAEN
ARAMITH
Brema River
Lorin Forest
Aramith Mountains
RHAEDA
Silondrian Mountains
FORWYTH
TERAMYL
Maelvor Forest
Xelrios River
VICIDOR
Tuiros River

CHAPTER ONE

Nesrelle, Empress of Death

THE CITY REEKED OF DEATH and ash, and I relished every breath. As I strode through the streets, I waded through puddles of blood and stepped over piles of corpses, charred beyond recognition. Blackened husks of stone buildings and shattered glass and channels of water tinted pink with gore—that was the sum of the dazzling white capital Inalgoth now.

It was perfection.

Smoke curled in the air, a constant haze that hovered over the city like a warning. *These streets belong to the Empress of Death now. See it and despair. Enter and suffer.*

Once, thousands had walked these streets, caught up in the division and hatred mortals always preoccupied themselves with. Now, all had perished, fled, or were in hiding—though most of those cowering souls had already been found and were our miserable captives.

Yet despite all of this, my faithful army was already growing restless.

I found Daedra beside a statue of the Life-Giver, his chiseled face gazing with cold disapproval upon the ashes drifting through the street. Her own eyes were nearly as dead as those of the marble effigy, her irises completely swallowed up by her pupils. Scales devoured a full half of her face, glistening in the dim, perpetual twilight of a city wreathed in smoke.

"When do we march on the rest of the empire?" she asked, bloodlust simmering in her gaze.

"Patience," I murmured, laying a hand on the Life-Giver's marble shoulder, injecting my power into the touch. Cracks spiderwebbed toward his face, crumbling it into pebbles that rained down at my feet. A smile pulled on my lips. "Success requires planning."

Daedra shifted, tossing her gaze toward the sky.

"Besides," I continued, "quick deaths aren't nearly as satisfying as slow torture. We want our victims to know the end is coming. To see and dread it."

Satisfaction settled upon Daedra's face. "So we can soak up their fear and pain."

"Exactly." I stalked toward a nearby bridge, setting my hands upon its charred stone railing and leaning over to watch a bloated corpse drift by. "Enjoy your playtime with our captives. Their fear is intoxicating. See if you can't sniff out more pathetic mortals hiding throughout this city—the capital is large enough that we can't have found them all yet. Let that be enough for you, for now. More death will come soon. And in the meantime, I have a visit to make."

I was gone before Daedra could comment, the air tugging at me as I envisioned my destination. Already, the Teramese emperor's thoughts called to me, a siren song beckoning me toward his suffering. Calling me to replenish my power in the presence of his despair.

Tucked away in a darkened room within an abandoned Hemlaen sanctuary, Revaed was sprawled out upon a settee, staring into the embers dying in the hearth across from him. His bloodshot eyes were glazed, studying nothing as he clutched a half-empty wineglass. His dark jacket had been cast aside, leaving him in nothing but an undershirt. Contrary to his usual polished appearance, he was a wreck, his tousled hair wild, his shoulders slumped.

Though on the outside, he appeared dejected and lost, rage boiled inside him. His thoughts were a tangled mess, full of loss and grief and the same pain of inadequacy and loneliness that had haunted him since he was a child. It was beautiful, poetic…almost enough to make tears swim in my eyes. But it wasn't enough, not yet.

Revaed didn't tug his eyes away from the fire as he spoke, his voice deadpan. "Ah, you again. You're not like any goddess I've ever heard about."

I shuffled forward, my bare feet leaving a trail of blood in my wake. My black dress, embroidered with gold, fire-breathing dragons mimicking Teramyl's sigil, whispered along the polished stone floor. "Oh yes," I said, "Tuiros, your god of death who looks like a hunched old man." I snorted in disgust. "Or Xeli, goddess of pain, who has the gnarled face of a hag." I stretched my arms wide, drawing his violet eyes toward me. "Did your people never consider that death could be beautiful?"

Revaed huffed out a humorless laugh. "Is that why you're here? To take me away to some underworld now that you've slaughtered my people?"

"Unfortunately for you, you still have more time left to live."

Sipping his drink, Revaed gestured about the empty bedroom. His guards shifted outside, but they couldn't hear us. I'd made sure of that. Not that there was anything they could have done to stop me. "Then what does some goddess of death want with me? Did you bring another heart?" His lips twisted in a mirthless smile. "Are you here to raze this city as well?"

"Most hearts left in Inalgoth have been burnt to ashes, I'm afraid," I murmured. "And no, I'm not waging another battle—yet. I'm here to discuss what's troubling you."

Revaed's brow pinched. "That would take a lifetime." He flicked his gaze toward me. "And you don't strike me as a goddess—or whatever you are—who enjoys listening to the pleas of mere mortals."

"I'm here to discuss *one* of the things that is troubling you," I clarified. "Your beloved heir, Caesiem."

Revaed's throat worked as he set his glass down on the table beside him, the embers of his fury stirring into something hotter. Life sparked in his eyes again. "Is he dead? Did you kill him?"

"I rarely resort to killing, young emperor. I merely usher the dead into—"

His voice pitched low and threatening, but he was unable to conceal the way his words trembled. "What did you *do*?"

I rolled my eyes. "He's not dead. He left you for the girl."

"He wouldn't turn his back on Teramyl," Revaed bit out, but doubt darkened his expression. His thought echoed clearly in my head: *He gave her his pendant.* His grief was all-consuming. After all these years, the one living person in his family who didn't hate him had abandoned him.

I cocked my head to the side. "You feared all along this could happen, once you saw he loved her. Are you so surprised he chose her people over yours? That he chose *her* over you?"

Revaed turned back toward the fire, his back rigid. Motionless, with his hands clutching his knees so tightly his knuckles blanched white.

Striding closer, I leaned in and whispered, "And how do you suppose he will aid her people, when you are the one who stands in their way? How will that battle go, I wonder?"

Repressing a shudder, he turned to me, eyes glistening with unshed tears full of loathing. I drank in the sight, inhaling the misery permeating the air. "He loves me. He wouldn't threaten me. He's…he's family. He knows I love him."

"You love him, yes, but you've also used him, and he knows about that. He's hurt, and he's dangerous. So now you must choose: whom do you love more? To whom do you owe the deepest loyalty? Caesiem, or your people?"

He leaned back, seizing his glass to take another swig. A few droplets spilled, dripping down his shirt, staining it like blood. He didn't seem to notice. "You're more twisted than the gnarled old hag we call the goddess of pain," he muttered. "Aren't you?"

I picked at my nails. "Call me what you want, but you know I speak the truth. This is why you sit here, cowering in Hemlaen, unable to think clearly. To plan. I thought leaders made the difficult choices. Survival above all else, correct?" I grinned. "What about survival for your people? Would you throw all that away for one measly heir?"

I knew the memories that were flashing through Revaed's head in that moment. The lashes he'd taken for Caesiem. The sleepless nights of worrying about him. The people he'd killed to protect him. The lies he'd told, thinking he could spare the boy pain. But in the end, he'd still manipulated Caesiem, even if he'd had good intentions.

Even mortals with good intentions wreaked plenty of chaos and damage.

Revaed's gaze was hard. "What does the goddess of death know of survival?"

"More than you would imagine," I breathed. "After all, I don't wish everyone to die."

He blinked, his churning thoughts turning skeptical.

I smiled, dipping my tone into something heartbreakingly gentle. "If everyone died, who would be left to suffer?"

Rising with a snarl, Revaed lifted his wineglass to toss it at me. "You sick, sadistic bi—"

I was gone before he'd finished his sentence, letting the glass shatter harmlessly as I returned to the glorious ruins of Inalgoth.

CHAPTER TWO

Jaliana of Alrenor

I KNEW HE WAS APPROACHING from the pattern of his footsteps even before the door creaked open, before his gold-flecked eyes met mine.

His jaw tensed, and remorse dimmed his gaze. The rumble of his words flooded the dank, shadowy brig with his musical accent.

"Jalie." Kovi stepped inside, closing the heavy door with a thud that reverberated through the floorboards groaning and shifting beneath my feet.

I tried and failed to force a taunting grin to my face, but it felt more like a grimace.

He betrayed you, Nesrelle's voice whispered. *Don't grieve over your enemy. He never loved you. He was always using you. He's probably here to command you again with his magic.*

Tension flooded my body, stiffening muscles that ached from hunching against the wall, gazing blankly at my wrists, which were shackled in front of me. I wanted to hate Kovi, and perhaps the part of me that Nesrelle controlled *did* hate him, but the corner of my heart that was all my own ached. I'd known better than to open up to my enemy. Mother had taught me better.

How could I have ever believed Kovi cared?

I'll fight for you. Always.

Those words taunted me, simmering in the air between us like an invisible barrier.

"What do you want?" My voice cracked from disuse. Time held no meaning in this dark, windowless space. Apart from the regular meals brought to me by a Forwyn woman who never spoke, never made eye contact, and a couple visits from a healer who'd threatened to leave me untended if I tried to hurt him while he cared for my wounded fingers, I hadn't even seen another soul since I'd been locked in the bowels of this Teramese ship.

Kovi's eyes flitted to my shackled wrists, briefly, before returning to my face. When I pushed with my power, sifting through his mind, I didn't detect fear of the curse I carried. Only fear of…me. He feared my touch itself, without the curse's effects. He dreaded the memory of my hand splayed against his chest, over his thundering heart. He ached at the thought of my fingers threaded through his, of the warmth of my body, of the taste of my kiss.

My mouth went sour, and I tugged my gaze from his. He didn't have a right to grieve the closeness we'd once shared, not when he'd been the one to break his promise to me. After that first awful time he'd used his magic against me, back when we'd first been enemies, he'd vowed to never command me again. I'd been a fool to trust him, to think he'd ever been anything but my enemy.

For a long moment, Kovi didn't move, didn't speak. Curiosity drove me to crane my neck and drink in the sight of him. Clothed in Aerekni red and gold that contrasted with his smooth, dark skin, he cut the perfect figure of a loyal soldier. Beautiful. Powerful. Untouchable.

Pain lanced my soul. *We always made it clear our people would come first,* I reminded myself.

See? Love is a lie, Nesrelle crooned.

My chest was hollow. I wanted to hate the so-called Empress of Death and her taunting words, but despite her betrayal, despite what she'd done to Inalgoth and my army, she was also the only one I had left. Only Nesrelle and the ghost of my mother kept me company in this brig. Only they shared in my hatred of the Teramese and Forwyn. Only they reminded me of my purpose to rescue my people from further destruction, to prevent another Alrenian city from burning to ash.

Kovi held his hands out, palms up. It was the most uncertain he'd ever appeared around me—he who had always seemed so sure in his convictions, so dedicated to his purpose. His gaze dropped again to my hands, but this time I realized his eyes lingered on the bandages wrapping my injured fingers, the ones that Revaed had severed. "No one else likes to risk their life to visit you, and it's time to change your bandages. I volunteered."

Bitterness coated my words. "Why would you do that? So you could control me again, or so you could tell me more lies?"

Kovi's usual soldierly mask fell back over his face, shutting me out. "You know it wasn't like that," he said. "I didn't *want* to break my promise."

"But you did," I retorted, sucking in a deep breath. I wanted to say more, but my chest hurt, full of too many swirling emotions for me to know which one to concentrate on.

Instead of responding, Kovi stepped closer. He gestured silently for me to stand as he drew out a pair of scissors from the inner pocket of his jacket. My heart hammered against my ribcage as he took my hand, his fingers steady and gentle as he cut through the old bandage and inspected my wound.

I flinched inwardly at the sight of my severed fingertips, but I was thankful that regular care seemed to be preventing infection. Slowly, Kovi applied an ointment that I knew would help with my pain, and then he wrapped my hand with a fresh bandage. The whole time, neither of us spoke.

As soon as he finished, Kovi stepped back, as if he couldn't wait to place distance between us. And yet…he didn't leave. "You broke your promise first," he said at last, his voice low, his gaze piercing. "You tried to kill a Forwyn. You broke our alliance."

I glared. "That Forwyn girl is my mother's *killer*. Surely you didn't expect me to let her go free? But I suppose I should thank you," I continued, renewed pain swelling. "When you broke your promise and controlled me, you reminded me of who you truly are. I can't believe I ever let myself fall for your deceptive—"

It was Kovi's turn to interrupt. "No." In two long strides, he was in front of me, pressing me against the wall, so close his breath whispered across my face. I wanted to hate it, to hate him.

Instead, I leaned in, my eyes dipping perilously toward his mouth.

Weak, Nesrelle scoffed. I could feel her influence clutching at me, as if she were straining to possess every last piece of my soul. But something about Kovi's presence grounded me, reminding me of who I was when I wasn't Nesrelle's executioner. When I wasn't lost in her dreams of vengeance and bloodlust, but was lost in Kovi's dreams of mercy and peace instead.

"I meant everything I said," Kovi murmured. "Just like I meant every promise I ever made." His throat worked as he swallowed. "*Please*, Jalie," he whispered. "Don't listen to the Dark Immortal. Don't fight against my people. I know your heart, and I know you want more than this. Choose our future—our dream. Choose us."

Maybe it was just his magic binding us, something in the way he had once been connected to my feelings that also drew us inevitably toward one another. That was what I tried to tell myself as my pulse thundered in my ears, as my breaths quickened, as our traitorous bodies pulled us closer together. Fevered and desperate, as if some part of our hearts hadn't yet caught up to what our minds had realized.

This could never be.

I knew it, but I kissed him anyway. I kissed him with every ounce of my heart that still belonged to me—that still belonged to him. We were a clash of contradictions. We were pain and joy, loss and hope. Each brush of our lips was fierce and angry, yet gentle and sweet.

Kovi cupped my scarred cheek with the softest of touches, his calloused fingers tracing the freckles that dusted my cheekbone. Something told me he was memorizing this moment, memorizing my face, as if bracing himself for an inevitable goodbye.

But I couldn't stop thinking about what Kovi had said. *He wants you to let your mother's killer live?* Nesrelle sneered. *He wants you to dishonor your own family? To choose him blindly, letting him control you with pretty words and kisses while his people fight against everything you believe? You know he won't even let you take the throne. He'll steal everything from you, all while distracting you with…this.*

"No," I said, breaking our kiss as suddenly as it had begun. "Lo killed my mother. I can't ignore that."

Kovi's eyes searched mine, pain darting across his face.

He's only hurt that you see through his lies, Nesrelle warned me.

"Then we can't do this," Kovi said, stumbling back. "I can't…" He shook his head, looking so overcome, so lost, that for an instant I doubted everything. What if Nesrelle was wrong? What if Kovi hadn't wanted to break his vow, and had felt like I'd forced him to?

I gritted my teeth, bracing myself as if for a physical blow. *No, I* thought. *Kovi is like his father. He has too much power, and he craves more. He's just subtler, more manipulative in the ways he seizes it. But he's using me just as Elder Ettonou did.*

Already, I could feel Nesrelle stretching, digging her claws further into me. The tender side Kovi had awakened was slipping away, plunging into darkness.

He was the last of my light, and he was going to extinguish it.

"I didn't want to command you," Kovi went on, and his voice trembled. *Trembled.* In the shadows, the gold flecks of his eyes seemed to glisten, and I realized they were tears. His gaze darted to my shackles. "I *don't* want to leave you locked up like this. I never wanted it to come to this." Drawing a deep breath, he stepped back even further.

Ice flooded my veins where before there had been a rush of heat. I knew this was it. This was where he drew the immovable line between us. This was where he declared that he was right, and I was wrong, and he could never stray into the darkness I'd aligned myself with. This was where he finally admitted that he couldn't save me, that I would always be Nesrelle's monster.

His monster.

He deserves your hatred, Nesrelle breathed, making the hairs rise on the back of my neck. I could feel her pull on me, drawing me toward her drive for bloodlust and chaos. Fueling my need for vengeance.

"But you threatened my people," Kovi went on, his words growing steadier. There was no trace of tears now, making me wonder if I'd imagined them. "You tried to kill Lo, the daughter of my general. And I can't turn my back on my people. Our alliance is over. Whatever…whatever was between us has to end too."

Before I could retort, he turned on his heel and left, the door rattling shut behind him.

All that is left for you is your throne, Nesrelle said, as I stared blankly into the darkness. *Forget him.*

Squeezing my eyes shut, I banished the memory of Kovi's hurt expression and forced myself to concentrate on what I had to do next. And this time, I couldn't let anyone—not even Kovi—get in my way.

CHAPTER THREE

Caesiem Adriatus

IT'S NOTHING BUT A CITY of ash and bones." Huvoki Mo'luhk—one of the soldiers from Aerekni Academy—voiced the obvious thought swirling through our minds as we stopped and stared. Though we'd meant to pause to survey the city and formulate a plan, none of us spoke. All thoughts of preparing were, for a few tense, awful moments, forgotten.

Even if Inalgoth wasn't exactly my home, my stomach still clenched at the sight laid out before us. It was sheer devastation, the air thick with ash and the lingering stench of flame and death. Even some of the stone buildings lining the street were lumpy, mishappen masses, their walls and glass melted by the intense heat. Apparently Nesrelle's unnatural army had the ability to wield fire as fierce and hot as dragon flame. Many other buildings, including the cobblestone streets, were blackened with a mixture of scorch marks and a layer of debris.

At my side, Vander was tense, his silver eyes wide with horror. His hands twitched, as if he were reaching for his wind magic out of habit…as if it could do anything in the wake of a lost battle. Out of the four of us Teramese who'd fled the battle with the Forwyn, only he and I had been permitted to join this scouting party. Vander's sweetheart, Tayla, and his sister Valentra had remained on the ship, doubtlessly watched closely by everyone aboard.

Huvoki glanced toward Kovi Ettonou, the solider who'd

commanded Empress Jaliana to stop when she'd nearly killed Lo. Kovi seemed to be close to General Ilowhe, and the academy troops clearly looked to the young man as a leader. Given the powerful compulsion magic he'd wielded against the empress, I wasn't surprised. I'd trained among countless mages, and I'd witnessed the Forwyn nuns' magic within the Circle of Serenity, but I'd never seen anything quite like what Kovi could do.

"The dark army is crawling northward. Something caught their interest." The melodic voice of Meli jolted us all from our thoughts as she shifted on her feet, the afternoon sun accenting the golden highlights glimmering on her dark skin. That flash of gold was a reminder that she was both Forwyn *and* Alrenian. She blinked in concentration, as if caught in a vision induced by her truth gift. "They're in one of the northern districts beyond the palace."

Huvoki scowled almost imperceptibly, as if annoyed Meli had spoken before he could ask Kovi what their next move would be. Maybe he'd forgotten the general had agreed to let her join our party. Maybe, with her Alrenian blood and gift, he didn't fully trust her yet.

Our party was one of many, but as General Ilowhe had chosen different scouts each day, it was our first time viewing the aftermath of Inalgoth's destruction. Seven days had passed since Nesrelle and her army had taken over the capital, and this was also the first time anyone with Alrenian blood—or Teramese, for that matter—had been included. I wasn't sure if I should be flattered that perhaps the general was starting to trust me and my intentions, or worried he was hoping I'd be killed on our mission.

"Then now is the perfect time to move, since the general wanted us to inspect the palace and grounds itself," one of the other Forwyn soldiers said. I hadn't caught her name, but she, like Huvoki and Kovi, was near my age. She wore her ribbons braided around one wrist rather than in her hair, which she kept in a tight bun.

"Meli," Kovi said in a steady voice, not removing his eyes from the city, "can you tell if they left anyone within the palace to guard it?"

Meli sighed, her shoulders slumping as she shook her head. "I can't tell, but it looked like a significant portion of their troops had left. Our best guess was that there were about a hundred that invaded Inalgoth, correct?"

Kovi's lips thinned. "I don't think any of us can make an accurate guess, when they were scattered throughout the city. And there's no telling how many joined them later." He crossed his arms. "There were…many more than that when Vander and I originally found them."

His dark eyes strayed toward my friend, appearing wary. There was clear tension between them. Kovi didn't trust any of us Teramese. "Would you agree?" he asked Vander hesitantly.

My friend nodded, no hostility in his expression. He'd told me more than once that he'd grown to respect Kovi on their mission to capture Jalie, even if they hadn't exactly been on the same side. "I agree. We need to be cautious."

"And can you sense anything in the air?" Kovi pressed.

Vander shook his head regretfully. "There were so many passing through in the recent battle, and the air is so tainted, it's difficult for me to be sure of anything. I'm sorry."

Kovi sighed, as if deciding to trust my friend. "It's all right. But warn us if you do sense anything." Then he pinned his gaze on me. I didn't have anything against him personally, especially not when he'd protected Lo, but it was obvious he held nothing but disdain for me. Maybe that was why I felt an irresistible tug on my lips, and the uncontainable urge to smirk at him.

He didn't react to my insolent expression, his face remaining as expressionless as stone. "Are you *certain* that all of your people retreated?"

Vander stiffened and rounded on Kovi, his silver eyes blazing. "You will address my prince with respect. His word is good. Whatever you think of the Teramese in general, know that we don't make vows or promises lightly. They are binding.”

I seized Vander's arm and tugged him back. “Your loyalty is appreciated, but unnecessary.” This time, my smile was forced. “Besides, I don't think most of the Teramese citizens would call me their prince now.”

Kovi watched us impassively.

“I'm certain,” I continued, my voice firm and unyielding. “Sephrode—the water nymph—saw them on the western coast, following the Alrenian, mere days ago. And it fits Revaed's character. He wouldn't risk his people by lingering once a battle was lost.”

Huvoki snorted. “What a caring tyrant.”

Meli settled a hand on my shoulder. “Caesiem is right. Despite the evils he committed against our peoples, Revaed is dedicated to his own citizens. If there's anyone near the palace now, it'll be Nesrelle's servants.”

With a sharp nod, Kovi turned and beckoned to us, and we formed a ring around him. A half dozen strong, we were small enough to infiltrate the city and hopefully go unnoticed, but we were made up of enough skilled soldiers and mages to repel an attack.

“This is how we'll approach the palace,” Kovi began, launching into a careful strategy.

Rubble crunched beneath my boots as I scanned the area, frowning at the fallen trees and charred remnants of oranges and lemons from the once-vibrant imperial garden. The palace grounds were as desolate as the rest of the city. Not a breath of life stirred within them. Even the lizards and birds seemed to have abandoned the space.

The air was heavy and oppressive, not just with the stink of smoke and death—though there was no sign of any corpses, with all either charred to ash or cleared away—but also with a sense of dread. My skin prickled. Portions of the palace buildings, along with some of the once-pristine white columns, had melted into shapeless forms, leaving numerous walls crumbling or tilting precariously. The main building that led to the throne room, however, appeared mostly unharmed.

One part of my mind stretched toward the distant water, the crash of waves dull from this height, as I approached the double doors. We'd all split up to scour the grounds for any survivors or helpful resources, and I couldn't help but wonder again if Kovi had intentionally suggested I search alone in hopes I'd be ambushed and killed. A wry smile tugged at my lips while I shoved open one of the doors.

The hallway was empty, with a high ceiling adorned with paintings and walls lined by columns. Beneath my boots, the marble floor glistened without a trace of soot or grime. At the end of the hall, another set of carved double doors led into the throne room.

Again, my skin prickled as if in warning, and I could have sworn the temperature dropped. I set a hand on my sword hilt and started forward with the same cautious grace I'd once used when pickpocketing for my survival. I was as quiet and unobtrusive as a shadow. When I set my hand on the door, I pulled it open with aching slowness so it wouldn't creak.

You're being absurd, I told myself as I peered through the crack. *It's abandoned.*

My gaze swept over the circular throne room. The glass ceiling remained untouched, allowing golden sunlight to fill the space. Shadows from the massive columns extended across the floor like wraiths stretching for something forever out of reach.

But the room was empty.

I sank back, feeling a little ridiculous that the atmosphere had put me on edge. More than that, I was annoyed that Kovi had requested I search this building first, of all places. It was unlikely that any survivors of the battle would have sought refuge here, especially with our enemies occupying the space, and the throne room certainly didn't hold any food or medicine.

"Leave no space untouched," Kovi had insisted. "The dungeons are below the throne room. Maybe the Dark Immortal has some survivors she's keeping there." He'd scowled at the thought.

But when he'd insisted I check the throne room first? I'd clung to the belief it was a waste of time. Rolling my eyes, I turned.

A woman with skin nearly as pale as the marble floor beneath her and hair as red as flame stood near the entry doors, as if she'd been there the whole time. Her blue eyes studied me intently, curiously. Like I was a display in a museum or a book on a library shelf.

I recognized her from before the invasion on Inalgoth, when she'd brought a bloody heart as a so-called wedding gift.

"Gods," I swore, furious I'd been taken by surprise. Had she materialized out of the air itself?

But the woman before me—Nesrelle, or the Dark Immortal as others had called her—only smiled. "Quite the opposite," she crowed.

Gritting my teeth, I concentrated on the sea. The rush of waves filled my ears, as steady and familiar as the pounding of my own heart. The salty tang stung my nose, grounding me.

"I meant to thank you, young prince," she said, her eyes gleaming. "You set the stage for so many deaths and so much pain in this empire." She inhaled deeply, like she'd been deprived of fresh air for too long and was savoring every breath. "The despair and sorrow have been absolutely…intoxicating."

My stomach lurched, and I set my jaw. "I don't serve you."

Her smile was sharp as a knife. "Are you sure? You've killed and shed blood and wrought terror. And all of that has increased your power more and more, hasn't it?"

I narrowed my eyes, fisting my hands. In my distraction, my connection with the water was severed, but the way Nesrelle was goading me made my fear disappear. Instead, it was swallowed by rage—cold, hard fury fueled by my endless guilt.

She was right.

"Your own people feared you and the darkness within you," Nesrelle grinned, crooning the words as a mother would a lullaby. She shuffled nearer, nearer, until I could see the shadows enveloping her in a cold, consuming aura. Until her eyes appeared less blue and more black—vast endless pits leading into despair. "Every kill increased your reputation. If the other mages and soldiers didn't respect you, at least they feared you, didn't they?"

My throat was tight. The room grew increasingly chillier, or maybe that was my own skin, slick with sweat yet ice-cold. "I didn't kill for power," I insisted.

"And yet it brought you power anyway." Nesrelle's smile reminded me of something sickly-sweet and utterly nauseating.

"So you're just here to taunt me?" I spread my arms wide, almost inviting her to attack. That seemed preferable to this. Gazing at her felt like peering into a mirror, filled with the deepest darkness lurking within me. Every reminder that the Forwyn were right to hate and distrust me, and that I wasn't worthy of Lo, would never be. That maybe, intentionally or not, I had served this Dark Immortal, and I had played a vital role in the fall of the Alrenian Empire.

"I'm here," Nesrelle said, pausing to lick her sharp teeth, "to remind you of who you are, and to thank you. Your pain and despair strengthen me too, as much as the blood you've shed has. And also to tell you that your precious guardian is hurting and angry. You should be wary of that." Her eyes shone wickedly.

I flinched. My emotions surrounding my guardian were still muddled and confused, full of betrayal and fury and aching sorrow. Did he hate me? Would I have to face him in battle now that I planned to fight alongside the Forwyn? Had he ever loved me like a son, like a friend, or had his love always been contingent on what I could do for him, how I could be a weapon in his arsenal?

"Wonderful things are coming," Nesrelle replied with a wink, as if she'd read my thoughts and relished the pain within them.

"Whatever you say," I snarled, "I don't serve you anymore. I won't."

She laughed lightly. "I promise, I'm not done with you, and you are certainly not done with me."

As quickly as she'd appeared, she vanished.

CHAPTER FOUR

Kovi Ettonou

MY SHOULDERS SLUMPED WITH THE weight of failure as I took in the destruction enveloping the once-beautiful palace buildings and gardens. Flowers Jalie had once picked, had once loved for their beauty and the memories they brought her, were now nothing but piles of black ash scattered in the dirt. Every time I closed my eyes, I watched the capital burn, smoke snaking over the buildings like a living thing, heavy and oppressive.

And each time I'd tried to sleep for the past week, I'd watched Rhi'il die in my arms again, blood spilling from his lips. I'd seen my cousin Marukio fall in the fight at the academy. I'd witnessed Jalie's expression of hurt and betrayal when I'd used my magic on her at the end of the failed battle for Inalgoth.

Everything I'd dedicated my life to was crumbling.

Worst of all, I couldn't shake the knowledge that I'd failed my best friend. I couldn't have saved Marukio, couldn't blame myself for Father's traitorous actions and the Teramese attack on the academy—but I could blame myself for Rhi'il's death. If it hadn't been for my mistakes, Rhi'il might still be alive. I'd let myself become consumed with the desire to punish my father for what he'd done to Jalie, for how he'd made her suffer. I'd let vengeance and anger consume me, rather than mercy.

When I'd had the chance to do the right thing, I'd been distracted with a vain hope of justice in a dark, ruthless world.

Huvoki detected the downward spiral of my thoughts while we approached the Dragon Keep. Emptiness filled my chest as memories of Jalie's delight and wonder over the dragons swept over me. My friend's eyes flicked to mine, over and over, his mouth opening and closing as if he wanted to speak, but knew words were worthless.

My earlier visit with Jalie wouldn't stop haunting me. I could still taste her mouth on mine, and I knew the memory of our final, searing kiss would be one I'd carry to my grave. The pain of regret cut me to the bone.

I was convinced I should have known better than to hope for a better outcome, and yet…

And yet…what was life without hope?

Part of me longed for the connection to her emotions I'd once had, forged after the first time I'd used my commanding magic on her. Somewhere along the way, probably when she'd almost died and only Nesrelle's power had saved her, my ability to sense her feelings had been broken. Now, even though I'd used my magic on her again, the connection was still gone. I suspected it was because Jalie was hardly herself anymore, lost instead in Nesrelle's powerful influence.

It was just another sign that I had lost her.

Lift your head, Kovi. Mother's oft-repeated phrase to me as a child echoed in my mind, and I forced myself to follow the instruction. I tilted my chin, meeting my friend's gaze as he waited at the Keep's mouth, wanting me to take the first step forward. To prove I was alert and ready.

There wasn't a sound. No enemies stirring nearby, no survivors, no dragons. Nothing. This mission felt as fruitless as all my efforts to strive for peace and mercy had been. To dream of a world where Jalie and I could be together, where my love for her wouldn't end in brokenness.

"Am I a fool, Huvoki?" I murmured. I'd already told him before of my failed visit with Jalie, of my hopes for an alliance between Alrenians and Forwyn.

But there was no world in which Jalie and I could be together, and despite the few Alrenians that Meli had brought with her to join our cause, imagining more living alongside us in peace was so preposterous it was almost laughable.

I had to let Jalie go. I had to atone for my mistakes, for chasing so recklessly into the palace after her and letting Rhi'il get captured in the first place. If I hadn't, perhaps he would have been surrounded by our brothers and sisters in battle, not singlehandedly trying to fend off traitorous former Elders and Revaed.

And if I hadn't been so caught up in the idea of preventing my father from harming Jalie ever again, maybe I would have rushed to Rhi'il's side sooner.

I'd committed my life to serving my people. Again and again, I'd vowed to put them first. But every one of my mistakes before and during that battle were rooted in one painful fact: I'd put Jalie first.

I couldn't ever do that again. Not now, when she'd proved exactly who she was. The water nymph's eerie warnings echoed in my ears, and another chill washed over me. *You still think death is the worst fate that can befall the ones you love.* I'd worried that Jalie was dead, back then. Now I realized perhaps that wasn't the worst way to lose her. Losing her to Nesrelle…I feared the living nightmare Jalie's life would become, bound to the Dark Immortal.

Everything between Jalie and me had always been ill-fated.

I shut my eyes, trying to block out the image I carried of her, hurt shining in her blue and gold eyes.

She hates your people, and she likely hates you now too. She's given herself to Nesrelle and vengeance. It's over.

Huvoki cast me a look that bordered far too close on pity. I gritted my teeth and straightened my spine.

The trouble with spending years living in close quarters with my friends, studying and training alongside them, was that it was impossible to conceal much of anything. Even when I tried to guard my thoughts and feelings, it was always easy for my best friends—Huvoki, Mhel, Oru, and Rhi'il—to read me. They could look at me and see straight through to my tangled, messy emotions.

"I'm sorry, Kovi," Huvoki murmured. "I don't think you're a fool. Just a man." He shrugged. "Love can cause us to…err, sometimes." He cast me a pointed look. "You might not have said it outright, but for reasons I don't understand, it's clear you love her."

Smiling bitterly, I nodded. "She wasn't…what I expected. And beyond falling for her, I even let myself think she and I—our relationship—could be the key to peace between our peoples. That maybe we could unite our forces, even temporarily, and fight off the Teramese. I let myself dream."

Huvoki shrugged again, uncomfortable. "I don't think it's foolish to dream of a better life. Or even…to have a soft enough heart to care about an enemy, or to fall in love. But I'm sorry it's led to this."

"This isn't who she is, not truly," I muttered, running an exhausted hand down my face. Weariness seemed to be my constant friend these days, accompanied by the burden of all the mistakes I'd made. The wrong choices.

From the look Huvoki gave me, I could tell he didn't believe my claim, but he was too kind to argue. Maybe he thought I'd fallen in love with a figment of my imagination, an idea of what I thought Jalie should be rather than who she truly was. But I knew better. I'd seen Jalie's heart—her passion for those she cared about, her courage, her strength, her rare moments of pure joy.

Quickly, I shoved the memories away. It was maddening, how spending only a few weeks near her had changed me so much. How a complete stranger—someone meant to be my sworn enemy—had become so utterly entangle in my life and heart that imagining the future without her left me feeling empty.

But I couldn't lose myself in those emotions. I had a mission to complete.

Forcing myself to step into the Keep, I seized a torch from one of the sconces and lit it using the supplies left on a shelf near the entrance.

My friend's and my footsteps echoing along the tunnel was the only sound for a long while until, throat tight, I dared to ask the question that had been tormenting me for days. The one I was afraid I already knew the answer to, deep down. I'd found it in General Ilowhe's tense face. I'd seen it in Huvoki's pitying expressions.

"Does the general plan to have her executed?"

Swallowing, Huvoki tossed me a helpless look. "She threatens our freedom—our very *existence*—with her claim to the throne, and she tried to kill his daughter. Do you think he has any *other* plans for her?"

I nodded, every muscle in my body taut. But I didn't miss a single step, didn't keep my eyes from calmly scanning every shadow and glancing toward every empty dragon den. The doors had been left open when their occupants had been removed. Now nothing remained of them, not even bodies left in the courtyard. Since the creatures couldn't be consumed even by the hottest of dragon fire, my only guess was that Nesrelle's army had disposed of them somehow. I cringed inwardly as I imagined the ways in which they might have accomplished that.

"I'm sorry, Kovi," Huvoki said again. "I wish it could be different."

I tried not to focus on the ache in my chest, tried not to wonder what I'd do. Could I sit back and let Jalie be put to death? But could I let her threaten my people? When it came to a decision between Jalie and my brothers and sisters, my general, my very empire—did I even *have* a choice?

There was only helplessness, and a growing dread that no matter what I did, I was destined to choose the wrong thing.

Nesrelle's words echoed in my mind, filling me with an icy sense of foreboding. *Do you know what's worse than the death you do not fear, soldier? Living to watch everything you love be destroyed.*

And then, tearing through my thoughts, piercing me with unexpected hope, a sound rent the silence. Huvoki and I paused, staring at one another.

"Could it be?" he whispered.

I picked up my pace, pulse thundering in my head, almost too afraid to believe my ears until we came to the den, until Huvoki hurriedly cranked the lever to lift the door and I held my torch aloft, its light catching on three sets of glistening scales. Until we were drinking in the miraculous sight awaiting us.

Dragon hatchlings.

CHAPTER FIVE

Lo'laeni Nolanhou

H E WAS DYING, AND THERE was nothing I could do to save him, not anymore. Days of trying and failing had led to this empty certainty. I didn't even know the man's name, didn't even know if he had any surviving loved ones who'd miss him. He couldn't have been much older than me, but his glassy eyes already seemed to peer into the Golden After.

My stomach clenched as my furtive pleas for his life, for Elhani's healing magic to save him, turned into our traditional farewell blessing. "May Elhani hold your hands and the guidespirits lead you home," I whispered as the light faded from my patient's eyes.

He was one of far too many who had fallen, succumbing to wounds and infection in the days following our retreat from Inalgoth. Though trained healers from the academy had worked diligently alongside my sisters and me, all of us using every ounce of knowledge and remedies and magic we had, it wasn't always enough. Sometimes, we didn't have the resources we needed. Sometimes, it seemed it wasn't meant to be, that the wounds were too grievous. And other times, long hours and utter weariness had consumed us all, dulling our senses until my sisters and I couldn't focus Elhani's magic at all. Until the healers who didn't know how to wield his power as we could were too exhausted to keep working, or found they just weren't fast enough to dart from patient to patient in time.

I was grateful we at least had found temporary safety on an entire fleet. The Teramese had poured forth from every one of their ships in the harbor during their retreat, leaving the vessels for us. The healthy soldiers had sailed them into Haven's Bay, where we felt that for the time being, at least, we would be unmolested by the Dark Immortal and her cruel army. Even if she seemed to know our thoughts and plans, she had apparently chosen to leave us alone. For now.

It was an illusion of peace, of respite. I sensed, deep down, she knew exactly where we were and could strike again whenever she wanted. For whatever reason, she was biding her time.

But with each soul we lost, with each time the search parties came back reporting that there were no survivors to be found, hope dwindled. In our close quarters, with trust either new or nonexistent between our peoples, tension sprang between the Forwyn, Teramese, and Alrenians among our ranks. Anxiety over what Nesrelle and Revaed planned to do next was growing in everyone's minds. Our food and supplies were limited, and what our scouts could scavenge from the city was sparse. Whether we spoke the words aloud or not, we all knew time was running short.

"Lo." It was Me'kali's voice.

Lost in my thoughts, I jolted in surprise at the presence of the young healer from Aerekni Academy, one of many I'd worked alongside in the past week. He paused beside me, his brow scrunched in worry. "Lo," he repeated, his voice gentle. "He's gone. It's over."

It was only then that I realized there were tears wetting my cheeks and I was still clinging to the dead man's hand, my last attempt at offering comfort and companionship as he passed on.

"You need rest," Pauni'a murmured, coming to my side to tug me into an embrace. Despite the fact that I was coated in a layer of sweat and blood from my long, sleepless night of working with our patients, I didn't resist. I teetered on unsteady, exhausted feet, breathing in her comforting scent, one that reminded me of freshly cleaned linens warm from the sun after we gathered them off the clothing line at the abbey. Perhaps it was just the lingering smell of the abbey itself on her, or the soaps and products she'd used to wash and moisturize the dark curls framing her face. With her hair hanging loose and free, she wore her ribbons braided around her neck.

When I pulled back, I realized I'd left a damp spot on Pauni'a's tunic, but she was as dirty as me and didn't seem to mind. My shoulders slumped. "How can I rest when…"

Approaching footsteps cut me off just as the infirmary door flung open, sending a stream of golden sunshine into the dim room. The narrow windows on the opposite wall were too grimy to properly allow light inside. Now, seeing the brightness, I realized it was afternoon already.

My head spun. When was the last time I'd eaten or drank anything? When had I last even sat down?

I blinked my burning eyes and swiped the tears from my cheeks as Mio'e stepped into the infirmary, her usually hard face softening when she took in the rows of cots and their occupants. Her gaze snagged on the newly still form I hovered over before darting back toward me. "Your father wants to see you."

With a sigh, I turned to my companions, who waved me away. I followed Mio'e out into the bowels of the ship, where countless eyes trailed us: a few of our Alrenian allies, ones Father had uneasily agreed to trust after they'd fought alongside us, and many more Forwyn. Likely, they saw the weariness on my face and the blood on my skin and knew we'd lost another soldier. But no one stopped me to ask about him. Maybe, like me, they were all too overwhelmed, too numb, to mourn the countless losses anymore.

"I'm sorry," Mio'e muttered, slowing her steps to match my pace. Her downcast eyes didn't meet mine. It was strange to have her at my side, consoling me over the loss of a soldier, when once she'd tried to hunt me down and kill me. Back then, she hadn't had any faith in my dedication to our people and our cause. Now, after many sleepless nights and long days, after countless bodies lowered into the water and endless moments of scrubbing off others' gore from my skin, there wasn't any questioning what I'd give to help the Forwyn.

And our uneasy truce looked like maybe, just maybe, it would last. Even if I wouldn't go so far as to call Mio'e a friend, I was grateful for her fire, for the help she'd lent our side.

Unsure what to say, I trailed Mio'e wordlessly up the steps and into the blinding afternoon glow on deck. My eyes watered as I blinked against the sunlight glancing off the glassy harbor.

Nearby, Karos's mournful cries rent the air, shredding my heart. I scanned the shore until I found his form pacing the rocky beach. Light glinted off his black and red scales, making him appear like a living flame, but everything else about his appearance was downcast and dim, more like a dying ember. His head hung low, his swishing tail dislodging pebbles as he keened, grieving the slain dragons.

Tears stung my eyes as I traced his path with my gaze, wishing I could undo the results of that battle, wishing I could make things right.

Nearby, Ryke trod his own way through the sand, smoke curling from his nostrils in rage, his muscles rippling beneath his flashing emerald scales. In their shared grief, the dragons had apparently formed an alliance, no longer locked in battle to protect the humans they were bound to. Instead, they grieved and raged against the evil that had been committed in slaughtering their brothers and sisters.

Behind them, over the cliff's edge, smoke churned over Inalgoth, a shroud of sorrow over a place of desolation. The sight left me aching, hitting me with fresh pain as intense as the first time I'd seen my home city burning.

Not long ago, I'd been so consumed with rage I'd wondered if the capital deserved to burn and fall. Now I knew I had only been feeling angry and betrayed in that moment. I'd never truly wanted to see Inalgoth fall into ruin. I'd never wanted to feel like I was losing my empire.

"It's awful," Mio'e whispered. With a nod toward my father, who stood across the deck, she hesitated a moment, as if considering saying something more, before she thought better of it and walked away.

Sighing, I approached Father. He leaned against the railing, his expression matching the heaviness that had settled on my chest. "Lo," he said, his eyes gentling when they met mine. "When was the last time you slept? Or ate?"

I shook my head uncertainly.

"Kei'on," Father barked to one of the men nearby. "Bring my daughter a hot meal." Turning to me, he grasped my arm and led me toward his cabin. Instead of taking me to the attached dining room in the captain's quarters, he took me to his bedroom, urging me to rest.

"I'm covered in blood," I protested.

His smile was bittersweet. "I'm a general. Do you think that troubles me? Besides, we can change the bed linens later. Rest and eat before you become our next patient."

I rolled my eyes but kicked off my boots and settled onto the bed, leaning against the pillows. Until that moment, I hadn't realized how much my feet had been throbbing and aching. I stretched my toes and sighed in relief.

As Kei'on brought me a bowl of stew and a large cup of water, Father settled onto the side of the bed, waiting until I finished every bite of soup and every drop of water. "Mostly I wanted to get you away and ensure you took care of yourself. But I also wanted to hear an update, because I'm thinking it's time we left," he admitted at last, when I'd set my empty bowl and cup on the bedside table. "We're losing too many, aren't we?" His eyes dropped again to the dried flecks of blood on my arms.

"We are," I said, glancing down at my hands, "and I don't think there's much more we can do for the rest of our patients alone. There aren't enough healers for all the wounded we have, and everyone is cramped aboard these ships. We need help. But where do you plan to go? From what I heard when I was at the palace, the Teramese occupy the rest of the empire."

"Forwyth," he said, drawing my surprised gaze. "It's closer than Misroth, and we need a place nearby where we can recover."

I frowned, thinking of how our ancestral kingdom had ignored us for the past three years. "Do you think they will help us?"

Father shrugged. "If they are dedicated followers of Elhani, they won't turn others in need away. We might not convince them to fight alongside us, but they'll at least give us a place to regroup and heal."

"Will they…accept all of us?" I asked hesitantly, thinking of the Alrenians and Teramese among us. Of Caesiem. When we'd first fled the battle, Father had wanted to turn Caesiem and his Teramese friends away or shove them into the brig with Jalie, only agreeing to let them stay among us when I'd insisted.

Now, I wondered if Father was regretting his choice to listen to me. If the people of Forwyth refused to trust us because of our Teramese and Alrenian companions…what then? Where else could we turn?

Father's lips thinned. "I hope so."

I leaned further back against the pillows, my eyelids growing heavy.

"Rest," Father said gently.

"I'm filthy," I muttered again, but he chuckled and brushed a calloused hand across my forehead, pushing a curl out of my face.

I was asleep before he left the room.

I woke to late afternoon light casting patterns across the bedcovers, and my stomach already aching with hunger again. When I opened the door, I found Father seated at his desk, wearily scanning a map. He tore his gaze away when he heard me, a grin immediately spreading across his face, even if it couldn't quite conceal the pain lingering in his eyes.

"What's wrong?" I asked, even if the question seemed a little ridiculous. Everything was wrong.

"I went to see Nihke, to give him a goodbye and be there for his send-off into the Golden After," he said sadly.

Nihke. That had been the name of the young man I'd failed to save. Another in a long list of men and women General Ilowhe and other officers at Aerekni Academy would have personally trained, and now were losing.

"I wish I was able to do that for each and every one of the soldiers." His eyes flicked sadly toward the window behind him, likely thinking of all the lives lost on other ships, gone long before healers could ever send notice to him. And for him to be there each time a body was lowered into the water? It was impossible, when there were simply too many dying, and too often.

"Anyway," Father went on, before I could try to offer condolences, "I'll have a bath drawn and give you some privacy."

A full bath was a rare luxury, and even then, the water brought in the large metal tub wasn't steaming like it would have been within Inalgoth. Still, it was refreshing to have the rooms to myself, to immerse my body and scrub the grime and blood off my skin.

As I did, Caesiem's pendant cooled more than usual against my collarbone, and the water seemed to ripple of its own accord around me. For a moment, I paused, watching soap bubbles creep along the water's surface, but then it settled again. Maybe it had only been my imagination.

Caesiem. The thought of him, the constant weight of his pendant hanging from my neck…it brought up tangled thoughts and emotions. Endless questions. There hadn't been time to speak with him, let alone find out what he thought of the strange situation we'd been thrown into—forced into a marriage ceremony all to create a distraction.

By the time I was dry and clothed in a fresh tunic and leggings, more food was already waiting for me, and I was rejuvenated. Though I couldn't have slept more than a few hours, my body was already accustomed to small amounts of rest from my frequent nightmares.

Father knocked at the door as I was finishing my food, a strained smile on his face. "How are you?" he asked, and my lips twitched as I held back a laugh. In the short time I'd known him, General Ilowhe had a commanding aura, one that demanded the respect and attention of everyone around him. He was powerful and stern and wise. But in my presence, he became a doting Father, worrying and fretting over me more than practical Naina ever would have.

It warmed me to know he cared. To know he wanted to get to know me.

"Much better," I said, managing a grin despite the heaviness of my heart. My hand went almost out of habit to the pendant hanging from my neck. The smooth stone seemed to radiate with power. It was the faintest tingle against my skin, a small sensation that reminded me of the protection it would grant me within the sea.

The water protects its own.

Father's eyes dropped to it. He'd seen me wear it daily, but each time he studied it, his brow furrowed.

"Lo," he said, his voice abruptly turning stern. I tensed immediately, preparing myself for an argument. This wouldn't be the first time he'd tried to broach the topic, but that didn't make it any less uncomfortable. "I know you've willingly given much of yourself to help our people," he went on. "But I don't want you to be trapped…not when it involves an arranged marriage to a man I'm not sure we should trust." He cleared his throat, almost awkwardly. "When we arrive in Forwyth, we can request that their Elders witness the dissolution of your marriage."

"I told you that I trust him," I said. "He helped me…"

"I understand," Father said, laying a gentle hand on my shoulder. "I'm grateful for what he's done, but I'm not grateful enough to want him to remain married to my daughter." His laugh sounded stilted.

"And I doubt he understands our customs or knows how meaningful that ceremony was for us. For you."

My cheeks warmed as I glanced down at my feet. In Forwyn culture, marriage was a sacred vow made before Elhani, as sacred as the promises I'd once made as a nun. It was considered a shameful thing to break such an oath without cause. Usually, the dissolution of a marriage required the presence of some Elders and proof the binding was not Elhani-blessed.

"Maybe he thinks he can pretend it never happened," Father said. "Or that you're his…property now." He cringed in distaste. "I don't know how the Teramese view marriage. But we can end this before—"

I lifted my hand. "I understand."

Father sighed. "I'm sorry. Of course you do. You're a woman now, and you're a dedicated servant of Elhani. You know all of this already." His smile was wistful. "I'm not sure how to do this, you know. It's hard to go from never having the chance to be a father to suddenly having a daughter, and a fully grown one at that."

Blinking back tears, I leaned into him, offering him a squeeze. It was an awkward hug at first, both of us unused to one another. We were little more than strangers, bound only by blood and a deep desire to be a family. "I don't know how to be a daughter either," I whispered. "But we'll learn together. I promise."

He brushed a curl behind my ear as I pulled back. "Of course," he said, his own eyes misty.

"I'll talk to Caesiem, and he and I will…" I shrugged. "We'll figure it out. But I promise, he would never consider me his property."

Father's mouth tightened, but he nodded.

I wondered if he knew I was in love with Caesiem, that I didn't hate the idea of a future with him, and that was the true root of Father's reservations.

But I couldn't blame him. If our roles were reversed, and he'd fallen for a Teramese woman, would I be just as worried about how trustworthy and honorable she was? About the risk of his heart being broken…or worse?

The sound of a commotion on deck drew us to the door. Father pulled it open, revealing a crowd gathered outside. The scouting party had returned.

"General Ilowhe!" Kovi Ettonou stepped forward, for once displaying joy on his usually stern, guarded face. In his arms, he cradled something. The sun glinted off the object so brightly that at first I thought he was holding a bundle of drae, as if he'd plundered the palace for coins instead of searching for surviving citizens.

But then the object moved, and I realized what he held.

I surged forward, gasping aloud. "A hatchling," I breathed, nearly weeping for joy at the beautiful sight.

"Three hatchlings," a familiar voice clarified, and I started, turning to face Caesiem. He held another small dragon closely to his chest.

Caesiem's bright eyes flitted to mine, the faintest hint of pain darkening his features before he cleared his expression and forced his lips into a carefree grin. For an awkward moment, my feet felt leaden, trapped to the boards beneath my boots.

As Huvoki and another Forwyn soldier joined Kovi to cluster around Father and give a report, I pushed myself to move until I was at Caesiem's side.

My gaze dropped to the hatchling, leaning one head against Caesiem's muscled forearm. The creature's scales were as black as a moonless night sky, rich and deep. Light reflected off each one, making them appear as if they were edged in gold. The hatchling nestled close to Caesiem's warmth, his sides gently rising and falling. Fast asleep and perfectly at peace, he was unaware that most of its kind in Alrenor had been callously slaughtered.

In general, dragon hatchlings tended to be sweet and tender creatures, trusting of their human caregivers. It wasn't until they were nearly fully grown that their wilder instincts began to overtake their affectionate side. That was when the dragons started to view all humans, even the ones that fed and cared for them, as potential predators or prey. That was when they needed to be tamed, often forming a bond with only one person at a time.

My throat burning with unshed tears, I brushed gentle fingers along the hatchling's side. Relief filled me to know the dragons hadn't all been annihilated, that these young ones had been spared.

"We found them safe in the Keep," Caesiem murmured, his gaze latched onto the dragon, his smile firmly in place. "I suppose that Alrenian army didn't bother with anything that wasn't human. Do you know this dragon?" He hesitated a beat. "It's a male, because of the larger wings, right?"

"I see you spent some time learning about dragons. Yes, this is a male." I smiled softly, and for an instant, his eyes swept over my face, snagging on my lips. Then he ripped his gaze away, dipping his chin toward the dragon in his arms.

"But I wasn't ever assigned to the young ones," I added regretfully. "Usually the Alrenians worked with them, since they don't pose much of a threat until they're a lot larger." I cleared my throat. "Besides, this is just a hatchling. If I'd ever tended to him, he'd be three years old now and nearly full grown. Based on his size, he's only a couple months old, if that."

I wanted to say more, but the others had overheard my words. Huvoki drew closer, studying the sleeping dragon in Caesiem's arms, and Father and Meli followed. Even some of my sisters had come up from belowdecks, drawn by the commotion. Pauni'a tossed me an encouraging smile, her amber eyes alight with knowing. We might not have had much free time over the past week, but there had been more than one night before we'd fallen asleep when I'd admitted how I'd felt about Caesiem…and how awkward it was to know I'd been bound to him under such strange circumstances. I could practically hear her thoughts: *Tell him how you feel, Lo. Take advantage of the time you have. Don't let it* become *awkward.*

But even if I'd had privacy and all the time in the world, I wasn't sure I could find the words. Wasn't sure I knew how to read the pain lingering in Caesiem's eyes. I could only imagine the weight he was carrying after spending years dedicated to serving both his people and his guardian, and then abandoning them during a critical battle.

Before I could try to break the quiet enveloping Caesiem and me, Kovi stepped near, a soft smile on his lips. When he wasn't wearing his severe soldier's expression, he seemed friendly…almost gentle. Perhaps, like my father, he was also softer than his hardened exterior gave on. "I couldn't believe we found one, let alone three," he explained. The coral dragon he'd been holding moments ago was now circling around his feet, fluttering her wings playfully as she flicked out her tongue to take in the scents of everyone on board.

Pauni'a, her heart-shaped mouth curled to one side in anticipation, knelt and stretched out a hand, letting the coral hatchling nuzzle against her palm. "She's beautiful," she whispered. She met my eyes, and we shared an awed grin.

Wing beats interrupted the excited chatter on board, and I glanced up in time to see both Karos and Ryke diving toward the ship, their large forms casting huge shadows. Men and women leapt aside as the dragons alighted on deck, furling their wings against their sides to make room. Their claws scraped along the wood and the ship rocked from the sudden added weight. I was overcome with the obvious joy emanating from the dragons.

Karos and Ryke crooned, the sound milder than anything I'd ever heard from a dragon before, each extending their snouts toward the hatchlings. Curls of smoke twined upward as they sniffed the young dragons. Even the black creature in Caesiem's arms stirred at the sound, leaping down to the deck. All three hatchlings chirped and dashed toward the adult dragons, fluttering their wings as they went, half-hopping, half-flying, in the awkward way of dragon hatchlings still strengthening their wing muscles.

They pranced around Karos's and Ryke's legs, chittering eagerly as the adults nuzzled them, continuing their crooning sounds. Warmth filled my chest and tears burned my eyes.

"The Elders sent word just before the Autumn Ball and the Teramese coup," my father said, and I didn't miss the glance he cast toward Caesiem, nor the way Caesiem tensed. "They informed me that Torla had laid a second egg in her lifetime—something they'd never heard of in all of Alrenor's history with dragons. Those two young ones would be hers, one fathered by Karos and the other by Zorven. And that one" -he nodded toward a pure silver female with scales rippling in shades of teal in the light- "that one is the offspring of Ziltha and Ivez."

The silver female was clearly older, already standing half as tall as a man, and considerably more graceful on her feet and in her attempts at flight.

"What are their names?" Vander, standing not far from Caesiem, asked, wonder in his eyes.

Father glanced at the young Teramese man. "We don't name the dragons until they're around three years old and close to fully grown. That's when their personalities truly begin to show, and we give them a name befitting who they are."

"What's that Alrenian saying?" Kovi asked. "*Whoever controls the dragons, controls Alrenor.*" He smirked. "I suppose this means we control all the dragons left in Alrenor now."

"You're right," Father agreed. "This is a gift from Elhani," he went on, raising his voice so the whole crowd could hear. "A sign that he hasn't forgotten us, and still hears our prayers."

Despite the somber mood that had hovered over us, heads nodded at Father's words. These dragons were a gift, a symbol. The first bit of hope we'd felt in days.

"But now it's time for us to move on. To make plans and seek help in a place where we can recover and prepare to take back our empire."

Scattered applause and cheers erupted, some soldiers eagerly crying out for vengeance, while others appeared graver, their eyes dim with the grief they bore. Fathers, mothers, brothers, sisters, loved ones—so many had died or disappeared when Inalgoth burned. It could be many months yet before we knew the full extent of our losses.

Father lifted his voice to a shout, his proud stance projecting courage and confidence. "Today, we set sail for Forwyth!"

CHAPTER SIX

Kovi

GENERAL ILOWHE GAVE THOSE OF us who'd scouted within the city time to clean up and grab a quick meal before he requested that some of us join him in his quarters for a meeting.

I changed into a fresh jacket and splashed some water on my face before hurriedly eating a bowl of the stew Kei'on had made. As I climbed on deck, I found the ship already preparing to sail, word having spread to the rest of the fleet. The hatchlings had been taken belowdecks where Forwyn more accustomed to tending to younger dragons could ensure they were well-fed and cared for. Karos and Ryke had returned to the beach where they could stretch their legs and wings, opening the deck back up for us. Excepting those who were preparing the ship for the voyage, there were few in sight compared to the crowd gathered before.

There was too much work to do to be idle. Too many decisions to make. Too many wounded to assist. Too many plans to determine.

Except…there was one notable figure lingering, as if lost or unsure of what to busy himself with.

The sight of the Teramese prince leaning against the railing, gazing out at the glistening water, made me pause on my way toward the captain's quarters. A strand of his dark, wavy hair fell across his forehead, adding to the careless appearance that irked me. Although Caesiem had been cooperative on our scouting trip, I didn't trust him.

Didn't like him.

I couldn't forget the calculating way he'd assessed me in my prison cell back at the palace, pinpointing my motives and weaknesses in order to compel me to work for him. This man was clever and dedicated, and he knew how to get what he wanted. Not to mention the fact that whispered gossip amongst some of the soldiers asserted that Caesiem was a former thief and spy. Though the man never seemed to still—always moving, always fidgeting, always drawing attention to himself—I'd noticed how quietly and gracefully he could be when he *didn't* want to be seen.

And he was married to Lo, my general's daughter. The *amara'rekni* herself. A leader among my people. My stomach clenched at the thought.

It's none of your business, I told myself.

But that didn't stop me from approaching him, leaning heavily on the railing.

Nothing within me felt like mincing words. "I'm surprised you've ingratiated yourself enough with General Ilowhe to not be locked up in the brig," I said.

Caesiem drummed his fingers against the railing before he tore his gaze from the water. His expression was…heavy. Not gloating or calculating, as I'd expected. "Well, there's still time for that, isn't there?" he murmured. "I know you probably hate what I did to the empress, but…"

"No," I cut him off sharply. "She deserved it." The words hurt, but they were true. I shifted uncomfortably. If my feelings for Jalie were that transparent even to this Teramese man, I feared they were too strong for me to ever push aside or ignore. It forced my brain to recognize the truth I wished I could run from: even if it destroyed me, I'd never stop loving Jalie.

I changed the subject, banishing the image of Jalie from my mind. "I suppose if anything, I should thank you for saving Lo's life. General

Ilowhe is like family to me, and that makes his daughter family too." Lowering my tone, I hoped he also caught the unspoken threat in my words. *Harm my family, and you will pay.*

Caesiem's fingers strayed almost absent-mindedly toward his bare neck, as if recalling the ribbons he'd worn during the wedding ceremony, a part of our traditions woven into the proceedings. "Of course," he said. "I *always* will protect her."

"You don't deserve her," I added, coldly. Though I hardly knew Lo myself, I knew the general, and could tell she'd inherited his determination and loyalty. She'd proven herself to be selfless and brave, willing to participate in the Teramese's ridiculous games, willing to give up everything in order to free the Forwyn and grant us a chance to regain our homeland.

Caesiem's smile was wistful. "I know. But I'll give anything for her," he added fervently. "And anything to undo the damage my soldiers have caused. I swear it."

I didn't bother with trying to conceal my skepticism. "Fine words, for a liar." Narrowing my eyes, I leaned in closer. "If you betray my people, if you leave a single scratch on Lo, I will gladly execute you myself."

This time, his grin was more like the cocky smile I'd expected from a pampered prince. "Not the first time I've heard that. You'll have to get in line."

Crossing my arms over my chest, I pulled back. "Gladly."

CHAPTER SEVEN

Caesiem

I WAS OUT OF COINS, leaving me with the polished buttons from my wedding jacket to barter with instead. As soon as Kovi vanished into the captain's quarters, leaving the deck mostly vacant, I leaned out over the water, watching it foam against the ship's hull.

Dragon wings thundered through the air as Ryke and Karos leapt off the beach, flying low alongside the cliff to stay out of sight of Nesrelle's army. They'd done this for days, eventually flying eastward to exercise and hunt game. But this time, their twisting flight was different—they flipped and spun in the air, each movement seeming…joyful, if dragons could be described as joyful.

They mourned the lost dragons, but they'd seen the hatchlings. A smile tugged at my mouth. Who'd have known that I, the renowned dragon slayer of Teramyl, would live to rescue young dragons and learn what social creatures they could be? That I'd find they were not only dangerous and deadly, but also loyal and gentle, affectionate and playful?

Revaed would laugh at my fancies before declaring how proud he was that I—

Cringing inwardly, I cut off those thoughts. The memory of Nesrelle's taunting words about his pain was fresh salt in my festering wound, and I didn't want to think about my guardian. Or what he was planning. Not now.

Tayla, Vander, and Valentra's approaching footsteps were a

welcome intrusion.

"To the shore, then?" Vander asked as he paused beside me, nodding toward the sands Karos and Ryke had just vacated. It had been an evening ritual for the past week, to all row ashore so I could step into the water and speak with Sephrode without the Forwyn surrounding us. Since the first time when General Ilowhe had demanded to listen in, he and the others seemed happy to give me privacy in order to avoid the water nymph's eerie presence.

At Vander's side, Tayla slipped her hand in his, their fingers threading together. Their closeness was a constant reminder of all that divided Lo and me, and that reminder grated on my heart. On my opposite side, Vander's sister Valentra was silent, inspecting the waves as if she expected a sea creature to rise up at any moment.

"To the shore," I agreed.

This time, I didn't even bother to try helping as my friends moved to ready the rowboat. I already knew any of my attempts would be futile, as all three of them still insisted on treating me like royalty. Instead, I climbed in silently as they did the work, lowering the boat into the water and tugging the oars through the foaming waves.

Although I'd insisted numerous times that I couldn't truly be called a prince anymore, both Tayla and the Arros siblings had insisted I was *their* prince. I'd managed to get them to address me like a friend, but otherwise, they were formal, insisting they served me. It didn't matter that I'd considered Vander a friend long before, when we'd trained as mages together in the Teramese palace.

"In fact," Vander had said our first evening after the battle in Inalgoth, "you're even more deserving of the title now. We've all seen that Revaed is becoming as corrupt as his father, and you had the courage to reject his choices, even when he is family to you. You'll always be my leader, because I trust you and I know you're not only dedicated to your people, but also to what is right. I'll follow you anywhere."

"And so will I," Valentra had agreed, dipping her head in reverence.

"And I," Tayla had added with a warm smile.

The ache in my chest hadn't abated at their words. My sense of betrayal ever since I'd discovered the extent of Revaed's cruelty within the Alrenian Empire, not to mention the truth about how I'd been used as a mage, continued to rankle me relentlessly. The grief from discovering that the only father I'd ever known had used and deluded me was unending.

Yet in spite of that, there was still a part of me that loved him, that wanted to trust him. That wanted to believe in his goodness.

Now, I soaked in the briny air whispering against my skin and the taste of the sea spray beading on my lips. Vander leapt out of the boat when we slid across the sand, and I followed, not caring as the water soaked my trousers up to the knees and lapped at my leather boots. Pebbles crunched underfoot as I strode toward shore alongside Vander and Valentra, who shaded her eyes with a hand to trace the dragons' winding path over the sea.

As usual, the pair was flying toward Forwyth, their shadows gliding over the waves. The island wasn't far away even by ship, and for a dragon it would be an especially short flight. Every day they'd gone there to hunt, making me wonder what the island citizens thought.

"Do you think we'll ever go home?" It wasn't the first time Valentra had asked the question, wistfulness dimming her eyes. While sometimes her irises appeared gold, this evening, in the dying light, they were pale silver. She tugged on the sleek braid trailing down her shoulder before meeting my gaze.

My shoulders were heavy with a hundred burdens. "I don't know," I said, as I'd answered far too many times already. I didn't want to abandon the Teramese—all three of us had vowed we'd do anything to help our people—but we'd also agreed that our first task would be to right the wrongs our army had committed within Alrenor.

And that meant facing our own army…and possibly not surviving to ever see home again.

And even if you do survive, what sort of home will you return to? a nagging voice asked me, over and over again.

I longed to speak with Lo and ask if she and her father would ever consider sending help to Teramyl, if a *true* alliance between our lands would be possible.

But the hope of getting any private conversation with her had been dashed that first day we'd boarded the Teramese ship, when her father had cornered me. "Stay away from her," he'd snapped, his hand on his sword hilt, his eyes alight with an inner fire that was all too familiar to me. I'd seen that same sort of deadly, protective expression on Revaed's face when he'd done anything and everything to defend me. "I don't trust you, and I won't hesitate to kill you. Just because you've fought alongside us, just because my daughter and a truth-gifted woman I just met both vouch for you…that means nothing to me. You're the enemy, and don't you forget it."

My chest had felt hollow as I'd nodded. There hadn't been a chance to see Lo much anyway in the past week, when she'd been needed to tend to suffering patients for nearly every waking moment. Hoping to be helpful as well, I'd dedicated myself to aiding in whatever way I could. When I hadn't been permitted to join scouting parties until today, I'd stripped my wedding jacket of its shiny buttons as payment for vials of theslynik from Sephrode. The miraculous, nymph-made healing tonic couldn't save all the wounded within our small fleet, but it had helped.

I knew everything I'd done wasn't enough to gain the Forwyns' trust. Even now, I had been excluded from the meeting General Ilowhe had called. I doubted they'd ever trust me, just as I wasn't sure Lo would forgive me.

And, truth be told, I wasn't confident I could ever earn her forgiveness. Now, after seeing the slaughter Revaed had ordered in the Alrenian marketplace mere days ago, after realizing the full extent of his brutality, I could understand how averse she'd been to working with us. To trusting me.

Nesrelle's words repeated in my head. *You set the stage for so many deaths and so much pain in this empire.*

Drawing a steadying breath, relishing the taste of the sea on my lips, I discarded my boots on the sand and waded barefoot into the water. "Stay back," I cautioned with a glance over my shoulder at my friends. It was a needless warning. They all knew how dangerous water nymphs could be.

These stolen moments ashore were the only true privacy my friends and I had, a chance for us to speak freely without the risk of prying ears. It wasn't as if we were planning to betray our new allies, but it was exhausting to always be questioned, always be suspected of duplicity. On board, we were quieter, more cautious in our choice of words. It would be too easy for our talk of missing home to be labeled as treacherous.

Tearing a button from my jacket, I tossed it into the sea and watched an incoming wave suck it into the harbor. A gull cawed and swooped low as I waited. Though even someone without water magic could summon a nymph to the surface with a tempting shiny object, it worked best if a nymph was already nearby. And after all the times I'd summoned Sephrode, I could sense her lingering close.

After a few moments, the nymph broke the surface, her white hair gleaming and dripping, seaweed woven through it like an accessory, as if she had carefully picked it out the same way a noblewoman would choose hair clips. The silver scales framing her face flashed in the sunlight, her yellow eyes luminescent and curious. In her webbed fingers she clutched my button.

"What do you want, my handsome mage?" she demanded, licking her needlelike teeth. Her eyes darted over my shoulder toward my friends, and I scowled.

"Ignore them," I said curtly. "Your business is with me."

She sighed. "Indeed."

"When Inalgoth burned and the Teramese army fled north, where did they settle?"

"First all the theslynik. Now important information." The nymph fluttered her eyelashes. "You ask a lot when you've only paid with a shiny button."

I drew on the water, calling droplets until they hovered around my hands, shimmering like diamonds. A subtle reminder of what I could do with little effort. "Consider your payment protection from the water creature. I can feel it lurking nearby, expecting to feed again soon when I've given it so many victims already. Do you want me to add you to that list?"

Sephrode curled her lips back in disgust. "Fine," she snapped. "The pretty emperor has settled his forces in Hemlaen. My sisters and I have watched them from the coast." Her mouth twisted into a threatening smile. Normally nymphs didn't venture this far from the ocean, but just like the Teramese army, just like the tentacled creature that preferred hovering in the deep and awaiting entire passing ships, it seemed I'd brought many dangerous things to Alrenor. "That's all the information one button will earn you, I'm afraid."

Guilt clung to me as I watched Sephrode sink back into the water, her tail splashing as she swam out toward the sea. Perhaps toward the Alrenian, where she could join her sisters and try to lure victims into the water. Or perhaps to stay nearby, hoping for more trinkets from me.

"Hemlaen," Vander muttered, coming up beside me to stare out over the bay. He'd told me how Jalie and her army had taken Aramith, so it wasn't surprising that Revaed hadn't led his forces there. Close to the sea, Hemlaen's harbor would be swarming with Teramese ships by now, making it the perfect location for Revaed's soldiers to recover before sailing back to the capital.

Because I knew Revaed. He'd be back to reclaim the capital.

And we needed to be ready to meet him.

When my friends and I clambered back on deck, Lo was outside of the captain's quarters awaiting us.

Though her hair was pulled back into a single braid, loose curls had escaped to frame her face. Golden sunlight highlighted each strand and brightened the emerald flecks in her warm brown eyes.

My chest tightened at the sight of her, at the way her gaze darkened with longing when it met mine. At the way her full lips twisted into a playful grin, making it feel as if things were simpler between us. For just that moment, the growing distance between us melted away.

"Caesiem?"

Vander's voice wrenched me from my thoughts and forced me to tear my eyes off Lo. My friend's smile was knowing as he studied my expression. "We're going belowdecks so you two can talk."

"*Please*," Tayla added, the emphasis she placed on the word telling me she'd noticed how downcast I'd been for the past week. Apparently I hadn't been as careful about hiding my emotions as I'd thought.

The memory of General Ilowhe's threatening glare flashed through my mind, but I shoved it away. I wasn't going to spend my life ignoring his daughter. Even if she couldn't forgive me, even if I could never deserve her…I couldn't let this time slip away.

Valentra winked as she strode past, trailing after her brother and Tayla, and I was tempted to roll my eyes at her. Instead, I fastened my gaze back on Lo, who was crossing the deck to meet me.

She was dressed in a plain tunic and black leggings, with a sword and daggers strapped to her sides. Over her shoulders hung a small pack. Her eyes scanned me up and down before she lifted her chin and tossed her braid over her shoulder.

"Would you like a weapon?" she asked me, as casually as if she were talking about the cool, sunny weather. "I have an extra for you, since I know Father wouldn't let you keep one." She tapped the hilt of one of her daggers. "But you'll need to pack quickly."

I blinked at her. "What?"

"Hold on—Karos should be close by now." Pressing two fingers to her lips, she let out a single shrill whistle. For an embarrassingly too-long moment, I stared at her mouth, recalling the taste of her kiss and the warmth of her in my arms. I longed to pull her into an embrace and breathe in the sweet scent of coconut that I knew clung to her hair, to tell her how I felt.

Throat tightening, I forced my gaze away.

"We're going to Forwyth," Lo explained as the steady beat of dragon wings thrummed through the air and a dark blot appeared on the eastern horizon. "Father and the others agreed that I should scout the area and speak to the residents before our entire fleet arrives."

I couldn't resist tucking a stray curl behind Lo's ear, letting my fingers trace its shell. She didn't pull away, didn't mask the way she shivered at my touch. Swallowing, I forced my own smile. "And he wanted me to go also?" I asked, not concealing the skepticism in my voice.

Lo set her jaw. "We're married. He's not going to tell me no." She hesitated a beat, vulnerability leaking into her beautiful eyes. "You'll come with me…right?"

"Of course," I murmured. *I'd go with you anywhere.*

Too surprised to formulate more words, I hadn't even addressed the other comment she'd made about our marriage, though my mind was swirling with questions and confusion. Did that mean she believed the ceremony was…legitimate? And did that mean she *wanted* to be married to me? Or did she resent me for that as well?

I opened my mouth to try to voice one of those questions, but Lo arched an eyebrow impatiently. "Hurry. Pack."

Turning, she watched Karos's black form draw nearer as he started to dive toward the ship.

"Right," I said, dashing to the cabin I shared with my fellow

Teramese to throw the few belongings I'd acquired into a bag. An extra set of clothes. A canteen of water.

"Where are you going?" Valentra demanded, and I hastily explained what was happening.

"Be careful," Vander said. "I'm not sure the people of Forwyth will like us very much."

I offered him a cheeky smile. "When am I not?"

Which was only partially true. We both knew I was a strange mixture of cautious and reckless. A life of thieving had made me bold when I needed to be, had taught me to run headfirst toward danger. But I was also one to always consider the risks, to always have an exit plan. To always know when to face a fight, and when to flee.

The ship rocked as I emerged from my cabin to find Karos on deck. He carefully tucked his wings and ducked his head, one huge eye studying Lo. In this moment, he seemed…docile. Not at all like the infamously untamable creature even the Alrenians and Forwyn had feared. Laughing softly, Lo strode forward and leaned into the dragon's warmth, brushing gentle fingers along his scales. When Karos tilted his head toward her, closing his eyes, he made a sound that reminded me of a cat's purr.

"Help me saddle him," Lo said as she pulled away, a contented smile tugging at her lips.

It only took a few minutes to gather the saddle and prepare Karos. Lo urged me to mount first, but I hesitated. The dragon huffed, his golden eye studying me warily, before he glanced back at Lo and seemed to settle. Smoke curled from his nostrils and his huge black sides heaved as he laid his head back down, allowing me to swing into the saddle and buckle myself in.

"Good boy," Lo murmured, patting the dragon before she seized the saddle and clambered up in front of me.

My pulse hammered against my ribcage at her proximity. With nothing else to hold, I was forced to wrap my arms around her waist. I squeezed my eyes shut as longing assaulted me again. It felt like the worst sort of pain to have Lo in my arms, only to know this was temporary. Her back pressed against my chest until I could feel her warmth through my shirt, until I was certain she'd be able to notice my racing heartbeat. With each movement of her head, her braid tickled my cheek, filling my nose with the scents of coconut and flowers.

I swallowed, half-certain this ride was going to be the death of me.

"Ready?" Lo asked as she finished buckling her strap.

I muttered something in the affirmative, while inwardly, I was cursing every Teramese god I'd been taught about since childhood. Surely the goddess of fate or the god of love was laughing at me in this moment.

At Lo's Alrenian command, Karos launched into the air, his wings unfurling to their full span and shadowing the water below us with his massive shape. When he dipped low, talons skimming the sea, Lo extended a hand and trailed her fingers through the water. Droplets swirled around her wrist and clung to her arm, beads as bright as diamonds catching the light in an array of dazzling colors.

"What—" Lo started to ask, before Karos soared toward the clouds, leaving the sea far behind. The droplets clinging to Lo's arm trailed off, plunging back toward the water.

Wind roared in our ears and stung my eyes as Karos picked up speed, his wings thundering. I squeezed my hands, tightening my grip on Lo as I turned back to watch our stolen fleet of ships melt on the horizon.

What would have been a two-day trip via ship only took an hour on dragonback. The land of Forwyth was three islands clustered together, the largest of them boasting the capital city of Rhaeda perched on its northern coast. From my vantage, I saw all three islands laid out like blots of green paint in a portrait of richest blue.

As Karos dropped into a dive, the largest island rose up to meet us. The jungle seemed to spring from the earth, a lovely smear of rich, vibrant hues. Unlike Teramyl, with its ancient and dark rainforests, Forwyth's appeared bejeweled. Tucked amongst the swaying trees were rivers of turquoise cutting through the land and verdant plants in nearly every color imaginable: violet and crimson, orange and gold, and every shade in between. Some were even as white as snowcaps atop a mountain or dark as the deepest night sky.

As Karos landed on the expanse of white sand stretching toward the jungle, I sucked in a breath when I realized everything was also *huge*. There were flowers with petals easily as large as my hand, and traipsing vines trailing from trees that grew so wide, I was sure it would take several men to wrap their arms around each trucks' circumference.

For a long beat, Lo sat rigid and silent, staring straight ahead.

"It's beautiful," she said at last, her voice strained. "I'd always wondered…" When she glanced over her shoulder, her eyes glistened with unshed tears. "It's not home exactly, and yet…it's where my ancestors grew up. It's the source of all my history and culture." A lovely, wistful smile twisted her lips. "Mother told me stories, sometimes. When she was able to sneak to me and sit beside my cot in the nights. I wish she could see Forwyth is even more beautiful than we imagined."

At a loss for words, I opened my mouth, trying to think of something consoling, but Lo leapt down from Karos, already shoving aside her grief. "We'll approach Rhaeda on foot," she explained when I jumped down, my boots crunching on the sand. She patted her dragon affectionately. "I don't want Karos to startle them and make them think we're hostile, so I didn't land directly in the capital. And the jungle is too thick for Karos to fly us through."

Shuffling on his feet, the dragon let out a strange noise that sounded like something between a whimper and a groan.

"Don't argue," Lo said when Karos leaned into her, snuffling as he pressed his snout against her shoulder. Lo laughed and gently shoved him away. "Wait nearby. I'll whistle if we need you, but I'm not sure you could even walk through the undergrowth. We'll come back to you. We should be ready to return by this evening," she added, glancing up at the sun high overhead. "But it depends on how long we'll need to speak with the citizens of Rhaeda."

Karos tilted his head and snuffed a stream of smoke into the air, as if sighing in resignation. I wasn't sure how much of our words the dragon understood, but Lo seemed confident he comprehended enough to obey her.

My eyes dropped to Lo's waist and the weapons strapped at her sides, remembering how she'd offered one to me earlier. "Do you expect trouble?"

"Not from the Forwyn," Lo said confidently as she turned toward the jungle. "But from wild animals in the forest? You can never be too prepared." Her grin was assured, but I didn't miss the uncertainty in her eyes.

If Forwyth refused to help her people, the war to reclaim Alrenor might already be over.

CHAPTER EIGHT

Lo

ALL OF MOTHER'S STORIES HAD told of a kingdom as beautiful as this, full of prosperity and wonder and magic. At the time, I hadn't known how to listen for Elhani's voice or wield his power, and hearing about our ancestors' abilities had seemed especially incredible. Now, I was overwhelmed by the fact that I was finally seeing the land I'd dreamt of my whole life, and eager to see if I could sense Elhani's magic more powerfully here.

"Stay alert," I warned Caesiem as we plunged into the jungle, the forest's thick canopy immersing us in shadow. The heavy scent of flowers mingled with the odor of damp earth. "Forwyth is known for being dangerous. My ancestors settled here because they could overcome the wildlife with their magic."

At my side, Caesiem scanned the mossy trunks of the huge trees enclosing us while we shuffled through the thick undergrowth, winding our way over huge roots jutting from the earth, as if nature itself wanted to block our path. "Well, in Teramyl's rainforests, most creatures are poisonous or venomous," he said with a grin. "So I won't attempt to eat anything I don't recognize."

As if to prove his point, a red frog that was undoubtedly poisonous croaked and hopped across our path, vanishing into a tangle of undergrowth.

I rolled my eyes. "Here, everything *actively* tries to kill and eat you.

Or so I was told. I don't know much about the animals here, because we forgot most of our history, but…we should be extra cautious." Pausing, I unfastened one of the daggers at my waist and passed it to Caesiem. "I'm sure you'll use your magic, but…"

His eyes were especially bright in the shadows of the jungle, while his bronze skin seemed to glow in the dappled light. My stomach flipped as his fingers brushed mine, lingering longer than necessary when he took the weapon from me. His trademark charming smile—the familiar thief's grin that seemed to mask more than it revealed—tugged at his lips. The one that had piqued my interest from the start, even if I'd cursed myself for it. "Thanks."

I started to step away, but Caesiem's hand darted out, gently clasping my wrist. His smile faded as he searched my eyes.

"What did you mean earlier, when you said we were married?" His brow scrunched. "I thought, since you were only doing it as a distraction, that ceremony didn't count."

Nervous laughter threatened to bubble up, but I clamped it down, gritting my teeth. His pendant was a cool, reassuring weight at the hollow of my throat. *He chose me. He cares about me.* But that didn't mean he wanted to be locked in this relationship, or that it even made sense. It didn't make my nauseating fear of rejection feel any smaller, or Father's talk of dissolving the union any quieter. It didn't make anything about this situation feel less insane.

"We made a vow before Elhani," I murmured. "And for my people, all vows to him are sacred. But we can break it," I added quickly, sure that was what he'd want to hear.

Caesiem's eyes widened, but he didn't pull his hand away. I wondered if he could feel my pulse pounding against his fingers. "I'm sorry." He shook his head and stepped back, dropping my arm to run a hand through his wavy hair. "You already broke vows before, all because I encouraged you to…and now this?"

I shook my head. "No, it's not like that at all." I forced a smile.

"Dissolving a marriage can be done in…well, an accepted and honorable way for many reasons. Being forced into one would count, I'm sure." I laughed again. "It will take another ceremony, but a quick one, and it'll all be over."

My chest ached even as I spoke the words. It wasn't like I'd planned to be bound to Caesiem like this. It wasn't like this was what I'd asked for. And yet, imagining that it would be a relief for him to break ties with me was painful. Because I wasn't sure what the future would hold for us afterward.

Was there even an *us* to speak of? My tongue seemed leaden, unable to ask the questions prodding at me. After all, weren't we destined for different paths? Even if my people managed to take back Alrenor, would Caesiem choose to linger in our empire, or would he return home? Would he be welcome among my people? My own father was loath to associate with him.

My words seemed to echo endlessly between us. *It'll all be over.*

But I didn't want it to be over.

Caesiem swallowed, his eyes darting over my face. A muscle worked in his jaw, but as his tension eased and his shoulders relaxed, I thought maybe I'd misread the flicker of uncertainty in his gaze. "Right. That sounds…good."

Drawing a deep breath and praying he didn't notice the hurt flaring in my eyes, I turned and gestured forward. "Be ready," I said, because those were the only words that made sense in my head in that moment.

Because everything else in my mind was a storm of pain and rejection.

Caesiem and I were silent for a long while as we trudged through the jungle, ducking, dodging, or shoving aside the vines and plants that blocked our way. When we couldn't do that, I drew my sword and sliced through them.

Though I'd expected hostile creatures or some sign of life the further we ventured onto the island, we were met with a heavy, strange sort of silence instead. Despite the sound of trickling water or the rush of the occasional stream we passed, despite the tittering of birds or the whisper of a breeze, there was nothing to mask the sounds of our presence. Each one of my steps seemed incredibly loud as I crunched branches or swiped at the leaves tickling my cheeks.

When I listened for Elhani's song, it sounded dulled in my ears, like I was catching strains of the notes carried to me on a distant breeze.

Shouldn't it have been *louder* and more powerful here?

My spine prickled in warning, and I kept my sword drawn.

The further we trekked, the more the humidity thickened the atmosphere, filling the air with a swirling mist that beaded on our skin. Sweat gleamed on Caesiem's face and made his shirt cling to his muscles. I tore my gaze away, annoyed with myself for noticing. My braid clung to the back of my neck while curls frizzed around my face, tickling and itching. Gnats buzzed incessantly around us, drawn by the heat of our bodies.

Stifling a curse, I flicked one away for the hundredth time and scowled up toward the forest canopy. Huge leaves swayed overhead, nearly blocking out the blue sky. An hour had passed, at least. Though there'd been no sign of predators stalking us, my unease had only grown. Sweat trickled down my back endlessly, the sticky heat almost unbearable, and Elhani's muted song made this beautiful world seem more eerie than serene.

Not to mention, there was no sign of civilization. I'd expected a path, or even some smaller villages built among the trees on our way to Rhaeda. Citizens armed as we were who could venture through the rainforest and brave whatever wildlife threatened them. *Something.*

"Lo," Caesiem whispered, pausing and nodding at one of the trees ahead of us. Its branches swayed as if by an unseen weight—perhaps from an animal creeping along its boughs, concealed by leaves.

Tensing, I tightened my grip on my blade. "Maybe it's just a bird," I muttered, even though I knew anything that could move a tree that much weighed far more than a bird.

We pressed onward, until the birdsong that had encircled us receded and only the sound of rushing water filled our ears. Ahead, the jungle thinned out until it reached a narrow wood bridge crossing over a deep ravine. Though I couldn't see the bottom from my vantage point, the noise of the splashing river below grew louder, and heavy mist clung around the bridge.

My heart leapt and I picked up my pace. At last, some proof of civilization. "We can't be far from Rhaeda now," I told Caesiem. Hesitantly, I sheathed my sword as I approached the bridge, studying the way it swung back and forth. When I paused on the edge, my stomach dipped. The drop was great, and the churning river below was wide and pocked with sharp rocks that would be a sure death for anyone who plunged toward them from such a height.

At my side, Caesiem scowled while he brushed his fingers along some of the frayed rope binding the bridge together. "This looks…old."

Swallowing, I studied the planks spanning the ravine, noting how insecure they looked. "It must not be a well-traveled path, so no one has bothered to keep it up," I said uncertainly.

But the sight of the rotting boards and rope only increased my uneasiness. Why did it feel as if Caesiem and I were the only people on this entire island?

"Let's go around," I said quickly, turning away from the bridge and trying to shake the chill running its fingers down my spine.

A blur of brown was my only warning before a weight slammed into me, the force of it sending me sprawling backward. Dirt and pebbles slid and tumbled down the ravine, reminding me how near I was to the edge. A pair of beady pink eyes glared down at me as the creature shrieked, revealing slimy fangs in its too-small mouth. I kicked, my boot striking the solid mass and sending it flying toward the trees.

Caesiem was already at my side, seizing me by the waist to help me up and steady me. The world tilted, and I realized there was something wet and noxious dripping down my neck. Saliva.

I wiped at it, but my hand came away wet with blood. My skin was burning. Hissing through gritted teeth, I spun toward the creature, hunched and snarling as it stared at me hatefully. Its brown, furry body reminded me of the descriptions I'd heard of monkeys, but its overlarge fangs, grotesque face, and swishing, barbed tail were something entirely monstrous.

And its saliva…something was wrong with it. The world turned hazy at the edges as I drew my sword. Burning pain flared down my neck, traveling along my skin like a living creature burrowing, burrowing. I bit down on the groan of pain that threatened to burst out of me and stepped toward the monster.

Caesiem was faster, sending a plume of water at the beast, immersing it completely and not relenting until the creature spasmed and lay still.

More animalistic shrieks pierced the quiet, making my hair stand on end.

Caesiem's eyes darted to the wavering canopy above us. Every towering tree, every vine-draped branch, felt like the perfect ambush. I imagined hundreds of pairs of eyes latched onto us, tracking our every movement, waiting to leap out unexpectedly or spew more venomous saliva at us.

"Run," Caesiem breathed, though it was hardly necessary.

Branches clawed at our faces and arms, catching at our clothing as we raced along the edge of the ravine. I sliced wildly at the dense undergrowth to force a path for us. My pulse ratcheted in my ears as the world tilted and my limbs grew weak and heavy. My chest felt tight and hot, like I was slowly burning from the inside out.

Lungs heaving, I stumbled to a stop, tears stinging my eyes. The pain was so fierce, I feared the venom was sloughing away my flesh, exposing muscle and bone. Hot blood coursed down my skin, wetting my tunic. Was I dying?

Before I could collapse, Caesiem caught me. In a few swift movements, he had my blade strapped to his own belt and my pack slung over his shoulder, joining the weight of his own. He scooped me into his arms, tucking me close against his chest, and sprinted onward.

"It's all right," Caesiem muttered, but I could see how tight his jaw was, how dark his eyes had turned. The same fierce intent that had filled them the night he'd found Renni flinging me off a cliff gleamed within them now.

Something hissed nearby, but Caesiem dodged. Blurs of movement darted from branch to branch overhead. A long, wickedly barbed tail flicked out, and Caesiem ducked, never losing his balance or his grip on me, despite the treacherous path.

His warmth enveloped me, and his pulse beat steadily in my ear, a soothing rhythm that helped me drown out everything else. Fear melted into a quiet, peaceful darkness as my eyelids drooped. Even the pain was dulling. Maybe dozing wouldn't be such a terrible thing…

You fool, focus! You can fight this. My thoughts were foggy, as muted and distant as Elhani's music in my mind. But they filled me with a familiar fire. I was a survivor. I wasn't going to die in the land of my ancestors because I couldn't fend off one measly beast.

"Stay with me, Lo. Just a little longer. Hold on," Caesiem said, as if he sensed how much I was struggling to keep my eyes open, to focus.

Hold on.

I remembered saying those very words to him once, when he was on the verge of death.

Inhaling deeply, I stretched out with my mind, seizing the tentative notes of Elhani's song. I forced them to stay near, to wrap around me. His power flowed in my veins, filled my lungs, coated my tender skin.

Hold on. Stay with me.

This time, it was the voice of that man on the beach, clothed in simple attire and smelling of nature. Unremarkable but for the aura of power surrounding him.

I slipped into comfortable blackness.

CHAPTER NINE

Jalie

I N THE UNENDING DARKNESS OF the brig, with only the redundant sounds of the groaning ship and the sloshing waves against the hull to keep me company, the sight of Mother's corpse was almost a relief. Her once-shimmering golden hair appeared dull in the shadows, and her beautiful blue eyes were nothing but black pupils, reminding me of hollow chasms. Congealed blood clung to her throat where a gaping wound had been carved into her flesh, mimicking the shape of her sharp smile.

Once, a chill would have crept along my skin at the sight of this wraith-like vision. Now, my chest filled with a cold sort of comfort. I was no longer alone with only shadows and regret and Nesrelle's voice for company.

"Daughter." Her hissing voice was like a frozen breath of wind rather than the commanding, vibrant tone I was used to. In life, she had been magnetic—beautiful and fascinating, adventurous and fierce, wonderful and horrifying. Everything an Alrenian empress was meant to be, and everything I should have been.

Still, I wasn't afraid. There was familiarity in her features. Her straight nose and high cheekbones and angular jaw all reminded me of my own face, and they reassured me I truly was hers. And if I bore her face, surely I bore her courage and strength too.

"There's something you must do to reclaim our empire. Don't let it linger in the hands of enemies or fall into ash and ruins."

I stood and approached. My shackles clinked at my wrists while digging into my skin, chafing it raw. "Of course, Mother. But what can I do now, from here?" I lifted my arms, and her soulless eyes fell on my shackles.

"You bear more power than these sorry wretches," she snapped, slipping closer. Her footsteps made no sound on the wooden boards, and when she seized my arm, her fingers were bony and icy, their chill seeping through my dragon scale armor. "You can escape. Fight back. And *kill the soldier.*"

Pain pinched my heart, and I tried to pull away. "Kovi?"

Mother scowled. Her face was terrible to behold as she sneered, her mouth a gaping hole. A scent of death and decay, sickly-sweet and nauseating, washed over me, and I choked. "Yes, him. Don't get moony eyed over an enemy and unbeliever who lied to you and used his dark magic on you."

My throat tightened at the memory. *Liar. He's a liar. He doesn't care about you.*

"He's the one standing in your way, the one holding you back from fully stepping into Nesrelle's power and being her executioner. From being the empress you were meant to be, and killing the empress-slayer so you can finally avenge me. You've let him make you *weak* with his talk of mercy." She sneered. "You've let him hold you back from your destiny. The throne is your birthright, your fate. You're better than this."

"I'm not fated," I said, my voice sounding like a pitiful whimper in my ears. I felt small and empty. "The Life-Giver cast me aside. He hasn't chosen me." The words tasted like bile in my mouth.

Mother scoffed. "Nesrelle has chosen you. *I* chose you. Isn't that enough? Make me proud. Make *your people* proud. Or will you leave our people to suffer and die?"

I swallowed thickly at the memory of Forwyn executions, of Elder Ettonou dragging a young man before me to slaughter him in my own bedchambers. And then I thought of the Alrenian cities caught in the Teramese army's grip, of the people—*my* people—their soldiers had killed in their takeover. "No, of course not."

Mother's clutch tightened until I had to grind my teeth together to keep from crying out in pain. When she leaned forward, a flash of Nesrelle's fiery hair and piercing eyes flickered across her face and then was gone, transforming back into Mother's features. "Kill him."

Mother vanished, but the bloodlust she'd stirred within me did not. The part of me that had asked for Kovi's comfort, that had leaned into his kisses, that had shielded him from harm and vowed to never hurt him—that part was shrinking, shriveling until it was as decayed and lifeless as my mother's ghost. Instead, the part that I'd given to Nesrelle grew, filling my veins with fire and strength. The curse crackled against my fingertips, electric and compelling.

All I could hear were Mother's and Nesrelle's commands, and all I could see were my people: burning, screaming, bleeding, dying.

Fear tried to weigh me down—fear of failure, of losing, of watching Kovi die. Of losing control of *myself.* But it was nothing compared to the need to fulfill the fate I'd chosen for myself—the one that Nesrelle and Mother had chosen for me.

Save my people. Be the empress they needed. Avenge my mother.

The Alrenian Dragon Keepers' vow, one beautifully wrought along each of the blades they were gifted when they were sworn into service, echoed in my mind. An old phrase, a powerful motto, one I hadn't even allowed myself to consider for a long time. A grieving girl imprisoned in her own home, I hadn't felt worthy to claim I lived by it.

O j'eh y'vonu.

I will not bow to fear.

I concentrated on my curse, letting its power consume and burn. That tingling, electric feeling crept up my hands, encompassing my wrists. My shackles snapped, a metallic shriek shattering the quiet as they broke apart and collapsed at my feet.

The vicious smile curling my lips was mine—and it was Nesrelle's.

At the door, Mother's form materialized once more, and she gestured to me. "Well done. Follow me."

CHAPTER TEN

Kovi

A S USUAL, GRIEF MADE IT difficult to sleep. Knowing it was
my fault that I'd never laugh or fight alongside Rhi'il again was an
unbearable weight, and knowing Jalie was under threat of being
executed was worse.

I knew my duty to my people. Once, I'd relished it. Now, it was an
endless nightmare, a burden I wasn't sure I was strong enough to carry.

*And if you stop her execution? What then? Would you sit by idly while Jalie
murdered your people? And do you think she'd spare you, you idiot? She hates you
now. Nesrelle has her heart. Whoever she once was is lost to the Dark Immortal
now.*

Stifling a sigh, I rolled over in my hammock, forcing myself to close
my eyes, to focus on the rhythmic rolling of the waves and rocking of
the ship as we sailed toward Forwyth.

Lift your head, Kovi.

Mother may have wanted me to be merciful, but never at the cost
of letting my people be murdered. Choosing one enemy life over the
lives of many innocents? That couldn't be mercy.

I wasn't sure I knew what was right or wrong anymore.

And who was I to be the judge of goodness and mercy anyway,
when I used my magic to command soldiers to be still so my brothers
and sisters and I could kill them without a fight? Who was I to judge or
be hurt by Jalie and the difficult, monstrous choices she'd made for her

people, when I was little better than a monster myself?

Worst of all, I couldn't stop wondering if I would have made the same choices as Jalie if I'd been in her position.

If I'd had the opportunity to avenge Mother by slaying Empress Karye, would I have taken it?

The thought haunted me endlessly. I liked to believe I knew the line between justice and bloodlust, between fighting for a righteous cause and murder, but sometimes…sometimes the world was cast in shades of grey rather than the black and white I wished colored it.

You were taught better than this. You were trained to be disciplined. To survive impossible conditions. Stop this nonsense and keep going. Serve your people. That's all that's worth focusing on. That *is the only right choice.*

But every time I closed my eyes, it was Jalie I saw. The hurt in her eyes. The betrayal…

If she was executed …I would never be the same again. It was the only thing I was sure of, and it was terrifying. If she died, the last goodness left in me would die with her.

The creaking of a floorboard jerked me out of my thoughts, alerting my senses that something was off even before my brain registered that there was someone hovering over me. I sat up and reached for my blade in one motion, but I wasn't fast enough. Jalie, impossibly free of her shackles and the locked brig, slammed her hands toward me.

Rolling, I crashed to the floor, the air rushing out of my lungs. Without waiting to catch my breath, I leapt to my feet and faced Jalie. My eyes flicked over the sleeping forms in the swaying hammocks around us as Jalie paused, her expression almost pleading.

"I need to talk to you," she whispered.

"Are you mad?" I demanded, taking in her bare wrists. "Someone could see and kill you. How did you escape?"

"Please."

The look in her eyes… I swallowed my questions, unable to resist her pleas. Setting my jaw, I nodded once, sharply.

Every one of my senses was on high alert as I trailed Jalie up the steps and on deck, where starlight bathed the ship in an ethereal glow. For an instant, I wondered if I'd fallen asleep after all, and this was a dream. But the tang of the sea in the balmy air brushing its fingers against my cheeks was real. I relaxed my fist, holding it at my side, even if the loose trousers I'd worn to sleep didn't have a belt, and I hadn't brought a weapon.

But I didn't need one against Jalie, and she and I both knew it.

As she turned to face me, I kept several feet between us, warily assessing the scene. There were no bodies, but the deck seemed eerily deserted. I glanced toward the helm, relieved to see Huvoki at his post, alive and well. His eyes locked on Jalie and me, widening, but I gestured for him to be silent. For now.

"How did you get out?" I demanded again, torn between fury and fear—and always that foolish, aching longing. "Did you harm anyone?"

Jalie lifted her chin, strands of blonde hair dulled by grime from battle and imprisonment clinging to her gold-sheened cheeks. "Did you really think you could hold me back with shackles and a flimsy lock?"

Gritting my teeth, I watched her impassively, waiting for her to continue.

"No, I didn't hurt anyone." Something flitted across her face, unfamiliar. Wrong. "I just needed to talk to you."

"So talk." I kept my expression taut, my body rigid. Though the person before me looked like the Jalie I knew, my mind wouldn't quit buzzing a warning. I couldn't forget the moment in the palace dungeon when she'd looked like Nesrelle, and I couldn't stop studying the shadows dancing around her now. It was a constant reminder of whom she'd pledged her allegiance to.

Her eyes darted toward the boards at her feet. "They plan to execute me, don't they?"

I tried to search her expression, to find a sign of the girl I'd fallen for…but she kept her eyes averted and her face lowered.

At my silence, her shoulders slumped. Her voice cracked as she continued. "I thought you said you'd always fight for me."

Pain rocked me back on my heels. I forced myself to step nearer, despite the warning in my mind. I wasn't afraid of Jalie, and I wasn't afraid of the power Nesrelle had gifted to her either. Nor the curse.

But I *was* afraid of seeing what Jalie was becoming.

"I did," I said, "but I also promised to protect and defend my people. When you and I formed our alliance, we both agreed we had to put our people first."

"So you're going to let them kill me?" she whispered.

My heart pounded in my ears. "I never said that."

Jalie snapped her head up, her eyes glistening with tears, but her face twisted in rage. For an instant, I saw a flicker of Nesrelle's eyes, Nesrelle's hair, Nesrelle's face. My stomach lurched as Jalie launched herself forward.

I seized her wrists before she could touch me, but she was strong…unnaturally strong. Nesrelle's power coursed through her. The shadows that clung to Jalie's form danced around us, churning so thickly they smothered my view of the stars.

Slowly but steadily, Jalie's fingers inched closer to my neck. Sweat beaded on my forehead. Her eyes gleamed sapphire bright, but as cold and empty as Nesrelle's gaze. The only sign that something inside her wavered—something of her heart remained—was the way her lips trembled, ever so slightly.

"Jalie." My arms quivered from the effort of holding her back, even as pain started to leak into my skin. Burning. Devouring. Every place where my fingers touched her arms, despite the barrier of her armor, was hurting. Perhaps *all* of her skin carried the curse now, and it would claim me after all.

It was difficult to cling to her wrists as the pain lanced through me. I was certain that if I glanced down, I'd find the flesh of my hands rotting away, leaving behind nothing but bone that would soon crumble to dust. Voices hissed in my mind, chanting in an unknown tongue. Loudest of all was Nesrelle's herself, laughing. Reminding me that I had spilled Alrenian blood, that I was a monster worthy of the curse's judgment.

I blinked, and every single kill I'd ever made or assisted my fellow soldiers in making filled the deck. Their empty eyes gaped at me as shadows twisted amongst them. I couldn't see Huvoki at the helm anymore—couldn't see the stars. There was only darkness and animated corpses and Nesrelle's laughter.

When I tore my gaze back to Jalie, even she seemed to have vanished, giving way to Nesrelle's form. Her taunting blood-red mouth twisted in a wicked smile as she revealed her fangs.

This is what it is to die by Jalie's curse, I thought as pain wracked my entire body, and I collapsed.

CHAPTER ELEVEN

Lo

I OPENED MY EYES TO a dim cave lit by dancing, sparkling light, moving across the stone floor as if underwater. Blinking, I sat up to find the world was steady and the wound on my neck no longer gave me pain. When I brushed my fingers along my skin, I felt no sign of injury beyond some dried blood crusted on my neck and the collar of my tunic. I'd wielded Elhani's healing magic more powerfully than I ever had before.

Whether I'd eradicated the effects of the venom as well, or it had only been a toxin that temporarily disoriented its victims, I couldn't say. All I knew was that my head was blissfully clear, and all discomfort was gone.

Blinking, I glanced around, taking in my surroundings. We were at the back of a small, dry cave, our packs lying nearby. On my left, the cave ended in a rough wall, while on my right, the mouth of the cave was concealed by a waterfall. The silvery light reflecting through it made me guess it was already some time after dark, though that glow was swallowed up by something far more magical: colorful vines and fungi lined the walls around us, illuminating the cave in a variety of colors. Silvers, golds, and deep crimson and rich emerald and sapphire and violet—they all stretched across the walls in a breathtaking, beautiful tangle that reminded me of constellations in the night sky, only more vibrant, more intense.

Perhaps strangest of all was the fact that the waterfall's sound was muted within the cavern, a soothing background noise rather than the roaring chaos that should have enveloped us. If I listened closely enough, I could even detect the sounds of the rainforest life beyond the noise of the water: chirping crickets, chirring insects, calling frogs, and the whisper of leaves and plants in the night breeze.

Underneath it all, in a far stronger current than I'd heard when first setting foot upon the island, was Elhani's song. It ran through me, warming my blood and calming my spirit. Refueling the strength I'd spent when I'd called upon his power to heal me.

I drew in a fortifying breath, a peace like I hadn't experienced in what seemed like ages filling me. This was the magic I'd expected to find in Forwyth. There was a strong presence here, a reminder that the people and this very land had been dedicated to our god, and that he had blessed us and Forwyth because of it.

Something must have gone very wrong for the monsters that had attacked Caesiem and me to run rampant as they did, but here…here I was reminded of my heritage. Perhaps once this cave had been used by my people, or perhaps it was simply Elhani-blessed because the whole land had been. But why did the rest of the land feel so…quiet? So ominous?

Caesiem leaned against the wall a few feet away, slumped in exhaustion as he studied the waterfall. His clothes were wet, his hair clinging to him in damp locks, as if he hadn't had the energy to change. There was no sign of the animals that had attacked us. How long had Caesiem been forced to carry me and fend them off?

Swiping a hand across my eyes, I frowned in confusion. "How long was I out?" It had to have been hours, if night had fallen. I scanned Caesiem's form, searching for injuries, but in the dancing shadows and light, it was difficult to tell. "Are you hurt? I'm sorry I passed out like that; that's never happened before…"

My words trailed off as Caesiem straightened and shook his head.

"It's not your fault, Lo." He met my gaze. "I'm not sure how long I ran, but…we were ambushed by so many of those creatures, I…well, I think our magic may be different, but we wield it in much the same way. It's all based on focus, and mental stamina…and eventually, I was too exhausted to continue drawing on mine. I found a river as the sun began to set, and that's when I realized those creatures didn't want to swim to get their prey. They're water averse, if not outright terrified of it. I figured this was the safest place we could rest and wait out the night. And being here, so close to the water, helps replenish my strength."

I knew what he meant. His exhaustion was physical from fleeing and fending off the beasts, but it was also magical. He must have been utterly depleted when he brought me here.

Glancing down at my own dry clothes, I frowned. "How did you get me across a river and through a waterfall without me getting wet?"

Caesiem tossed me a cheeky grin. "You might not believe it, but I *do* know how to take care of a lady." I rolled my eyes, resisting my own smile in response as he explained, "I crossed in the shallows, and I was able to climb into this cave and slip behind the waterfall rather than through it. There was a path. I'm drenched from using my magic more than anything."

Realizing he had avoided one of my other questions, I sat up on my knees and leaned forward until I rested a tentative hand on his shoulder. He started, and my chest ached as a feeling of rejection washed over me. When had he gone from pressing me against a wall and kissing me to flinching at my touch?

"Are you all right?" I repeated. Before he could answer, my eyes flicked down to the blood staining the front of his torn shirt.

"It's not deep," he insisted, but I scowled at him, crossing my arms. "Let me look at it."

Stifling a sigh, Caesiem reached for the hem of his shirt, slowly peeling it off and dropping it to the cavern floor. Warmth rushed through me, an annoying tangle of desire and embarrassment, but I shoved it away. I'd seen him shirtless before, and I'd seen dozens of other half-naked soldiers in the past week I'd been tending to our wounded. Trying to ignore the way the sight of his bronzed skin and toned muscles made me feel, I focused my attention on the cut just below his ribcage. It wasn't bleeding heavily, but it was deep enough to warrant stitches.

"What happened?" I murmured, reaching for my pack. I dug through it until I found painkiller and a salve to clean the wound and stave off infection, along with the mending kit I'd brought. Naina had taught me to sew up skin, but I'd never had the need to perfect the skill until the past week.

"I wasn't fast enough to avoid one of their barbed tails," Caesiem said with a wry smile. "It felt like a knife."

Tearing my gaze off his face, I leaned forward and focused on tending to the injury, cleaning the wound and urging him to take some of the painkilling herbs I'd brought. He remained obedient and quiet, only hissing when I pulled the first stich through.

"I don't understand why you're doing this," he said through gritted teeth.

I tugged on my thread again as I made the next stitch. "You don't understand why I'm helping you when you're injured?" I demanded incredulously. "It's what I *do*. What I've always done. Who do you think I am?"

"No." His voice turned soft. "I don't understand why you asked me to come with you. Or why you want to associate with me, or how you can stand to be kind to me at all."

My eyes flicked to his and I paused, freezing under his piercing gaze. That haunted look was back in his eyes, turning their brilliant blue a darker shade.

Breaking my stare, I frowned at his wound and made another stitch. He didn't understand why I wanted to be around him? How couldn't he see? How didn't he *know*?

But Caesiem continued. "I thought I understood before why you couldn't forgive me, but now..." He drew a deep breath. "I saw what Revaed did, what he told our soldiers to do to your people," he whispered. "I saw the bodies in the Akytha square. I saw your sister..."

Tears burned my eyes and my fingers trembled, forcing me to stop, waiting for my hands to still. I pursed my lips. The memory of Eloiyah's song pierced my heart, the words still ringing in my ears. I couldn't stop seeing the peace on her face as she accepted a brutal death—murder at the hands of her enemies—all to ensure I didn't reveal myself and could keep fighting for our people.

"I don't know how you can even stand to look at me," Caesiem muttered.

Throat tight, eyes on my needle, I blurted out the words. "I told you at our wed...at the ceremony that I trust you. Well, I also forgive you."

Caesiem froze, and I forced myself to glance at him. "I don't deserve it."

Clenching my jaw, I shook my head. The pendant at my neck was heavy, a weight pressing on my chest, crushing me with both anger and sorrow. "That's not for you to decide," I snapped.

He flinched. "All I ever did was make excuses for myself, for my guardian, for my people. I'm sorry for what I did, and I'm sorry I was such a fool. I'm sorry I didn't see Revaed for what he is sooner."

Tying off the thread, I sighed. "Revaed took you in when you were young and half-starved, didn't he?"

Caesiem nodded, his eyes unfocused as he stared into the waterfall.

"I understand what it's like to long for a family, for someone to love you like a parent. That's what Naina was to me. A mother figure after I'd lost mine." I swallowed painfully. "Revaed cared for you, and so it was natural for you to trust him, to be loyal to him. I understand why you did what you did, and I forgive you."

Caesiem swept a hand through his hair, tousling it until it was as wild as the windswept waves of a stormy sea. A lock fell across his brow. "I'm going to have to confront him." He squeezed his eyes shut, as if the very thought caused him physical pain.

I hesitated as I finished applying his salve, leaning back on my heels. Reaching for my tin of herbs once more, I poured some more of the dried leaves into his hand. "You can chew some of these every few hours to ease the pain."

When Caesiem had finished chewing, I sighed and screwed the lid back on my tin. "I think Revaed does care about you, in his way."

Caesiem studied me sadly. "That's what makes everything he did even worse. He's the only father I ever had, and I was just a weapon he sharpened to use for his own purposes. Even if he cares for me...even if he doesn't fully realize it because it's what his father taught him to do...he's been using me, manipulating me. Now that I'm not his weapon anymore...will he still love me?"

I shook my head, at a loss for words. "I'm sorry." Turning from him, I busied myself with putting away my supplies. "Are you sure you want to be caught up in all this? In our war?"

"I'm not a heartless monster who wants to see your people suffer."

"I didn't say that," I said quickly, fumbling with the tie to close my pack. I thought again of the way he'd tried to evade my touch, of his earlier comment about thinking our marriage ceremony hadn't been real. "I guess I just expected you to return to Teramyl, since I know your people are also suffering."

"Even if I didn't care about you or your people," Caesiem murmured, the tenderness in his voice lending me the courage to turn around and face him, "going back to Teramyl without a plan would be suicide. Revaed's father hates me. If I returned now..." His voice trailed off, his eyes once again growing distant. "I suppose by law, I'm still a member of the imperial family, but that could end soon enough. Even so, I owe my people, if we survive this war, but I'll have to make careful plans to find a way to help the Teramese."

I smiled sadly, but I injected some lightness into my tone. "Your confidence in our cause is inspiring."

Plucking a fresh, dry shirt out of his pack and tugging it over his head, he leaned back against the wall. When he searched my face, his expression was earnest. "I'm not going to abandon you, Lo. I meant it when I said that you deserve better. I'll make sure that happens, or I'll die trying."

"Thank you," I said, too overcome to say anything else. As I met the intensity of Caesiem's gaze, heat unfurled in my stomach, leaving me confused and uncharacteristically shy. I forced myself to breathe evenly, and my fingers strayed to the cool pendant at my throat. *Just because the nymph said he loves you, doesn't mean she was right. Or that he couldn't have changed his mind,* I reminded myself.

The weight of Caesiem's pendant grounded me, clearing my head as I reached up to untie the leather cord fastening it about my neck. "And thank you for giving this to me, but I think you need it more than I do right now. Won't it help you replenish your strength faster?"

Caesiem shook his head, and my fingers stilled. "I won't need that. Let's rest here, and I'll be fine in the morning." His eyes flitted back to the waterfall. "You should eat something and get some rest. I'll keep watch."

"You don't need to." I gestured around, as if he too could hear Elhani's song permeating the air. "Look at this place. It's Elhani-blessed. We'll be safe here, and his magic will restore our strength. You can sleep too."

His eyes scanned the space, taking in the colors as if seeing its beauty for the first time. "And here I thought I was just drawn to it by the magic of the water. I did think it was strange we could hear each other and even the jungle outside so…clearly."

I grinned. "Another sign it's Elhani-blessed. If anything approaches, we'll hear it coming."

"What makes you think Elhani's power will restore *my* magic?"

Caesiem asked after a long moment.

As I found some dried meat, a hunk of bread, and one of the apples I'd packed, I rubbed the fruit against my tunic and leaned against my pack. "We Forwyn believe all magic comes from Elhani," I explained. "Alrenian gifts, Teramese elemental magic…you name it. We believe as the creator of all life, he is also the source of all power and strength. Even that of the Dark Immortal—Nesrelle." I scowled, thinking of the Immortal who had taunted me with my own failure to save Edi and Naina from death.

Caesiem raised his eyebrows. "But Nesrelle and many of the Alrenians use their powers in such brutal ways." He pressed his lips together. "And…I've used my magic to kill people who…maybe didn't deserve death."

I glanced down at my apple. "Well, that's where our choices come in. Even Forwyn magic can be used for cruel purposes."

A heavy silence fell as I ate, broken only by the crunch of my apple. It was loud, echoing in the small space, and only made the quiet between us more uncomfortable, but I was too hungry to care—much. At last, as I tossed the core away, Caesiem stood and shrugged a little awkwardly. "I'll rest. But first, I need to change out of these wet pants."

My face heated. "All right," I said. "I'll…look away."

I turned my back to him and sat rigidly staring at the wall. Embarrassment made my entire body warm, but every sound Caesiem made as he stripped off his pants and pulled on his new ones seemed impossibly loud in the cave. My mouth was dry, painfully aware of how little space we had. Somehow, it hadn't occurred to me until now that with only the two of us on this journey, we'd be sleeping beside each other, sharing every moment together. Mostly because I'd never expected it would take this long for us to reach Rhaeda, and I'd imagined they'd have separate rooms for us when we arrived. Even with the distance that had settled between us, there was still intimacy in that. Even though we'd shared the same chambers at the palace, those rooms had seemed vast. Here, if I breathed too loudly, the noise reverberated off the walls. It'd be easy for him to hear me if I murmured in my sleep. Easy to roll so close I'd feel his body heat enveloping me.

I swallowed, hard.

"It's safe now," he said, amusement edging his tone.

I turned and tried to scowl. "You think it's awfully funny, don't you? Embarrassing me just because I used to be a nun?"

He settled against the wall and ran his hand through his damp hair, shaking out some of the water droplets. Once again, a lock fell against his bronze forehead, and I had the wild desire to step forward and brush it back, to run my hands through his hair. To kiss him like I had before. To press *him* against the wall. My stomach clenched and I forced the thoughts away.

He's pulling away because he's meant to return to Teramyl. Nothing would have ever lasted between you two, and now this forced marriage has made things even more awkward and painful.

"I didn't mean to make fun of you," Caesiem said. "It's just endearing, how modest you are about these things, when only moments ago you were touching my bare skin."

I rolled my eyes. "That was…different," I stammered.

"Plus, I so rarely see you frazzled," he went on, his smile growing until I could see the hint of dimples. My stomach flipped. He was so ridiculously, painfully beautiful.

"You just enjoy it because you're the one making me frazzled," I said, before I realized what I was admitting. I bit my lip, my eyes widening a fraction.

Caesiem's smile faded, something else crossing his face. Longing? Desire? It was gone in another instant, as he turned away and cleared his throat. "We should sleep."

"Yes," I said, immediately seizing my pack to use as a makeshift pillow and stretching out. The ground was cool and hard, but it was mostly flat, and my muscles already ached anyway. Long hours of tending to the wounded aboard the ship had made every inch of me sore.

As I listened to Caesiem settle down, his earlier promise ran through my mind. Some part of him cared, I thought, but building any sort of romantic relationship required more than love. Things had always been complicated between us, always forbidden. Even if I found the words to confess how I felt about him—I wasn't sure it could change anything. We would fight for my people's freedom, and if Elhani willed it, we would win, and Caesiem would return to Teramyl to aid his own land.

My heart throbbed painfully. As I forced my eyes closed, it took everything in me not to stand up and go to Caesiem, not to throw my arms around him and beg him to stay.

CHAPTER TWELVE

Jalie

My head pounded as hands seized my arms, wrenching them painfully behind my back. I hardly registered the sensation, hardly noticed the racing footsteps across the deck or the panicked shouting as I gaped down at Kovi's sprawled form. While one part of me gloated, victorious and hopeful that I'd finally made Mother proud, there was another part, tucked away in a dark corner, that shrieked in misery and horror.

One step closer to your throne, my sweet young amara. The voice sounded both like Mother's and Nesrelle's, as if the two of them had become so intertwined in my brain that I couldn't tell them apart. Both lent me courage. Both were strong figures who'd nurtured and supported me. And I longed to make both proud.

Quieter, underneath that pleased voice, a terrified thought that was wholly mine ran on repeat. Almost stifled, it cried out in vain. *Stop! You can't kill him. You can't. This is* Kovi. *What will you do if he dies? What will be left of you?*

Though Kovi was motionless, his chest rose and fell evenly, indicating he was only unconscious. Not dead. There was no stench of decay, no sign his flesh was rotting or burning away…

A strange combination of elation and disappointment burned within me.

"Kill her now." The sharp words snapped me from my daze,

drawing my gaze to General Ilowhe. There was no hatred or fear in his eyes, only grim determination. "We can't have her posing a threat to our people. The time for compassion and mercy is over."

There wasn't a word of protest, not even from the Alrenians gathering on deck, intermingling shamelessly with the Forwyn and studying Kovi with the same sense of horror the general's own people displayed. A healer knelt beside Kovi, checking his pulse.

"He's alive. He's…" His voice trailed off as Kovi stirred.

Inhaling deeply, Kovi snapped his eyes open and sat up, his stare locking on mine. The arms on either side of me shoved me to my knees, slamming them into the wooden floorboards. The force shuddered through my bones and made my teeth clatter together.

Kovi's gaze was dark and unfathomable, carefully concealing whatever emotions brewed behind his mask. If he hurt, if a part of him was screaming and weeping like that small, lost part of myself, he showed no sign. "No," he said quickly, firmly, dragging his eyes away to look at the general. He stood, straightening his stance and setting his jaw, once again the disciplined solider. He showed no sign of pain, no indication of weakness at all. He was utterly coherent, and it was clear he'd heard what the general had said.

Had my curse failed? Or had that part of me that didn't want to kill him kept him from dying? Bile swam in my mouth.

"You're not worthy of the title of empress." I turned, finding my mother's corpse sneering at me. As if I weren't worth another second of her time, she turned her back on me and strode away, once again vanishing, melting into shadow and blackness. No one else reacted to her presence, reinforcing my belief that she haunted me alone.

I squeezed my eyes shut.

"Soldier?" There was an edge of warning in General Ilowhe's tone as he studied Kovi.

Kovi, however, had turned his eyes back to me. I opened mine to meet his gaze, still finding it impenetrable. Carved from stone. There was no hint of the young man I'd once begged to lie in bed beside me and keep the nightmares at bay, the one with whom I'd danced and kissed and dreamed of impossible things. The one who had made promises to me, promises he'd *broken*.

I snarled and spat at him, but I fell short of my mark, and he didn't move. "I'll do it," he said, every word steady, echoing clearly in the nighttime stillness.

For a long moment, the world seemed to freeze. The only movement was the cool breath of wind as it fluttered strands of hair into my face. The only sound was the gentle rhythm of the waves splashing against the hull and matching the beating of my heart.

I'll do it. His declaration rang in my ears endlessly. *I'll do it.*

Horror and pain clawed at my chest, matched only by…elation. *Now he shows who he really is,* Nesrelle hissed. *Now you can set your sentimentalities aside and kill your would-be executioner.*

I was split in two, half of me full of bloodlust and fury and excitement, and the other half aching and sorrowful and broken.

"When we reach Forwyth," Kovi continued, studying me as if I were a foreign creature whose weaknesses he needed to memorize, and not the woman he'd once held, once protected, once…

I cut the thoughts off, letting the heat of my curse burn through my blood. *I can overpower him. He's nothing but a lying traitor,* I thought fiercely, *and I will be glad to kill him.*

"Let me face her in a duel to the death in the land of our ancestors," Kovi continued. "Let the people of Forwyth bear witness, and see we have the strength to face our enemies and win back our empire."

Surprise and eagerness stole through me. A duel? It was almost too easy. Did Kovi have a death wish?

And yet…my eyes scanned his body, recalling how my curse had done nothing but strike him unconscious. Just like when I'd attempted to avenge my mother and slay Lo, my curse had been ineffective. Was it losing its power? Was something wrong?

Fear threatened, until I remembered the way I'd broken my shackles, and the other powers Nesrelle had bestowed upon me. I had plenty of fearsome weapons at my disposal. And even without the otherworldly gifts the Immortal had given me, I had been trained by the finest of Alrenian warriors. I could hold my own in a fight, even against an Aerekni Academy graduate who wielded unnatural Forwyn magic.

"We should discuss this," the general cut in firmly, but Kovi set his jaw, meeting his superior's eyes.

"Do you doubt it would send a powerful message to the Forwyth?"

"No, Officer Ettonou," General Ilowhe said, "but is the empress truly deserving of the chance you give her in a duel?"

Kovi was calm. Serene, almost. The sight made my blood boil. Had the brokenness I'd seen in him earlier been an act? Had he really been playing me all along, in an awful game that took advantage of all my emotions—my loneliness, my grief, and my longing to be loved?

You don't care, I thought firmly, imagining myself constructing a barrier around my heart. *Shut him out, as you should have done from the beginning. You were weak to let yourself feel anything for him. Don't be weak again.* Never *again.*

"Are you doubting I can win?" Kovi asked, placing a hand on his sword hilt.

"Not at all."

A muscle twitched in Kovi's cheek. "Take her to the brig. I'll guard her myself until we arrive. She won't escape again."

There was a pause. I couldn't tear my eyes from the soldier in front of me. It felt like my world was crumbling apart and rebuilding itself. Countless emotions writhed in my stomach, and a vague part of me wondered if Kovi had spoken the truth when he said he could no longer sense my feelings, or if the commanding magic he'd used on me during the battle had reconnected us. If he could sense my emotions now and was behaving this coldly, then everything he'd ever done must have truly been an act.

Nesrelle had been right. Nesrelle had always been right, from the very beginning.

My heart was a fortress. A frozen shard of ice. A hunk of untarnished steel.

All along, only Nesrelle had been on my side. Only she had ensured I'd never again be alone.

She was all I had left. All I'd ever had.

"Very well, Officer," the general said. "I trust your wisdom and your abilities. You'll defeat the empress in a duel, and you'll show the Forwyth we have the strength to overcome our enemies. You will exact justice on Jaliana, daughter of Karye, and you will help us forge a new alliance to reclaim Alrenor for the Forwyn people. Empress Karye's terror and cruelty will die with the last of her line."

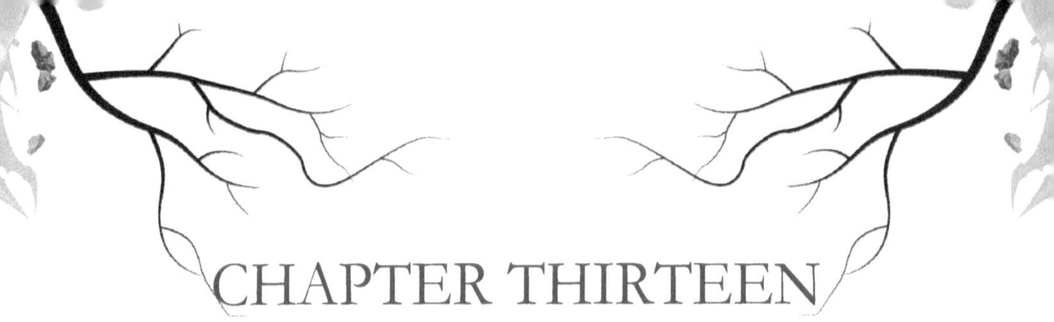

CHAPTER THIRTEEN

Kovi

—✦—

THE INSTANT MY EARS POPPED, I knew General Ilowhe had called upon Elhani's magic, enveloping us in a sound barrier to keep our conversation private. As he paused before the door I guarded, I straightened. His dark gaze flitted briefly toward the brig before settling on me.

"If you're here to try to persuade me differently, it won't work, sir," I said stiffly, not quite meeting the general's eyes. "All I can ask is that you don't order me to change my mind."

General Ilowhe's brow furrowed, some of the sternness in his expression slipping away. "Kovi," he said, dropping his formal tone. "I just wanted to see…" He pursed his lips and shook his head, compassion stealing over his face and overtaking the disciplined mask he usually wore. "I know you care about her," he continued, lowering his voice even though his magic already protected us from prying ears. "I'm sorry for everything that's happened—what this has come to—but you don't have to be the one to do it."

My throat tightened as I tried to lock away the memory of Jalie's burning gaze. I couldn't detect her emotions, no matter how hard I tried, so I could only guess how much of her was left, buried deep beneath Nesrelle's control.

My only hope that she wasn't fully lost was the fact that somehow her curse hadn't killed me. Maybe that was a sign she hadn't actually wanted me to die. Maybe somewhere, deep down, a part of her true self remained, refusing to give in completely to Nesrelle.

"I *do* have to be the one to do it," I muttered. Finally, I forced myself to meet the general's eyes.

He set a hand on my shoulder, grief flickering across his face. "You are…" He sighed. "You are a soldier first, always, but you're also a man. It's all right to let yourself grieve, to fall apart now and then. It's all right if you let someone else carry your burdens sometimes. I've always asked so much of you, always relied on you…" He swallowed. "I just want you to know that I care about *you*—not just for who you are as a soldier, or what you can do for your people. You're young, not much older than my own daughter, and…" He hesitated. "I want to ensure you'll be all right. If you're the one to kill her…that memory will live with you for the rest of your life. You'll never be the same."

Drawing a deep breath, I leaned against the wall, letting myself relax for the first time in what felt like hours. Nothing seemed quite real, like I'd been caught in a nightmare for the past week. Everything since Rhi'il's death and Jalie's imprisonment had been a miserable blur as I tried to hold myself together. No—it had been like this for longer than that. I'd been broken inside since the massacre at the academy, since I'd lost my cousin and so many other friends and fellow soldiers. Since I'd felt my father's betrayal cut more deeply than it ever had, and since I'd thought Jalie had died.

And now, here I was, planning to be the one to kill her.

It was like planning to destroy myself.

"I have to do it," I murmured, squeezing my eyes closed as if I could shut out my current reality and will a new one into being. "I can't stand by and *watch* it happen. It…it has to be me. At least then I…I can make sure it's fast and painless. I can make sure she doesn't suffer." My chest was hollow, and my body was numb. None of my words sounded right in my ears, as if someone else was speaking for me.

I couldn't face Jalie in a duel to the death. I couldn't kill her. But I couldn't let her escape her prison and kill all my brothers and sisters aboard this ship, either. I couldn't let her continue to give in to Nesrelle's control and murder my people.

Lift your head, Kovi.

Mercy was a lie.

There is no room for kindness in war. Maybe we're all monsters. Jalie's earlier words mocked me, along with the terrible declaration the water nymph had made, what now felt like ages ago: *You'll have to choose, in the end.* In my mind, I could see her yellow eyes, her gaze cold and unblinking. **You still think death is the worst fate that can befall the ones you love. Perhaps it is, if it comes at your own hand.**

When I looked up, General Ilowhe's gaze was gentle, a sharp contrast to my memory of the taunting water nymph. "Are you sure?" he asked. "I can find someone else who will be merciful."

I squeezed my hand into a fist. "I'm not going to change my mind," I declared, staring levelly at the general. Let him believe I wasn't wavering. Let him believe I knew what I was doing. Let him believe I didn't already feel like I was dead inside.

After a beat, he nodded and retracted the sound barrier with another muted popping noise. I stood to attention as he stepped back.

"As you were, soldier," General Ilowhe said, his mask already back in place.

He retraced his path back up the stairs, leaving me alone, with nothing but the crashing of the sea against the hull and the thundering of my pulse to keep me company.

CHAPTER FOURTEEN

MY TANGLED, TROUBLED DREAMS MELTED away as birdsong drew me from sleep. When I opened my eyes, my body stiff from sleeping on the unforgiving cavern floor, I found the space awash with golden light that danced from the movement of the shimmering waterfall. Inhaling deeply, I extended a hand and called upon my magic, finding the action as effortless as breathing.

Little droplets pulled away from the cascading wall of water, settling atop my fingers with the same grace and gentleness I imagined a butterfly would perch. They glistened like shards of glass, cool against my skin. I couldn't hear the song Lo had talked about last night, but something about this space had drawn me—even stronger than my pull to the water, that warm current always calling me home. Something even more reassuring than the familiarity of my magic. There was peace and strength here. Safety. A sense of home in a foreign land.

Rising, I glanced over my shoulder to find Lo still asleep, her dark braid twisting over one shoulder as her chest rose and fell in a steady rhythm. My stomach clenched at the sight, at the way the golden lighting shimmered in the frizzy black curls framing her face, at the way her full mouth relaxed in a straight line, for once at perfect peace as she slept. No nightmares haunted her here. The hard front she usually put up to protect herself had vanished, its absence highlighting her every soft and gentle feature. Somehow, that only emphasized the strength and power that I knew lived inside her.

She was beautiful and stubborn and untamable. Empress-slayer. Nun. Vigilante. Leader.

My eyes fell to my pendant hanging from her neck.

What if you told her everything, and she committed to you as fully as she committed to everything else? She'd honor her vows to Elhani… Maybe she'd even love you, as fiercely as she loves her people.

Banishing the selfish thought before I could lose myself in a senseless daydream, I tore my gaze away to approach the waterfall. I plunged my hands into the clear water and splashed some onto my face, scrubbing off as much of the dirt and grime coating my skin as I could. Then I ran some through my hair and tried to rinse off my hands and arms. The coolness was a welcome reprieve from the gathering humidity of morning. Even in the cave, the air was already growing stifling.

When I leaned out of the cave's mouth to peer around the waterfall, the jungle showed no sign of the venomous animals that had attacked us yesterday. Rather than eerie stillness, the trees and plants were full of life, with birds flitting to and fro and lizards darting along tree trunks. Beyond the churning of the waterfall, the edges of the pool glistened, smooth and undisturbed by anything but the colorful, harmless fish I'd discovered when I'd waded through it the first time. My worry eased.

Perhaps today we could reach Rhaeda without incident and begin gaining the promise of Forwyth's assistance, before our ships arrived. My thoughts turned to Lo's father, and I wondered if he'd be more likely to forgive me for joining Lo on this mission if we actually secured help. And…if he knew I would agree to whatever ceremony we must perform to dissolve the marriage.

If only he knew I was as dedicated to securing Lo's happiness as he was, even if it meant losing her forever. I almost scoffed at the thought. I'd never *had* her. Lo had always been unattainable and forbidden. But now it was also clear how undeserving I was of her, how much better off she would be when I was back in Teramyl and out of her life for good.

My chest ached when I thought of home. Of Revaed. Of the High Imperator.

My head throbbed with the start of a headache. Did Revaed consider me a traitor already? Or did he think I was a prisoner of war— or wounded or dead? Did he mourn me, or did he already hate me?

Eventually, my only choice would be confronting him and everything he'd done. And that meant open rebellion. That meant…possibly having to fight him.

Movement behind me alerted me that Lo was waking. "You look well rested," she said, and I forced a smile on my face as I turned to her.

"You were right about the cave and what it would do for my magic." I called upon the water again, letting it swirl around me, twisting in a silver ribbon that flashed every color when the morning light struck it.

Lo rolled her eyes and bit back a grin. "Show off."

Wordlessly, I sat, and Lo plucked food from her pack for both of us. As we ate, silence fell over us, but it wasn't quite as heavy as it had been last night. Things felt…easier, more natural between us. Even if the knowledge that Lo forgave me couldn't ease my guilt, it did comfort me to know that she cared.

"We should reach Rhaeda today," she announced at last, her eyes distant as she studied the walls of the cavern. In the daylight, the fungi and vines that had glowed so vibrantly were dull shades of green and grey and brown, appearing completely ordinary. "Which is good," she added, "because by now we won't arrive much sooner than Father will."

"I can hardly believe you convinced him to let you and me go on ahead," I said, half-smiling at the thought of how protective the general was of her. "He's been so worried for your safety."

Lo smirked around a bite of jerky. "That's exactly why he agreed—

I told him he needed to stop treating me like a fragile child, like he didn't trust me." Her expression sobered. "He's still trying to…figure out how to be a father. I think in his mind, I'm still the little girl he saw at the palace, before he was sent away."

I couldn't help asking the question, even if I knew it was dangerous. "You didn't really answer me last night. Why did you choose *me* to come with you?"

Shrugging, she didn't quite meet my eyes as she replied, "Nia is a fighter, but she's still a nun and a healer first. And who else could be spared?"

Excuses. But I didn't question her further. It was safer for both of us that way.

Another silence descended, and my thoughts turned to the citizens of Rhaeda. If the beasts in the rainforest were this vicious, if we'd found no other signs of civilization before now but for that decaying bridge, what would await us in the city? To survive this land, their capital would have to be heavily fortified. And would the citizens there be willing to accept us? Lo would be easier for them to welcome—even if she was Alrenian born, she was tied to their culture, to their way of life. But would they accept *me*?

"What will they think of a Teramese man?" I blurted. "What if I hinder your mission just by being here with you?"

Lo's gaze was steady. "If we explain what happened—that your people invaded but we have you and others like you on our side—I think they'll see there is hope. *You're* that hope."

My mouth twitched in a half-smile. "So *that's* why you brought me."

For a second, I thought I saw hurt pass over Lo's face. Once again, she shrugged rather than answer.

It didn't take long for us to pack and approach the waterfall, gazing out through the gap between the water and the cave's mouth. The jungle remained still and peaceful.

"I'll go first," I said, following the narrow, rocky trail that I'd discovered last night. The waterfall left a cool mist against my skin, refreshing in the gathering heat, and within moments, I was wading through the pool. No creatures waited for us on shore, and there was no sound but for the calming notes of birdsong. Behind me, Lo stepped gingerly through the water, pausing when some of it rippled and moved toward her rather than away. I stopped and glanced back as she gaped at it.

"What's happening?" she whispered, her eyes round with awe.

My heart slammed against my ribcage, but rather than answering, I merely gestured toward my throat, where my pendant had once hung. In response, her fingers drifted up, cradling the pendant, tracing its smooth surface. She nodded in understanding, a soft smile quirking the corners of her lips.

But she didn't know the full extent of the truth.

I turned away and pushed onward, listening while her own footsteps sloshed through the pool.

As Lo and I pressed through the undergrowth, we found no paths, no indication at all that we were nearing the capital. Sweat clung to the back of my neck as I scanned the trees for any signs of another ambush. The chirr of insects and the chirping of birds became a steady, soothing rhythm, mingling with the nearby burbling of the river.

"Maybe…" I began doubtfully, but my words trailed off when I noticed the sudden silence descending over us.

At my side, Lo stilled, her fingers tightening on her sword hilt. My pulse pounded in my ears, and I focused on the river, on the foaming water…

As a flock of huge birds that had been concealed in the branches overhead dove, sharp beaks glinting in the sunlight, I seized Lo around the waist and ducked, pulling her to the ground with me. The wall of water I'd called roared and stretched overhead, creating a barrier between us and the birds. Enraged squawks filled my ears as the water pummeled into them, knocking them off course and throwing some to the ground, where they lay still and dazed. Feathers in shades of vibrant red and gold rained around us.

Most of the birds fluttered off, furious and wet, abandoning the ones left ruffled on the forest floor. I waited several more moments before I called off the water, enough time to become aware of just how close Lo was. Despite the oppressive heat of the jungle, her warmth was welcoming, the lingering scent of coconut oil in her hair tickling my nose. I'd pulled her against my chest, near enough that I wondered if she could feel my erratic heartbeat.

Embarrassment trickled through me as I waited for the water to swirl back toward the river, as I caught my breath and slowly, carefully, loosened my grip on her hips and retracted my arms.

Lo leapt to her feet and, in a blur of silver, slammed her sword through the nearest bird, skewering it to the earth. I drew my dagger and hurled it at another as she finished off the remaining two. For a minute, we gaped at the mangled bodies, at the foot-long beaks as sharp as blades, at the broken wings that spanned easily as wide as a man was tall.

Wiping the sweat off my brow, I offered Lo a wry grin. "Well," I said, "I don't know about you, but I'm fully awake now. No coffee needed."

Lo rolled her eyes, but it didn't quite conceal her uneasiness. "Something's wrong," she murmured, her eyes distant. "I can barely hear Elhani's song out here, and these creatures shouldn't be running rampant like this. There should be signs of civilization…something…" She swallowed before shaking her head, as if trying to shake off her concern. "Come on," she added, her voice steadying.

As we pressed onward, the sense of wrongness that had been prickling at both of us grew. The rainforest thinned out abruptly, leaving us in an eerily desolate expanse of grey ash and debris. Piles of rocks and bits of old, decaying tree limbs littered the ground all the way to the coast. Our boots crunched over pebbles, the only sound aside from the crash of water onshore.

There were no towering buildings, no people traveling toward a bustling city, no roads. There was only desolation, leading toward Forwyth's single peak: Mt. Nu'ohni. My body froze as I took it in: the empty crater where the summit of the volcano had once been. The utter lack of any sign of life for miles. The dismal grey coating everything, including the distant lumps and smudges—the ruins of the capital city of Rhaeda.

Beside me, Lo was utterly still, breathing out a single curse before stifling a sob. "It can't be," she whispered, her eyes sparkling with unshed tears as she scanned the ash and sand. "They're here. They have to be. Didn't the Elders say they'd exchanged letters with them within the past three years?"

My stomach clenched, and I reached for her. She leaned into me, letting me wrap my arms around her even as she continued to stare, her right hand still clutching her sword hilt in a death grip.

"I'm so sorry," I murmured. "I don't think anyone has lived in Rhaeda for a long time."

CHAPTER FIFTEEN

INSTEAD OF RAGING AND SCREAMING when I was shoved into the brig, I found myself enveloped in an overcoming sensation of numbness. The inferno that had been my emotions chilled, until I could have been carved from ice, frozen over both inside and out. I'd been a fool to ever trust Kovi. To ever think he could have cared…

Shaking my head, I collapsed against the wall, letting Nesrelle's glee overtake me instead.

I'd kill him. I'd kill all of them. And I wouldn't regret it. I couldn't. I'd strangle that weak, sentimental part of me that was breaking until I could silence her for good. Until there wasn't room for anything else but Mother's strength and Nesrelle's bloodlust.

My throne and my crown and my people—that was all that mattered.

At some point, I drifted into sleep. A memory floated through my mind, some parts hazy from the passage of time, but others…the emotions of grief and comfort I'd experienced, the scent of my mother, the warmth of her embrace…those were as real as if I were living them all over again.

I was thirteen and I was weeping, crumpled up on my bed, devastated that even with the allure of being the imperial princess, I hadn't managed to secure the attentions of the boy who'd caught my eye. Instead, he'd spent the duration of the feast we'd had that night laughing and dancing with another noble girl. My young heart had been crushed and frustrated, full of a mingling sense of grief and the horrible realization that in spite of who I was, I couldn't control everything that happened to me. I couldn't have everything I wanted.

In my short life, losing in such a way was a novel concept to me, and it stung fiercely.

But as usual, Mother had been swift to notice my distress and had found me in my rooms after the party. She settled beside me on my bed as I cried.

"My strong one," she murmured, pulling me gently into her arms until I could tuck my head beneath her chin. I drew in a shaky breath, filling my nose with the scent of vaeletta, the flowers she loved to adorn our chambers with. "He's not worth your tears."

Ironically, just four years later, I couldn't even remember the boy's name, could scarcely recall his face. But the emotions I'd experienced had been as tumultuous as the ones raging inside me now.

I jolted awake, startled to find my cheeks were wet.

"He's not worth your tears."

This time it was Nesrelle's voice, but it was no longer in my head. I lifted my face to see her leaning against the door, lazily picking at her too-long fingernails. When she peeled her gaze from her hands to meet mine, something peculiarly like empathy flitted across her expression. Her pale eyes darkened, and the lines of her mouth grew taut. But the look was gone as quickly as I'd noticed it, making me wonder if I'd imagined it. If I'd only hoped to see it when I longed for comfort.

But when my only allies were Nesrelle and my mother's ghostly spirit, I wasn't sure I'd ever find comfort anywhere again.

My voice sounded gravelly. "Are you prying into my memories as well as my thoughts?" I asked. It was strange looking at Nesrelle now, knowing I both loathed and admired her. I wanted her to leave and never return about as much as I longed for her attention, for her pride, for her affection. When had I begun to see her like a motherly figure?

When had I started to rely on her for advice, for help, for *comfort?*

Was I mad?

Nesrelle straightened with a clink of metal and swept toward me. Tonight, she wasn't attired in one of her elaborate gowns, but in dragon scale armor in shifting shades of ebony and purple as deep as vaeletta petals. Silver veins ran through the scales, startlingly bright against the midnight darkness. A sword with a finely wrought black hilt, covered in silver markings I didn't understand, hung at her side. Her hair hung loose down her back, the only warm thing about her.

When she smiled, it was vicious, the expression of a warrior. "I'm here to help you, little empress. You know this. You've always known this."

My laughter was harsh, grating against my ears. "You're here to help *yourself.*" I nodded toward the door. "Can he hear us?"

She listed her head, red curls tumbling over her shoulders. "Do you *want* him to overhear?"

I swallowed down my rising panic and pain at the thought. As if Kovi could hate me anymore. As if he didn't already know I cavorted with the goddess of demons and darkness.

"He can't hear us," Nesrelle continued. "And I don't think I need to remind you that my interests and yours have aligned for quite some time now." She quirked a single, perfect eyebrow. "Those you want to kill are the same people I'd love to greet as they draw their last. And helping you gain the throne? It would be a pleasure." She swept into a mock curtsey.

Scowling, I drew back. "Are you sure you don't want to keep my throne?"

Nesrelle laughed, the sound like the cheerful tinkling of bells, and yet somehow it sent a chill skittering along my skin. "I have a throne already, a beautiful throne built of bones." She waved an elegant hand through the air. "My nestrae, my devoted worshipers, assembled it for me themselves. I don't need your throne. I'd rather see you rule Alrenor and continue to use your curse." She grinned. "It can happen, *if* you kill Kovi."

"He should already be dead," I snapped, voice bitter. "Why did the curse fail me? Surely the Life-Giver has seen the blood Kovi has spilled. He's a soldier. He's not like Lo was..." I scowled at my hands, confusion twisting my thoughts.

Nesrelle glowered, her eyes piercing into my soul. "Did the curse fail, Jalie? Or did *you?*"

I paused, silence hovering between us. Did she mean I hadn't willed Kovi to die? That some part of me had held back?

"You can't fail again," Nesrelle continued. "You need to win."

The curse burned through my blood, filling me with strength so powerful, it was nearly painful. My fingers twitched as the urge to use it, to fuel myself with the intoxicating feeling it gave me, flooded me.

I lifted my chin and met Nesrelle's gaze unwaveringly. "You know I'll win."

Nesrelle's smile was almost doting when she stepped forward, resting one chilly hand on my shoulder. "Of course you will, if you don't let sentimentality get in the way. Kovi's magic is no match for the gifts I've bestowed upon you. He's been a bothersome obstacle for you from the start—the only thing standing between you and everything you've dreamed of achieving for *years*. Vengeance. Power."

"Helping my people?" I added, my throat tight with longing.

"Of course."

"All along, that soldier has tried to fill your head with thoughts of mercy, of how being a monster would be a bad thing. But he's only manipulated your emotions for his own benefit. He knows and fears what you are capable of becoming, and he's tried to prevent that from happening. He's used you and lied to you in order to protect himself and his people. To *weaken* you."

Nesrelle's nails dug into my armor, the sharp points piercing through to my skin. But the pain didn't make me flinch or pull away.

Instead, it grounded me, reminding me of what was at stake.

When I closed my eyes, I could see Elder Ettonou. I watched my people being murdered. The woman being burned alive just after she'd found me in the crowd and cried for me to avenge the empire. Elder Ettonou slitting the young man's throat in my own bedroom. I thought of Lo slaying my mother, of the Forwyn stealing the dragons, of the Teramese pillaging Alrenor.

I opened my eyes and curled my fingers into fists. "I won't be used again," I vowed. "I'll show them how right they are to fear me."

CHAPTER SIXTEEN

Lo

RHAEDA WAS UTTERLY DESOLATE, NOTHING but an expanse of ruins and dust left in the wake of a terrible disaster. Caesiem didn't leave my side as I trod through the city, tears welling in my eyes when I beheld each new horror. Here and there, where wind and time had displaced mounds of debris, were skeletons in every size imaginable, buried within the rubble or half lost amidst the ash. Some of the bones were far too small, and I had to look away, unable to bear the thought of the children lost here.

My knees grew weak with each new sight: cracked, decaying boards that had once belonged to houses or businesses, crumbling stone adorned with faded paintings, rotting remnants of palm trees and gardens long left to wither beneath the scorching sun. I hadn't known these people, hadn't known anything about Forwyth and what my homeland's culture was truly like aside from the few stories Mother had told me. And yet, I felt leaden with grief.

Mt. Nu'ohni had destroyed an entire city, leveling buildings and erasing its traditions. Hundreds—perhaps thousands—of lives had been blotted out. It was a staggering, awful thought, one that left a lump in my throat and a weakness in my limbs.

Had anyone on Forwyth survived? The rainforest had been overrun with dangerous beasts, and the destruction Caesiem and I now walked through seemed to stretch on endlessly, appearing to extend even beyond the mountain looming on the distant horizon. Was there anyone left on this main island? Did the survivors flee to the smaller islands to the west, or had this destruction wiped out all their resources? Had they suffered and died, unknown to the rest of the world?

If they were all gone… I would never have the opportunity to witness the glory of my people, to learn all the wealth of information the Forwyn of the island possessed regarding Elhani's magic. I wouldn't walk the streets of their cities and learn about their architecture, their art, their traditions.

And we would have no one to beseech for help.

"I thought the Elders said Forwyth responded to their request for help," I whispered, repeating my earlier statement in my shock, "and said they wanted to stay out of our affairs." My throat was tight with unshed tears. I shook my head, at a loss. "But I think this happened longer than three years ago."

At my side, Caesiem reached out silently, taking my hand in his warm, calloused one and threading his fingers through mine. His touch buoyed me, reminding me I wasn't alone. When I glanced at him, his blue eyes shone with a grief that mirrored mine. "Maybe that was just the assumption the Elders made when they received no answer from Forwyth at all?" he suggested softly.

For a long time, we climbed through what was left of the city in silence, stumbling through piles of ash until it clung to our boots, our clothes, our skin. I wasn't sure what I was searching for, what I hoped to find, and Caesiem didn't ask. Patiently, quietly, he stayed by my side, never taking his hand from mine.

I didn't want to admit, even to myself, how much his presence comforted me, or how grateful I was for the physical contact. Even if I knew he had to return to Teramyl. Even if I knew we were destined to never be, and that maybe, while the thought pained me, he was fine with that, and only wanted to comfort a friend because he was as horrified by the destruction as I was.

At last, I froze in the middle of a street, too overcome to go on. Dust swirled in the air, stretching toward the sandy coast on one horizon and up toward the volcano—the deadly cause of all of this—on another. Everything was eerily still, like we were ghosts haunting an empty city, clinging to memories that weren't even ours.

"What do we do now?" I breathed, trying to keep myself from trembling, from collapsing right there in the ruins and weeping. These weren't my people to grieve and yet…how could I not be moved? And how could I not feel waves of hopelessness knowing that the help we Forwyn had been depending on might not even exist?

The shuffle of footsteps emerging from the rainforest at our backs made my pulse jump. As one, Caesiem and I whirled around, his fingers tightening on mine.

An entire group of Forwyn men and women stood mere yards away, their eyes roving over us in curiosity. But there was no warmth, no kindness in their expressions, only something feral and hungry. Clothed in animal furs and armed with daggers and spears, they appeared ready for battle…or a hunt. My stomach dropped with unease as my mind blared a warning.

The foremost man cracked a smile, but it was too toothy and full of an eagerness that unsettled me. "How fortuitous," he declared in Forwyn. "It seems that fate has sent us new sacrifices for the Dark Immortal."

"What did he say?" Caesiem hissed in my ear.

I took a step back, assessing the number of Forwyn clustered before us, scanning their weapons. A dozen stood here on this street, but who knew how many waited in the jungle, preparing to ambush us if we tried to flee back into its shadows?

"They want to sacrifice us to the Dark Immortal," I said, glaring at the man.

Caesiem laughed, but the sound was harsh as he lifted a hand, calling the sea to him. The noise of crashing waves grew louder, and a wall of water rushed forward, preparing to engulf the Forwyn.

Together, Caesiem and I ducked, letting the foaming wave plunge toward the Forwyn and immerse them in its watery grasp. I waited, one breath, two…unable to see our opponents in the churning water, but certain I'd notice when their bodies collapsed to the ground.

Instead, it was Caesiem who lurched at my side, ripping his hand from mine. He let out a strangled groan and tipped forward from his crouch until he was crashing to his knees. His entire body trembled as he sucked in air, his blue eyes darkening in agony. He extended a fist as if in one final effort to keep control of the water, but his arm fell limply. The water tumbled downward, spraying around us and plastering loose curls to my face.

"Caesiem!" I grasped his arm, trying and failing to rouse him from whatever had its grip on him. His eyes were glassy as he ripped them from the Forwyn emerging from his failed water attack and pinned them on me.

Caesiem shook his head, clarity flaring in his eyes. "Run," he choked out, raising his hand to call on the water again. "Get out of here."

"Not without you, you idiot," I snapped, seizing his arm with both hands and wrenching him to his feet.

He staggered, his weight falling against me and nearly knocking us both back to the ground. The water came again, churning and frothing like it felt the same rage Caesiem did, but it was clear he was distracted—lost. His attack went awry, slamming into the ruins of an old building rather than into the warriors advancing toward us.

"Caesiem, snap out of it!" I plead, drawing my sword. I couldn't fend off a dozen warriors on my own.

Gritting my teeth, I forced every ounce of my concentration into listening for Elhani's song over the pounding in my ears. When I'd been a nun dodging danger in the streets, any attacks had spurred my anger and cleared my head. But this time, my fury was diminished by rising panic. Something was wrong with Caesiem. He squeezed his eyes shut, groaning and muttering something under his breath.

Wrapping shaking arms around him, I started praying frantically in Forwyn. "Elhani, take this away!" I shouted.

Our enemies cackled, scraping their blades together until the shriek of steel on steel filled the air. When I focused, I could see something swirling around them—blackness, like living shadows.

This wasn't the magic of Elhani. This was darkness. Death. Despair.

"Nesrelle," I snarled. Somehow, this was her doing.

With a deep breath, I shouted again. For Elhani. For that man on the beach who'd told me I was a world-changer, meant to fight for those I loved.

His song rushed through me all at once, powerful and all-consuming, bringing relief and steadiness to my shaking limbs. In an instant, Caesiem's body stilled, as if he could feel the effects too. Maybe, through my embrace, I was instilling some of the strength I'd been given to him.

Warmth tingled through my entire body as I called on the easiest form of magic I knew how to wield: rendering us both invisible. Caesiem vanished, giving me the illusion that my unseen arms were clinging to nothing. "Hurry," I hissed, pulling him away.

His hand found mine again, and we ran. Our feet displaced ash and rubble as we went, stirring up a cloud of dust, but I prayed our invisibility would be enough to confuse our pursuers. *One, two. One, two.* My steps found my old running pace easily, and the familiarity brought an extra wave of comfort as sounds of charging footsteps and scraping steel trailed us.

I fled toward the beach. Was Karos near enough to hear me if I called? Had Caesiem recovered enough from whatever strange trance he'd been in to use his magic?

Stretching my thoughts, I recalled the feeling of sending terror into my enemies, compelling them to obey or to flee. Just as I had when I'd rescued a girl being kidnapped, when the Alrenians had attacked the abbey, or when I'd spoken to the crowd at the palace after the wedding ceremony.

One of the warriors leapt forward, and, as if not fooled by our invisibility at all, slammed a hand into my shoulder. I nearly lost my balance, but the strength of his grip held me in place. I cried out, trying to swipe at him with my sword.

 Pain crashed through me, hot and intense and so consuming it shut out all thought. With a muffled cry, I faltered and collapsed, yanking Caesiem down with me. I lost my grip on my magic and my hold on our invisibility disintegrated. A cloud of dust wafted around us, choking me. My muscles spasmed from the overwhelming agony shooting through every tendon, every bone, every inch of my skin.

I was dying. I was being drowned on land, burned to death in invisible flames, skewered by a hundred unseen blades. Black dots danced across my vision and the world quaked around me.

Dully, barely able to comprehend anything beyond the pain, I realized Caesiem had crumpled beside me, as incapacitated as I was. The warrior was grasping both our shoulders, laughing and taunting us, not even bothering to attack with the blade still strapped at his waist. More footsteps pounded toward us, accompanied by jeering shouts.

I groaned, trying to force my shaking limbs to stand, to fight back, to do anything but lie here and accept my fate. Blood and bile filled my mouth. *Not like this*, I thought. I'd survived slavery and attempted murder and gruesome battles. To fall apart now seemed like the worst sort of failure to both my people and myself.

Caesiem's hand seized mine, and with a glance over my shoulder, I found his gaze. Despite the clear agony he was in, his blue eyes were clear, reminding me I wasn't alone. The determination in his stare filled me with courage, somehow giving me the strength to shove my feet off the ground. Together, we stood, leaning on one another, lending each other strength and pushing our attacker's hands away.

With my free hand, I wiped blood from my lips and shakily lifted my sword. My mind was blank of everything but hazy pain and a desperate need to defend. Elhani's song was a distant memory, and I wasn't sure if I even had the strength to call for Karos.

But Caesiem's hand in mine was my reminder that I wasn't alone.

When I stepped forward, lunging for the warrior, he easily dodged my swipe. His laughter was dark, his expression cruel. "Yes, come closer, so I can let you feel the Dark Immortal's pain again."

I gritted my teeth.

Caesiem sent another wave crashing into the man, forcing him back, but our enemy wasn't fazed, even as his body jerked, starved of oxygen in the swirling water. His eyes continued to stare into mine, the look on his face utterly insane. I repressed a shiver as he collapsed.

The whistle of displaced air was the only warning I had as a dagger whirled straight toward me. My shaking knees didn't feel strong enough to dodge, so I dropped to the sand. Squeezing Caesiem's fingers, I tugged him down with me, watching the blade skid harmlessly across the beach. I licked my parched lips, but I couldn't speak. Could barely keep my head up as more Forwyn charged. When I glanced at Caesiem, I saw the darkness swirling in his eyes, fatigue turning the lines of his mouth taut. Weakened as we both were from the warrior's dark magic, we wouldn't be able to call on our own powers again.

Another blade flew toward us, glittering in the sunlight. Another. They flew like rain, oddly beautiful. The world tilted and roiled around me, and with a jolt, I realized there was no way I could duck or dodge them all in time.

Gritting my teeth, I braced myself. *Elhani,* I thought weakly, wondering if he could protect us, or lend us just enough strength to get away and recover.

But the blades stopped mid-air, slamming into an unseen force— and dropping to the ground. Ash scattered around them. Scampering to a stop, the Forwyn gaped toward the sky.

Vision clearing, I spun around as my ears detected what they hadn't noticed earlier in my panic: the thundering of wings. *Dragon wings.* Hope swelled in my chest. As one, Caesiem and I stood.

It wasn't Karos diving toward the beach, or his vast wingspan blotting out my view of the sun. This dragon's scales flashed in brilliant, contrasting shades of gold and ebony, and its sleek form and smaller head indicated it was a female.

As she landed, shuddering the earth with her taloned feet, I gaped in awe and shock. I *knew* this dragon, knew the two riders astride her.

And I knew the power that had stopped those daggers, that even now held the shouting, furious warriors at bay like an invisible wall. Our enemies pounded at it in vain, faces twisted in fury, in concentration. But despite the shadows writhing around them, despite their attempts with their own dark magic, the protective shield held fast.

I tugged my gaze from our enemies to stare once more at Reyva, a magnificent dragon who'd once belonged to Empress Karye herself.

"Hurry!" The foremost rider, a young woman with wavy brown hair escaping from her braid and framing her pale face, leaned over the saddle to extend a hand. *Halia.* Though it'd been three years since I'd last seen her, I would have recognized her anywhere. "Avrik can't hold them back for much longer."

Shoving aside my disbelief, I launched into a sprint, Caesiem matching my stride, our hands still locked. Dust and sand and pebbles kicked up under my feet, their resistance making my calves burn. Strength I didn't know I still possessed coursed through me, fueled by my adrenaline and hope. Reyva dipped her head and furled her wings against her back so we could easily approach.

As the second rider—Avrik—slid toward the front of the saddle and wrapped his arms around Halia's waist, I released Caesiem's hand to swing into the second seat. He was behind me in an instant, leaving no space between us as he landed in the cramped space, his chest pressed into my back and his legs tangled with mine. With shaking fingers, I seized the buckle and strapped us in, feeling ridiculous when I realized I was more unnerved by Caesiem's proximity than I was by our enemies who could no longer reach us.

"Ready?" Avrik asked, glancing over his shoulder. His short, chestnut brown hair was tousled from flying, making him appear almost boyish, but his expression was intent as he concentrated on wielding his gift. A gift that had saved my life once before, three years ago.

Thank Elhani, I thought, even as I questioned how these Misrothians came to be as far south as Forwyth, of all places.

I nodded, and Halia shouted to Reyva, commanding her to leave. The dragon launched into the air with a lurch that made my stomach fly into my throat. Caesiem's arms tightened around my waist, his heart thudding against my back. The warmth of his body seeped through my clothes, and his breath tickled my neck. I repressed a shudder, trying to focus instead on the wind whistling in my ears and stinging my eyes, on the glistening waves foaming and crashing below us as Reyva glided over the water.

Nearby, other huge forms arose, three more dragons flanking us. My heart soared when I recognized Karos. He emitted a short cry, like a greeting to an old friend, and Reyva called back to him. Soon, his huge wings guided him toward us, and he settled into a similar rhythm as the female, his great gold eye finding mine. I grinned, and I could have sworn the puff of smoke and tiny, almost playful growl Karos returned was his way of telling me he was relieved I was safe.

The two other dragons also carried riders, though it was difficult to make out who they were from here. The dragons, however, I recognized easily: the green and black one was Kova, and the ivory and sapphire one was Jozek. Both were the other two beasts we'd gifted to the Misrothian princess and her friends after they'd helped us slay Empress Karye and take over the palace.

I couldn't resist my smile at seeing them again, at knowing my

Misrothian friends were, impossibly, here.

Reyva turned northward, toward Elha'tonu, one of Forwyth's smaller islands, and Karos followed. Though the wind chilled my bare arms, Caesiem exuded a distracting warmth I could have melted into. Instead, I sat rigidly, pretending that I could force space between us, pretending I wasn't hyperaware of every inch of me that he touched. *Idiot,* I kept reprimanding myself.

Soon, my smarting eyes detected a smear of green on the horizon, my first sighting of the island of Elha'tonu. Unlike the main island of Wenu, overtaken mostly with thick rainforest but for the huge volcano on its northernmost coast, Elha'tonu was dotted with expanses of both jungle and rolling hills. From above, it was a soothing, beautiful sight: all vibrant emeralds and glistening hues of turquoise and sapphire where streams cut through the earth and plunged in beautiful waterfalls over small, rocky cliffs and into foaming pools.

Halia guided Reyva toward the beach, where the dragon landed on the glistening white sand, followed by the other three. I leapt off immediately, scarcely giving Halia time to dismount before I'd thrown my arms around her. She staggered back in surprise before returning the hug.

"*Melhona,*" I cried, using the Forwyn word for princess. "I mean…" I corrected, remembering the news we'd received, that she was now the queen. "Your Majesty."

Halia simply laughed.

Pulling back, I shook my head in disbelief. "It's good to see you."

Even though I hadn't known Halia for long and it had been years since we'd last seen one another, I felt an enduring connection with her. She'd not only been the first person to teach me how to defend myself, but she'd also aided the Forwyn uprising against Karye. And the man she loved, the one who stood at her side even now, grinning in that careless way of his…if it hadn't been for him, I never would have lived long enough to slit Karye's throat.

I owed them everything.

Suddenly feeling awkward and uncertain about my familiar outburst, I bowed. "Thank you for helping us."

Already at my side, Caesiem shot me a surprised glance before dipping his head in respect toward Halia. "Queen Halia of Misroth?" he guessed.

Halia's mouth twitched, as if holding back a smile. From what I remembered of her three years ago, even that restrained display of amusement was more than she usually showed. "We don't need to waste time on formalities. Halia will do just fine." She turned to me. "It's good to see you too, Lo. And I know who you are, Caesiem," she added smoothly as she glanced at the young man. Though her face was stoic, her posture and tone all grace, even with her clothes covered in sand and her hair disheveled from our flight, I caught a gleam in her bright green eyes. Like Meli, Halia possessed the truth gift, making me wonder what visions she'd seen of Caesiem—or maybe of Caesiem and me together. It was clear that she trusted him. "And this is my husband and captain of the guard, Avrik."

"The first title is more impressive," Avrik interjected with a smirk. "Not every commoner can claim to be married to royalty. She couldn't resist my charm." He winked.

Halia ignored Avrik and nodded over Caesiem's shoulder, making us both turn to the two approaching figures, having just dismounted the other dragons. "Lo, I'm sure you remember my advisor, Jennah, and my ambassador from Toryn, Narek."

Jennah was a tall, lithe woman with gold-tinted dark skin, hinting at her mixed Alrenian and Forwyn ancestry. In her late twenties, she had a motherly quality that extended, I knew, beyond the children in her own home to all she met. She'd been the one to comfort me after I'd killed Karye and realized nothing would ease the ache of Edi's murder. She had been the one to gift me my gold ribbons.

With a warm smile, she closed the distance between us and pulled me into a tight embrace. "You look well, Lo," she murmured as she stepped back, glancing at my ribbons and grinning.

Her presence emanated strength and courage, an emotion that filled me to the brim at her touch. While Alrenians had only recently recovered their missing courage and war gifts, Misrothians had never lost them. And Jennah bore the courage gift, one she liberally shared with those around her.

Though I recognized the man with dark hair and onyx eyes too, I didn't know him as well as the others. He'd always been more reserved, more guarded. Narek dipped his head in a silent greeting, his face expressionless.

"We're here because I've been having visions about Alrenor…and you." Sadness seeped into Halia's tone. "I saw the battle in Inalgoth. I'm so sorry."

I nodded, unable to form words. In my mind's eye, I saw the dragons perish all over again, watched the Forwyn fall to Nesrelle's army, witnessed Inalgoth burning, burning…

In all my years of loving and hating that city, I'd never imagined how soul-crushing it would be to watch it fall.

"When a vision showed me what awaited you here in Forwyth, I knew we had to help."

"Mostly, she means I had to help," Avrik cut in, shrugging.

Halia narrowed her eyes and elbowed him. "There's so much I want to tell you, but right now, there isn't a lot of time. We need to warn your friends and allies to avoid Wenu." She hesitated. "And I don't want to worry the Forwyn on Elha'tonu with our dragons. I think you two should go ahead on foot to introduce yourselves and make it clear we mean no harm." She nodded toward the swaying palms adorning a lush, misty slope. A winding path followed it, cutting past one of the many waterfalls on the island. "I saw a vision, showing me a thriving city here on this island. One not…given over to Nesrelle's power." She grimaced. "We'll intercept your ships to tell them to come here, and then we'll rejoin you."

I still felt at a loss for words, overjoyed to see my friends here, alive and well. "Thank you."

Halia pressed her mouth into a firm line. Though she rarely let her feelings show, usually carving her face into an unreadable mask, I detected a hint of regret in her bright eyes. "This is such a small thing, and I wish we could do more to help you. Far more. But we can't stay for long."

The ember of hope that had sparked in my chest at the Misrothians' appearance dimmed, but I forced myself to smile through the disappointment. "We didn't expect Misroth to have the resources to aid in our war," I admitted. "That was why we came to Forwyth in the first place, hoping they could at least help with their magic."

Halia nodded. "I hope so." She shot a glance at her companions. "Let's go." Turning back to me, she offered a small smile. "We'll be back."

As the Misrothians again mounted their dragons and took to the sky, I approached Karos, who snorted and nuzzled against my shoulder in greeting. "I missed you too," I murmured, running my fingers along his smooth scales. "But I'm going to need you to wait here, just for a little while."

Karos leaned into me, pawing at the sand and churning up a small dust cloud. "I know, but we'll be all right."

Amusement laced Caesiem's tone. "Does your magic let you read dragons' thoughts too?" he teased.

I glanced over my shoulder to roll my eyes at him, but the sight of his dimpled smile made my stomach flutter. "Once you spend enough time around the dragons, it's not difficult to read their body language. Or the sounds they make," I added with a laugh as Karos snorted again. I could have sworn he sounded indignant, still frustrated I was leaving him behind.

Bidding my dragon goodbye, I joined Caesiem in trekking beyond the beach and into the vegetation beyond, where a well-tended dirt path assured me that this island, unlike Wenu, was civilized…hopefully a sign the people would be far more welcoming. The backdrop of lush plant life and swaying palms, singing birds and chirring insects, sea breeze and fragrant floral scents all created a soothing atmosphere—a vast contradiction to our grueling climb. Sweat trickled down my back as we clambered over jutting stones and ducked beneath hanging vines.

Along the way, I explained my story with the Misrothians to Caesiem—how they'd sought to outmaneuver Empress Karye's schemes, how Halia had trained me to defend myself, and how in return I'd taught her how to tame and bond with Reyva.

"The empress-defier and the empress-slayer," Caesiem said when I finished, casting me an appreciative look. There was so much respect, so much *awe* in it, that heat flooded my veins, and I averted my gaze to brush a dangling vine away. "I can't believe when I first was sent to find you, I expected to find a meek nun. You've always been fearsome."

I laughed. "I am what Karye created me to be. She was cunning and vicious, so I had to be more cunning. And if not vicious…well, capable of withstanding anything." Elhani's words to me echoed in my head. "An…overcomer. It's ironic, in a way. If it hadn't been for her, I wouldn't have learned how to defeat her. I wouldn't have had to learn to fight to survive, or to sneak around in the shadows, or to be calculating and a bit reckless. I wouldn't have let my pain and anger strengthen me. In a way, she created the cause of her own demise."

Caesiem was quiet for a long while as we rounded a bend in the path, passing a trickling stream. If he'd been about to speak, he was interrupted by the sight before us. The path opened onto a stunning view of a lush valley, encircled by rocky outcroppings and a series of misty waterfalls. There was an entire prosperous city here, stretching out for miles, tucked away at the center of Elha'tonu. Miles of farmland and grazing livestock surrounded the heart of the city itself, where homes and walkways were built among the huge trees on one side and buildings with thatched roofs lined orderly dirt roads on the other. And though from this distance it wasn't easy to make out the people, I could see them everywhere. Walking along the roads, talking, or tending to livestock in the grasslands. They were thriving here, safe and hidden away from the rest of the world.

The sound of shifting feet pulled my attention away from the beautiful city below.

Because blocking our path was an entire row of heavily armed Forwyn, their spears and bows and blades all pointed at us.

CHAPTER SEVENTEEN

Kovi

FOR WHAT IT'S WORTH, I'M sorry."

The voice startled me from my futile attempts at sleep. After hours posted outside Jalie's cell door, Mhel had insisted I retire to my hammock and rest. "Her power may be unnatural and powerful, and you might be strongest with your magic, but that doesn't make the rest of us helpless against her," he'd insisted. "And you're not invincible. If you're going to…fight her, you'll need your strength."

I'd been weary enough mentally and bodily to give in, though the sleep I'd had was not restful, and I'd spent a lot of time staring at the rough-hewn boards overhead, listening to the creaking of the ship.

Now, I sat up, swinging my feet over my hammock to face Mio'e. Her gentle tone and unexpected words had startled me. The last thing I'd expected to hear from her was an apology. Honestly, I hadn't expected much from her at all. We'd rarely spoken, and aside from delivering the news of Rhi'il's death to her, when she'd stood rigid and dry-eyed, I hadn't even tried to approach her.

Maybe that was another mistake. My best friend had clearly started to care for her. Maybe I should have tried harder.

Though Mio'e's jaw was set and her posture tense, there was a softness in her dark eyes that I'd never seen before. She looked as exhausted and pained as I was. The sight of her sent a jolt of shame and guilt through my chest. I'd been so caught up in my own grief and my conflict with Jalie that I hadn't spent much time considering how my best friend's death had affected Mio'e. Though the two hadn't known one another for long, it was clear that Mio'e must have returned Rhi'il's growing feelings.

"I don't understand your attachment to Jaliana," Mio'e continued, her eyes flicking around to the other empty hammocks as she leaned against the wall, "but I know loss. We all do. But…"

Her unspoken words hovered in the air between us, and I knew what she meant. She was thinking of Rhi'il, of the way his death hurt her similarly to how Jalie's loss hurt me now. It was an especially crushing sort of grief, to lose the one your soul was bound to in this world, the one you cared most for—the one you would give anything for.

Maybe it was too soon for whatever connection Rhi'il and Mio'e had formed to be considered love, but maybe not. Sometimes…the heart just knew. Sometimes the impossible happened, just as it had when I'd fallen for the woman I should have hated.

I couldn't pretend to know Mio'e's heart, but I had known Rhi'il's, and after the losses he'd borne, he hadn't grown attached easily. But when he did, it had been a loyal, fierce kind of love.

And it was that loyal, fierce love for you, as his brother and friend, that led him to his death. If you had been there in those final moments for him the way he'd been for you, he might still *be here now.*

"Rhi'il thought highly of you," I said at last. "And…I'd give anything to have him here. He deserved better."

Mio'e blinked furiously, keeping her tears at bay. "We all deserve better." She glanced away, her jaw tightening as if she feared she would break down, and she couldn't bear doing so in front of me.

"I'm sorry I haven't talked to you more," I said, "but I want you to know you're not alone. If you need to talk about him…I'm here."

"Thank you," she whispered.

I stood, listening to the footsteps of others moving around on deck. Somehow, the endless night had passed while I'd guarded Jalie's cell, and everyone else had returned to their duties aboard the ship by the time I'd come here to drift in and out of sleep. I imagined it was late afternoon by now. I wondered how close we were to the islands of Forwyth.

"Anyway," Mio'e went on before I could say anything more, "I also came down here to tell you we're closing in on Forwyth. Some Misrothians flew dragons here. They're on deck now, speaking with General Ilowhe and telling us to sail to Elha'tonu instead of Wenu."

My stomach clenched at the name. *Elhani-Blessed.* It was the name of one of the islands of Forwyth, but also the nickname Rhi'il had teasingly called me.

"I thought you'd want to be up there as we prepare to drop anchor."

As we near the moment I'll have to duel Jalie, I finished in my mind. The thought made me numb, as if every emotion that had been churning within me for hours had at last emptied me of all ability to feel anymore.

"Thank you," I murmured, and Mio'e ducked her head in response and turned toward the stairs.

I waited until she'd left before I sank back into my hammock, dropping my head in my hands. *Elhani, there must be some way out of this. Please, show me how to spare Jalie. Show me how to save both my people and her. Show us a path toward peace, toward an alliance. Don't let that dream die.*

But when I lifted my head, I couldn't hear the notes of Elhani's song. I didn't feel the warmth of his magic.

There was only an icy chill spreading through my chest.

General Ilowhe was already at the prow, studying the island of Elha'tonu as our ship drew near. Overhead, two new dragons, their riders clinging to them expertly, circled and dove around Ryke in an aerial dance, emitting snorts and chuffing noises that I assumed were greetings. On deck, a stunning black and gold dragon I recognized to be Reyva, Empress Karye's former mount, brushed her snout against the three hatchlings like a content mother cat checking on her kittens.

Nearby, Meli spoke with two strangers, a woman and man both only a few years older than me. The woman had windswept, wavy brown hair and was clothed in black dragon scale armor. The man had tanner skin and wore the blue and red uniform of a Misrothian Royal Guard.

"My visions have shown me how far you've come in learning to use your own gift," Meli was telling the woman. "I'm so proud of you."

I stepped forward, and our coral hatchling fluttered her wings and darted about my feet as I passed, causing Meli to turn and laugh. "Reyva was always a queen among the dragons," she said fondly. "It seems the hatchlings recognize that."

When the Misrothians turned to me, I noticed that the woman's eyes were a startlingly bright green, reminding me of the Teramese.

Meli gestured toward me. "This is Kovi Ettonou, esteemed soldier and graduate of Aerekni Academy. And this," she added, sweeping her arm to the Misrothians for my benefit, "is Queen Halia of Misroth and her king consort and Captain of the Guard, Avrik."

"Don't bow," Halia blurted out, holding up a hand before I could move. Her serene face broke into a grin as the man beside her—Avrik—started to laugh.

"She's spent most of her life as a royal," he said, his brown eyes twinkling mischievously, "and yet just a few short years in a nowhere town, living among her people, changed her. Now she despises formality."

"We're among friends." Halia lifted her chin. Whatever Avrik claimed, it was still clear his wife was a queen. She had a quiet yet commanding presence, and the way she carefully reined in her emotions, masking them nearly as well as we soldiers had been trained to, was the pinnacle of diplomatic training.

I quirked an eyebrow. "Friends? You know Meli?"

"She trained me in my truth gift when I was in Alrenor three years ago," Halia explained.

"And you have much to thank Halia for," Meli added with a proud smile. "She and Avrik helped Lo slay Empress Karye and lead the Forwyn into freedom. And now they're here, thanks to Halia's visions, to help us again. They warned us about Wenu and the Forwyn capital, and that is why we'll be landing on Elha'tonu instead."

I stiffened. "Warned us?"

Halia brushed a lock of hair over her shoulder. "Rhaeda is in ruins, and the people on the island of Wenu…" Her voice trailed off. "My visions weren't entirely clear about what had happened beyond the volcano erupting, but they're not friendly. Your best hope of building an alliance lies on Elha'tonu, where the citizens appear to be peaceful. Lo is there already, hopefully convincing them that we mean no harm."

I glanced at Meli. "You didn't see this in your visions?"

Meli's brow crinkled. "Our truth gift doesn't show us everything, unfortunately, and I'm afraid I've been so focused on trying to see what is happening back in Alrenor, I failed to concern myself with looking ahead. I'm ashamed I didn't see this, but…"

"The Life-Giver showed me the truth instead, and brought us here," Halia cut in. "Clearly, it was supposed to happen this way. Even if we can't stay for long." She glanced at the dragons still diving and twisting through the air. "I wish we could. I wish we could do more."

Meli laid a hand on her shoulder. "I've seen some of the work you've done not only in Misroth, but also in Toryn. That is where you are called to be right now."

Avrik's gaze fastened on a point ahead of us, and he straightened. "We've arrived."

Turning, I saw he was right: the island of Elha'tonu was rising on the horizon. Its shoreline gleamed golden in the sunlight, but beyond, a thick jungle inclined steeply, interspersed with flashes of silver and blue from streams and waterfalls. Wispy trails of mist and rocky outcroppings crowned the peak of the island. It looked like paradise, colorful and lovely and thriving with life.

But all I could think of was how this was where I'd be forced to face Jalie. This was where my people would be depending on me to execute her and protect them from her thirst for revenge. This was where I was supposed to sever all possibility of her taking the throne ever again.

CHAPTER EIGHTEEN

Lo

THE FORWYN WARRIORS DIDN'T WASTE time with questions. Instead, the twang of bowstrings was my only warning before a volley of arrows launched toward Caesiem and me, cutting off my protest before I even had a chance to voice it.

For an instant, I sensed more than saw water rippling and glistening in the sunlight, pouring forth from the nearest stream and tumbling through the air. It felt like an extension of me, an unquenchable power drawn by a mere thought. I'd wanted protection, and the water answered my silent call, roaring and swirling between the Forwyn and us to form an undulating wall. The pendant hanging from my neck pulsed with power, growing even cooler against my skin.

I gaped as the arrows splashed into the water, only to be flung back out again, spinning as if they'd struck impenetrable stone—or a whirlpool. Arrow shafts snapped and splintered, cascading in a worthless pile before the Forwyn. But the wall of water itself was translucent and deceptively calm in appearance, giving me a perfect view of the Forwyn staring at me. They shouted, shooting again, but all in vain.

"What demonic trick is this?" one of the men demanded, stepping close to the water and examining it suspiciously. I was startled to hear him speak in the merchant language rather than Forwyn. After years of being cut off from Alrenor and perhaps the rest of the world, I hadn't expected the people of Forwyth to use the common tongue.

At my side, Caesiem slipped his hand into mine, his calloused fingers comfortingly familiar. I wanted to inquire what was going on myself, but I couldn't tear my awed gaze from the water. Part of me feared one glance away would bring it all splashing down, leaving us vulnerable to another wave of attacks.

And another part…another part was thinking of the nymph and what she'd said about the water caring for its own. Was this in answer to my need for protection, all because I wore Caesiem's pendant? But if so, why did I feel a connection to the water in a way I'd never had before? Why did the distant thunder of the waves match the pounding of my heart? Why did the glistening wall of water swirl and move according to my will?

"It's not demonic, and it's not a trick," Caesiem responded, his voice steady and firm. "This is Teramese magic, and it just saved our lives when you attacked us simply for setting foot on your island."

The man who'd spoken before sneered. Tall and lithe, he appeared older than the others but still in his prime. Muscles rippled along his bare arms as he crossed them over his broad chest. He wore loose, flowing pants and a sleeveless shirt, both in shades of bright orange and gold. In sharp contrast to his comfortable attire were the rows of daggers lining a leather bandolier strapped over his chest and the twin swords sheathed on his back. But braided around one wrist was a familiar sight: ribbons of all imaginable colors woven together.

When I scanned the other men and women, all clothed and armed similarly, I found that they too wore ribbons around their wrists or necks or wound through their hair. Some were in shades I had never seen Forwyn within Alrenor wear, but others—gold and black and purple and orange—were ones I knew.

"Stand down and speak with us," Caesiem went on, "and we will call off our magic." His eyes flicked to me, and I wondered if he knew that I wasn't sure I *could* make the wall of water collapse. It was as if the magic was attuned to my own defensiveness, and I had a feeling I'd have to trust we were no longer in danger before I could force it to fall.

"Why should we trust you?" the man snapped. His dark eyes flared with anger as he fingered the hilt of one of his daggers. "We saw the dragons. We know you're not alone. Why bring beasts controlled by Alrenian conquerors if you have peaceful intentions?" His eyes lingered on me, as if disgusted by the mere thought that someone descended from Forwyth could be allied with Alrenor.

Frustration bubbled through my veins. "Because we didn't fly those dragons up here to burn down your city!" I bit out. "And we didn't draw our weapons on you! If we'd wanted to attack you, we would have already." Drawing my sword, I tossed it to the ground for emphasis. "We mean no harm."

At my side, Caesiem followed my example, discarding the dagger I'd given him when we first arrived on Wenu. I unsheathed the second one strapped to my waist and tossed it beside his.

"We came seeking help," I continued, my throat tight. "Once, our ancestors lived here, before they were unfortunate enough to become slaves to Alrenor. Despite all we Alrenian Forwyn have suffered for generations, we still remember Elhani and his magic, but we've also forgotten much. And now, Alrenians and Teramese are killing us, and if we can't find refuge and allies here, I'm afraid we don't have anywhere else to turn. Please, let us speak with your Elders. Show us mercy, in Elhani's name."

The man stiffened, his eyes scanning me before snagging on the gold ribbons at my throat. "You wear our ribbons," he mused, tilting his head in consideration. "But...what is this about the Teramese killing your people?" His eyes flicked to Caesiem.

I gritted my teeth. "They broke their alliance with our Elders and overthrew our government. Some, like Caesiem here, have chosen to ally with us and our cause—along with some Alrenians—but it is a long story, one I'd prefer to start from the beginning. And," I added, "it is a story that is in *your* best interest to hear, because these islands lie in Alrenor's shadow. There is no reason to believe the Teramese won't come here next, seeking the resources you possess." I gestured around us, at the lush plant life. For soldiers coming from a land fighting disease, starvation, and homelessness in the wake of dragon attacks and other disasters, I could only imagine what a paradise this island would be.

"She speaks the truth." A woman who was perhaps in her fortieth decade stepped forward from behind a row of taller warriors. Unlike the others, she was clothed all in blue and silver, and her loose pants ended at the knees. A sleeveless robe embroidered in images of nature trailed behind her, rippling like water as she walked. A pure silver sash tied it about her slim waist. She wore her black hair in short curls, and her ribbons in long, woven ropes layered around her neck. Rows of earrings adorned her ears, and her eyes shone an ethereal shade of silver. Though she bore no visible weapons, her bare arms and legs were corded with lithe muscles, proving that she could be a fighter, if she wanted to be.

As she paused before the wall of water, her intelligent eyes drinking it in, the Forwyn around her dipped their heads in respect. Every eye latched onto her.

The woman met my gaze. "I am Yelaia, youngest of the Elders, appointed for my ability to wield Elhani-blessed Sight magic," she proclaimed. "However, not every one of my visions is clear. Forgive me. I saw danger approaching our peaceful island, and when we spotted the dragons circling near, I mistakenly thought it came on their wings. But I can see now that the danger will not be from you." She dipped her head, a gentle smile tugging at her lips. "If you will drop your water barrier, you may enter our city, with our blessings, and explain to myself and the other Elders what is happening in Alrenor."

Passing under the first arch curving over the road, my heart swelled, full of wonder. Everywhere, the sounds of birds twittering and waterfalls churning mingled to create a peaceful song, falling to the background of my consciousness as I took in the sounds of the city. Towering on either side of the road, statues of Elhani stood beside others made into the likenesses of revered Elders and priests, their pedestals surrounded by flowers, some with petals nearly as large as my hand. Ahead, large sandstone buildings containing rows of curtained windows decorated with baskets overflowing with flowers awaited us. Forwyn clothed similarly to the warriors leading us into the city—except for their lack of weapons—chatted with one another, milled through shops, or drove wagons laden with crates or pulled carts full of produce. The scents of coconut, banana, passionfruit, and other deliciously tempting foods wafted through the air.

Beyond the heart of the city, I could see more roads and streams snaking throughout the valley, passing grazing livestock, orchards, and huge copses of trees where ladders or steps led to homes interconnected by wooden walkways, like a second city layered above the first. And all around this hidden valley, rocky outcroppings and flashing waterfalls encircled us, like a natural barrier.

I couldn't help the tears that stung my eyes when I walked past people wearing ribbons like me, living peacefully, speaking our language freely. The warmth and energy of Elhani's magic coursed through the air, and his song ran in a smooth, whispering melody beneath the rich tones of rushing water, chirping birds, and braying livestock.

This…this was the sort of life so many of my brothers and sisters in Alrenor had fought and bled and died for. A life where our children could laugh as they played in the streets, like those darting behind their mothers' legs and peering at Caesiem and me curiously. A life where we could wear our ribbons proudly, without being harassed or jeered at in the streets by contemptuous men and women who thought they were better than us. A life where we could pursue our dreams without fear of an impending war, or the constant terror of being stolen back into slavery or murdered in the middle of the night.

Caesiem was silent beside me, his bright eyes drinking in every sight with a look that I imagined mirrored my own. This must have appeared like a paradise for him as well. Plentiful food and water. No wild dragons threatening the city. No sign of oppressive leadership or injustice or plagues.

Of course, I knew as well as he did that tyrants understood how to disguise themselves. But still…these sights gave me hope I hadn't dared to cling to in a long while. Here, there was peace on the citizens' faces, peace that wasn't feigned. If the Court of Elders on Forwyth was full of tyrants, I couldn't imagine the people would look like *this*.

At last, we reached the edge of the city, leaving behind the wider road in favor of a narrow path climbing over and around hills. We passed more livestock and farms, the men and women tending to them pausing to nod as we walked by. When we stood at the base of the tallest, rockiest hill, a stream burbled past, while the sound of a nearby waterfall filled my ears.

We wound on and on, up and up, circling past the waterfall and an open patch of grass stretching beyond its pool. Mist clung to my face, making the curls that had escaped from my braid cling to the back of my neck. Finally, we reached a tall temple that reminded me somewhat of an Alrenian building with its height and intricate stone detailing. But this one was made of warm sandstone that gleamed golden in the afternoon sunlight, not ivory. Its wooden doors were flung open wide, welcoming all into a spacious room lined with windows and decorated with colorful, woven rungs and circular tables where countless people sat and talked or prayed together.

This was a temple of community, of warmth—not a temple dedicated to exclusive gifts where warriors of old had once trained in violent arts and communed alone with their god. And this building wasn't like my abbey, either—here, the atmosphere was more informal, more suited to how my sisters and I behaved at our mealtimes or sparring matches than how we conducted ourselves in our sanctuary with the public. Here, everyone seemed like family, talking and laughing as if they were attending a party, not solemnly seeking divine guidance.

Yelaia guided us beyond this first room into a cool, dimly lit hallway. Pushing open a door, she led us into a space that again felt familiar to me. A circle of twelve chairs rested in the middle, each of the seats occupied but one. Every other Elder was grey-haired and wrinkled, making Yelaia appear especially youthful as she assumed her own spot.

Extending from another door on the opposite side of the room, a line of citizens stood waiting patiently against the wall. One man currently occupied the center of the circle, speaking to the Elders with respect—but also without fear. He didn't grovel, and the Elders didn't peer down their noses at him.

I sighed inwardly, imagining how differently life in Inalgoth could be, even now, if our own Elders had conducted themselves with just as much humility and wisdom in their rulings.

As soon as the other Elders saw Yelaia, they wrapped up their conversation with the man. One of the male Elders stood and faced the line of waiting citizens. "Please let us adjourn for a short time before we return to hearing your requests and concerns," he announced.

The people began to shuffle from the room as the same Elder glanced to the warriors surrounding Caesiem and me. "If Elder Yelaia trusts these foreigners, I don't think your presence is needed. You may be dismissed."

Once the warriors had left, shutting the door behind them and leaving Caesiem and me alone with the Elders, the man gestured for the two of us to approach the center of the circle.

"If you truly come in peace, then welcome to Corapaxu, the heart of Elha'tonu," the man began. "I am Elder No'haleo." His narrow eyes flicked over Caesiem and me, alight with a mixture of curiosity and distrust. "Who are you, and what brought you to Forwyth?"

Straightening my spine, I refused to be intimidated by his doubt. Whenever I'd dreamt of exploring the home of my ancestors, of learning more about Elhani's magic and our traditions, I'd never imagined a hostile or chilly reception. But I swallowed my disappointment. They *would* accept us. They would help us. They *had* to. I would make sure of it, and guarantee that in this crucial way, I did not fail my people.

"I am Lo'laeni Nolanhou," I began, "firstborn of Lai'ell Nolanhou, a slave of the former Empress Karye. My birthright was enslavement and suffering. From the moment I drew my first breath, I belonged to the Alrenian empress. Until recently, I never knew my father, as my parents kept their relationship a secret out of necessity, and soon after my brother's birth, Father was sent away from the palace, sold to another master."

The Elders shifted in their seats, some looking uncomfortable while others at least appeared perturbed. *Good,* I thought. *It's time you understand how we've suffered and feel some compassion. We are Elhani's people too.*

"Every day of my life was full of fear and hatred," I continued. "Slaves were beaten and murdered daily. We didn't receive care from healers unless the empress deemed us especially worthwhile to invest time and effort in. Usually, she didn't care, as she had plenty of other slaves to take the place of the dead. Other times, she slew us on purpose, for the sport of it.

"To survive, it was better to be invisible, to not be noticed by the empress or her court. If you were noticed, you became a target. You would be abused even further, or raped, or assigned more important or difficult work that would put your life in greater danger if you made a single error. We were tools and pawns, instruments to be used to tend to their every need and whim, and then cast aside when we were no longer useful." I swallowed thickly, trying to calm the tremble building in my body. Grief burned my throat, and familiar hatred flamed in my chest.

Caesiem slipped his hand into mine again. I concentrated on the warmth of his fingers as he squeezed, on each soothing brush of his thumb along my knuckles.

Raising my voice, I stared straight into Elder No'haleo's eyes as I recounted the day my mother was sold and sent away, and the moments Edi and I had stolen to talk and grieve together. Then I told the Elders of Edi's murder and Karye's callousness, of my growing hatred and longing for vengeance. I didn't spare any of the gruesome details, didn't shy away from the pain. As Naina had once said, that pain had been mine to bear these long years, but it was now mine to overcome.

At last, I explained how the Misrothians and I had slain Karye and overthrown her tyrannical government. "But we continued to struggle," I said, telling them how our Elders quickly fell to the temptation of greed and corruption. I shared about my people's fear, about the nightly murders and other abuses the Alrenians had managed to get away with. Finally, I explained how the Teramese had capitalized on Alrenor's weakness to claim the divided empire for themselves.

By the time I told them of the battle for Inalgoth and the slain dragons, of our wounded and ragtag band of allies, Elder Yelaia was studying me with tears shining in her eyes. Even Elder No'haleo seemed stunned into silence. The others were more difficult to read.

Let them see we mean no harm, I prayed. *Let them see how desperately we need their help, and how eventually, their survival may depend upon ours.*

"If you don't help us," I finished softly, "do you think that whoever wins Alrenor—the Teramese or this vicious new Alrenian army—will spare Forwyth? Do you think they will be content to conquer our land only? Even if you don't take compassion on our suffering, then I hope you see how necessary it is for you to act to protect what you have built here." I gestured around the room. "I saw what has become of Wenu, and I see how wary you are of outsiders intruding upon this haven. Surely you would protect your city at all costs."

One of the women cast a grey braid over her shoulder, making the ribbons around her neck rustle. She stood slowly, carefully, her form hunched but still strong. Her eyes pierced into me, until her gaze flicked to Caesiem. "Miss Nolanhou, your story is quite stirring. My name is Elder Olahni, and I have been an Elder of Corapaxu longer than anyone else here, and it troubles me that, with the fall of Rhaeda, we never heard of the changes within Alrenor. And we certainly didn't know the extent of your struggles—or even if any Forwyn slaves had survived the centuries trapped within Alrenor, cut off from the rest of the world." She sighed. "But one thing does not make sense. You spoke of Teramyl invading your home, and how their people threaten us as well, yet you have not explained why one of theirs stands at your side. Who is he?"

Caesiem cut in before I could respond. "Caesiem Adriatus. I am an ally of the Forwyn and Alrenians Lo has been working with."

Elder No'haleo sneered. "You trust this man, Miss Nolanhou?"

"I do," I said, squeezing his hand more tightly in mine. Before I could regret it, I blurted out, "He's my husband. We established a marriage alliance between our peoples. He entered the contract willingly."

The Elders blinked, some turning to mutter to one another.

"Why didn't you say that from the beginning?" Elder Yelaia asked, a smirk twitching her lips. "If you trust and care for the man"-her eyes fell to Caesiem's and my laced fingers- "then we will welcome him gladly. We will welcome *all* of you gladly, as followers of Elhani seeking refuge and bringing us an important warning."

Elder No'haleo and Elder Olahni scowled at Yelaia. "We haven't made a unanimous decision."

Elder Yelaia shrugged. "And what other decision is there? Cast them out and ignore the approaching threat? We know what the Alrenians are like, and the Teramese invasion tells us to expect much of the same from them. Whoever wins Alrenor will not be satisfied with its borders alone. They'll come for us."

Elder Olahni flicked another braid over her shoulder, looking annoyed. "We don't have an army. Our numbers are small, and those warriors we do have merely train to protect the city. We are all that's left..."

Another Elder interrupted, nearly knocking his chair off its legs in his haste to stand. "And if we hide away, this haven will eventually be destroyed too, and our grandchildren will be enslaved to vicious masters just as this young woman and her people were." He gestured toward me for emphasis, but Elder Olahni didn't tear her gaze from him.

"We have Elhani's protection on this island," she murmured, waving at the air around us. I could feel the truth of her words in the powerful tingle creeping through my blood. The very earth seemed to sing with his music and strength. I could only imagine how easy it would be to harness his magic here, to wield it in new, impressive ways I'd only ever dreamt about. "And we have the high ground. An army trying to invade would be at a severe disadvantage, and we'd see them coming for miles before they even anchored their ships. We could defend ourselves well, if they ever dared to come at all."

"Just like our ancestors defended the island when we lost so many to slavery two centuries ago?" Elder Yelaia demanded. Though she remained seated, one leg crossed over the other in a deceptively relaxed pose, her gaze was sharp.

"I think the point here is that allowing these strangers here brings an unnecessary risk—" Elder No'haleo started.

Elder Yelaia stood, lifting her hands to quiet the onslaught of arguments bursting around us. Nearly everyone in the circle of Elders had risen to their feet, many lifting their voices as they discussed different options. "Everyone, enough!"

Silence settled, all eyes turning to the youngest Elder. "My Sight showed me Lo'laeni and her allies' arrival this morning. At first, I confused them for coming danger, but now I see that the armies Lo'laeni speak of are the ones who pose the true threat. My magic tells me she shares the truth, but I *don't* need my Sight to also tell me that Elhani would wish for us to aid them. They have wounded and dying aboard their ships, and we could not call ourselves the Chosen People if we turned our fellow Chosen away." She drew a deep breath. "However, I have seen nothing beyond this, and I don't pretend to know all of Elhani's will. Today, let's welcome and tend to our guests with food and healing. Tomorrow, I will pray and seek another vision that will guide us in our decision about what to do beyond this. If Elhani means for us to join in this war, he will make that clear. And his will is *ours*."

One by one, the Elders dipped their heads in agreement.

"I will share whatever I see, and we will use any visions gifted to me to discern his will."

I swallowed, throat tight. I trusted that the Elders meant well, and that Elhani's magic was powerful here, but I also knew how easily it was for a ruling body to grow corrupt. What if these Elders failed us as the ones in Alrenor had? What if Elhani granted Yelaia a vision commanding that they help us take back Alrenor, but they twisted his meaning to match their desires?

"We welcome you," another male Elder said as the crowd quieted, stepping forward to offer me his hand. "I'm Elder Ah'koni. While we await your fleet, we'll find a place for you to stay and ensure you have everything you need. Now, tell us more about these allies that are coming so we can prepare for them."

As I began to list off the approximate number of both healthy and wounded allies we had approaching, as well as the number of ships, the Elders convened amongst themselves again. They tossed around various ideas, mentioning farmhouses and cabins, vacant businesses and unoccupied treehouses, and even a collection of tents they could erect in a makeshift camp for our soldiers.

At last, Elder Ah'koni turned back to me. "I'm confident that we'll find enough room to shelter and tend to the rest of your allies. Our people will be ready hosts at our request, in Elhani's name. We have many talented healers to help with your wounded, and more than enough food. Elhani has greatly blessed us with provisions."

"Thank you." I cocked my head to the side, hesitating, not wanting to press their generosity to its breaking point. "And…what about our dragons? They won't hurt you—they obey us. Will they be welcome too?"

The Elder blinked, folding his wrinkled hands together. "Will they eat our livestock?"

I grinned. "We will tell them to hunt elsewhere."

Elder Yelaia nodded. "My Sight showed me the dragons and their loyalty to their riders. You and your Misrothian friends can bring your dragons to our city. In the meantime, I'll take you to your accommodations myself."

I exhaled with relief. "And I'll call my dragon."

"We will meet your dragon *first*," another Elder interjected gruffly, a stern-looking bald man.

"Yes," Elder Olahni agreed, her braids brushing her back as she nodded. "Some of our warriors will join us. We won't threaten your dragon unless it threatens us. But we need to be sure before we just…let him wander the city."

"Of course." I would show them Karos was not to be feared—not as long as they proved to be allies, and not our enemies.

Despite Elder Yelaia's and my reassurances, the line of warriors tensed and fingered the arrows in their quivers as Karos swooped toward the valley. His black, umber, and red scales caught the light reflecting off the nearby waterfall, forcing me to squint. Eliciting a piercing cry that sounded suspiciously like a gleeful squeal, he dove straight for the pool the fall spilled into, splashing with the joy and energy of a hatchling.

Caesiem laughed with me, lifting his hands and stopping the water before it could reach us. He commanded it as instinctively as breathing, flicking it effortlessly back in a graceful stream toward the pool.

Elder Yelaia cast a sidelong glance at him, but no one commented on his magic this time.

At my neck, the pendant pulsed and tingled against my skin.

"Karos!" I said, launching forward to meet my dragon at the pool's edge. I sensed the warriors stiffen behind me, but they must have realized Karos wasn't a threat. In his playful mood, I couldn't imagine how anyone could fear him.

Leaping out of the pool and shaking a cascade of water all over me, Karos nuzzled against my shoulder. Wiping away the water dripping down my cheeks, I stifled a laugh.

"How do we know he won't eat our livestock?" Elder No'haleo repeated gruffly, and I rolled my eyes.

"I told you, he'll listen to me," I said, not bothering to turn and face the man as I ran my fingers along Karos's head. I laughed outright when he dipped a wing toward the pool and splashed me. "Dragons are highly intelligent and loyal, so he'll do as I ask."

It took a while before the warriors and Elders seemed convinced, but eventually, after watching me talk to Karos and splash around in the pool with him, they began to disperse. All but Elder Yelaia, who waited patiently at Caesiem's side.

"I'm sorry," I said, bidding Karos a quick farewell and wading out of the pool, wringing the water out of my soaked tunic. "I didn't mean to keep you waiting."

Elder Yelaia's lips curved in a smile. "It's no trouble. It's amazing to see a dragon up close like this." Her deep brown eyes scanned Karos with wonder and appreciation, and my chest warmed at the sight. "But I'm sure you're tired and hungry. Come, follow me."

As Yelaia led us on a winding route toward the eastern side of the valley, passing the pool with its misty waterfall and climbing a rocky path heading upward, she told us about Corapaxu's history. "We're not always at ease here, you must understand," she began. "I know this seems like paradise after the destruction you saw on Wenu, but the inhabitants of that island…" Her voice trailed off. "Many decades ago, when Mt. Nu'ohni erupted, the Forwyn on Wenu grew desperate and lost sight of Elhani's ways. The ash from the eruption tainted their water supply and killed most of their wildlife. Even the fish surrounding their island fled further out to sea. The heartiest of the wildlife was also the deadliest, and that fact only further endangered the people there."

"And they didn't leave the island?" I asked. "Why not come here?"

"It was pure chaos for years afterward, and all of the islands, even Elha'tonu, struggled," Yelaia explained. "Everyone was starving. Everyone was suffering. And so many of our people died in the eruption itself. Many more died in the years following."

"They couldn't leave Forwyth either," Caesiem muttered, kicking a pebble out of his way as we turned a bend in the path and the incline grew steeper. "That would have been when the barrier still kept these kingdoms to the west of the Terebrys shut off from the rest of the world."

Yelaia nodded. "It was a dark time. Some turned to Elhani, resulting in this paradise you see here. We thrive under his protection. There are plentiful resources, even if the island is small. But the people of Wenu…they turned to the Dark Immortal."

"Nesrelle." I muttered her name like a curse.

"Their magic is terrible and…well, the Dark Immortal demanded human sacrifices in exchange for granting them that power. And food." Yelaia shuddered. "Though I suspect most of their food, at least at first, came from those they sacrificed to her."

Bile crept along my tongue.

"But Wenu's resources are nothing compared to what we have. Its people are constantly trying to get past our defenses. Our warriors are always alert, ready to fend them off." Yelaia sighed. "It's one reason why the Elders are so suspicious of outsiders, and why some of them are reluctant to even consider helping you, let alone joining your war. They fear losing what we have here. If we send warriors to aid you…well, we don't have many to spare."

"You know that if we don't stop the threats in Alrenor, you won't be able to keep them from invading Elha'tonu, right?" I asked.

Yelaia nodded. "I see that, though I'm not sure the other Elders are convinced. Helping you won't be simple." Her eyes were sad. "We don't have much to offer."

I smiled grimly. "I understand."

"For now, though," Yelaia went on, "you're our guests. Take time to rest. We'll send someone to notify you when your allies' ships dock."

She gestured to the path ahead. Palms and flowers lined the way, and birds and lizards flitted through the foliage. Far below, the sea crashed against the shore, while nearer, a stream burbled. Tucked a short distance before us was a small cabin with a thatched roof. Flowers bloomed in baskets hanging below each curtained window, and the door was painted a bright, welcoming orange.

"You can join us in the temple for your meals, but there's also some food stocked here. Cabins like this one are used for meditation and prayer away from others to train in Elhani's magic or discern his will. Or…" Her grin grew sly. "For honeymoons."

Heat spread through my body at her insinuation.

"Thank you," Caesiem said, his grin the charming, confident one I remembered from when I'd thought he was merely a thief. The one I now knew was a mask to conceal his doubts and fears. Yelaia laughed as she bid us goodbye and strolled down the path.

As soon as the Elder was out of earshot, Caesiem turned to me, brows raised. "I thought you wanted to dissolve our marriage, not be given a honeymoon cabin."

I shrugged. "I needed them to trust you."

"And they'd only trust me if we're married?"

"First of all, we *are* married for now, like it or not. And second of all, sorry for trying to save your life," I snapped, storming toward the cabin. I needed a hot bath and something to eat. "I figured *that* was the priority, and we could talk to them about dissolving the marriage later, once they didn't want to kill you."

I shoved open the door, pausing on the woven mat and sighing at how small the cabin was.

With its one bed.

And its washroom that opened to the outside, where there awaited a steaming hot spring that looked glorious…but was entirely too exposed to the rest of the cabin. Only a sheer screen to keep out insects partitioned it off.

"I'm taking a bath first," I announced, dropping my pack on the floor and turning back to Caesiem. "I'll let you know when you can come inside."

His face was a mask. "That's fine," he said, turning to a fork in the path, leading down toward the east—and the beach. He plucked a gold button from his pocket, one of the many he'd torn off his wedding jacket and used to talk to a water nymph when we'd been in Haven's Bay. "I have something I need to do."

CHAPTER NINETEEN

Caesiem

THE PATH TO THE SEA was narrow, but smooth and well-trod, as if past occupants of the cabin had made numerous trips here. As the crashing of the surf grew louder and the scent of brine heavier, I drew a deep breath, feeling the tension in my muscles ease. With a flick of my wrist, I drew water toward me, letting it dance around my arm, sparkling every hue imaginable in the sun.

The sea itself glistened in countless shades of gold and crimson as the sun sank below the horizon.

I strode to the shore's edge, sand crunching beneath my boots, and tossed my button into the water. For a moment, there was no sound but the rhythm of the waves and the cawing of gulls. Then, with a quiet splash, Sephrode's white hair emerged like sea foam. She stepped out of the water in human form, clothed in a clinging white dress that matched her pale hair. The scales along her face and her inhuman yellow eyes, however, remained—a reminder that she was not safe.

Even with my magic, even knowing she was duty-bound to protect me because of my connection to the element she called home, I didn't trust her.

"Seeking more news?" Sephrode asked, barely covering her mouth to conceal her yawn.

I scowled. "Is Revaed still in Hemlaen? Has his army moved at all?

Have you overheard *any* of his plans?"

As much as I relied on the nymph to learn about Revaed and his army's position, I knew that *he* was likely using her to track me as well. It wouldn't have been the first time he'd risked approaching the water nymphs for me. And if he was doing so now, then he would also know that I'd betrayed him…

"He's still in Hemlaen." Sephrode blinked her long lashes at me. "Honestly, I thought by now you'd just send him a message yourself." She picked at her nails, as if fascinated by them. Maybe she was. It wasn't as if I'd seen her take on a human form often.

I clenched my jaw, suddenly suspicious. It wouldn't be unlike her to taunt me about information she didn't want to give up easily. "*He* hasn't sent me a message, has he?"

The nymph twisted her lips into a pout. "You're so demanding. Not fun at all." She sidled closer, and I took a step back. "You only gave me *one* shiny thing, prince." She lifted a hand, showing off the button glinting in her palm. "Give me another, and I'll answer your questions. Or," she added, extending her fingers to brush a lock of hair off my forehead, "we could play a game, and you can forget everything that's troubling you."

I swiped her hand away. "Is. There. A. Message?" I bit out. "If Revaed gave you one, he already paid for it to be delivered."

Sephrode smirked, her teeth needlelike. "No, I don't have a message from the handsome emperor, sweet prince. I have one from someone else. Shall I recite it for you?"

My blood thundered in my ears, unease prickling along my skin. Who else would be using Sephrode to send a message to me?

"The water takes care of its own," Sephrode said in a sing-song voice, "but what happens when it discovers a new master? What happens when a haven becomes a battlefield?" She licked her lips. "What happens when your strength becomes your downfall?"

"What kind of nonsense is that? Are you sharing a message, or did you see something?"

Sephrode smiled again, stepping backward and letting the water lap at her knees. "They have been bored for many long years. Too long those who ventured among the trees and along the Terebrys were only wary, but now caution has turned into daring and desperation. Or perhaps it is merely greed. A deal will be struck. A price will be paid." Her teeth flashed. "But who will pay it?" In the fading light, her yellow eyes shone like beacons.

"Are you threatening me?" I tightened my fist, my mind already seeking the power of the sea. It hummed through my veins, as ready as ever to heed my call and defend.

Sephrode cocked her head to the side. "I am sharing what I know. What I've seen. What I've been told."

"In Hemlaen?" I frowned. "Are the nymphs attacking there? What deal are you talking about?"

"Too many questions. Dive in with me, and I'll answer them all," Sephrode taunted, laughing as she threw herself backward into the water with a splash. She sank rapidly, her only goodbye a flick of her tail as she transformed back into her true form and swam out into deeper water.

Reaching for my pendant out of habit, my fingers found nothing. If the message wasn't Sephrode's, then I wasn't sure who would have sent such a vague warning.

But if it was also something the water nymph had seen… Was she saying my magic was under threat? Or that something or someone else was gaining the water nymphs' allegiance?

Whatever she'd meant, I had a feeling we were running out of time before the small chance we had of saving Alrenor was gone forever.

CHAPTER TWENTY

I DIDN'T NEED TO MATERIALIZE in the hall outside the Teramese throne room and storm past mosaic tiles and intricate tapestries and openmouthed guards—and I certainly didn't need to throw open the double doors to make my entrance.

But it elicited a grander reaction, including plenty of fear from the guards I'd rendered immobile with shock, terrified I was one of their vengeful gods or a violent specter. It annoyed the High Imperator, who jolted upright from his lounging position on his throne, wide awake where before he'd been drowsing the afternoon away. He huffed and narrowed his eyes in annoyance, clearly more put out by the fact that I'd caught him off guard than by my threatening presence.

He'd learn, soon enough, to fear me properly.

"Guards!" he snapped, silver eyes alight with a lust for death.

I smirked and waved a hand toward the approaching men, slapping my palm against one's face. Agony made his muscles spasm until he collapsed in a heap, chainmail clinking uselessly against the tile floor. The others hesitated, their bright eyes watching me warily.

Now I had the arrogant imperator's attention. He stood, his sword hissing from its sheath. Once, he would have been as handsome as Revaed, but time had etched his face with wrinkles and painted his hair in shades of grey. It was clear from his proud stance and his lean body that he kept himself fit, though. He wasn't just wearing his blade for show.

"Who are you," he demanded, "to enter the throne room without permission and attack my guards?" His eyes flicked toward the man still prone on the floor.

I paused to sweep my veil away from my face, letting the sheer gold fabric trail down the back of my silk outfit. It was in rich shades the Teramese favored and was also heavily embroidered: all lush gold and deep green and flashing silver. The tunic and loose pants were fit for the imperial family. I was nothing if not a respectful guest, always keeping my attire befitting the lands I visited.

The imperator scanned my face, taking in my pale skin and red hair, so unlike the appearance of his people.

"I'm Nesrelle, the Queen of Death, or the Dark Immortal, as some like to call me," I said. "Although for now, I've enjoyed calling myself Empress of Death while I keep the Alrenian throne warm." I smirked to myself, and the imperator stiffened. He must not have heard any reports from his son yet. Revaed was too afraid to admit to his recent failures.

"There is no Queen of Death, only the god Tuiros—"

I was in front of him in a single breath, seizing him by the throat, immersing him in delicious, intense pain. Choking, his hands scrabbled against mine, but his strength was that of an aging mortal—inconsequential and futile. "Don't disrespect me again by mentioning your fictitious god to me," I snarled. "I am the goddess of death and pain. The only deity's name on your lips will be *mine*."

Releasing him as swiftly as I'd grabbed him, I pulled back, sighing and rearranging the loose sleeves of my tunic as I waited for him to recover and collect himself.

When he dared to speak again, his voice was hoarse. "What do you want, goddess?" He dipped into a low bow, and I beamed.

"I want your allegiance. You and I have a war to win."

CHAPTER TWENTY-ONE

Kovi

J ALIE'S CELL DOOR GROANED IN protest as I shoved it open. My heart thudded like a drumbeat as I stepped within, the scent of mildew greeting me. In the darkness, Jalie sat motionless, peering at me through her lashes. Though she was silent and still, there was a raging fire in her eyes, one that seared me.

Looking at her was agony, but looking away would be weakness. *Lift your head, Kovi.*

Perhaps the time for mercy had ended and there was only room for justice, for war, for bloodshed. Pain was my longtime friend. Sacrifice was my purpose. Grief was my constant burden. I wouldn't shy away, even if I was confused and lost and broken inside.

I stared at her, one hand resting casually on the hilt of my sword. "We're going ashore."

I'd expected protests and anger, passion and defiance. Something that revealed her fear and her heart. But Jalie stood without a word. The only sign she knew what my words meant or that she believed I was dedicated to my earlier vow—that I would duel her on the island—was the way the light in her eyes went cold.

As she marched behind me, her shackles clanking, I had the unnerving impression that the Jalie I knew and cared about was already dead, taken by Nesrelle.

Everyone else had already gone ashore with the Misrothians to meet the Forwyn of Elha'tonu, leaving me to escort Jalie when she couldn't hurt anyone else. But the question was—even if Queen Halia and Meli had been confident their truth gifts had shown them visions of the Forwyn agreeing to welcome us—what would the people of Elha'tonu do when they saw me bringing a dangerous prisoner ashore?

Jalie didn't protest or resist our departure. She settled into the final rowboat with the poise of an empress, only the feathering of her jaw giving away the emotions churning within. Even with dirt and ash from the battle layering her face and dulling her hair, she was stunning. Her scar had faded somewhat, already appearing more white than pink where it traced her skin from her cheekbone toward her jawline.

My muscles strained as I lowered the boat into the water with a muted splash. Moonlight danced along the surface of the sea, and for an instant, I thought I saw a flash of white hair and silver scales. Memories of the taunting water nymph—the one Caesiem had called Sephrode—flitted through my mind. But when I blinked, there was nothing but the quiet harbor where our ships lay at anchor.

It was clear the Forwyn of this island didn't travel often beyond their shores, not after being cut off from the rest of the world for two centuries. Other than our ships, there were only a handful of others.

Rather than look at Jalie where she perched rigidly on the bench across from me, I trained my eyes on the brewing clouds smothering the stars. I threw every muscle into the work of rowing, tugging the oars with more aggression than was necessary.

Who was I if I killed the woman I loved? Who was I if I let her live to slay my people?

Duty. Discipline. Purpose. The words repeated in my head like a mantra with each dip and splash of the oars. If I didn't execute Jalie, someone else would. Better for it to be me. Better for it to be someone who didn't want revenge, who wasn't fueled by hatred or rage... Better for it to be someone who wanted it to be merciful and quick...

And that was only if I could convince the Elha'tonu citizens not to kill her on sight.

I tugged the boat ashore, passing creaking docks, empty of any signs of life. Jalie trailed me as I followed a path climbing through a thick jungle and toward the sheltered plateau at the peak of the island. I didn't bother using compulsion magic on her—the thought of it sickened me. The last time I'd used it, I'd commanded her not to hurt another Forwyn. Clearly, that order must have already worn off, as it hadn't stopped her from attacking me. Or Nesrelle's power had granted Jalie immunity to my magic.

Just as I didn't try to wield magic on her again, Jalie didn't try to attack me, either. She didn't need to.

We would be fighting to the death soon anyway.

Insects chirred and frogs croaked beneath the rainforest canopy, a lovely rhythm on a beautiful island. I would have felt peace and even a thrill to be here, to explore my ancestors' homeland, if not for the heavy weight I brought with me. Now every flower made me think of poison, and every animal seemed venomous. Instead of beauty, I saw death.

As I shoved aside a vine overhanging the path and watched a lizard scurry up a trunk, I let myself consider a different outcome for the first time. If Nesrelle's power flowed so powerfully through Jalie, would it be possible for her to *win*? And if she killed me, could Jalie get away before General Ilowhe and our soldiers slew her?

Impossible. And yet, escaping the brig last night should have been impossible for her as well. I swallowed thickly and shoved the apprehension away.

"Does it ease your guilt if you pretend I'm just another Alrenian stranger you've been ordered to kill?" Jalie's voice was cool behind me.

I glared ahead, not wanting to turn and meet her eyes. I wasn't afraid of what she could do to me. She'd already dealt her worst blow. But it did hurt to look at her, to be reminded of everything broken between us each time our gazes met.

"Do you feel no guilt at all, for trying to murder me?" I retorted, keeping my tone level.

"You *betrayed* me," she seethed, and strangely, relief flooded me to hear that familiar fire return to her words. Better that than the chill that reminded me of Nesrelle.

I swiped aside some leaves and followed a bend in the path. Roots and rocks littered the way, but it was clear and worn, obviously used often. From the height we'd reached, I guessed we were nearly to the island's summit. "We already went over this. You betrayed me first by breaking our alliance. You agreed it would end if you ever hurt a Forwyn, and you tried to kill the daughter of my *general*." I fisted a hand before catching myself and releasing it. Exhaling a breath. For the first time, I paused and turned to her. "General Ilowhe is more like a father to me than my own ever was, and you tried to kill the person who means the most to him in this world."

She froze on the path, her dragon scale armor blending in with the emerald plants surrounding her. Her golden skin was bright even in the dim shadows, catching every bit of light and sparkling. And her eyes…her eyes swirled not with hatred, not with anger, but with pain. Grief. "Lo murdered the person who once meant the most to me," she said. "If my mother was alive, are you saying you wouldn't have tried to kill her, after she took your own mother? Even if it jeopardized our alliance?"

It was the same question that had haunted me.

I gritted my teeth and turned away, scowling into the forest. "You chose vengeance over…us."

Her voice shook. "I didn't choose vengeance. I chose love. I chose honoring my mother's memory and a promise I made long before I ever met you. That was and still is *my* duty as an Alrenian daughter."

Inhale. Exhale. Your emotions are a mask. They are secondary to who you are as a soldier. Duty, discipline. Discipline, purpose.

It didn't matter. My feelings were cracking my mask and carving a hole into my chest. When I met Jalie's gaze, I didn't try to conceal my grief or my anger. My words came out low and fierce as certainty solidified in my heart. "If Karye had been alive on that battlefield, I wouldn't have killed her. I wouldn't have chosen revenge. I would have chosen *you*."

For a moment, Jalie stared at me, struck silent by my confession. Then her lip curled into a sneer. "You've made it clear you don't truly care, so don't keep lying. Don't try to soften me with talk of mercy and dreams."

"Jalie—"

"Don't start. We will fight, and I *will* kill you," she snapped. "Like you, I have a duty to myself and my people, and I'm going to put it first, as I always should have. I won't be weak, and I will *never* trust you again." Her eyes sparkled with unshed tears.

"I'm glad we're in agreement then," I murmured, whirling on my heel and pressing forward, deeper into the forest.

We didn't speak again as we climbed the final feet to the top of the island, where rocky outcroppings overlooked a large valley. Ribbons of silver from burbling streams and crashing waterfalls curled through a blanket of verdant green. Pastures and farmland encircled a city, while on its western edge, even more massive trees extended toward the sky, these ones covered in homes and bridges.

There were miles stretched out before us, but it was easy to pick out the enormous dragons in the countryside. Already, they had made themselves comfortable for the night. Ryke, Karos, and the Misrothians' dragons were curled in a protective circle around the three hatchlings. Smoke curled up from their snouts and their sides heaved in a gentle rhythm as they snored.

I wanted to drink in the sight, to rejoice that my brothers and sisters had found a refuge where we could recover and plan. I wanted to believe that maybe we'd also discovered allies who would be strong enough in their magic to help turn the tide of our war. But I was numb, the hole in my chest like an endless void.

A row of heavily armed men and women waited at the top of the path leading into the valley. "Welcome to Corapaxu," the foremost man said, a smile twitching his mouth. "I am Elder Ah'koni. We were warned of your coming, Kovi Ettonou, and who you brought." He dipped his head toward Jalie. "But General Ilowhe also informed us of your strength in wielding Elhani's magic. It's impressive."

"Thank you," I said. All my senses were attuned to Jalie, where she stood frozen at my side. I didn't glance in her direction, didn't try to determine her emotions.

"We appreciate that you escorted her here, but we will take her off your hands now," the Elder went on.

My pulse spiked, but I was careful to conceal my concern. "What do you plan to do with her?"

"We understand you want the honor of executing her, to show that your people are worth standing beside in battle." Elder Ah'koni shrugged. "We Elders agreed to that plan. Understandably, your people will want to execute the one who wronged you yourselves. And we need to know your forces still have some strength and skill, that if we did side with you to reclaim Alrenor, we wouldn't be bearing the full weight of the burden of war, fighting alongside forces that depended on our might alone."

I breathed out through my nose, despite my annoyance at the man's words. Would the Elha'tonu citizens really shy away from helping us and choose to hole up on this island instead? Did they really think the Alrenians—or the Teramese, for that matter—would leave them alone if they gained full control of Alrenor?

"Until your execution—"

"Duel," I interrupted, voice flat.

"Duel to the death," the Elder said with a wave of his hand, "which we recommend take placc tomorrow…we will keep her under close watch. Your people—and ours—will be safe."

I shifted on my feet, studying each of the warriors.

"Trust us," a woman said, stepping forward and giving me a warm smile. "Our abilities with Elhani's magic are greater than you know, and no power the empress possesses is a threat to us. No harm will come to anyone, not even her, until your duel."

Something about the woman's eyes—an unusual shade of pale grey, striking against her dark skin—made me feel as if she knew more about my emotions than she let on. Like she knew I wasn't just uneasy about surrendering my watch over Jalie, but that I was also concerned about them hurting her.

Which was absurd, since I was supposed to kill her anyway.

"Very well," I said, letting half the warriors lead her away, while the others guided me down the path and into the valley.

With every step, I told myself not to look back. Not to think about tomorrow. Not to feel.

By the time I gave in, sparing a single glance over my shoulder, Jalie and her escort were gone.

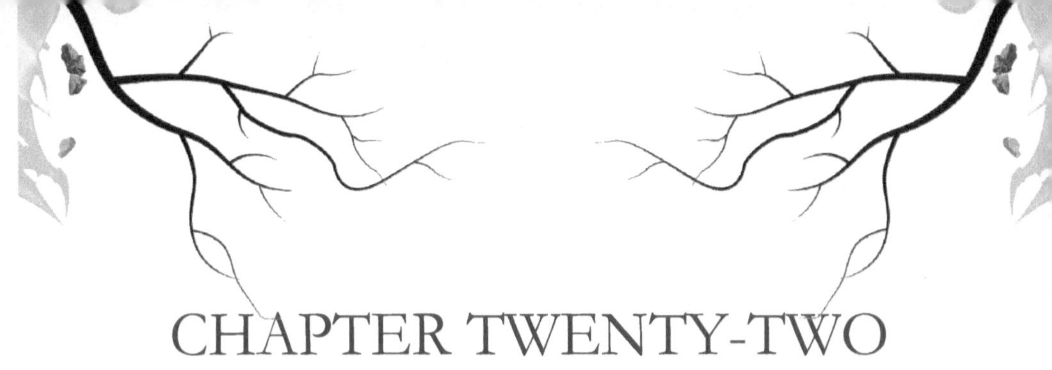

CHAPTER TWENTY-TWO

Emperor Revaed Xalenos

Ten Years Ago

I WASN'T SURE EXACTLY WHEN I'd drawn the final line in my mind, thinking of my father as the High Imperator more than my own flesh and blood. It had been a gradual process, as each of his disappointed lectures turned into angry outbursts, and angry outbursts turned into punishments.

Today, the High Imperator leaned back in his seat as he pondered his next move in our game of chess. "Auleia Venari is of noble blood," he mused, "and her grandfather was an earth mage. It's possible that his magic could be passed down to a future generation, and she could help you produce a magical heir. One that would hopefully not suffer your…affliction." His lip curled in disgust.

The possibility of passing on my so-called affliction to potential offspring was my one bit of relief from the High Imperator's endless pestering. Once, he'd insisted it was my job as his heir to the empire to ensure I married and then fathered its next ruler. He'd berated me about duty and honor, about how marriage and parenthood were not choices for us, but necessities. How love and companionship and romance were not expected or essential to these tasks of ours. "We do what we must, whether we want to or not," he'd snapped.

But over time, he'd realized I didn't just have an aversion toward being forced into a potentially loveless marriage—I had no interest in ever having anyone warm my bed. The High Imperator had done everything he could, trying to tempt me with beautiful female guests, and when that failed, he'd begrudgingly invited men. On more than one occasion, I'd entered my quarters to find one of the High Imperator's own scantily clad mistresses waiting for me. I'd left my rooms fuming and disgusted.

Anyone would throw themselves at me when ordered to. It was revolting to know that so many of those the High Imperator tried to dangle before me desired my power and prestige—perhaps even the body they called handsome—but never companionship. Never friendship.

Their attempts to touch or kiss me didn't work. I didn't feel desire, not as they did, and I didn't want to. All I wanted was for the endless loneliness growing within me to be assuaged. With a father who ruled by fear and a mother dead mere hours after she'd birthed me, I had been all but alone in the world. Tutors and servants, advisors and fellow nobility—no one dared get too close. No one was truly my friend.

Everyone wanted something from me, something I either couldn't or wouldn't give. Even my own father.

And so, when kindness didn't work, the High Imperator resorted to tactics he usually reserved for rebellious servants and citizens. He ordered his guards to whip me or beat me. He frequently lectured or mocked me, labeling me the vilest of names. Over and over, he made it clear how I'd disappointed and disgusted him, how I was failing my empire.

But he didn't want to force me into a marriage or a bed anymore, either. Because with his growing abhorrence of me and my…affliction, as he called it…he'd also started to fear that I'd pass it down to a son or daughter. Like he thought my indifference—or even, sometimes, outright disgust—toward any romantic involvement was a disease.

Now, even when I thought perhaps I'd force myself into some loveless marriage and resign myself to a woman who wouldn't want to be my friend, who would only use me for my body and my power, I was starting to fear it would be for naught.

The High Imperator would still hate and punish me, even if I found a woman and she bore my child. If it weren't for the fact that it was widely known that I was his only legitimate heir, the odious man would have likely named one of his bastards as his new successor instead. As it was, I was conscious that I was probably running out of time. Though he still occasionally broached the subject of marriage with me, he wasn't trying as he once had.

Maybe he'd marry and father a new child and leave the empire to it. Maybe he'd choose one of his illegitimate sons anyway and force the people to accept him. There were endless possibilities, and all of them ended in my death.

Because I wouldn't be useful to him anymore. I'd only be the embarrassment that plagued him—and anyone that plagued him, he killed.

There was only one thing that made the High Imperator tolerate me now, and that was the fact that all the fine tutelage and training I'd undergone had made me cunning and shrewd. Even if I had no friends, I was well-liked throughout the palace, and I was excellent at reading others. I was invaluable as a diplomat at dinner parties, and I was adept at navigating court politics. In short, I tempered the peoples' fear of the Xalenos family with outward charm—and I aided in strengthening my father's reign by learning secrets about the nobility, or even members of the royal court of Brevinn—the kingdom to the north and our tentative allies—that he could leverage.

"Ah," I murmured as I moved one of my pawns forward on the board, "so you'll risk that my heir might have my *affliction* if there's a chance magic could be passed down as well."

Thankfully, the guards posted around the room ensured the High

Imperator wouldn't fly into an all-out rage for the sake of appearances, but I could see the fury simmering in his eyes. He only had a select few of his men whip me, ones that he knew would carry out his orders but keep their mouths shut about it. He didn't want to sully the Xalenos name by making me appear weak, so he kept most of our darkest discussions or my worst punishments a secret.

Silence fell over us as we continued to play the game the High Imperator had taught me as a boy. "You need to know how to be cunning, to always be one move ahead of anyone who might oppose you," he'd said back then. "Politics and war are all much like a game of chess."

Even now, when it was clear we despised one another, we continued the tradition of playing in the High Imperator's quarters at least once a month. He insisted we needed to keep our minds sharp. At least I was still useful to him for that.

Each of our moves was precise. I studied not only the board, but also the High Imperator himself, searching for his tells. The way his lip quirked ever so slightly downward. The way his brows occasionally knit together before he smoothed them into a carefully neutral expression. The way he leaned forward or settled back into his plush armchair.

But it only took two moves for my confidence to shatter. The High Imperator didn't bother to smile as he knocked over my king.

"I used your skill against you," the High Imperator said, rising from his seat and not even sparing me a backward glance as he retreated deeper into his rooms. "I know how well you read others, so I used the expressions that have given me away in the past to send you the wrong messages. I let you get confident, thinking you had me backed into a corner. You were too distracted to see what I was planning all along." He paused and snorted. "That's something else you need to learn to survive as a leader. Once you know your opponents' greatest strengths, you can use them against them."

Present

The memory evaporated, but the High Imperator's words lingered in my mind as I set the chess pieces out on the board.

Once you know your opponents' greatest strengths, you can use them against them.

Leaning forward, I took a long sip of the wine resting on the side table by my elbow, my eyes unfocused. I wasn't truly seeing the game board anymore. Instead, in my memory, I watched the flash of fire and dark wreaths of smoke swirling over the city of Inalgoth. I saw bloodthirsty Alrenian soldiers with scale-like growths marring their necks and faces. Those soldiers bore unnatural powers: the ability to drop their enemies by immersing them in hallucinations of their greatest fears, and the ability to control flames while remaining impervious to the fire's destructive nature themselves.

Nesrelle, the Empress of Death, as she called herself, had led them to us. *She* had granted them their powers. *She* was their greatest strength.

My skin chilled as I remembered her visit, the way she'd taunted me about Caesiem's disappearance. I didn't want to believe her, but doubt and unease had latched their talons into me and wouldn't let go.

In the time since I'd called our retreat from the capital and led my forces into Hemlaen, I'd barely had a moment's rest. With injured soldiers to tend to, more forces to call upon from surrounding cities and towns, plans to form, scouts to send, restless citizens within Hemlaen to contend with...I was exhausted. There was scarcely even time to consider whether my heir had willingly joined the Forwyn or not.

I couldn't remember the last time I'd slept a full night.

No matter what plans my best men and women came up with, no matter what strategy I laid out myself, I had no idea what Nesrelle and her army would do next. The mere fact that she'd visited me made her an enigma. Her whole purpose was to sow chaos and suffering, and that meant she could meddle anywhere, without any loyalties, any allegiances. And she was immortal, without ties to anyone. She truly had nothing to lose.

If I didn't know how to use her strengths against her, how could I defeat her or her army? Most of my best mages were gone. Darix and Vander hadn't left Inalgoth with us, so I was left to assume they'd fallen in the battle. Caesiem had vanished, and I could only pray he was alive and not willingly helping our enemies. Even if we rallied the Forwyn throughout Alrenor to fight with us—even if we convinced some Alrenians to join us as well—our sheer strength in numbers would mean nothing against the magic Nesrelle and her unnatural soldiers could wield.

I took another sip of wine and moved the chess pieces about listlessly, listening to the crackling of the fire in the hearth and the whistling of the wind outside. This far north in Alrenor, the leaves had turned fiery shades of gold and crimson to welcome autumn, and the air was turning cold. Gusts of chill wind regularly blew in from the sea.

Though she was utterly silent, as unobtrusive as the shadows in the corner of my room, I sensed when Nesrelle appeared.

"Have you come to savor my suffering some more?" I asked dryly, not lifting my eyes from the pawn I'd shuffled forward. No matter how many times I'd imagined the chess pieces were my army and the opposing ones were Nesrelle's, I couldn't get in her head. Couldn't begin to guess her moves. Still, I couldn't stop trying, and though I hoped I could conceal the emotion, I was pleased to see the Empress of Death had returned.

Another conversation might help me understand her better.

Nesrelle's smile was sharp as she strode forward and seated herself across the table, assessing her chess pieces. "I've come to play." With a snap of her fingers, a glass of blood-red wine appeared on the table by her chair.

My lips twitched as I finally tugged my gaze up from the game board to study her. As usual, her hair fell in loose waves over her shoulders and her eyes were fiercely bright. Tonight, she was clothed in a dress fashioned of gold dragon scales, one that flashed blindingly each time she shifted. "I didn't think deities cared about the games we mortals amuse ourselves with."

Nesrelle was unexpectedly quiet as she tapped one of her pieces with a long fingernail. It was her turn, but she was in no hurry to make her move. "I was a mortal, once," she said contemplatively.

At that, I couldn't conceal my surprise.

"Yes," she went on, her smile broadening. "I too was haunted by misery. Betrayed. Lonely. Desperate."

I chuckled darkly. "So you've come to take pity on the mortal whose throne you stole? Come to seek a friend?"

Nesrelle quirked an eyebrow. "My power is enough companionship these days. *Your* weakness is caring too much about your people. Your heir." She lifted her wineglass and sipped delicately. "You hope to uncover my secrets, but your earlier thoughts were true, Revaed. I have no weaknesses. You can't kill me. You can't hurt me. But I do enjoy spending time with you, because your pain is potent, and it serves me well."

At last, she made her move, taking out one of my pieces in a single fell swoop. Just a pawn—but still. She was vicious, even in a game. She flicked it to the floor, where it rolled under the table and past my boot.

"You read my thoughts." I swirled my glass of wine, training my eyes on the liquid glistening within. It gave me a moment to compose myself, even if concealing my emotions would do no good when faced with someone who could sense them. But the High Imperator had trained me well, and it was still a matter of pride to not show my feelings in my expression.

And it was clear Nesrelle felt emotions, too. Emotions that maybe I could read and use to my advantage.

I pushed another of my pawns forward, curious to see what she would do. Wanting to know if she was the type to rise to the bait or to bide her time.

Nesrelle shrugged gracefully. "Yes, I can read your thoughts. I'll know everything you plan. Everything you hope to do. I'll always be one step ahead of you." She slid one of her pawns forward. The move wasn't surprising—an immortal had plenty of time to be patient.

"Isn't that a little dull, never being surprised? Never having an opponent that's a *challenge*?" I prodded as I made my next move.

Her eyes were cold, fathomless…but the slightest twitch of annoyance flashed across her brow. There and gone in an instant, it would have been undetectable to anyone who hadn't spent years analyzing facial expressions.

She moved another piece forward, her eyes glinting. "I don't need a challenge. It's not the thrill of victory I chase, for all mortals die in the end, and I always win. All I crave is the thrill of your misery."

"But clearly you wanted the throne," I mused as I took out her pawn, dropping it with a thunk on the table.

Nesrelle leaned forward, teeth flashing in the firelight. "I'd rather place a mortal on that throne. Once, I thought young Jaliana would do well. Her emotions are powerful; her pain…beautiful." She sighed. "But those emotions also make her weak. And she refused to embrace the beautiful army I created for her. I'm not sure she'll be strong enough, in the end."

"So you've come to me, because you enjoy my suffering." I couldn't help the dark chuckle that escaped. It seemed my whole life revolved around someone enjoying my suffering. First the High Imperator, and now this immortal, sadistic being. "But you already know my pain stems from my defeat." I waved a hand around the room. "Your army is unbeatable."

Nesrelle tsked and lifted her wineglass. "Come now, if you truly had given up this easily, you would already be assembling your remaining ships to retreat to Teramyl."

Her reminder of the fleet we'd left behind in the capital harbor and—according to my scouts—had since disappeared stung. Another failure.

I scoffed. "If I slunk back to my father, he'd have me executed on sight. Better to die here than at his hand."

"What if there was magic you could wield?" Nesrelle demanded. "Magic powerful enough to counter that of my army *and* that of your beloved former heir?"

I gritted my teeth at her painful reminder of Caesiem's absence—or abandonment—and she smirked in response, always relishing my grief. "I didn't know magic was just lying around for the taking."

"In some ways, yes," Nesrelle said. "The old Alrenian gifts have started to return, and many Forwyn have learned, albeit weakly, to tap into their ancestral magic. And there are beings who are able to drain that magic to use for themselves—or grant to others."

I straightened, my wine and the game forgotten. "You mean the water nymphs. But Caes is a water mage—they would never work against him."

"Purebred water nymphs cannot, yes," Nesrelle agreed. "But there are other nymphs. Many, such as the wood nymphs, haven't been seen in quite some time—especially here in Alrenor, as they prefer the deep mountain forests in northern Teramyl and southern Brevinn. But I was once a mortal from Brevinn, and I'm familiar with their ways and how to wake them."

Nesrelle leaned forward, casually knocking over another of my game pieces. I barely noticed. "And occasionally, some of the nymphs crossbreed."

I frowned in confusion. "I thought they were all female."

Nesrelle rolled her eyes. "Don't be dim. They're magical, but they reproduce just like any other creatures. Ignore the nonsensical rumors you mortals bandy about. Some of the wood and water nymphs bred generations ago, and their offspring—half water nymphs, half wood nymphs—are forces to be reckoned with. They aren't bound to water mages as purebred water nymphs are, and they carry both the power of the water and the power of the forest. Wouldn't they make wonderful allies?"

I studied her warily. "Why would you help me defeat your own army?"

She scoffed lightly, running a fingertip along the edge of her glass. "I don't take sides. I created those soldiers, but I take just as much enjoyment from their suffering and deaths as I do from those of any other mortal. Besides, maybe someday they could be *your* army." She stood, her skirts swishing about her. "All I'm saying is that I like to back the mortal who gives me the most power and can elicit the most suffering from others." She licked her sharp teeth. "And tonight, my bet is on you." She glanced down at the game. "Don't you love to use your opponents' strengths against them? What would it be like, to throw their own magic back in their faces?"

I gaped at her.

"Consider it, young emperor," Nesrelle murmured. "Instead of wracking your brain to defeat me, you could be my ally, and we could stop the Forwyn and their supporters together."

Before I could respond, Nesrelle was gone, leaving me to my churning thoughts.

CHAPTER TWENTY-THREE

Lo

THE STEADY THRUM OF MUSIC pulsed through the air as I took my first bite of the dinner the Elha'tonu people had prepared for us. There was hearty fish stew that melted in my mouth, creamy and rich; fresh vegetables and fruits from their abundant gardens; juicy chicken marinated in a tangy citrus sauce; and toasted coconut sweetened with sugar. Elder Yelaia had explained that their sugar, along with coffee beans and other resources, were harvested from Puneli, the third island of Forwyth and another haven where more Forwyn resided, away from the dangers on Wenu.

Contentment and hope swelled in my heart as I ate and scanned the feasting, music, and excitement around me. The residents of Corapaxu appeared to have welcomed us with open arms as soon as Father anchored his ships, immediately taking our wounded to infirmaries, where they tended to our soldiers with their superior skill in Elhani's magic. They settled the rest of my allies in tents erected outside the heart of the city, or in various other homes, from vacant tree houses to more lone cabins to residences where the families were willing to house guests. Though I could tell the Elha'tonu people were wary of the Alrenians and Teramese among us, they treated us all with the grace and kindness expected of Elhani's Chosen People.

Now, they were even warming up to our dragons. While the adult dragons played in the grass, pouncing and rolling around with the hatchlings, the citizens gradually drew nearer, watching in awe. A few even played with the hatchlings, laughing and chasing them as the small creatures tried to strengthen their wings, rapidly flapping and hopping after the humans. I giggled at the sight.

I knew even Ryke, who paced agitatedly down by the pool Karos had splashed in earlier, posed no threat. He was uneasy because of Jalie's absence, but he knew and trusted me, and he was clearly comfortable among the other dragons. As long as the other creatures felt safe, he wouldn't do anything drastic. But…it did hurt to see him so upset. He flicked his tail and sniffed the air, growling and calling out, as if hoping Jalie would answer his cries.

My stomach twisted when I remembered that after tomorrow, he might never see her again. No matter how I felt about Jalie herself, seeing a dragon in mourning was a terrible sight.

I set down my fork, trying to shove aside my pained thoughts and focus on the hope tonight had brought. Long tables had been set up outside of the temple, since its gathering room was far too small for the crowd that had assembled to visit with us strangers. Somehow, in just a few short hours, the people of Elha'tonu had put together a feast, filling tables with the delicious food I was enjoying.

After spending time this afternoon exploring the city with him, Father had given me space when I requested it, my thoughts turning dreary. Now he sat down the table from me, talking and laughing with Huvoki, Oru, Mhel, and a few other soldiers I didn't recognize. Normally Kovi would be near that group, but I hadn't seen him since everyone else had arrived on the island. Another twinge went through me. There was no avoiding the pain he'd have to face, either.

As for Caesiem…I'd barely seen him since we'd parted ways at the cabin. After I'd bathed and dressed in a brightly colored, patterned tunic and pair of leggings I'd found in the cabin, Caesiem had returned, and I'd given him privacy to bathe. I'd been eager to help our people bring our wounded ashore, and then to venture through the beautiful city with Father. Elder Yelaia had been happy to escort us, showing us her favorite places to eat, the best shops for beautifully woven tapestries or brightly colored clothes, the smithies where their weapons were forged, and the market full of fresh fruits and vegetables harvested both from around Elha'tonu and Puneli. We'd tasted their freshly brewed coffee—made, she said, with hints of cacao that gave it a smooth, slightly sweet flavor. We'd played tag with some especially brave and curious children, who wanted to know all about Alrenor. Finally, we'd paused in one of the streets to listen to a group of musicians playing a lively song, some of the citizens joining the fun by starting up a dance full of stomping and twirling and laughter.

"This," I said breathlessly as Father finished spinning me around at the end of a dance, "is what Mother told me stories about." My eyes burned with sudden tears, and I blinked them away. "This is what Edi and I dreamed of seeing someday, when we were free."

Father nodded, his own eyes shining, and pulled me into a warm embrace. "They're rejoicing with us right now, watching from the Golden After." His grasp tightened as confidence filled his words. "We *will* win back Alrenor, Lo. We'll see peace in our lifetime. This, more than anything, shows me that Elhani has blessed us."

Sniffling, I pulled back, uncertain. Elder Yelaia was talking several feet away with several citizens, giving us a moment of privacy for me to voice my concerns. "What if the people of Elha'tonu won't fight with us?"

"Well, then they've already given us a chance to save our injured soldiers and return to Alrenor stronger. Elhani is on our side."

Now, I clung to his words as I studied the happy faces at the feast. My eyes snagged on Caesiem with his Teramese friends, just for a moment, and unconsciously, I reached for my pendant. Ever since our fleet had arrived, Caesiem had stayed with his friends, finding solace among others who felt like outcasts.

"You're troubled." Halia's voice cut into my thoughts. I wasn't sure if she was reading my expression or had seen something with her truth gift, but it hardly mattered. There was no hiding what I felt from her.

"This welcome gives me hope, but…" I sighed. "Kovi Ettonou, who has been close to my father for years…he seemed to think that Jalie would help us form an alliance with *all* Alrenians. And now instead, he's going to be executing her. If we can't even succeed in allying with the people we live with in Alrenor, how can we expect to forge an alliance with foreigners who barely know us? The Elders of Elha'tonu…" I trailed off, shaking my head.

Halia nudged my shoulder. "The empress-slayer is doubting that she can save her empire again? You already did it once."

"But the empire was always in disarray," I muttered, tugging on my braid. "I never truly saved it."

Halia's expression grew more solemn than usual. "I understand. I saw some of the unrest in my visions. If there is more we can do…"

"No," I cut it, glancing around at Avrik, Jennah, and Narek, who all sat close by. On my opposite side, Pauni'a was quiet, soaking in our conversation. She was fascinated by the fact that I was friends with Misrothian royalty, and now, while I visited with them before they returned to Misroth, she was latched to my side, speechless with awe. "Lending us your dragons is a great help. I know you're still trying to rebuild Misroth."

At the start of the feast, Halia had explained that, along with rescuing us from the corrupted citizens on Wenu, they'd come to offer us some of their dragons to help us in our war. She'd tried to leave Reyva with us, until I'd insisted they take her when they flew home the next morning. Reyva was, without a doubt, Halia's dragon, deeply loyal and closely bonded to her, especially after three years together. Instead, we'd agreed that Kova and Jozek would stay behind, until we won or lost our war.

Halia picked at her food thoughtfully. "Our rebuilding efforts have gone well. The main reason my Council won't approve sending soldiers to Alrenor is because I've already sent so many into Toryn." She gestured to Narek. "Iyleth, Toryn's new Captain, and Narek have been steadfast friends to Misroth. I knew as soon as we were able that we'd help Toryn purge itself of its monsters and rebuild its cities."

"Honestly, we probably could do more for you here, but those Councilmen are old and stubborn." Avrik scowled. "They still like to pretend they know better than Halia because they've lived longer and have something else between their legs."

"Hush, Avrik," Halia said, seizing his hand, even as her lips twitched in her effort to hold back a smile.

"Well, they didn't defeat the Queen of Death in battle or fend off the nestrae in Toryn," Narek cut in, his voice smooth as his onyx eyes swept proudly over Halia, like a big brother bragging about his sister. He flicked his gaze to me. "But I'm truly sorry our efforts in Toryn are keeping the Misrothian army from helping you. I know what it's like to watch your home be destroyed."

I shook my head. "It's all right. You already did so much for us, and I couldn't ask Misroth or Toryn to give again. Your people need your armies and their leaders with them. I just have to trust that Elhani will lead the people of Forwyth to help us."

Jennah's smile was warm, almost motherly. Even though she wasn't old enough to be my parent, her fierce love and courage made her a natural comforter. Her eyes swept to the golden ribbons gracing my neck. "As you said earlier, you told them your story. That alone is powerful. I believe that, just as before, you will lead your people to freedom."

As soon as Halia and her companions bid me goodnight, I slipped away from the crowd. I wanted a moment alone with Caesiem, a chance to ask him about the water magic I'd somehow wielded. Was it truly all because of his pendant? Or maybe we could discuss how we would broach the topic of dissolving our marriage with the Elders. My throat ached at the thought, even if I knew it was inevitable. Even if Caesiem did care for me, that didn't mean he wanted to be tied to me forever in marriage, not when he had his own people to think about. Just because he was choosing to work against Revaed and his army didn't mean he would abandon the suffering Teramese citizens.

I slipped away from the music and chatter, my gaze drifting once more to where Caesiem sat with his friends. Like when I'd first met him, Caesiem joked and laughed with a carefree air, masking the weight of every burden he carried. Concealing the darkness and doubt I knew churned within. In a moment of weakness, I let myself remember what it felt like to be in his arms… Cringing inwardly, I brushed aside thoughts of kissing him.

He doesn't want you, and this was never meant to be anyway, I tried to tell myself. But another part reminded me of the water nymph's words as she'd described how Caesiem's pendant protected the one the mage loved most in this world.

"Good to see I'm not the only one who isn't in the mood for festivities," a deep voice said, shattering my tangled thoughts.

I glanced up to find Kovi Ettonou lingering further up the path, where he could overlook the party but remain apart from it. He stood as stoic and motionless as if he were on guard duty, except for the fingers that drummed restlessly on his sword hilt. As always, his Aerekni uniform was pristine, making me wonder when he'd found the time to keep it so wrinkle-free on the voyage over. Then again, based on the shadowed look in his dark eyes and the way he was fidgeting, I guessed he probably hadn't been sleeping much, a fact that would have granted him plenty of quiet hours in which he'd want to keep busy.

My smile was more like a grimace as I swept my braid over my shoulder. "Is it that obvious?"

Kovi's mouth twitched in an answering half-hearted grin. "You're leaving the celebration so quickly—and alone." He glanced toward Caesiem before turning back to me, but he didn't voice the question in his eyes. "And I was trained to read opponents who were taught to conceal their emotions."

I laughed. "All right, yes, that was a silly question." Sighing, I leaned against the trunk of a nearby palm tree, joining Kovi in staring beyond the people to the dragons playing together. "To be honest, I've been wishing for a chance to talk to you for a while. You're probably the closest thing my father has to a son. You probably know him better than anyone else."

"He cares deeply about all his students," Kovi replied softly. "He's felt every loss keenly."

And so have you, I thought. I'd heard whispers aboard the ship about Kovi having lost his best friend in the battle for Inalgoth. Between that and the obvious tension between him and Jalie, I could tell he was suffering, even if he worked hard to mask those emotions. "Still, you two seem especially close," I pressed.

Slowly, Kovi's expression lightened, the gold flecks in his dark eyes dancing with mirth. "Are you trying to ask me for advice about getting closer to your father?"

Embarrassed, I shrugged helplessly. "You've known him for years. I've known him for *days.* He's my own flesh and blood, and we've had some good—I don't know—bonding moments? But…I'm learning how to talk to him. Who he is. What it's like to be a daughter. To…to not be alone."

Kovi nodded thoughtfully. "I understand. It was like that when I first found out my father was alive…until I realized what he was." The darkness in his voice stabbed me with pain. I'd never held any fondness for Elder Ettonou, and I could only imagine what it would have been like for him to be my own father. Before I could offer condolences,

Kovi continued. "I don't know you well, but I see a lot of General Ilowhe in you. You're both confident in who you are and what you believe in. You're both dedicated to your people and everyone you love. He has had to make harsh choices as a general, as a protector of our people…but within, he is kind."

I sighed as I watched my father laughing with his soldiers and officers. When he dropped some of his formality, when he let himself be at ease, he looked like he was among family. And I could tell he cared for me, but caring wasn't the same as *knowing* me, as trusting in my strength and abilities. Compared to the men and women he'd bled and laughed and grieved alongside, I was a stranger—his love for me not unlike his love for our people. Strong and beautiful, but out of passion and duty and instinct, not knowledge of who I was. What if he didn't *like* me?

As if understanding my churning thoughts, Kovi went on. "He always takes his coffee black. He prefers the sunrise to a sunset, but he's often up late poring over work. Though he was our highest-ranking officer at Aerekni Academy and no longer had to directly teach any of our classes, he always took time to get to know his hundreds of students. He didn't love the Court of Elders, but he respected them and tried to believe they would do what was best for our people. His faith in Elhani and our people's abilities runs deep, as does his optimism. He loved your mother deeply, and his greatest regret in life is not finding a way to sneak her and his two children out of the palace after he was sold away."

Tears stung my eyes.

"It takes time to build a relationship," Kovi murmured, his tone gentle compared to the firmness I was used to hearing from him. "But love is already there. He has loved you all these long years that you were apart. Trust me, a day hasn't gone by that he hasn't thought of you. He talked about you—about all three of you—all the time."

I inhaled sharply. "Thank you," I whispered. For a long moment, we stood still and silent, listening to the chirring of insects and the distant cooing of birds in the forest. The backdrop of nearby streams and waterfalls mingled with the sound of softly rolling waves far below. Those sounds stood out especially sharply to me now, like a siren's song, endlessly calling to me. It made me wonder if, even without my life under threat, I could call upon the water right now, the way Caesiem could.

"Where is she?" I asked at last. I didn't need to say Jalie's name. I knew he would understand who I meant. "Where did they put her?"

Kovi's expression was a mask. "They said they would keep watch over her until…"

Until the duel tomorrow.

Condolences would be empty in the face of the pain I knew Kovi was facing, so I didn't waste my breath. Instead, I voiced the thoughts that had troubled me ever since Father had told me of the plan. "I don't think Elhani wants her to die."

Kovi straightened almost imperceptibly, but he didn't tear his eyes away from the feast.

"The night of the Teramese coup, Caesiem and Mio'e and I attended the Autumn Ball with the intention of assassinating Jalie," I explained. "We wanted the murders of Forwyn citizens in her name to end, and to stop her from using her curse on anyone else. But in the chaos, when Caesiem betrayed us, I felt compelled to chase after Jalie when she fled. One of my fellow vigilantes had coated his gloves in vylae to poison her, but I stopped him. Elhani didn't want her to die that night, and it was because of him that I chose to save her life."

"That was in the past," Kovi said stiffly, shifting on his feet and tightening his grip on his sword hilt. "Perhaps his will has changed because of the choices the empress has made."

It didn't escape my notice that he avoided saying her name. The connection I'd seen between them, the closeness they'd shared…I was sure it wasn't in my imagination. He cared for her, perhaps as deeply as I cared for Caesiem. I knew the sting of her betrayal ran deep. I understood the vicious grip of his grief.

But to choose to be the one to execute her? I couldn't fathom the level of discipline and dedication to his duty and his people that would take. My heart broke a little at the thought.

"I will *not* let her slay my brothers or sisters. I've lost enough." Kovi's voice was low, almost tremulous, the only indication of his sorrow. When he turned to me, his expression was firm and unyielding. He knew what he had to do, and he was willing to pay the price.

"You're right," I muttered. "Maybe she's too far gone to save. But for what it's worth…I wish it wasn't so. Goodnight, Kovi."

And with that, I slipped down the path into the darkness, trying to ignore that last look Kovi had given me, one brief glimpse at the vulnerable emotions churning behind his soldier's mask. It lasted only an instant, but it was full of such dark pain, such helpless grief, that it haunted me all the way back to my cabin.

When the door to the cabin creaked open a few hours later, admitting a sliver of starlight, I was wide awake, staring at the shadows pooling in the corners of the room. Caesiem crept inside, pausing when he noticed me shift in bed. Shadows lurked in his blue eyes, as if he were at last too weary to conceal the weight he carried.

"I didn't mean to wake you," he whispered as he approached a chest at the foot of the bed, withdrawing a couple of blankets.

I sat up, brushing my braid over my shoulder. "I wasn't asleep."

A crease formed on his brow. "Nightmares?"

I shook my head, and he spread the blankets out on the floor. Frowning, I sat up further. "What are you doing?" I demanded.

Caesiem smiled tightly. "If there was room to stay with my friends, I would have gone with them, but since there isn't…" He gestured to the blankets. "I hope you don't mind if I sleep here."

I rolled my eyes and slid over. "There's no reason for you to sleep on the floor when there's enough room for us both in bed. It doesn't have to mean…" I hesitated awkwardly. "We're only sleeping."

Caesiem froze, his eyes dark in the dim room. "Lo," he murmured, my name sounding like a confession on his lips. "I…"

My heart thudded against my rib cage, but I ignored it, telling myself not to be ridiculous. Or hopeful. Eventually, he would return to Teramyl. Even if some feelings for me lingered, it was becoming clear from the growing distance between us that he didn't want me.

Caesiem shook his head, as if clearing it. "I don't want to make you uncomfortable," he finished at last.

"Well, you won't," I said firmly.

Caesiem didn't speak as he stripped out of his shirt. My mouth dried at the sight of his bronze skin and the flexing muscles of his back. When he turned around, his smile was almost sheepish, and I quickly averted my gaze.

Slowly, as if he expected me to change my mind, Caesiem settled into the bed. He lay on his back while I remained curled on my side, facing him. For a few heavy moments, stillness settled between us, broken only by the rhythm of our breathing. I watched his chest rise and fall in the darkness. He was too close and yet too far. I was intensely aware of the inches separating us and of the warmth of his body. When he shifted slightly and his leg brushed against mine, the touch sent a jolt of electricity through my entire body.

Caesiem sighed, squeezing his eyes shut. "Lo…" he whispered again.

My breaths were shallow, and my skin was hot. I couldn't speak as my heart pounded in my ears. In the darkness, it seemed easier to admit my feelings, to beg him to stay. I could taste the words on my tongue, sweet and dangerous. Because if all he wanted was to return to Teramyl and forget I'd ever existed, I was afraid I'd break.

Caesiem paused, and whatever he'd been about to say was swallowed up by something else. "Earlier, I went to the shore to speak with Sephrode and learn the latest news from Hemlaen." His breath caressed my face as he spoke, and without really meaning to, I found myself inching closer. "She's always speaking in riddles and taunting…but tonight, it almost seemed like she was threatening me. As if…she believes my own magic could turn against me."

My head cleared, and a jolt of fear darted down my spine. "She told me the water always protects its own." I clasped the pendant at my neck. "Wouldn't it be impossible for it to turn against you?"

Caesiem sighed. "I'm not sure, but I was thinking…I need to go back and speak with Revaed."

"What?"

"Think about it, Lo." He sat up, the covers sliding down and exposing more of his chest. My whole body heated, and I dragged my eyes back up to his.

"I am, and I don't like it," I bit out.

"If he'll listen to anyone, it'll be me," he went on stubbornly. A muscle in his jaw worked as his gaze fixed on the window behind me, turning distant. "If I can convince him to ally with us to stop Nesrelle's army, and then withdraw his forces from Teramyl…"

"Do you think he would?"

Caesiem closed his eyes, tension etched in every line on his brow, in the creases around his mouth. "I don't know. I thought for years that I knew him, but…now I'm not so sure. And the trouble is, if he does give up Alrenor and retreat to Teramyl, his father will consider him the worst sort of failure. It's highly likely he'd execute Revaed. Revaed knows this. And…when someone is backed into a corner like that? Desperate to ensure his people's survival—and his own? I don't think Revaed will give up easily. He's never been one to do that. Why would he stop now?"

"He loves you," I reminded him gently. "Maybe he'd be willing to work with you to find a different way."

"He also lied to me." Caesiem's tone was bitter as he lay back against his pillow, running a hand through his hair until its waves were as wild as those of the sea he loved so much.

There was a moment of silence as I grappled with words. What comfort could I offer him? My father was kind and honorable and loving, while the only guardian he'd ever known had deceived him for years. Of course Caesiem felt used and betrayed. How couldn't he?

"Would Karos let me ride him back to Hemlaen?"

"He'll trust anyone I tell him is a friend, and he's familiar with you. But you can't go alone."

He shot me a look. "I absolutely can. There's no guarantee Revaed wouldn't order his men to kill you on sight. But if I showed up alone? He might believe I'm not entirely against him and listen to me. And I don't want to be against him, if I don't have to be. If all else fails, I can pretend your army captured me and gather information."

I brushed my hand against his. Even if he'd held my hand to comfort me many times over the past few days, twining my fingers with his while we were lying side by side felt much more intimate. "Caesiem…"

"I have to do this," he cut in sharply, jerking his hand away from mine. "If it weren't for me, Naina would be alive. You'd still be a nun. So many of your people wouldn't have lost their lives. You'd probably still have Alrenor."

My eyes burned. "You don't know any of that."

"I do," Caesiem whispered, and when his gaze met mine, the starlight shimmering through the window glistened in his unshed tears. "I told you, I saw the dead in the Akytha District. And what happened at the abbey…and then the academy…"

"That was *his* doing, not yours."

"I worked for him, and I was blind." Caesiem's expression was tortured. "All that time, you saw him for what he was, and I argued with you, trying to justify the killings and the violence. I'm as guilty of crimes against your people as any Alrenian. I've hurt *you*." His voice wavered, and he dropped his head in his hands, body trembling.

"You didn't know."

"I should have. I don't have an excuse." He lifted his head, jaw set. "That's why I'm going to do whatever it takes to make this right, starting with meeting Revaed."

His eyes dropped to my throat, and he lifted his thumb, gently brushing my neck. My ribbons must have fallen loose, revealing my scar. As his skin caressed mine, my breath caught, and I was sure Caesiem could feel my pulse pounding against his thumb.

"You and your people deserve better than the suffering you've endured," he muttered, slowly dropping his hand.

I wanted to reach for him, to reassure him that I cared, to remind him I'd already forgiven him, but I swallowed back the words. A memory of something Naina had once told me, back when guilt had haunted me endlessly, echoed in my mind. *You'll never believe others' forgiveness is sincere until you forgive yourself first.*

Until Caesiem believed he was worthy of my forgiveness, he wouldn't fully trust it, no matter how earnestly I offered it to him.

But with this realization came a wave of peace. Caesiem *did* care. I could tell in the way he looked at me, in the way he'd touched me just now. He wasn't rejecting me—he just didn't believe he deserved me. If I could help him walk through the darkness of his guilt and regret, maybe he'd finally realize that he was exactly what I wanted.

My throat tingled where his calloused skin had so tenderly brushed it. "If you're going to Revaed, then you'll need this," I said, unfastening the leather cord holding his pendant and leaning forward to fasten it on him instead. As I wrapped my arms around his neck, his scent—spice mingled with the tang of the sea—enveloped me. His shoulders were warm and solid, and I could feel every muscle in his body tense beneath my touch.

Caesiem inhaled sharply, closing his eyes. Leaning closer, he pressed his forehead against mine. My pulse thundered in my ears and my fingers grew clumsy as my own eyes drifted closed. *Kiss me,* I thought, pleading with him in my mind.

"Don't." His voice was low, his breath warm and intoxicating against my face. "It's yours now. Keep it. I don't need it—trust me."

I swallowed thickly, suddenly loath to move my arms.

"This is torture," he whispered, his nose grazing mine. I held my breath when I sensed him inch nearer, bridging the gap between us until his mouth was finally on mine. His lips were hot, his kiss hungry. I gasped, pulling him closer.

And then—he yanked back, out of my grasp. I dropped the pendant, and he shoved out of bed.

"I'm sleeping on the floor," he said huskily.

I didn't try to argue.

Swallowing, I plucked the pendant from where it lay on the sheet and fastened it around my throat with shaking fingers. When I pulled the covers back over myself, I was too warm. Too wide awake.

I lay there listening to Caesiem settle onto the floor, his breathing as erratic as mine.

"Promise me you won't leave right away," I whispered at last. "Wait until we know if the people on Elha'tonu will help us, and then, if you still believe you must go, we'll make a plan."

Caesiem's voice was strained. "I promise."

CHAPTER TWENTY-FOUR

Jalie

WIND WHISPERED THROUGH THE PALM fronds as I gazed at the distant stars, trying to identify the constellations Mother used to point out to me when I was a child. There was the Dragon Keeper and her dragon, the Emperor, the Warrior, and—what had secretly been my favorite as a girl—the Mother and Daughter. It reminded me of what my own mother and I had shared, in the way the stars forming the mother's arms wrapped around her child, in the way the girl's face gazed into her mother's loving expression. Of course, the cold, faraway stars didn't give the constellations much warmth, but in my childish imagination, they had been a glorious, shining pair, adorned in silver armor as they held one another close and shared stories about their day.

Now, my stomach clenched painfully, and I had to look away. Instead of the loving voice I remembered, I could only hear the new, ghostly version of Karye that haunted me. The one that reminded me of the monster she'd been to others, and of the brutal way in which she had died. The one that urged me to avenge her and make her proud, that made me worry I wasn't enough to follow in her footsteps and fight for my crown—for our people.

I glanced down at the ruby ring that had once been hers, glistening on my finger. Once it had been a comforting reminder, a way to keep her memory close. Now, I wasn't sure how I felt about it. About her.

Angry, I stood and scanned the ground outside the lone cabin the Elha'tonu residents had brought me to. Supposedly, their magic created an invisible barrier around the space, isolating me and not permitting me to leave until they fetched me tomorrow for my duel. But I hadn't bothered to test it and see if it truly could hold back Nesrelle's power.

I had no desire to leave this haven until it was time for me to face Kovi, the traitorous *garash*, and finally shove him out of my life and my heart. Permanently.

When my gaze landed on a stick, I lifted it, breaking it in two until it was the approximate length of a blade. Naturally, I wouldn't have any weapons before my duel, but I could still practice. I could stretch my muscles and direct some of my seething energy into something productive and distracting.

Because every time I closed my eyes, I saw Kovi's face and heard his words. *You chose vengeance over us. I would have chosen you.*

It made me want to scream. *Liar.*

He wouldn't have. He would have chosen his people every time, just as he had when he'd broken his promise and used his magic to control me. Just as he had when he'd shoved me into that brig and slammed shackles around my wrists. And just as he had when he'd chosen to take on the role of my executioner.

Drawing a deep breath, I sliced the branch through the air, relishing the rushing sound it made and imagining it was steel cutting toward Kovi's neck instead.

And yet...

I faltered, chest heaving and eyes burning. Another memory invaded, one I wished I could burn to ash and forget forever. His warm mouth on mine, his deep, gold-flecked eyes studying me earnestly, devotedly. *I'll fight for you. Always.*

Blinking furiously to fight the tears, I twirled and swung my stick again and again, fighting my imaginary opponent. The night air was cooler than it had been during the day, but it was still balmy and thick, and sweat soon beaded along my forehead. Strands of my hair, which hung loose down my back, stuck to my damp face. Though my dragon scale armor was made to withstand the heat, it couldn't stop my own body temperature from escalating with my building fury.

"You smell much better than you did in that brig. It's good to see your new captors at least gave you a place to bathe this time, and you bothered to stop moping long enough to take advantage of that fact."

Nesrelle's voice pierced my thoughts. I dropped my stick to my side and spun to face her. My lip curled in disgust, even as the rune her nestrae had carved into my cheek burned in response to her presence. "Ah, the other traitor in my life," I drawled.

Nesrelle laughed. "I've already told you. Do you think that I truly have an interest in ruling over mortals? I'd gladly help you onto your throne so you can lead your people through their miserable little lives and allow me to feed off their pain and suffering. *If* you use your power to be my executioner." Her white dress slithered behind her bare feet as she stepped closer. "As it is, I'm not sure you will succeed."

I swallowed hard. "You think I'm weak. Are you going to go back on our deal and take the power you gave me?"

She shook her head, laughing lightly. "No, I truly hope you succeed and kill that soldier. But he's always been your weakness, and I'm not sure you'll follow through." She tilted her head, studying me thoughtfully. "You're full of so many contradictory emotions and ideas."

"Stop reading my thoughts," I snarled.

Nesrelle raised her eyebrow. "If you want to wield my power, you have to welcome me inside."

I gripped my stick more tightly. "I hate you."

"And the pain your hatred fills you with is beautiful," she crooned. "But you need to hate the solider more. Kovi Ettonou must die tomorrow if you ever hope to win your throne. Get him and his ridiculous notions of love and peace out of your head. Focus on the coming war. Don't be weak."

She stepped close, holding out her hand as gently as a mother would reach for her child. I blinked and glanced down as my armor transformed, forming into a smooth gold breastplate with a protective emerald shirt, like a gambeson a warrior of old would have worn under traditional armor, yet lighter. This new outfit was heavier than my old, but stronger. Dragon scales in matching gold layered over new pauldrons, while the sleeves of my shirt concealed the black scales growing along my own skin.

"And then, what happens after I kill him?" I asked, forcing my voice not to tremble and to remain cold, forcing myself not to think about how safe I'd once felt in Kovi's arms or how my heart ached when I imagined killing him. "Will you help me escape these new captors before someone else steps in and executes me? Will you help me find Ryke and return to Alrenor? Will you return the army you stole from me and ensure they no longer murder my people?"

Nesrelle smirked. "If you are strong enough, of course I will, little *amara*. And then you and I will make the Teramese and the Forwyn suffer."

My smile was knife sharp. "Good."

"Get some rest," Nesrelle went on. "Get your emotions under control. Tomorrow, we have work to do."

CHAPTER TWENTY-FIVE

Revaed

THE SCREAMS WOKE ME FROM a restless sleep, even before Zalec threw open my door and stormed into my bedroom. Two other soldiers trailed him, all on high alert as they scanned the shadows, their firsts clutching their drawn swords.

"Your Imperial Majesty! Are you all right?" Zalec demanded.

Leaping out of bed and reaching for where I'd draped my jacket over a nearby chair, I threw it over my shoulders and began buttoning it as I walked, not bothering with an undershirt. "I think it's clear the sounds are coming from outside," I snapped. Still dressed in the loose pair of trousers I'd been sleeping in, I didn't stop to grab my belt, and instead seized my sword and drew it from its sheath, holding the naked blade aloft. I didn't miss a beat as I stepped into the boots by my bedroom door and strode down the hall, the guards racing after me.

The streets outside were full of chaos, with men and women sprinting in every direction, some toward the danger and others fleeing.

As I broke into a run, Zalec matched my pace, determined to protect me. But the sight that awaited us…I wasn't sure how anyone could protect us against it.

I staggered to a stop in the middle of the street, lungs heaving.

"Tuiros's blade," Zalec cursed at my side.

Huge branches protruded from the earth, as if a tree had sprouted in mere minutes, cracking the street and spewing rubble. Bodies hung from their ends, men and women who had been skewered. Blood coated the broken cobblestones surrounding the tangled branches. One of the bodies was still thrashing.

Bile rose in my throat.

From the shadows, figures emerged, their luminous eyes glowing unnaturally in the moonlight. Their inhuman gazes reminded me of Sephrode's, but their long, flowing hair was in shades of earthy brown and mossy green as well as pure white and pale blue. And the scales on their skin was coupled with *bark*. Twigs hung from their hair, and more sprouted from their limbs, even from their webbed hands.

"Hybrid nymphs," came a purring voice.

I whirled toward Nesrelle, narrowing my eyes and lifting my blade.

Zalec gaped at me as if I'd gone crazy. Apparently, I was the only one who could see the goddess of death.

"What have you done to my people?" I demanded.

Nesrelle's eyes flashed with glee. "I told you…these nymphs could fight for you. I wanted you to see how powerful they are, how…eager they are to please me."

I snarled. "So you had them murder my soldiers?"

She shrugged elegantly. "Now you know what they're capable of. Normally, they prefer to feast on magic, to drain their victims of it. But they can be persuaded to kill even nonmagical mortals outright."

More screams tore through the night, along with a terrible cracking, breaking sound. Was it from more branches ripping through stone and spearing through flesh? My heart throbbed inside my head.

"Will the killings stop if I agree?"

Nesrelle grinned. "Yes. And you'll have the magic you need to oppose even a powerful mage like Caesiem."

Her remark cut me to my core, but I ignored it. Instead, I focused on this chance to spare my people tonight, and perhaps win the war later. Rather than viewing it as an omen, I decided to take it as a miracle that the wicked immortal who had torn my empire from my grasp was offering to partner with me—and maybe even offer me victory.

"All right." I extended a reluctant hand, and she placed her cool one in my palm.

Nesrelle licked her too-sharp teeth, and we shook.

CHAPTER TWENTY-SIX

Lo

I MET HALIA, AVRIK, JENNAH, and Narek outside of the Corapaxu temple first thing that morning, Caesiem at my side. Meli joined us too, pulling Halia into a hug as soon as she saw her.

"I wish we could stay longer," Halia confessed, her green eyes straying from Meli to me. "I wish we could join your fight."

Shaking my head, I offered her a bright smile, perhaps more hopeful than I felt. "You've already done so much, and your own kingdom needs you. Thank you."

When I threw my arms around her, she laughed and returned the hug. "This isn't goodbye, you know," Halia declared, loud enough for all to hear, but before I pulled back, she dipped her head to my ear and whispered, "By the way, my gift showed me how you feel about your husband. You need to tell him."

Embarrassed heat flushed through me at her words, but when I glanced around, I realized that no one had overheard.

Jennah embraced me next. "You're strong, and always have been." Her fingers brushed my gold ribbons. "I might not be able to share my courage gift with you across the miles, but I hope this is a reminder of how brave you've already been. May the Life-Giver fight alongside you."

"Safe travels," I told the group as they mounted Reyva and secured themselves in the saddle. It was a cramped fit for four, but from Avrik's smirk as he wrapped his arms around Halia, I knew at least one of them didn't mind.

Meeting my eyes, Halia grinned, and before I could open my mouth, she began repeating the Forwyn blessing I'd once offered her, the first time we'd parted. "May Elhani hold your hand."

Even though my heart ached with the goodbye, I matched her smile as I finished: "And the guidespirits lead you home."

Then Reyva leapt into the air and unfurled her wings, her gold and black scales flashing in the rising sun as she soared toward a perfect, cloudless sky.

When I turned away, I held back my sigh, thinking of all today would bring.

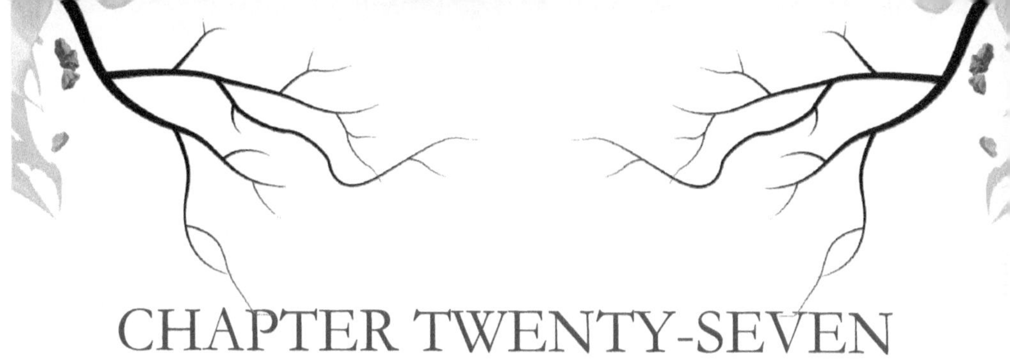

CHAPTER TWENTY-SEVEN

Kovi

I WAS IMMENSELY GRATEFUL THAT General Ilowhe didn't attempt to speak to me as he brought me my sword. He gave no false words of comfort. No prolonged declarations about how proud he was of me, or how justice needed to be dealt to our enemies to save the lives of our people.

Instead, he walked forward silently, handing me my sword and clapping a hand on my shoulder.

Nearby, the Elha'tonu Elders stood in a row near the pool's edge. Here, it lay calm and clear, but further out, a misting waterfall poured endlessly into its depths, churning and frothing its surface. Clustered near were Huvoki, Oru, Mhel, Lo, Mio'e, Caesiem and his Teramese friends, Meli, and an assortment of other soldiers and Alrenian allies.

If I craned my neck, I could see the temple towering above the steep incline rising past the waterfall, and some of the citizens of Corapaxu that had gathered to watch from a distance.

Elder Yelaia dipped her head toward me. "I appreciate that you're showing us your ability to overcome your Alrenian enemies," she said, "but know that we would gladly execute the empress ourselves, according to our customs." Something in her eyes made me wonder if her Sight magic, which she'd told me about last night, had revealed my feelings for Jalie. If she could sense the numbness filling my chest.

"No," Elder No'haleo intervened, shaking his head at Yelaia. "We haven't yet decided if an alliance is worth the risk. Let's see if the Forwyn from Alrenor are capable warriors. We need to know that they will be strong allies able to defend our own people in a fight…not weak dependents who will prove a liability to our people."

Yelaia pursed her lips, but she didn't argue.

"Thank you for the offer," I said, "but Elder No'haleo is right. This is something I must do."

But as I turned away, my heart pounded painfully against my ribcage.

I can't do this. This is wrong.

Letting your people die is wrong.

I closed my eyes, and all I could see was Jalie with her darkened eyes, those yawning depths reminding me of Nesrelle. The shadows surrounding Jalie consumed her, and the black scales sprouting along her arm multiplied.

It's not her. It's Nesrelle controlling her.

Still, Jalie had made the choice to ally with Nesrelle, to let the Dark Immortal control her and her actions. She'd given herself wholly to her cause of revenge and spilling blood.

And the tender, vulnerable side I'd seen within her? The joy and the passion to love and protect those around her, to lay aside her prejudices and pursue a dream that granted us a peaceful future? I was afraid that woman was gone forever.

I swallowed thickly and tightened my fingers around my sword hilt. *Lift your head, Kovi.*

What would Mother think if she saw me now, caught between love and duty, between justice and mercy? Between what I was told was right and what I hoped and longed to be right?

As I stepped onto the open patch of grass the Elders had announced would be today's battleground—or perhaps it would have been more accurate, with so many witnesses, to call it a stage—Lo moved away from her spot, catching my eye.

"Kovi." Her hand was gentle yet firm on my arm. When I turned toward her, the same fire I often saw burning within her father's dark eyes shone in hers, strengthened by the bright flecks of green in her irises. "You're making a mistake."

The uncertainty with which she'd talked about Jalie last night was gone. Now, she spoke as if she'd heard Elhani's voice.

I shook my head. My words came out rough yet full of conviction. "Doling out justice is the price I must pay for keeping our people safe. I made a vow as a soldier, Lo."

Pain flashed across her face, revealing the depth of her empathy. She threw her arms around me in an embrace, murmuring a reassuring blessing that Forwyn families might have once spoken over their fathers and sons and brothers. It was the first part of the same traditional blessing given during goodbyes, whether temporary ones, or permanent ones in death. "May Elhani hold your hand."

When Lo pulled away, I glanced at General Ilowhe's stoic face, and he nodded his reassurance. His daughter returned to the line of spectators. I straightened my spine and stretched my shoulders, awaiting the inevitable.

Jalie

The warriors surrounding me were stoic, their expressions infuriatingly composed as they escorted me down the path toward…a duel to the death. Toward Kovi.

Birds flitted from palm branches, and the humid air was heavy with the scents of life, a stark contrast to the burden of death I carried. In my mind, Nesrelle's voice urged me on, honing my focus, sharpening my resolve. She eased the ache of betrayal and grief threatening to swallow me whole with her reminders of my purpose—my goal of regaining my throne and leading my people.

When I closed my eyes, I focused not on Kovi and his deep, beautiful eyes as they'd once studied me with desire and something else—something softer and stronger and too overcoming to name—and instead thought about Revaed. My wounded fingers ached at the memory of his dagger slicing toward them, of his violet eyes scanning me with disgust as he proclaimed that I was a monster. A monster he didn't fear.

If killing Kovi was the price I had to pay to get to Revaed, to wrest the throne from his greedy, arrogant hands and finally lead my people into the glory we were meant for, I would do it. I *had* to do it. Mother wouldn't have hesitated, not for her people.

Leading means setting aside your own dreams. It means putting the needs of your people ahead of your own. That was one of the earliest lessons she'd taught me, her expression earnest, even if her sapphire eyes had glimmered with repressed sorrow. I'd often wondered what she'd sacrificed for Alrenor, but I'd never asked.

Now, I had an idea of just how weighty such sacrifices could be.

You'll do this for your mother, Nesrelle urged me. My cheek burned where her rune marked me, and it filled my blood with fire and a lust for battle. It raged with a fury that quenched my sorrow, leaving no room for doubt or grief or the sting of betrayal. There was only resolve, only what I must do for my people. For Mother. For Nesrelle.

He lied to you, Nesrelle said. *He used you, just as I warned you he would. Loving men…it comes at a horrible price. Make him feel your pain. Make him suffer for what he's done. Make sure he never hurts you or holds you back again.*

As I followed the final bend in the path, sweeping down to a grassy expanse clearly chosen as our battlefield, I squeezed my fists. *I will never be weak again,* I reminded myself. I couldn't let my heart waver. Not when the price would be my peoples' suffering. I held on to the memory of Inalgoth burning, of my people screaming in pain, and used that as my motivation. Kill Kovi, so I could return to them. So no more Alrenian cities would burn while I let an enemy soldier distract me with foolish dreams.

Kovi

I couldn't stop my sharp intake of breath as Jalie came into view, winding down a path lined with swaying palms. She was flanked by half a dozen heavily armed Elha'tonu warriors, every last one of them taller and larger than her, and yet the sheer magnetism and power of her presence made them seem like shadows next to her. Her armor was new, in shades of shimmering gold and emerald, with dragon scale pauldrons. Even her arms were covered, concealing the black scales growing along her skin. Instead of tying her hair back into a braid, she'd left it to flow loosely down her back. It streamed like a golden banner as a breeze washed over us, one full of the tang of the sea and the heavy perfume of the island's flowers.

When Jalie's eyes met mine, there was caution in them, like she'd erected a wall to conceal her emotions. The passion I was used to seeing was replaced with icy blankness. It was far too similar to the way the Dark Immortal tempered herself, and the sight chilled my blood.

My mind swept back to the first moment I'd seen her, back at the palace when Elder Ettonou had insisted upon a celebration in my honor after my graduation from the academy. Even then, before she'd reclaimed one of her dragons, escaped to freedom, commanded an army—or made a bargain with Nesrelle for her dark powers—Jalie had drawn every eye to her naturally. Against my better judgment, she'd drawn *my* eye too, just as she did now. And just like on that day, she studied me intently, like a predator sizing up her prey.

Our earlier promises ran through my head. *I'll fight for you,* I'd told her. And both of us had vowed we would never harm the other, even if one day we found ourselves looking at one another across enemy lines.

Now, here we were. My palm was slick against my sword hilt; my heart drummed like a war beat in my ears. Every memory and every dream I'd had with Jalie coursed relentlessly through my mind, forcing me to relive each moment with her as vividly as if they were happening all over again. The warmth and softness of her body when I carried her from the arena after she'd witnessed the execution of an Alrenian woman and had dissolved into horror. The wide, vulnerable fear and hurt in her eyes—the surprise and softening toward my gentle touch when I'd dumped her into her tub and brushed her hair away from her face. Her cinnamon and vanilla scent enveloping me when I'd slept by her side as she tossed and turned, delirious and terrified, while her body fought against poison. Her unrestrained joy and laughter as we'd ridden Ryke together, diving and soaring over Inalgoth. The warmth and kindness in her eyes when she'd caressed my cheek with a gloved hand in the battle for Wynlaen and confessed that she couldn't lose me. Her promises and kisses when she'd sent me away from her army to save my life. And the way she'd leaned into me, the way I could tell she trusted me and found comfort in my presence, when we'd been reunited in the palace dungeon.

I gritted my teeth and shoved aside the recollection of her kiss, the thrill of her embrace. I stifled my dreams of a future together. I forced every one of those moments away, letting them burn up and drift away like ash on a breeze.

Because now, they couldn't mean anything. Not when Jalie had wholly committed herself to Nesrelle and destroying my people. The girl I'd shared those moments with was dead.

All of it had been futile. Maybe Rhi'il had been right after all. Maybe Jalie had only used me and manipulated me for my power and what I could do to help her. Maybe I'd only ever been a pawn in her game.

The doubt cut me to the core, needling into my heart like a thousand icicles. But it helped steel me for what I had to do.

I lifted my gaze to meet Jalie's once more. For the briefest instant, I thought I saw something like grief flash across her face. Then it was gone. Her jaw hardened and she lifted her chin, quickening her stride until she stopped across from me.

Only a few feet separated us. A few feet, but it might as well have been miles. Years. Lifetimes.

"Jalie." My voice was raspy. "No magic, no powers, and no use of your curse in this fight—we face each other in an honorable duel of skills to the death, as your ancestors would have done."

Her eyes were cold. Her mouth twitched, and I thought maybe she would frown, maybe she would give some indication that her heart was as broken as mine…but she stood as still as stone. "I accept," she said at last. Her eyes narrowed. "No magic, no powers. No curse. Not unless you break your vow. *Again.*"

I didn't take the bait. This time, I lifted my voice so everyone watching could hear. "Empress Jaliana, daughter of Karye, you have been declared an enemy of the Forwyn people and our cause for peace within the Alrenian Empire. You have attacked both soldiers and citizens without provocation, threatening their lives." I drew a breath. "For that, you have been sentenced to death."

"When we give the signal," General Ilowhe announced smoothly, drawing Jalie's and my gazes to him, "you may commence."

It was Elder Ah'koni who offered the final word. "May Elhani determine the rightful victor."

Bile coated my tongue as I lifted my blade. Steel sang when Jalie drew hers from its sheath, one that her warrior escorts must have granted her when they'd readied her for this moment. It clearly wasn't an Alrenian sword—there were no words etched into the blade itself and the hilt was plain—but it was still a beautiful weapon. The Elha'tonu people were clearly gracious, even toward their enemies.

It felt wrong, to offer this gift to the woman we planned to kill, like embracing her only to stab her in the back.

"The duel ends when one of you deals the killing blow." There was a pause in which the world seemed to still, the distant chirping of birds ceasing and even the dull roar of the waterfall softening. "You may begin," Elder Ah'koni finished.

Jalie struck first. Our blades elicited a hair-raising screech as they crashed together. Once. Twice. Again. She whirled and stepped and dodged with the grace I expected from an Alrenian warrior, her hair swirling around her and her eyes flashing with emotion she could no longer conceal.

But I'd grown up being taught everything the Alrenians knew. I'd trained in their fighting style, and I'd lived and breathed their conquering, brutal culture. General Ilowhe and every one of his officers had ensured we perfected the art of battle just as the Alrenians had—and then we'd studied how to take advantage of their weaknesses.

While Jalie depended on feinting moves and the strength of her attacks, always pressing the offensive and pushing in close to me, I relied on patience. Her passion was like a roaring fire, consuming her as she let it grow hotter. Eventually, she would tire, and my defense would turn into offense, preying on the weariness that would make her sloppy.

I forced myself to think objectively, as a solider. To see an enemy. Not Jalie. If I let myself look too closely at her face, let myself remember…

I would break.

No, I was already broken. There was nothing but numbness in my chest. Ending her would end me.

Perhaps this was the price I'd always been destined to pay for the ways in which I'd wielded Elhani's magic. For the violent life I'd been forced to live as a solider. For the blood I'd spilt in questionable ways to protect my people above all else, even above my own conscience.

Maybe this had always been meant to happen—a cruel twist of fate that would force me to become my own undoing.

Jalie's mouth pursed into a thin line as she stepped nearer, her breathing ragged, her jaw tense. I couldn't avoid her expression this time. Couldn't help but see her emotion written plainly across her face: rage. It was better than the coldness I'd seen from her earlier, but also worse. It reminded me of the woman I'd fallen for rather than the Dark Immortal she'd allied herself with.

And worst of all was the flash of bitter betrayal that shone in her eyes.

"You think it's merciful to fight me like this?" she snarled, her voice lowered so only I could hear. Already, she'd backed me toward the pool, where the roaring of the waterfall tuned out the murmurs of our crowd of witnesses. Mist soaked the back of my jacket, and the grass beneath my boots turned slick with mud. "It's still an execution."

"Better for you to die standing on your feet." The words sounded mechanical coming from my mouth. Did I believe them? Did I believe anything I'd been trained to trust in, to do, or to *become* anymore?

Jalie's laughter was harsh. She pressed harder, her blade a flash of silver as she slammed it against mine again and again. Sweat glistened on her golden brow, and warmth flushed her freckled cheeks and glowed like fire in the bright flecks of her irises. "It all ends in you murdering me. You, who spoke those honeyed lies of fighting for me, of caring for me—" Her voice cracked, and she broke off abruptly, grunting as she launched a kick to my side.

She should have learned from our very first fight in the training hall, but she was distracted, her emotions a storm I could sense even without the magical connection that had once bound us together. I seized her boot, shifting her off balance until she tilted backward. Jalie maintained a tight grip on her sword, her free hand shooting out to seize my jacket collar. We plummeted together—Jalie sprawled on her back, chest heaving to catch her breath. Though I caught myself before I could be tangled up with her completely, I was still down, my knees pressed into the damp earth as I straddled her hips. I sat up to keep my face away from hers. Even with her armor and my uniform between us, I could feel the heat of her body seeping into my skin.

For a long moment, we froze. I held my sword to her neck while her own blade brushed against mine, pressed toward my throat. We were trapped in a tense stalemate, each of us hyperaware of every breath, and the way the steel nicked at our skin. Blood bloomed from my neck, a warm trickle that traced its way down to my collar.

I tried to will myself to do what needed to be done. To end this and accept the pain.

Jalie

The moment I lashed out with a kick and Kovi grabbed my boot, I inwardly cursed myself for a fool. It was the same move that had failed me the first time we'd dueled, back when the only thing that could cut had been our angry words. Back when all that had been at stake was the pain of hearing him call my mother a monster.

This time, I was just as horribly aware of the heat of his body and his nearness. His breath was steady, his muscles poised and controlled. When I stared into his eyes, pressing my sword to his throat just enough to make him bleed, he kept his soldier's disciplined mask tightly in place.

Kill him now, Nesrelle snapped. *Don't wait. Don't let him lie again. Don't let him trick you. Emotions are weak.*

But I couldn't deny the part of me that ached, hoping to find *something* in his eyes. Some hint of regret or longing. Anything to match the pain searing my heart, anything to tell me that deep down, he still cared. That he'd always cared.

What happened to always fighting for me? I wanted to scream.

I should have never let my walls crumble down. I should have known exactly what sort of havoc he'd wreak on my heart.

Kovi's sword was cold against my neck, a clear threat that if I moved to harm him, he would retaliate. And yet… Neither of us moved. He was as motionless as I was, his face inches from mine. His breath brushed my cheeks, warm and familiar, and I could smell coconut and soap, leather and steel, emanating from him.

My eyes blinked at the blood trickling onto his uniform collar, slightly darker than the vibrant red of his jacket. If I killed him, there would never be a Forwyn-Alrenian alliance. If I killed him, the world would feel…

I would feel…

Nesrelle snarled in my head and the pain at my cheek flared again. Cold bloodlust seized me in a relentless grip, shoving the part of me that wavered and ached so far down inside myself that, for an instant, I wasn't sure who I was anymore. Nesrelle's hate claimed me instead, reminding me of the rage Kovi had filled me with as she taunted me with memories of the shackles around my wrists, of the dark brig he'd led me to. Of my own people that he'd killed.

Enemy, Nesrelle reminded me.

My eyes burned. I pressed my blade a little harder against Kovi's throat, waiting for his own to bite back into mine. Wondering if this is how we'd both die.

Kovi

"Go ahead," Jalie whispered, defiance flashing in her eyes. "Kill me. That's the revenge you've wanted, isn't it?" Her voice shook, and her eyes glistened for a moment, making me suspect she was holding back tears. "From the moment you met me, you wanted to see me suffer because of what my mother did to yours. You admitted it before. Why not admit you *still* feel the same?"

But that wasn't true. She wasn't the enemy I'd been told she was. She wasn't like her mother, and I wasn't like my father. Her mistakes didn't make her Nesrelle, either…they made her lost and grieving, hurt and afraid, strong and determined.

In this moment, the woman beneath me didn't look like the one who'd bargained with the Dark Immortal and tried to murder me. She looked like the one who'd been so lonely and afraid she'd sought my comfort. The one who grieved her mother because she'd loved with an intense ferocity, the way she embraced everything and everyone dear to her in this life. The one who wept for her people's suffering and defied my father's cruelties.

Tears stung my eyes. *Elhani, I am a fool.*

When Jalie blinked, her own tears were gone, replaced with something cold and threatening. "Use your magic like you want to and command me to kill myself. Just like you slay all your enemies."

With a cry, I whipped my blade away from her and rolled backward, away from her reach. The scratch on my neck was shallow, but a chilling reminder of what was at stake. I leapt to my feet at the same moment Jalie shoved to hers, the expression on her face feral.

"You're not going to bait me," I said as she stalked around me, sizing me up.

"Fine," she snapped, and without warning, she charged again, pressing an attack that forced me back and around the pool. I retreated, letting her rain her fury upon me, listening to the way the rhythm of her breathing grew more rapid, watching the flush on her cheeks and the sheen of sweat on her face grow more pronounced.

Mist shimmered around us, and a final step sent me behind the waterfall, where its roaring filled my ears and pounded in my chest, and cool droplets slicked my skin. It was a shocking contrast from the heat filling my body as I whirled toward Jalie. Pointing my sword downward, I seized her arm to twist her weapon away.

She cried out as I shoved her against the rocky cliff, out of sight of all who'd come to witness our duel. Her eyes flared bright in the shadows, light from the waterfall reflecting in their gold flecks. Mist plastered strands of hair to her face as she tilted her chin toward me, defiance sparking in her expression.

"Is this the part where you kill me like a coward?" she shouted over the thundering water.

Ignoring her, I leaned in close, pressing my body against hers and letting my lips brush her ear. "Run," I urged.

I felt her body tense against mine, every one of her muscles locking in place. The rhythm of her breathing was ragged, each rise and fall of her chest making her armor dig into me. This close, she didn't have to yell as loudly as before to be heard.

"What?" she demanded.

"Run, while they can't see. Get out of here. Find Ryke and go."

Jalie jerked her head toward me, so close our breaths mingled and her face was all I saw. Mouth agape, she was clearly at a loss for words. "This is a trick."

"No," I ground out. "But you'll need to be fast."

"I don't believe you. What about the threat you say I pose to your people?" Her eyes narrowed.

"Never lay a hand on them again." My body trembled, unable to hold back the tangled emotions rising within me: fear, doubt, and horrible, all-consuming desperation. "Get far away from here. Go to Alrenor, another island, across the sea… Take back your throne or choose a different life. I don't care. Just *go*. Live."

Her laughter was harsh. "You would kill me before I took my throne."

I leaned my forehead against hers, breathing in her scent. *Elhani help me,* I thought, *but she is my downfall.* "I can't kill you. But if I let you go, or I let you kill me, they'll execute you immediately. There is no way the Elha'tonu or General Ilowhe will let this duel end without your death—you were right. And I can't let that happen. I *can't.*"

Jalie shivered, but when I leaned back, I realized it wasn't with tears or sorrow or fear. No…it was…

I blinked, confusion and hurt slashing into my chest as she kneed me in the groin and launched forward, seizing me by the throat and squeezing.

Gone was the woman who'd been watching me with vulnerability, with a tinge of hope. Gone was the vivid hue of her eyes, the golden flecks like fire or the first brush of dawn against the sky. Gone was every trace of humanity, every last piece of the one I loved.

Her eyes were black pits, and she was *laughing.*

Jalie

Another trick, Nesrelle breathed into my ear, sending a chill down my spine. *He's lying to you again, the son of whores and infidels and tricksters. End him, before he ends you.*

The agony that lanced through me, spreading from my cheek throughout my body, was unlike anything I'd felt before. It was more intense than the pain Nesrelle's demons had inflicted on me with their claws, and more awful than the bone-deep suffering the Queen of Death herself had subjected me to with her touch. It was a fire licking across my skin, a devouring plague rippling through my body and consuming every organ. My feelings, my thoughts, my memories—everything plunged into darkness, like I was freefalling into the depths of a churning sea, never to see the sunlight again. Nesrelle took over, her desire for blood raging inside me.

And she had to be sated.

Glee tore through my being, the same vicious joy I'd experienced before the battle of Aramith when Nesrelle's thirst for death and suffering had first claimed me. She laughed. I laughed. *We* laughed, as we slammed a knee into Kovi's groin, taking him by surprise. He staggered back, pain and confusion at war on his face as we grasped him by the neck and squeezed.

"You're fortunate we like to keep our word, mortal," we breathed, close enough he could hear our words even over the roaring of the waterfall. "Or you would feel the fury of the curse tearing through your flesh, even now."

His despair and terror—not at the possibility of death but at seeing Jalie vanish into Nesrelle's clutches, at seeing her become *us*, the executioner and the empress—they were beautiful emotions. We could taste them on our tongue, sweet and intoxicating. They fueled our power, sending a pleasantly warm flood of strength through our limbs and feeding our bloodlust. And yet, the craving for death and pain never ended.

We needed *more*.

Kovi

I'd been trained to pry myself from chokeholds, but Jalie's strength, fed by Nesrelle's unnatural power, was harder to free myself from. And yet…this was still Jalie's body—not that of the Dark Immortal. In a few deft moves, I broke free, staggering backward, grasping at my neck. My throat was swollen, each breath shooting daggers of pain into my chest as my lungs heaved for breath.

With a snarl, Jalie leapt for the blade I'd knocked from her hand, only giving me an instant to retrieve mine. Her onslaught was more furious and graceful than ever, leant extra force since she'd given herself entirely to Nesrelle. Her eyes were endless black pools as she stared at me, slamming her blade into mine, whirling around me in a deadly dance.

Sweat beaded on the back of my neck as we left the privacy afforded by the waterfall. Its roar dulled a little in my ears, allowing me to hear indistinct shouts coming from where General Ilowhe, our allies, and the Elha'tonu Elders stood. Perhaps they were calling out encouragement. Or maybe they were crying out for me to end the fight already.

Steel shrieked against steel as I faced Jalie—or whatever was left of her. *You should have taken the chance I offered you,* I thought wildly. Now…now I wasn't sure if Jalie would be able to escape. And if she did, would she simply turn around and slaughter my people while under Nesrelle's influence? Had she given her own free will away so easily?

If Jalie had made that choice, then that left me with only one.

One I refused to accept.

Every muscle in my body burned. It wasn't often I faced an opponent with as much endurance and skill as me, and I was growing weary. Jalie, on the other hand, hadn't worn herself out at all. Her ferocity seemed only to be growing.

"Jalie," I croaked, voice hoarse, "this isn't you. Don't give in. Come back to me."

She twisted her blade against mine, trying to fling it from my hand, but my grip held firm.

"This *is* me," she bit out. Despite her words, I was relieved to see a spark of blue in her gaze.

"No," I retorted, ducking a swing and dodging her follow-up attack. "The Jalie I know would never let someone else control her words and actions. Giving in to the Dark Immortal's influence and letting *her* will consume yours? That's even worse than the compulsion my magic wields. And Jalie would *never* surrender her will to another."

This time, Jalie staggered back, frowning and shaking her head as if to clear it. When she glanced at me, her eyes were her own again, but they still gleamed with fury. "Stop trying to confuse and distract me!" she snapped, lunging for me again.

"I'm not," I said, stepping back and throwing away my sword. It hit the grass with a dull thump. I could sense more than hear the murmuring of the crowd. Where I stood, there were only the sounds of the steady rush of the water and birdsong echoing through the trees behind Jalie. "And I refuse to fight you another moment."

I dropped to my knees, the muddy earth soaking into my trousers. I let my empty hands fall to my sides and met Jalie's gaze straight on. "I declare this duel over. Run and live. Or kill me, if you must. But I won't hurt you."

Never had I given myself so fully to such a mad plan. There was no strategy, no logic behind my move. It was a wild, desperate choice. It was potentially disastrous—even traitorous.

But I wasn't afraid.

Lo had said that Elhani had led her to spare Jalie's life once, and she'd been the one to tell me, even after Jalie had tried to kill her, that she didn't think this duel was right.

And maybe, it was time I trust something wild and mad, full of emotion and hope and faith that would have made Rhi'il proud. Maybe it was time to surrender the control I'd wielded so long against others.

Maybe this was the only way.

Elhani, may your will be done.

Jalie stared, her blade flashing in the sunlight as she held it aloft. An endless storm of emotions played out across her face, ranging from confusion to horror to glee. In the end, her jaw tensed and her mouth became firm. As she tightened her grip on her sword, her knuckles turned white.

I dipped my head, accepting my fate.

"That's…foolish," Jalie said at last. "You're an Aerekni solider. You don't surrender. You fight till your last breath. You made a vow to your people."

"And I made one to you," I murmured. "That I would fight for you. So I'm fighting for your life. Take this chance, Jalie. Live."

"You've lied before," Jalie protested, stalking closer, the blade still tight in her hand. "This is just another mind game. But you won't win."

I didn't move except to lower my head further, waiting for the blade to fall.

Lift your head, Kovi. How ironic to know that the woman who'd encouraged me with those words would be proud of me in this moment, with my head lowered, waiting to die.

But I'd rather die than kill the woman I loved. Even if that woman was all but lost.

There was a flash of silver as Jalie's sword dipped, and a whoosh of air. I wondered, distantly, if Rhi'il and Marukio and Mother would be waiting for me together, prepared to greet me in the Golden After.

Jalie

"Stop hesitating, you fool." Nesrelle's voice was a snarl, and when she dug her fingers into my shoulder, her nails felt like claws. "There's no room for wavering in leadership. No room for sentimentality."

And no room for kindness in war, I thought, the words echoing hollowly in my head. *I am the monster my people need.*

Empress Plague, monstrous enough even to slice a sword through the neck of the man she loved.

My heart stuttered as I raised the blade.

Loved.

Why had I let myself think that word in this moment? Only Mother had ever loved me and cared for me above all others. Only she had been my safety and my home.

Other than the love I held for my people and my empire, there wasn't room for anything else in my heart. Love, I'd learned, ended only in loss.

I wouldn't lose again.

I blinked my eyes closed, imagining the throne awaiting me. My crown. Mother's proud smile, if only she could see me now.

When I opened them, Nesrelle grinned at my side, ready to leech the pain out of Kovi's miserable death.

I won't lose again, I vowed, forcing all my strength into the swing as I brought my sword down.

CHAPTER TWENTY-EIGHT

Lo

WHAT IS HE DOING?" ELDER No'haleo shouted, his eyes shooting daggers toward Father. "Is this the type of foolishness your people display when fighting against the enemies of Elhani?"

"No," Father said, an edge of terror in his words. He stepped forward, as if to run to Kovi and protect him, but one of the Elders seized his arms. An Elha'tonu warrior shuffled over to take his other arm.

"You cannot interfere with a duel," Elder Yelaia murmured, though her eyes betrayed her pain. She was sorry for him. Perhaps even sorry for Kovi.

My heart pulsed in my throat as I gazed across the pool to where Kovi kneeled before Jalie. The Alrenian stood frozen, her blade lifted but motionless. For one breathless, wildly hopeful moment, I wondered if perhaps she wouldn't strike. Maybe whatever she felt for Kovi would stay her hand, and I'd been right about Elhani wanting Jalie's life to be spared. Maybe this duel didn't have to end in death at all, but in an alliance my people desperately needed.

Then Jalie swung.

Though I barely knew Kovi, I couldn't hold back the cry that tore out of me. At my side, Father stilled, catching his breath.

There was a flash of silver as Jalie's blade cut through the air. It took me a moment to realize that the trajectory was wrong, that rather than slicing downward into Kovi's neck, it slammed…into air.

Or what had been only air. In the moment between blinks, Nesrelle appeared at Jalie's side, with the empress's blade lodged in *her* throat.

Shock curdled into horror as I noted there was no blood, no noticeable damage to the Dark Immortal at all.

I swallowed. Of course not. She couldn't be killed.

Trembling, Jalie wrenched her sword out of Nesrelle's flesh—or whatever immortal stuff she was composed of—and staggered backward, her face contorted with rage. Nesrelle swept her fiery curls over her shoulder, laughing lightly as if everything were a joke to her. A horrible game.

As quickly as she'd appeared, Nesrelle vanished.

"What demonic plague did you bring to our shores?" one of the Elders shouted, spinning toward me, her eyes shining with anger and fear.

"I…"

But another shout interrupted us.

Jalie

The moment Nesrelle vanished, I felt every power she'd granted—even my curse—leech out of me. It was a jolting sensation after all this time, when they'd been as ever-present as my shadow, as stabilizing and strengthening as my armor. My knees wobbled and a wave of dizziness rushed over me as another burst of pain slammed into my marked cheek. Then the pain melted away, leaving nothing but a burning feeling like that of an old wound that had scarred over.

A cracking sound snapped my gaze to my arm, where the black

scales that had been growing along my skin fell and crumbled, dispersing into ash-like swirls that vanished on the breeze. Even my armor had changed, returning to the damaged, grimy pieces I'd worn until Nesrelle had altered them. The gaping hole in my side returned.

Realization struck an instant before agony lanced through me. There wasn't a dragon claw digging into my side this time, but the wound was the same, tearing deep. Twisting. Blood gushed and I collapsed, my body already turning cold and numb.

I was dying all over again, sent back to the moment Nesrelle had saved my life and proclaimed me her executioner. The moment I'd truly had to make good on my vow to become hers.

"Jalie!"

I blinked, struggling to focus on Kovi, to recognize and savor the feel of his warm arms around me as he held me close, cradling me to his chest.

"Someone get a healer!" he shouted. "Help!"

Darkness tunneled my vision, until all I could focus on was Kovi's dark eyes and the embers of gold that simmered within them. I tried to swallow, but my mouth was too dry. Lifting a trembling hand with the last vestiges of my energy, I managed to brush my fingertips against his cheek. *You were right,* I wanted to say, but my lips refused to form the words. *I couldn't lose you.*

Kovi

Distantly, I was aware of other screams, of pounding footsteps and shouts, but all I could focus on was Jalie's still form and closed eyes. The warm, sticky sensation of blood coated my hands and pooled through the front of my uniform. Too much blood.

"Move aside." Lo shoved me firmly, her tone brooking no protest. She moved with the assurance and authority her father would have, and I didn't think twice about releasing my hold on Jalie and letting Lo seize her instead. When Lo looked up at me, there was fire in her brown eyes. "I can try to save her, but you'll just be in the way. Go. Help the Elha'tonu. There's been an attack."

Numb, I forced myself to my feet, glancing at the blood staining my hands. Jalie's blood.

Lo was already singing, her voice rich and low as it wove effortlessly through the notes of Elhani's song. She kneeled over Jalie, brushing back blonde strands of hair with an unexpectedly tender hand. Everything in me wanted to stay, but Lo was right. I didn't know how to wield healing magic. As much as I hated it, there was nothing I could do here.

And the screams echoing through the trees ahead warned me that something else was going very wrong.

Caesiem

The screams came from the other side of the island, instantly sending everyone into high alert.

"Our guards!" Elder Yelaia cried. "They're under attack!"

The Elders sprinted into action, General Ilowhe and his allies following.

Vander spun to me as I ripped my gaze from Lo, where she was kneeling beside Empress Jaliana. "There's a scent on the wind…" he said thoughtfully, his fingers toying with his pendant.

Tayla grasped his elbow, her brow knotted with concern.

"It reminds me of the forest by the river in Alrenor, cool and dark and woodsy. Mixed with brine. And…" He drew a deep breath. "Magic."

I shook my head. Vander had always claimed that magic possessed a distinct scent, one that he could never quite describe to me because he said it was unlike anything else he'd encountered in this world. Other wind mages often stated the same thing, declaring that their magic allowed them to sense it, carried on the wind.

"Come on," I urged, charging after the others, toward the screams. My heart pounded out a warning as I remembered Sephrode's taunts. Had she brought her sisters to the coast to attack the Elha'tonu residents? But why?

Vander, Tayla, and Valentra fell into step beside me, sprinting along the path leading through the palms that Jaliana and her warrior entourage had walked only minutes ago. I turned when the path forked, descending toward the coast. The rhythm of the sea instantly called to me, matching my pulse.

But louder than the water were the sounds of battle and the cries of the dying. As we rounded a final bend, the scent of blood filled my nose and a baffling, terrifying sight met my eyes.

Creatures the like of which I'd never seen before were attacking the warriors who'd been posted along the coast to hold off the potential threat from the inhabitants of Wenu. And the creatures were vicious…plucking their victims into pink-tinged water and tearing them apart with fangs and claws, or shoving them down deep beyond the frothing waves to thrash and drown. They held out arms cloaked in moss and ivy, calling upon the earth itself, drawing on the branches and roots of palm trees and extending them unnaturally far, until they coiled about the warriors, choking the life out of them.

Vander shouted and a blast of air followed, slamming toward the strange creatures, who, when they stepped onto land, appeared like women…and yet not. Like the water nymphs, their skin was adorned in scales ranging from bright silver to deepest black, and their eyes glowed unnaturally. But unlike them, moss and ivy and bark wrapped around their bodies, until it was impossible for me to decide if they wore pieces of the forest like clothing, or if the growths were part of their bodies. Their hair hung in long strands of green, blue, brown, or white. When they opened their mouths and stretched out their hands, I saw animalistic fangs and claws already dripping with blood.

Before Vander's gust of wind could strike the creatures, one of them leapt forward, gesturing with her bark-covered arm. A huge tree trunk erupted from the sand, knocking us backward. Branches, fronds, bark, and roots ripped through the earth. I teetered and fell, blinking at the sky and coughing on a cloud of sand, grit burning my eyes.

"Tuiros's blade," Valentra cursed, her shoulder smacking into mine as she flailed beside me, gasping against the onslaught of sand. "What *are* those things?"

Another cry pierced the air as I leapt to my feet, just in time to see one of the creatures slip around the trunk to launch herself with unnatural speed and strength toward a warrior. She dodged the man's blade with ease and sunk her teeth into his neck, tearing flesh. Blood spurted as the man's body jerked, weakening until she kicked him casually away, wiping the gore off her chin. Her slitted silver eyes met mine and she lifted her hand.

And then…a wave of water roared toward me with a force that made my skin prickle. I reached toward it instinctively, the magic in my blood calling to the sea. But something was wrong—a disconnect where before there had always been a sense of rightness, a sense of home and belonging. This water felt foreign, and it didn't answer my pull, didn't heed my silent command. I couldn't shove it back, couldn't bring it toward me. Couldn't do anything.

Fear and betrayal like I'd never known shot through me. I'd thought Revaed's deceit had hurt, but this…I'd never imagined facing water magic wielded against me and finding myself helpless. I'd never expected to grapple with water and be unable to call to it. I'd never known that my connection to the sea—or the absence of it—could hurt this much.

"Caes!" Vander screamed as the water rushed forward, a frothing wall of death coming straight for us.

I gritted my teeth, redirecting my focus on the sea behind the attacking creatures. If I couldn't control the water they were wielding, maybe I could draw on the waves beyond them.

The wall of water slammed into us, nearly knocking me off my feet again. It swirled and raged, filling my ears with its recognizable roar. But nothing about this cold, hungry beast was familiar. Another chill swept up my spine as I tried to concentrate—not on my burning lungs, already aching for air, but on the churning waves off the beach. Somehow, my magic was weaker, the tether between the sea and me seeming distant. It felt like trying to pull water from a desert.

Vander gripped my arm, his fingers digging in urgently as bubbles burst from his mouth, his brow furrowed in confusion. Strands of his black hair floated around him like a halo as he tried to focus. And that's when I realized he was struggling with his magic too. He was trying to bring air to us, but it wasn't coming.

Heart pounding, I pulled harder on my magic, desperate. My lungs were screaming now, while the force of the water locked my limbs in place. My friends were equally trapped, unable to fight back, unable to draw on magic or strength to reach for oxygen. It was eerie, knowing how my past victims must have felt as they'd drowned on land.

Clenching a fist, I focused on the waves, recalling the feel of the briny wind on my face and the splash of sea spray along my skin. *Come to me,* I commanded.

Then requested.

Then begged.

Nothing.

I squeezed my eyes shut as bone-numbing terror seized me in its talons. The water had betrayed me. The water wasn't answering.

Never in my life had I feared the dangerous creatures that lived in the ocean or the seas, never had I concerned myself with the possibility of drowning. But now…now the thought of succumbing to the very element I'd always loved, always felt safe with, was too much to comprehend. It was an overwhelming ache, an all-consuming terror.

Opening my eyes, I scanned the water for help, for inspiration, for anything at all.

Keep fighting. No matter how many times I reached for the water, no matter how many times it remained silent, heedless of my pleas, a part of me refused to believe this is how it all could end.

Please. Please. PLEASE!

Black spots danced across my vision, and my knees grew weak. I couldn't kick to the surface, couldn't walk across the ground or swim up to the top of this wall of water. My legs struck the beach, a dark cloud pooling around me as I stirred up grit. At my side, Vander's grip on my arm slackened when he fell. His other hand threaded through Tayla's as he clung to her, and they exchanged a heartbreaking look. It was as if I could read their thoughts: at least, in the end, they had one another.

My chest ached when I thought of Lo. Was this really how I'd leave things with her? Would I really die here, betrayed by the water, never having told her how I felt?

On my other side, Valentra tried and failed to thrash against the water, her face twisted in fury. The same magic that turned Vander's and mine against us also seemed to have sapped us of all strength, locking us in place.

Eyes fluttering, I tried to focus on Lo's face, willing her to somehow know how I felt about her. Waiting for the awful end when my aching lungs would give in, seizing, and suck in nothing but water. Waiting for the blackness to consume.

Survival above all else. The mantra mocked me, the same way Sephrode's earlier words had. She'd known. She'd known my magic wouldn't work—

Sephrode! It was a last desperate attempt, a hopeful wish that somehow the water nymph's magic would be strong enough to fight against whatever was holding us here, that she could banish the sea back to where it belonged and save my friends and me. *Call back the sea. Take it back. Please.*

I'd never begged her for anything before. I'd never had to. Now, I wasn't sure if she would listen.

Before, she'd been bound to protect me, but now I feared the same rules that had allowed these other nymphs to use my magic against me had broken the tie I had with the water nymphs as well.

I felt a tug, first in my bones and then all around me as the water moved. It rushed away, receding into the sea with the force of a vicious current. Frothing and bubbling, it obeyed an irresistible pull, retreating from us and back over the beach, slamming into the creatures prowling toward us. It whirled around the bodies of both the dead and the living, and then cascaded into the sea with the grace of a winding serpent.

Thank you, I thought, even though I knew Sephrode couldn't hear specific words. She could only sense my will, the same way the water understood me when I called upon my magic. Besides, she hadn't rescued us because she had the desire to, but only because she was compelled to. Because my magic made her.

Gulping down air, I stood, relishing the looseness of my freed limbs. The strange nymphs hadn't been affected by the wall of water when Sephrode called it back. Instead, they stalked forward, some returning to their attacks against our allies and others setting their sights on us. Their eyes glowed in the sunlight, their needle-like teeth showing in their ominous smiles. Scales flashed among the clusters of bark and vines and moss clinging to their bodies, and their stringy hair dripped sea water.

Before they could use whatever power had frozen my magic before, I reached for the water. I did it desperately, like a starving man grasping for food. Relief soothed my soul as the water responded, and I felt my connection restored.

Coughing and gasping, Vander worked his magic instinctively alongside mine. We'd done this countless times before in training sessions and in real fights—me pushing water forward while Vander used wind to propel it more forcefully, until reckless whirlpools drove toward our enemies. The strength of our combined magic was too much for the nymphs to withstand.

With the first wave, they were knocked off their feet, squealing angrily as they thrashed in the sea, fighting to swim toward us as the current pulled them away. The second shoved them further from the beach, from their potential victims. Branches swayed and the earth shook, as if the nymphs were trying and failing to call on whatever powers they'd used to attack before.

Another wave shoved them into the depths of the sea.

Exhausted, Vander and I gasped for breath, waiting for the creatures to resurface. Waiting for them to turn the water magic back against us, or leap from the sea and tear into another unsuspecting victim's throat.

We crept closer to General Ilowhe and the Forwyn, Alrenians, and Elha'tonu warriors who clustered around him, some dripping blood from minor wounds and some kneeling beside their fallen companions—but all staring out toward the sea. Waves pounded against the coast, frothing and bubbling along the sand. Gulls swooped and dove as if nothing evil or unnatural had just risen from the Great Sea's depths. A breeze rippled through my wet clothes and, despite the warmth of the island, sent a chill over my skin.

But there was nothing. Whatever had brought those nymphs to us, whatever had driven them to attack, that urge was gone and the creatures had vanished.

For now.

CHAPTER TWENTY-NINE

Revaed

REPRESSING A SHIVER, I WATCHED the seawater swirl around my knees, soaking my trousers. Moonlight danced along its surface, lazy and enticing. After growing up with the thunder of the ocean in my ears and its tang in every breath I breathed, I'd always found the water beautiful.

Tonight, though, it was chilly and eerie. Unlike Caesiem, I wasn't connected to the element, and that meant I wasn't connected to the nymphs. Each time I summoned Sephrode, who had come to recognize me after bringing me countless messages from my heir while he'd spied in Alrenor, I knew I was gambling. I didn't possess any magic that would tempt her, but nymphs were still fickle creatures, easily bored, always wanting to trick humans and play games. There were countless reasons why she could choose to sweep me out into the sea and drown me.

Each time I called on the nymph myself, it was always worth the risk. Once to obtain theslynik to heal Caesiem, and twice now to determine if he was all right.

I cast a single glance over my shoulder to ensure my guards were staying back like I'd ordered them. They didn't enjoy this, but I refused to let them risk themselves for me. This was a danger only I would face.

Tossing a gold coin, I waited, watching the waves churn over sand

and pebbles. Watching the water foam.

Sephrode's white hair flashed in the sea first, before her luminous yellow eyes hovered over the surface, taking me in curiously. "The sad, handsome emperor wants to talk again?" She cocked her head. "Do you know I could take away your sorrows?"

I swallowed thickly, questions swirling in my head. Nesrelle's words were taunting me. *Are you so surprised he chose her people over yours? That he chose* her *over you?*

Was he safe? Had he truly betrayed Teramyl? Was he really willing to fight against his own people? Or had Nesrelle been playing mind games, preying on my doubt and misery to breed even more sorrow for her to feed upon?

Sephrode tsked impatiently. "Are you going to make your request, or stare at me all night?" She fluttered her lashes. "Or are you considering my offer? The water is deep enough to make you forget all your troubles."

This time, I couldn't stop myself from shivering. "I'm not trying to die," I snapped.

Sephrode laughed lightly. "You could have fooled me." She steepled her hands thoughtfully, and her eyes turned distant. "Do you want to ask me about the future?"

I cleared my throat.

"Of course not. You want to know about the handsome prince. He's also full of sadness…" Her expression turned solemn. "But I'll only answer one question. I have restless sisters to watch. I'm curious what games they'll play next."

Foreboding crept down my spine, but I caught my words before the question spilled forth. I wouldn't let her bait me into using up my one question on something else.

I sighed, considering. I longed to know where Caesiem was, and what he was thinking. What he was planning. But…as much as anxiety and worry and betrayal tried to steal my attention, there was only one question that mattered.

"Is he safe?" I didn't trust that Nesrelle had spoken the truth when she'd claimed he wasn't hurt, that she hadn't killed him.

Sephrode grinned. "Oh yes, he is safe."

Something in her smile made me regret my question. Maybe I should have taken more care to word it differently. I twisted the question around and around in my mind, trying to discover if there was some loophole in which she could have answered truthfully yet still misguided me.

I gritted my teeth, cursing my stupidity. *What if she means safe in the afterlife?*

Sephrode sighed, something almost like compassion filling her gaze. "Poor, sad emperor. I won't taunt you. You're too pretty to suffer this much, so I will leave you with a gift: more information, for free. Yes, your heir lives, and yes, he is unharmed and safe."

She drifted closer in the waves, flicking her tail. "But I'll warn you. I've looked into the future, and it is dark."

Frowning, I stepped deeper into the water. "What does that mean?" I demanded, but the nymph was already diving back into the sea, disappearing among the waves.

CHAPTER THIRTY

"WHY DON'T YOU…LET HER die?" Elder Yelaia's question didn't sound vicious or callous, merely curious. Yet I couldn't help but be taken aback.

Pauni'a had arrived at my side not long after I'd rushed to Jalie, joining me in calling upon Elhani's song and weaving his magic over the empress to stop her blood loss and knit up her skin. Once we'd stabilized her, Elder Yelaia had helped us move her into a room within the temple. Other than its bright woven rugs and tapestries adorning the walls, offering splashes of vivid color, the space was plain enough to remind me of my old bedroom at the abbey. Its bed and chairs and single dresser were all simple yet solid. The two glassless windows afforded plenty of light, and the Elder opened the curtains over both to permit more fresh air.

It was hot and sticky, but each breeze brought relief and the scents of fruit and flowers. The temple was surrounded by trees and shrubbery, a lush garden that could have rivaled the one at the Alrenian palace, before it'd been burnt. The ever-constant burble of water filled the air, helping to calm my racing heart.

I sank into a chair Yelaia had brought in. Pauni'a was already in another, using a cloth dipped into a bowl of water to wipe off Jalie's sweaty, blood-splattered face. I glanced at my hands, coated in a layer of dried blood. It was everywhere, slicking Jalie's armor and everyone's skin. She'd lost a lot. Enough that, even with Elhani's sustaining power,

I wasn't sure we would save her.

Again, I thought of Elder Yelaia's question. Why not just let Jalie die?

It's not Elhani's will for me to let her die, I thought, but I didn't say the words. Surely, with her gift, she already knew enough about Jalie's and my past to be both understanding and puzzled. To know that this wasn't the first time I'd rushed to Jalie's aid. To know that I'd been the one to kill Jalie's mother, and for years, Jalie had craved revenge against me.

Even now, I wasn't sure what Jalie would do if she opened her eyes and saw me hovering over her. Would she latch her hands around my neck? Would she reach for her lost blade—left somewhere near the pool where she'd fallen—and demand *I* face her in a duel to the death? Or would she be thankful, especially now that the shadows and scales that had been a part of her were gone?

But just because Nesrelle's influence on her had ended didn't mean her hatred of me had.

"If you were in her place," Elder Yelaia went on, "I'm sure *she* would let you die."

I gritted my teeth. "Do you think that her death would bring peace to Alrenor any faster?" I asked. "What does your Sight tell you?"

Elder Yelaia shook her head, her silver eyes trained on the gold-skinned empress. "The future shows so many different outcomes right now, it's impossible for me to say. But I do know that she's caused much pain and death and suffering. Does she deserve this mercy you offer her?"

"I'm sick of death," I snapped, my voice rough and angry. "I'm sick of hate. Maybe Jalie will have to be executed when all this is over, but she chose to spare Kovi's life when she could have easily ended it. She chose *him*, a Forwyn, and that has to mean something."

Elder Yelaia nodded solemnly, her eyes finally meeting mine. "I understand," she said smoothly. "An alliance could be a powerful thing, if she can convince more of her people to follow her example. But I think you and I both know how stubborn both the Forwyn and Alrenians in your empire can be."

I shrugged. "Who can say? But I believe Elhani led me to help Jalie for a reason. Now the question is if she can make the rest of the recovery on her own."

Pauni'a glanced at me, her amber eyes full of exhaustion. Our extensive use of Elhani's magic had drained us both. "She did lose a lot of blood," my sister agreed. "But she seems…at peace."

Elder Yelaia stepped forward, resting a hand on each of our shoulders. "Go get cleaned up and rest. Until she wakes, there isn't much you can do." She turned pointedly to me. "And maybe it's better if your face isn't the first she sees when she *does* wake?"

"Maybe not," I admitted.

As Pauni'a and I left the temple, I drew a deep breath of fresh air. I'd been so focused on listening to Elhani's magic and saving Jalie's life that I hadn't been aware of the sounds around me. Now, I realized I couldn't hear the distant shouts anymore.

"Do you think they're all right?" I asked Pauni'a, but before she could answer, footsteps pounded toward us.

A figure tore through the trees and down the path from the coast, sprinting toward the temple. Kovi, bloodied from catching Jalie and the battle he'd come from, his jacket sleeve torn. An angry, bloody scratch trailed along his skin.

As soon as he spotted us, he raced forward, his eyes entreating. "Is she all right?" he demanded, catching his breath. His gaze strayed to the dried blood adorning my hands and clothes. "Did you save her?"

"We closed the wound, but she lost a lot of blood. She's resting, and only time will tell if she can pull through. For now, she's stable." Before he could say anything else, I asked the question weighing on me. "Where's everyone else? Are they all right?"

"We were attacked by creatures I've never seen before," the soldier said, his eyes distant. "The Elha'tonu people lost the warriors guarding their coast, but Caesiem and Vander were able to send them away with their magic. And yes, Caesiem and your father are both unharmed. They're coming here, to the temple, and joining the Elders in an emergency meeting."

"What sort of creatures?" Pauni'a asked, tensing.

Before Kovi could say more, approaching footsteps interrupted us. "They can explain." His throat worked as he swallowed. "I'll join the meeting later, but…can I see Jalie?"

Pauni'a tossed me a sideways glance. "I'm not sure Elder Yelaia would let you in to see her," she said. "You were just fighting her to the death, after all."

I shrugged. "I'm not sure the Elder would care," I muttered.

Kovi dipped his chin toward the temple. "Is she in there?" When I nodded, he added, "I'll talk to her and see. Thank you, Lo." He turned to my friend. "Pauni'a."

Pauni'a grinned. "Call me Nia. And…of course. We'd be remiss in calling ourselves followers of Elhani if we hadn't used his magic the way he'd called us to."

As Kovi vanished into the temple, Father and several other Forwyn soldiers appeared at the foot of the path, surrounded by Elders. As soon as I met Father's eyes, finding him well and whole and smiling back at me, I ran to him, pulling him into an embrace. Lifting my head, I instinctively sought out Caesiem.

He noticed my wandering eyes. "The Teramese left last," he said, his gaze searching mine. I couldn't tell if he was disappointed in my concern, or if part of him was beginning to understand, to maybe even trust Caesiem. "He's all right, Lo."

As the others shuffled wearily into the temple, Pauni'a came up behind me, squeezing my arm. "I'm going to wash and rest," she murmured. "I'll give you and Caesiem some privacy."

I rolled my eyes. "We had plenty of that last night, stuck in the same cabin, and he *still* is closed off to me."

"Tell him how you feel, Lo," my sister urged. "Tell him everything you've told me." She paused. "*Including* about Elhani's sign."

My heart slammed into my chest at Pauni'a's reminder. *Elhani's sign.* The other important secret I'd been holding back from Caesiem and my father.

"Nia, he was just in a battle against Elhani-knows-what," I protested. "Now is not the time."

She shrugged. "When will there ever be a good time? All I'm saying is, you shouldn't put it off. Don't be afraid. Why *wouldn't* he want you?" With a final nudge, she turned and headed in the opposite direction, away from the temple and toward the forest full of treehouses, where she and some of my other sisters had been given lodging.

Caesiem and his friends came into view a moment later, descending the path at a slow pace. My gaze instantly latched onto Caesiem, scanning his body despite everyone's reassurances that he was unharmed. His clothes were soaked, the loose red pants and white shirt he'd found in our cabin clinging to him. His bronze skin and taut muscles showed through the thin fabric of his top, making my stomach flutter. Waves of dark hair hung across his brow, dripping water into his face no matter how many times he tried to brush the locks back.

He was talking with Vander, Tayla, and Valentra, all of whom looked exhausted and worried. Caesiem noticed me first, flashing me a tight smile and dropping the conversation to pick up his pace and come to my side.

"That's not your blood, is it?" he asked.

"Of course not. *You* were the one in a battle. Are you all right? What happened?"

Caesiem's expression turned solemn as his friends joined us.

"We almost weren't fine," Vander proclaimed, his silver eyes intense. "Those creatures took away our ability to use our magic and almost drowned us on land."

I frowned. "They have water magic?" My fingers strayed to the pendant around my neck, before I remembered the blood staining my hand and dropped it back to my side.

"They have *more* than water magic," Valentra cut in. "They wielded the earth against us, moving whole trees." She shared a knowing look with Tayla. "There are stories about such creatures, crossbreeds between wood nymphs and water nymphs. They belong to both the forest and the ocean, and because of that, they wield the powers of both. And all nymphs can steal magic. They stole Vander's and Caesiem's and rendered us all helpless."

Caesiem ran a hand through his hair. "I think the children's stories we grew up with are exaggerated. Those nymphs didn't steal our magic permanently—or completely. I could still call out to Sephrode for help, and Vander and I were able to use our magic to send them back."

I swallowed. "Send them back *where*?"

Tayla's green eyes were wide. "That's the question, isn't it? We know that water nymphs mostly live in the Terebrys, and wood nymphs prefer cooler woodlands, like those found in the mountains in Teramyl or Brevinn. I don't know if there are any on your continent, which means they probably came from ours, all the way across the sea. But it's rare for them to interbreed like that…and no one knows where these crossbreeds prefer to live, as they are not bound to water or trees."

I frowned. "Breed? All the nymphs I've seen so far are female."

Caesiem's lips twitched. "That's because their females are the warriors, while the males stay hidden away. Nymphs may be bound to nature—the ocean or the forest—and the magic that stems from it, but they are forever craving and seeking more magic. At least, that's what the stories Tayla and Valentra keep talking about say."

"And that's how they overcame your magic, and the magic of this island? Because they can…drain it from people somehow?"

"It seems a strange coincidence these hybrids showed up after we arrived on the island," Vander muttered, studying Caesiem.

"Revaed wouldn't know anything about them, or have any way to send them after us," Caesiem protested, but I noticed the furrow in his brow. He was thinking furiously, his eyes dark and distant.

"Anyway," Vander continued, "the Elders called for an emergency meeting. I'm not sure what that means for your alliance." He looked genuinely sorry when he turned to me. "We have time to clean up and to tend to those with minor injuries, and then they want us all back at the temple at the thirteenth hour."

I blinked at the sky, suddenly dizzy with weariness. From my estimation, that was only two or three hours from now. It was already late morning, the sun high and hot in the sky.

Tayla twined her fingers with Vander's. "We'll see you soon."

Caesiem's jaw worked as he nodded, watching his friends leave, walking in the same direction Pauni'a had taken only minutes ago.

"And *we* need to talk," I pressed, keeping my voice firm despite my exhaustion.

Caesiem's gaze latched on mine, and for one annoying minute, my breath caught. I wasn't sure I'd ever grow accustomed to those beautiful eyes, or the warmth that spread through my chest whenever I was around him. *Tell him how you feel,* Pauni'a had urged, but I had so many other things swirling through my brain, the words wouldn't come.

I brushed the pendant with my fingers again, and Caesiem's eyes followed my movement. "If my magic doesn't protect me, I don't think even that pendant could stop those nymphs," he murmured.

"That's not my question. I need to know how *I'm* using water magic. You said it's the pendant, but this never happened before. Maybe if you explain to me how to use this magic, I can at least...well, find ways to send away these hybrid nymphs like you did."

Gently, Caesiem grasped my elbow and steered me toward the path, trudging up toward our cabin. He sighed. "You're right. The reason you're wielding water magic now...it's more than just the pendant."

He paused, drumming a rhythm against his leg with his free hand before facing me.

"It's…well, it was the marriage ceremony." He scratched the back of his neck. "Mages can…share their power."

I blinked. "What?"

"It's the only known way a mage can give magic," Caesiem went on hurriedly. "And I'm not exactly sure how it works. But the water magic…it's a part of you now."

"A legal ceremony bound your magic to me?" I asked, skeptical.

"It's like you said—it was more than that. You made vows before Elhani, making the ceremony a sacred thing. I'm sure you having my pendant helped," Caesiem said, his voice dipping lower, softer. His neck flushed. "And I sort of…willed it to happen."

"Why didn't you tell me before?"

Caesiem searched my gaze, something vulnerable and dark flitting across his face. "I told you. It's because of me that you lost Naina and so many others. I have their blood on my hands. I didn't want you to…" He grimaced. "I couldn't have transferred any of my magic to you if I didn't…"

Releasing his grip on my arm, he scrubbed a frustrated hand across his face.

"What are you *talking* about?"

"I don't deserve your forgiveness, Lo," he breathed. His wet hair was tousled about his face, and my hands were still crusted with blood when he seized them. He leaned closer, his breath a caress against my cheeks. "I've never deserved it. Not when you were a nun and I foolishly let my feelings get in the way, not when I betrayed your trust and helped overthrow your government, not when I naively thought Revaed and I could help your people." He inhaled sharply. "You have every right to hate me or to never forgive me…and I didn't want you to know I'd given some of my magic to you."

I scowled. "How about you let *me* decide if I can forgive you?"

A muscle flexed in his jaw.

"Besides, you already know that I've forgiven you," I continued, "but you refuse to forgive yourself."

Caesiem released my hands.

My throat was tight, and my heart slammed against my chest as the full weight of his confession struck me. "You gave up some of your magic for me?"

"Of course I did," Caesiem murmured. His lips twitched into an almost bashful smile. "My magic is strong enough for both of us. And just like with the pendant…it will protect you."

The pendant protects the one the mage loves most in this world, I thought. I opened my mouth, determined to get more answers, but Caesiem took a step back.

"But your water magic, along with all your other magic, could be drained during an attack from those hybrid nymphs. This just proves I can't put off going to see Revaed, Lo. I don't know if he had anything to do with this…but even if he doesn't have answers, I'm our only chance of talking some sense into him and maybe getting him to side with us against Nesrelle and her forces. I'd bet anything that *she* is behind this attack. I need to leave. Soon. I know those nymphs will be back."

"I know," I said, my mind feeling sluggish as I tried to follow the change in topic. "But first…we have the meeting. You'll stay for that, right?"

Caesiem nodded. "You can bathe first," he added as we neared the cabin. "I'll change when you're finished."

I glanced down at the crusted blood on my arms. "Oh. Right. Thank you."

He peeled off his drenched shirt and laid it on a nearby rock. Sitting down, he leaned against it, soaking up the sun. For an embarrassing moment, I froze, staring at his bronzed skin gleaming in the sunlight and the chiseled planes of his jaw as he closed his eyes, stretching his arms behind his head. He looked as content as Karos did when he curled up for a nap in the sun.

Even more shocking was the white mark that stood out against the brown of his skin. It formed a braided pattern, like an intricate but small scar along his chest. Right over his heart.

My pulse thundered—I'd known I'd find it, but it was still strange to see it with my own eyes. To confirm a fact that had been buzzing in my brain for over a week now. I wondered if Caesiem thought it strange, if he had any idea what it meant, or if he'd explained it away as a scar he must have received in battle.

Prying my eyes from him, I darted into the cabin, internally scolding myself. But as I scrubbed the blood and grime off my body in the hot spring, watching steam curl around me, I couldn't stop thinking about what Caesiem had admitted. He'd given up his pendant and now some of his magic for me.

If only he would stop pulling away. If only he would forgive himself. I'd never felt closer to him—and yet so far away at the same time. I'd never been so absolutely sure of how much I loved him.

With shaking fingers, I reached up and brushed my own mark—one that had appeared the evening of our wedding. The only other soul who knew about it was Pauni'a, as I didn't even know how to explain it to my father, afraid he'd try to deny it. It was pale against my dark skin, forming a pattern over my left breast—over my heart. A mark that perfectly matched Caesiem's.

Kovi

My heart lodged in my throat as I shoved open the creaking temple door and stepped into the cool, dim interior. I couldn't erase the image of Jalie collapsing, of her blood pooling beneath her. Even now, her blood was drying on my skin, mingling with my own from where one of those creatures had dug her claws into my arm.

Though everyone had witnessed Jalie choosing to spare my life, I wasn't sure that would change anything. And in the process, I hadn't proven anything to the Elha'tonu Elders except that I'd risk my own life for Jalie's, jeopardizing our potential alliance. They probably still viewed her as a threat, an enemy. What if, after all of this struggle to save her, General Ilowhe and the Elders still insisted she had to be put to death?

I ground my teeth. I'd already chosen Jalie over them. I'd already risked my own life for her. I wouldn't let them heal her only to turn around and slaughter her later.

I'll do anything to protect her, above anyone. The realization felt natural, as if it had been there all along, under the surface. I'd prided myself on being a loyal soldier, on being unswervingly dedicated to my people.

But I'd crossed a line during the duel. I'd made a choice I couldn't unmake.

Lift your head, Kovi.

I didn't regret it, either. What kind of person would I be—what kind of soldier was I—if I couldn't defend the woman I loved? If I wasn't willing to lay down my own life and upend my whole world for her? If I couldn't show her mercy, how could I ever enter the Golden After and look Mother in the eye, knowing I'd betrayed my own heart? Knowing I'd forsaken the first thing she'd taught me?

Most of the temple sat empty and still, but soft footsteps drew me toward a small room near the back. The door was ajar, affording me a glimpse of the bed upon which Jalie slept, her golden hair spread out across the pillow. Elder Yelaia paced the floor, her eyes unfocused as if she were deep in thought or lost in a vision.

But as soon as I stepped forward, she whirled toward me, her nostrils flaring and her eyes piercingly bright and clear. "What are you doing here?" she demanded. Her gaze flicked to Jalie and back to me.

"I wanted to make sure she was all right."

Yelaia pursed her lips. "The future is too noisy; there are too many pieces in place and too many decisions ahead. I can't see you or your path clearly." She straightened. "All I know is what I saw of your past, and what I saw at the duel. I don't know if you're here to check on her or to kill her."

"You saw how I ended the duel," I murmured. "I would *never* kill her."

"You would have, once," Yelaia cut in sharply.

"Once, I was taught that she was my mortal enemy, trained to slaughter my kind as ruthlessly as her mother had. Once, I thought she was a heartless stranger. I know better now."

Yelaia crossed her arms, uncertain. "And who's to say she feels the same?"

I leaned against the doorway. Being a whole head taller than the Elder, it was easy for me to glance over her shoulder and study Jalie. "She might wake up and decide she still hates me. I don't know. But I needed to see if she was all right."

The longing in my tone seemed to convince Yelaia. Sighing, she plopped into a chair beside the bed and gestured me forward. "I can't see her future yet, either. She's still fighting for her life. She lost a lot of blood. And when if wakes…who's to say what she will think or feel."

"She broke ties with the Dark Immortal," I said. My hand twitched at my side, but I resisted the urge to brush Jalie's hair back from her face. She looked so peaceful in sleep, I didn't want to disturb her.

Don't lie to yourself, I thought. *You're afraid she'll open her eyes and curse you. You're afraid to see the hate in her expression.*

I couldn't stop remembering that moment in the duel when Nesrelle had taken over and Jalie had tried to strangle me. Though, in the end, Jalie had freed herself from the Immortal's influence, I wasn't sure how much of Nesrelle's power would linger. The rune on Jalie's cheek was a constant reminder of the connection that had existed between them.

But you have a connection to Jalie too. Drawing a deep breath, I laid my hand over hers, watching her chest rise and fall. In my mind, I imagined my message entering her thoughts, seeping into her consciousness the same way my words had once crossed the miles between us. *You're strong, Jalie. You can survive this. Come back to me. Remember what we dreamed.*

Footsteps and voices echoed from the front of the temple, drawing my attention away. Yelaia sat up.

"Until we know what they're thinking, you probably shouldn't be here," she warned me.

My stomach clenched. I didn't want to imagine General Ilowhe's disapproval if he found me now, cradling Jalie's hand. I wanted to believe he'd understand and choose mercy…but what about the other Elders? They wouldn't want to risk their own people in a war that wasn't their own, fighting alongside soldiers who chose to sacrifice themselves rather than slay their enemies.

"Go get cleaned up," Yelaia said gently. "The other Elders want to meet and discuss the attack in two hours. Come back to the temple then. We can persuade them to reconsider their plans for your empress, too."

I nodded wordlessly, letting the Elder guide me out of the room and down the hall toward a back exit. Emerging into a verdant garden full of waving palm fronds and bright flowers, I wound my way around the temple and toward the forest on the other side of the island. A curving dirt path led into the trees, where just this morning children had laughed and played, and mothers had hung laundry to dry on clotheslines. Now, when I stepped into the shadows, relishing the cooler temperature, there was nothing but birdsong to greet me. The people had retreated into their homes, waiting quietly until the bell at the temple rang to signal all was clear.

At regular intervals, wooden staircases led up to the trees, each with trunks as wide as several men and covered in layers of bright moss. I approached a set of steps leading to my own treehouse and ascended, watching lizards and dragonflies flee from the noise. I followed a walkway past other doors leading into other trees until I reached the one given to Huvoki, Oru, Mhel, and me. My friends were nowhere to be found, but I expected they'd be back soon, and I wasn't eager to answer their questions in the wake of Jalie's and my duel.

Stepping inside, I passed through the small kitchen, its screened windows looking out onto waving branches and twisting vines, and down the hall to one of the bedrooms. Stripping out of my torn jacket, I studied the scratches tracing up my arm. Gathering soap, gauze, and ointment, along with a fresh outfit the Elha'tonu people had supplied, I left the house, hurriedly making my way to one of the many pools scattered across the island.

With everyone else in hiding or still returning from battle, the pool, tucked deeper within the forest, was abandoned. A small waterfall, barely a quarter of the size of the one beside which Jalie and I had fought, cascaded into it. Stripping off my grimy clothes, I waded into the water and scrubbed at the layers of dirt and blood staining my skin. I didn't waste any time dressing and tending to my cuts, applying ointment to clean them and then wrapping them in gauze.

I tried to distract myself with these mundane tasks, but my mind wouldn't stop replaying the duel and the tears in Jalie's eyes. The hatred. The grief. It haunted me endlessly.

Then there'd been the moment Jalie had stabbed Nesrelle instead of me. The instant she'd collapsed, far too much blood flowing from her wound. I feared she wouldn't recover, that she'd given her own life to save mine.

How would I live with myself, if she died for me, believing I thought she was my enemy?

❧

Caesiem

"What do you think of my latest recruits?"

The taunting voice sent a chill snaking down my spine. My eyes flew open. This wasn't Lo's voice—she was still inside our cabin bathing. I sat up and glanced around, my gaze landing on a figure whose very presence leeched all the warmth from the sunlight soaking into my skin. Her fiery curls and pitiless blue eyes gave her away immediately.

The Forwyn and Alrenians alike called her evil and twisted. The Dark Immortal, Nesrelle.

I sneered at her. "So I was right. Those hybrids nymphs are *yours*."

She shrugged, sweeping aside her long green skirts to stride across the grass on bare feet. "In a way. Yes, they wield the power of nature and are bound to the laws of earth and water magic. But they pledged allegiance to me." Her grin turned feral. "And they also answer to Revaed."

Blood pounding in my ears, I stood. I could sense the sea crashing against the coast, could feel each wave thrumming through my veins. It rushed to me in a coiling, glistening stream, misting about my face and beading in my hair, before I was fully conscious of pulling it to me. It was always there, ever faithful, like a living presence, sustaining me. Grounding me. Protecting me.

It was relieving and empowering to know the nymphs' attack hadn't wreaked any long-term damage on my magic. "Revaed doesn't have earth or water magic," I declared. "And he doesn't have any earth or water mages left in his army. He couldn't summon those hybrids."

Nesrelle laughed, her teeth so sharp they looked like fangs. "Who needs elemental magic when they have an Immortal's power?"

I gritted my teeth. "You lie. He wouldn't side with you."

"Revaed is desperate," Nesrelle crooned. "Don't underestimate him and what he can do when pushed. Even against *you*. He's been betrayed by his own blood before. If he grew to despise his own father for all the ways in which he destroyed him, how much more will he hate you when he realizes you have chosen Lo over him? That you're prepared to fight against his army?"

Fury exploded in my chest, fueled by desperation, by grief, by raw terror. The water roared forward, frothing as it rushed at Nesrelle. But she was gone before the wave struck, leaving it to pummel through the air and pour back toward the sea in a tumultuous waterfall.

Lo

"I don't think the appearance of those strange creatures coming right after your arrival was a coincidence," Elder No'haleo remarked gruffly as we gathered in the temple's main room. Caesiem stood at my side, his gaze distant and his body tense, but when I'd asked him what was wrong, he'd only shaken his head.

"Trust me, we've never seen their like," Father said from his position at my other side.

Elder Yelaia glanced around the room thoughtfully, taking in the faces of fellow Forwyn, Alrenians, and Teramese. They snagged on Meli, whose mouth was pursed, her brow furrowed. "My Sight is clouded— too full of the many choices and paths that lie before us. Has your gift shown you anything, Meli?"

Drawing a deep breath, Meli closed her eyes, her forehead pinching as she concentrated. In seconds, her eyes flashed open. "Nesrelle sent them."

One of the Elha'tonu warriors stirred. "The Dark Immortal? I thought you said she already had an army of Alrenians she'd twisted with her dark powers."

"It seems we've been drawn into your war whether we like it or not," Elder No'haleo muttered, turning accusing eyes on me. "If the

Dark Immortal's followers have already attacked our people, there's no guarantee that they will leave us alone even after your departure."

Elder Yelaia straightened, running a hand over her hair. "Maybe, maybe not. But from what I've seen in visions, I think Elhani brought these fellow believers to us for a reason. It's time we stop hiding and start fighting. It's time we consider the world around us, and not just our own survival. It's time we think of what the world could look like generations from now. We could help build a peaceful union with Alrenor, one that will establish trade and travel. Our children and their children could see and experience the world beyond our small borders." Regret flashed across her features. "I could use my Sight to know more of the world and its needs, instead of ignoring it as I have."

"Or we'll be slaughtered before we can ever see such a future," one of the warriors protested, waving a well-muscled arm. A necklace of shells clinked around her neck as she moved. "Those creatures wielded powers that drained us of our ability to fight back, even with Elhani's magic."

Anxious murmurs arose. Some Elders paced, while others took advantage of the chairs scattered throughout the room to sit and muse. The air was tense, fraught with fear.

"There are only two choices here." Kovi's voice was steady, its deep timbre echoing off the walls. Everyone fell into silence, and even my father paused, turning to him with deference. "Either you bide your time and pray you can defend your island from another surprise attack, or you take the fight to Nesrelle and her army on your own terms. Either way, there will be bloodshed. Lives will be lost no matter what. But allying with us increases our numbers and resources, giving us the greatest chance of success. The benefits are undeniable, for you as well as for us."

"Says the soldier who couldn't even slay his worst enemy," snarled a bulky warrior, his dark eyes flashing with fury as he twisted his lip in disgust. "You are a disgrace."

More arguments burst forth, some people insisting that Kovi's choice of mercy showed dedication to Elhani while others shouted for Jalie's death.

And then Caesiem stepped forward, lifting his hand and bringing with it a gentle stream of water that danced around his arm, graceful as a coiling vine. The action demanded attention, silencing everyone. "In Teramyl, we're familiar with nymphs and their powers, as their magic is similar to ours, grounded in nature."

"Granted to you by false gods," one of the female Elders sniffed.

I opened my mouth to protest, my fingers lingering on the pendant I wore. Surely Elhani had bestowed magic on the Teramese, just as he'd given the Alrenians their own particular gifts. But Caesiem pressed on, unperturbed by the woman's interruption.

"Wherever it originates, we've also grown up being taught that nymphs forever crave more magic, more power. If they're water nymphs, they're restricted to the water. Forest nymphs cannot stray far beyond the borders of their wood. But they can drain all magic from humans—temporarily from a distance or permanently if they make contact for long enough. Stealing human magic grants them additional powers, breaking down some of the restrictions the laws of their magic place upon them. I'm not sure how many of these stories are true, but today's battle proved at least parts of them are."

"So these creatures are nymphs? But they used earth *and* water magic," the female warrior said, fidgeting with the shells at her neck.

"Sometimes, the nymphs interbreed and create hybrids that can wield the magic of both their parents." Caesiem's forehead wrinkled as he dropped his arm, releasing the water to rush back out of the temple, swirling through the open front doors and out of sight. "We don't know much about them, but it has come to my attention that these hybrids are working with Revaed Xalenos as well as Nesrelle. I can fly one of our dragons to Hemlaen and confront Revaed. It's possible he'll listen to me and stop these attacks. Maybe even give up his war effort."

Across from me, Huvoki snorted. "Yes, let's send a man who was just recently our enemy into the heart of enemy-occupied territory to speak with their leader. *And* we'll give him a dragon. Sounds foolproof."

Caesiem tensed, annoyance flashing in his eyes before he forced one of his dimpled smiles onto his face instead. "I'd welcome a companion on the journey, but it would be suicide for them. Revaed would kill anyone who wasn't Teramese and ask questions later. Care to join me?"

Elder Yelaia held up a hand. "This is enough! Enough bickering! Enough mistrust! This young man and his friends abandoned their army and risked death to side with you. My Sight shows me no deceit in their actions or words. And the young empress fighting death in this very temple chose to spare a Forwyn life during their duel, even when she knew there was no chance that you, as spectators, would spare hers."

Silence fell heavily.

"I think it's time we put aside our differences and our fears and accept that Elhani brought us all together for a reason." Her gaze flicked to Meli. "You already have learned that a woman born with both Alrenian and Forwyn blood can lead a rebellion composed of Forwyn *and* Alrenians who seek peace." Her eyes darted to me. "You already found that a Forwyn and Teramese could unite in marriage—and whether that ceremony was part of a distraction or not, here they stand, together, fighting on the same side. Fighting for each other." She gestured to Kovi. "You've already seen an Aerekni soldier battle against the Alrenian empress herself, and both emerged from their duel alive— each prepared to give their life for the other." Elder Yelaia shifted, cocking her head as a smile stretched her mouth. "I think Elhani has made his will clear, my friends. Of course we are afraid. Our enemies are strong. But we are stronger together. This is our path toward a new future, toward peace, if we dare take it."

"Or our path toward death," a warrior muttered darkly.

Elder Yelaia shrugged and laughed. "Miss Nolanhou already

reminded us that some things are worth dying for. Freedom. Peace. The chance to breathe easily, without fear of enemies murdering or enslaving us. I've seen some of the enemy's plans with my Sight, and I promise you, we would not be spared, even if we chose to sit back and fool ourselves into thinking we were choosing safety by avoiding this war. As Kovi said, the creatures that attacked us have proven that the war has already come to us. And it will *continue* to come."

Father glanced at me, his expression soft, before clearing his throat. "You're right. I am prepared to stand alongside all of you, as allies and friends, and face death for the chance to ensure peace for future generations. My daughter has shown that enemies can become allies, and I trust her judgment." He waved to Caesiem. "And I trust her husband to fly to Alrenor and speak with Emperor Revaed on our behalf. He has my blessing *and* my trust."

I straightened at Father's declaration, warmth spreading through my chest.

Huvoki grimaced, looking chastened. Dipping his head, he murmured, "I follow my general."

One by one, and then in groups, the gathered assembly of Alrenians, Teramese, and Forwyn agreed to fight together.

Until at last, there was only me.

Elder Yelaia looked to me expectantly.

My footsteps echoed in the temple as I stepped forward. "Thank you for your wisdom, Elder Yelaia. You already know I'm prepared to fight for peace and freedom. I refuse to watch my people suffer any longer." My eyes snagged on Kovi, whose expression was stoic, his body rigid. He looked out of place in the Elha'tonu outfit he'd been given—a white shirt that clung to his muscled form and orange pants patterned with the Forwyn rising sun—but he was still the perfect picture of a disciplined soldier. He was restraining himself, waiting for the right moment, but I knew he was longing to argue for Jalie's life. "But before we finalize this alliance, I have one more request," I went on, turning back to the Elder. "If we are choosing to fight together, choosing to look past what once divided us and focus only on what unites us, then we need to spare Empress Jaliana's life."

Murmurs broke out, but I pressed on.

"As you already said, she spared Kovi Ettonou. The two of them share a bond that goes beyond my understanding, and if he believes in her, if he knows there is more to her than a desire for revenge…well, I choose to trust him. Let's give her a chance. She could be the key to gaining more Alrenians to our cause. She could be the one to help us end the generations of hate between Forwyn and Alrenians. Elhani already called me to save her life once. I know he's doing the same now. The only way to end all the killing is to embrace mercy."

"That's foolish," Elder Olahni said, standing so quickly she nearly knocked her chair off its legs. "Mercy has its place, but so does justice. We saw the darkness in the empress, the shadows that clung to her and the power of the Dark Immortal residing within her very soul. She's chosen her fate. She's beyond saving."

"The very fact that she broke free of Nesrelle's influence and chose *not* to kill Kovi proves otherwise," I snapped.

Father took my hand and squeezed it gently, reassuringly. "With all due respect, Elders, the empress is my prisoner. I trust the judgement of my soldier and my daughter, and I choose to give the empress a chance. Trust me, if she threatens more lives, I'll be the first to execute her. I will never put her safety over that of your people or mine."

His tone was firm, brooking no argument. Even Elder Olahni seemed appeased, nodding and slowly sitting back down.

"Well then," Elder Yelaia said, her smile so carefree, so full of joy and peace and confidence I could have imagined she was speaking at a party, "we have made our decision. It's time to plan for a war."

CHAPTER THIRTY-ONE

Jalie

YOU FAILED ME." MOTHER'S EYES flashed with undisguised contempt, her mouth a cruel, vicious line as she turned her back on me. "If you spared the soldier, how can I trust you'll avenge my death? How can I believe that you'll fulfill your vow? Are you a true Alrenian with honor, or are you a disgrace? Are you my daughter—or not?"

My chest ached. I knew, deep down, that this woman wasn't truly my mother. Mother was long dead, defeated by the enemies she'd used to take joy in tormenting. People like Kovi's mother, whose only crime had been to be born to a race that worshipped differently and wielded powerful magic we didn't understand.

Still, this figment of my imagination felt real. We stood in the throne room, golden sunlight streaming through the glass ceiling, each thick marble column casting a long shadow. Mother was clothed in a thigh-length dress in the style she preferred—adorned in dragon scales and leather, as if she were prepared for battle rather than sitting at court. With each step she took, her long legs rippled with muscle. She was taller than me and as lithe as a predator. Her hair fell in a shimmering curtain down her back, braided and decorated with countless scales of black and ivory that matched her dragon Reyva's colors. And every inch of her dripped with weapons—curved daggers strapped to her thighs and calves, a sword on her hip and another attached to her back, and more that I knew were hidden beneath her clothes. If I remembered correctly, she even had a few small yet deadly blades bound in her hair.

"He didn't deserve to die." My voice wavered. In this moment, I felt as small as a child being scolded. Not the woman I'd become, independent and strong in my mother's absence. Not the one who'd escaped her enemies and led an army.

Mother turned back to me and sneered. "He's an infidel who doesn't follow the Life-Giver. He's not Chosen to rule, as we are. If he's standing in the way of your god-given destiny, of course he deserves to die."

I gritted my teeth, fisting my hands. For the first time, a wave of fury and disgust washed over me as I studied my mother. She was proud, confident that she was right. So sure that the blood she shed was justified.

"Do you think killing is a game?" I demanded.

Mother blinked, her expression cool. "It is your *responsibility* if it means ensuring you can lead and protect your people."

"But you take pleasure in it," I said, speaking in the present tense as if she were still alive, still harming the Forwyn. "In watching the slaves suffer and die."

She sniffed. "What if I do? Fear encourages their obedience. And obedience is their only purpose in life."

When I closed my eyes, I pictured Kovi and his deep gaze flecked with gold, watching me tenderly. I could feel the gentle brush of his hand as he tucked my hair behind my ear. His warm breath on my face. His embrace. The taste of his kiss. My stomach churned when I imagined what Mother would have done to him, if he'd lived too long within the palace. He could have been long dead before I'd ever had the chance to meet him.

Before I'd ever had the chance to learn how merciful and kind and thoughtful he was. How strong and brave and loyal.

"No," I whispered, my throat tight.

"What?"

"No," I repeated, my voice growing stronger. "Obedience isn't their only purpose. They're more than that."

Mother burst into laughter, the sound harsh and mocking and utterly unlike the way she'd treated me in life. It grated against my ears, making my blood seethe and my stomach turn. This wasn't my mother, not truly, and yet everything in this moment felt so real. It made me wonder—if Mother were alive, if this conversation were happening in the world of the living, would she behave the same? Would she turn her back on her only daughter, when once she'd doted on me? The doubt that clawed through my chest made me uneasy, made me question everything I'd ever thought I'd known.

If Mother had been a monster to her enemies and her slaves, was it possible that she could have turned her monstrous nature on *me*?

The sound of her laughter continued to echo in my ears as my eyes flew open. My entire body was weak, and my throat felt parched and scratchy, like I'd swallowed several spoonfuls of sand. Sunlight pierced my eyes and made them water, forcing me to blink rapidly as I tried and failed to sit up.

"I'd lie back down if I were you," a female voice said, startling me. I didn't resist her suggestion, sinking against the pillow. "Considering you almost bled out, I don't think you're ready to sit up or move around quite yet. I can bring you some broth, but first you'll have to promise you're not going to kill me when I get near you."

Her dry tone seemed familiar, but it took me several moments to place it. Lo.

Peeling my eyes fully open, I turned my head to meet the woman's eyes. I was in a small bedroom with two windows, both permitting an abundance of light that made my head ache. Lo stood across from me, leaning against the wall. The green flecks in her eyes burned with an inner fire as she assessed me, as if preparing to fight. A self-satisfied smirk twitched my lips at the realization that she didn't underestimate me, not even when I was prone on a mattress and half-blinded by the daylight.

My mouth was so dry, it was a challenge to get the words out. "What if I don't make any promises?" I asked.

Lo pushed off from the wall, taking a step closer and rolling her eyes. "You'll die of dehydration and all my work pouring Elhani's magic into you will have been wasted."

Licking my lips, I hesitated, studying her curiously. I wasn't sure how I felt about this woman, who'd apparently saved my life twice now. Was her story of grievances against my mother as terrible as Kovi's?

Resisting the urge to smirk again, I gave in. "I won't try to kill you."

Besides, I was pathetically weak and vulnerable. Trying to kill my savior would be the epitome of idiocy. And the power that had once flowed through me…both the new abilities Nesrelle had granted me and the curse I'd carried…they were all gone. I could sense the fact with every beat of my heart, with every inhalation of breath. Where once there had been surging energy and a listlessness for violence, there was only emptiness. It left me both hurting and relieved, a strange mixture of emotions I wasn't about to try to sift through yet.

"All right," Lo said. "I'll be back. Don't do anything stupid."

Lo was only gone a few moments, giving me time to adjust to the sunlight and push up against my pillows enough to peek out the nearest window. A view of waving palm fronds and bright red blossoms greeted me, with a backdrop of forest that I knew marched down toward the coast. Inside this building, I couldn't detect any other sounds or movement, leaving me to believe Lo and I were alone, for now.

When she returned, bearing a plain clay bowl full of steaming broth and a crude-looking spoon to match, she settled into a chair beside my bed. Everything about this island was simple compared to the life of luxury I'd known, but the broth smelled delicious, and my mattress, though small, was comfortable. The simplicity of life on Elha'tonu was peaceful, a welcome respite from the pressure even my best days at the palace had carried. If I wasn't worried about the residents' desire to kill me, I had a feeling I would have loved it here.

"Please tell me you can feed yourself," Lo said.

It was my turn to roll my eyes as I plucked the bowl from her hands. The chicken broth was as rich and hearty as I'd hoped it would be. Lo didn't move away from her chair but didn't speak again either as I finished every last drop. When I glanced at her expectantly, she took the bowl with a raised brow. "Let your stomach settle before you fill it to bursting. You can have more later."

I settled against the pillows, even though my stomach was still growling. "Why did you save my life?" I asked bluntly. "*Again?*" A day ago, if I'd seen her bleeding out and had the healing power to save her, I wasn't sure I'd have offered her the same mercy she'd given me. Not when every time I blinked, I pictured her attacking Mother and watching the life drain from her eyes.

"It's not your time." Lo's words were simple, her voice light. When I met her gaze, there was no animosity in it, but no affection either. She made the statement with the same ease she would have commented on the weather—indifferent and factual.

"Your god told you this?"

Lo shrugged, setting the bowl on a table, one of the few pieces of furniture in the room. "For some reason, he thinks you have something more to do in this lifetime." Her gaze turned piercing, the warmth in her brown eyes giving way to something hard. *That* was the type of look I'd expected on the face of my mother's killer. "Maybe he thinks you can atone for all the suffering you've caused."

In my mind's eye, Inalgoth was in flames again, my people screaming, fighting, dying. Despite the air's warmth, a chill rushed over my skin. I hesitated, the question that I didn't want to ask lodging itself in my throat as I pictured Kovi kneeling before me, offering his own life in place of mine.

Foolish. Merciful. I swallowed hard. *I don't deserve him.*

"Does…" My throat was still gravelly. Lo reached for a cup of water resting on the table and handed it to me. I gulped it down eagerly, until Lo, sighing and smacking me gently on the arm, pried it from my grasp.

"I told you, go slow or you'll make yourself ill."

I scowled. "You're like a fussy old nursemaid."

Her stare didn't falter. "*You're* like a careless child. Do you want to heal or not?"

Huffing, I glanced away, ignoring her question. Silence descended once more before I tried another question. "Does everyone else agree with you? About it…not being my time?"

I listened to Lo moving about the room, pushing open another curtain to let in more of the fresh breeze. Birdsong filled the air, soothing and reminiscent of the steady melody of home, when my balcony doors were thrown open to the palace gardens. A swell of homesickness filled my chest.

The gardens would be burnt now.

"They've agreed to let you live, for now," Lo said at last. Her tone turned pointed. "But everyone is waiting to see what you choose to do next."

I smirked. "They expect me to leap from my sickbed and go on a killing streak?"

"Don't jest. They know what you're capable of."

I glanced at my hands, lifting them to study my palms. They were calloused and coated in grime and dried blood. The three mutilated fingers on my left hand mocked me, still a little painful, but freshly bandaged.

I weighed the risks of confessing the truth to Lo, the girl who'd stolen everything from me, the girl I was meant to kill. The girl who'd saved my life.

Sighing, I stared at the ceiling. "You're not a monster," I blurted out. When I finally dared to meet Lo's eyes, her expression was unfathomable. For a long moment, we gazed silently at one another, until I started to feel ridiculous.

Then Lo's mouth twitched, the flecks of green in her eyes shining with repressed mirth. "That makes me feel so much better, knowing the person who tried to kill me doesn't think I'm a monster."

"You know what I mean," I snapped. "Don't make me say it."

Lo tossed her braid over her shoulder, the smile spreading across her face turning positively devious. "You're glad you didn't kill me, so I could save your life."

I shrugged. "And because…" I glanced at my hands again, considering. "You're not who I thought you would be."

Lo raised her eyebrows inquisitively. "What do you mean?"

"For the longest time, I imagined the one who had killed Mother had been someone like Elder Ettonou, who took pleasure in bloodshed and making people suffer." I blinked, banishing the threatening memories, the phantom pain of long-faded bruises and injuries. "Someone who enjoyed the chance to rip the empire away from my people and lord his power over us, relishing every opportunity he had to execute us in brutal ways. You're not like him." I drew a deep breath. "How…how did it happen? How did you kill her?"

For several seconds, Lo gaped at me. "Why would you want to know that?"

"I'm not delusional about who my mother was, not anymore. And I know her throat was slit. But I think I need to know, to really be able to let everything go. Did you plan it? Were you an assassin? How did *you* kill *her*?" My eyes flitted over her form. She was confident and strong, but it was difficult to imagine that she, who would have stood at least a head shorter than Mother, someone who would have been a slave unable to use her magic and ignorant in the ways of fighting, overcoming Empress Karye.

Lo burst into laughter. "An *assassin*? No, I was a slave in the palace." Her smile fell away, and her eyes turned distant. "She killed my little brother in front of me. Slit his throat, like she loved to do to slaves who displeased her. She'd been upset with me, but Edi stepped between us to protect me. I couldn't save him, couldn't stop her." Her voice trembled and her eyes became glassy, but she turned back to me, not avoiding my stare. "When the Misrothians visited, I saw my chance to avenge his death. Halia trained me to defend myself, and I helped her tame Reyva. That night, your mother discovered our plans to defy her and threatened the Misrothians… by killing slaves. She was going to kill me." Reaching up, she drew away the braided gold ribbons wrapped around her neck, revealing a pale scar tracing the skin across her throat. "I took her by surprise and slew her first, with her own dagger."

I inhaled a shaky breath, licking my parched lips as I processed everything she'd said. "Self-defense."

Lo nodded. "It was kill or be killed. And…revenge. For my brother." There weren't tears in her eyes anymore, just a hard, determined expression. She didn't regret what she'd done, though it was clear the night haunted her.

"I don't hate you," I admitted. "I would have done the same thing, in your position."

"She was still your mother. You must have loved her." Lo hesitated. "And as you know now, I understand the urge for revenge when you've lost someone you loved."

I blinked back threatening tears, refusing to cry in front of this woman. "But that's why I don't hate you. In Alrenian culture, it's expected to avenge a loved one's death to honor them. You did right by your brother. I tried to honor my mother, but…" I shook my head. "If I had, I'd probably be lost in Nesrelle's clutches still. And *she* is the one who's stolen my empire. And my mother…she wasn't who I thought she was. Killing children…" I lifted a trembling hand, pushing a strand of hair out of my eyes. "I don't even know how I feel about her anymore." I glanced back at Lo, half-smiling. "Besides, just because I say I understand you and don't hate you anymore, doesn't mean I *like* you or forgive you. I only mean I respect you and your choices. You did what you had to do. I did what I had to do. And now…"

"We all have to live with the results," Lo finished solemnly.

I nodded, laying my head down on the pillow and staring out the window. "I'd like to be left alone now."

"If you need anything, just call. There are other healers in the temple, and they won't be far away."

Lo gathered my empty bowl and walked toward the hall, floorboards creaking with her steps. I knew I should thank her for everything she'd done, for fighting to save my life. But just because she wasn't my enemy anymore didn't make her my friend, and my throat was tight, full of unshed tears. I didn't regret hearing her story, knowing exactly what had happened the night of my mother's death. And I'd meant what I'd said—Lo had done what I would have.

Mother had deserved the death she'd been given.

I glanced at my ruby ring, fidgeting with it and watching the light dance in its crimson depths.

And yet…I was still a motherless daughter. I still loved the woman I'd known, the one she was for me and the one I'd thought she'd been. I still missed her.

I still needed to grieve.

CHAPTER THIRTY-TWO

Lo

CAESIEM AND HIS FRIENDS WERE gathered outside the temple, standing in a tight knot and speaking solemnly.

"We know the Xalenoses," Vander was saying. "We have *every* reason to think Revaed will kill you on sight."

"It's *Revaed*," Caesiem protested. "Think of everything he's done for me. He'll want to hear me out."

"But in the end," Tayla said, her voice smooth and unyielding, her green eyes sharp, "he will behave like his father."

Valentra nodded, laying a hand on Caesiem's shoulder, squeezing gently. My ridiculous heart lurched at the sight, as if it had reason to be jealous. "I'm sorry, Caes, but what Tayla says is true, and you can't deny it. Revaed may love you, but he was taught to follow in the High Imperator's footsteps. Any threat to their power or their people is always removed swiftly. You saw the bodies in the square. You saw what measures he's willing to take."

Caesiem stepped back, his eyes trained on his boots. "I know," he murmured. "But you know this is something I have to do. It's a risk I have to take…and no one else," he added pointedly as Vander opened his mouth. "He'll be swifter to attack if he sees others with me. If I go alone…"

Vander sighed, turning and running a hand through his hair. It was shaggier than Caesiem's, quickly becoming unruly. "Fine," he snapped. "I know you can take care of yourself. But don't put your guard down just because he's been family all this time. You know who he truly is."

"Speaking of the High Imperator…" Tayla's voice trailed off. "I know we haven't finished our work here in Alrenor, but please, think about what happens afterward. If we survive this fight only to return home and be executed by the imperator for our failure, it's all for nothing. And our people will be left with no hope."

"We'll find a way," Caesiem said, but his body was taut, revealing his concern.

As I stepped forward, the group turned, finally noticing my presence.

"How's the empress?" Valentra asked.

"She's resting," I said evasively, my eyes darting over her to Caesiem and lingering. "Where's…everyone?"

"The Elders went to spread the news of our alliance to their people," Vander explained, nodding toward the city proper behind him. "And General Ilowhe wanted to meet with his soldiers. He agreed our meeting about Caesiem's trip was our first priority, so he left us to talk." A knowing smirk spread across his face. "But now, we're going to join them and leave you two," he added, eyes flicking between his friend and me.

While he, Tayla, and Valentra retreated toward the treehouses on the western side of the island, I turned to Caesiem, heart pounding uneasily against my ribs. "I don't think going to see Revaed will do anything," I announced bluntly.

Caesiem's eyes were dark. "Are you saying it isn't worth trying?"

"No, it's worth trying," I murmured. I squeezed my eyes shut and breathed in deeply, inhaling the scents of the island, of flowers and fruits and water and sunlight, all reminding me that it was vibrantly *alive*. A haven for a people who were being dragged into our war. For a miserable instant, I wished we could have hidden away here forever, that those hybrid nymphs hadn't found us, and we could just leave Alrenor to rot. But that wasn't an option I could live with.

Opening my eyes, I let my gaze trace the face of the young man before me. If I was honest with myself, it was his discussion about returning to Teramyl that was truly weighing on me. Nothing about our relationship had been planned—and certainly not our wedding—and yet, here I was, aching at the idea of being parted from him.

He couldn't abandon his people. I couldn't leave mine. Our marriage had been a farse, our growing feelings cursed from the start. And yet…Elhani had left his mark of approval on our union. The proof was on my own skin.

It was madness. Was it all because he knew what Caesiem and I could accomplish together to unite the Forwyn and Teramese? Maybe we weren't meant to survive the war, and the future was inconsequential.

All these thoughts wound through my mind on an endless cycle, vicious and confusing. I grasped the pendant around my neck.

I wanted to tell Caesiem a thousand things, ask him countless questions. But it all seemed hopeless, pointless, and his departure to meet with Revaed loomed over us. Along with all that would come after.

At the least, I could ask him to help me prepare.

"Teach me how to use water magic," I said. It was useful, but it was also a distraction, and he probably knew it. But he didn't protest.

Instead, with a nod, he took my hand and guided me down the path that led past our cabin and to the shore. The tension in his shoulders was evident as he scanned the waves, but there was no sign of anything amiss. His voice was low and musical when he leaned in close to me. "Close your eyes."

I did, sensing him take my other hand, until he was clasping both in his. A breeze stirred the loose curls framing my face, tickling my cheeks, but it was difficult to concentrate on anything but the feel of his thumbs brushing over mine.

"Focus on the sea."

I listened to the rush of the waves, their steady rhythm as they tumbled over the sand. I breathed in deeply, inhaling the salty scent of the water.

"You have to feel it here." Caesiem released one of my hands and placed his palm over my heart, right where my mark traced its pattern over my skin. My pulse skipped a beat, but I tried to shove the sensations away and ignore the heat flowing through my body. "You can call to it," Caesiem went on, "but the sea has to answer back."

I swallowed and turned my thoughts toward the water again, imagining it glistening in the sunlight, gulls soaring over its surface. My mind went deeper, picturing and feeling what it was like to be submerged in its depths, cradled in a chilly, dim embrace with fish darting around me. With the light fading…

I shivered involuntarily. Caesiem pressed his forehead to mine. "The water protects its own," he whispered, his breath warm. "You're safe." His proximity grounded me, tugging my old fears of water creatures away as he reminded me that I no longer had any reason to worry.

In my thoughts, I called to the water, picturing an invisible tether binding it to me. It twisted like a silver ribbon through the air and coursed toward Caesiem and me, rippling about us in a twisting circle. And then the sound went from imagined to real. I opened my eyes and saw the sea wrapping around us, misting against my cheeks.

A smile twitched Caesiem's lips as he pulled back just enough for his gaze to meet mine.

"Try again. Send it back."

I did, marveling at the way the water obeyed me, swirling over the beach and then cascading back into the sea. I laughed outright, thrilled by the rush of power running through me, the tingling feeling along my skin. Suddenly, I knew what Caesiem meant about the sea being home.

"You helped me, didn't you?" I asked.

"You did most of it on your own," he admitted with a grin, stepping back and releasing my hands. "But now try it completely on your own."

I averted my eyes before I found myself staring at the dimples I loved so much, or the playful glint in his eyes that warmed my chest.

Drawing a deep breath, I closed my eyes to shut out the rest of the world, turning all my thoughts toward the sea. It took several tries, my mind losing its grip and sending the water tumbling back into the waves each time I opened my eyes and lost my focus in my excitement. But at last, I pulled, and the sea came, twisting around me in a gentle whirlpool on land, sending another thrill of joy through my entire being. The sea filled me with energy, with life.

Over and over, I sent the water rippling through the air, twirling and dancing. My concentration wrapped up wholly in the effort it took to wield the water, to keep my hold on it from slipping away.

I'd lost all track of time when I noticed Caesiem step near again. My thoughts were hazy and sluggish, and I realized it was taking all of my mental energy to continue working with the water. I lifted my hand toward the liquid coursing overhead, imagining it pouring back into the sea. But my grasp on it snapped, and instead, the water dropped, splashing over us both.

Gasping and spluttering, I choked on my laughter as I shoved my drenched curls from my eyes and took in my soaked clothes. When I glanced up, Caesiem was equally wet, locks of dark hair plastered to his forehead, but he was laughing too. And then our eyes met, lingering on one another, and our grins melted away.

The words tumbled from my lips before I could consider the consequences. "I don't want you to leave."

Caesiem froze. "Tomorrow?"

"Later. To Teramyl." I pressed my lips into a firm line. "I know you can't abandon your people but…I don't want you to abandon *me*."

The confession left me feeling utterly vulnerable, and for an awful moment, it hung in the air between us as we stared at one another.

Caesiem reached for me. The emotion in his eyes was overwhelming—full of openness and longing. "Whatever happens with Teramyl—it doesn't have to be forever. If you want me, I will always come back to you."

I shook my head in disbelief, holding back my tears. "How could you think I don't want you?"

His brow pinched, regret knotting his features. "Because…I know you didn't ask for any of this, Lo. Not long ago, you were a nun, not planning to ever be trapped in some political marriage, and…"

"Stop," I whispered. "That life I had before? It was as much of a lie as your old life was. I was running from my past and my true calling. I was never meant to be a nun, and though I don't regret that time because of the sisters and the training it gave me, that wasn't *me*. Elhani spoke to me and told me my purpose has always been to fight for my people, and I'm not afraid of that anymore." I sucked in a shaky breath. "And I think we were always meant to meet, always meant to—to fall in love. To be the ones to show the Teramese and Forwyn that there can be peace between our peoples. I didn't want that marriage ceremony, not like that, but I don't regret that it bound me to *you*."

Caesiem blinked, looking a little dazed. "You…love me?"

I couldn't help laughing. "Yes, you fool! I love you."

And then he was kissing me. His hands cradled my hips as he pulled me closer, his lips painting a trail from my mouth down my neck. He paused, his whole body trembling as he whispered in my ear, his breath sending a jolt of pleasure down my back. "I don't deserve your forgiveness. I don't deserve *you*. But I love you. You are the best part of my life, and I will do anything to be worthy of you."

He pulled back, tears shining in his eyes as he caressed my cheek, gently pushing away a dripping curl. I caught my breath, torn between the desire to laugh, the urge to cry, and the need to throw myself into his arms and kiss him again.

"You're the only future I want," he declared.

My mind reeled. I reached up, tracing his jaw with a finger. He leaned into my touch, his eyes searching mine as if I carried the answer to every question he'd ever asked. Before I could begin to respond, he dropped to his knees in the sand, clasping both my hands in his.

"When a mage is brought to the Teramese palace to serve the Xalenos family," he murmured, "we are forced to take a vow binding our magic and our lives to the empire. To tether ourselves to Teramyl and the Xalenoses' wills until the day we die. But now, those vows are my promises to you." His eyes met mine, his gaze burning into me as he recited the words. "I offer you everything that I am. Each day of my life I pledge to be faithful to you alone, to defend you with my strength, my magic, and my life. I am bound to you, under penalty of death, until my end. May the go—" he paused and, with a smile, corrected himself. "May *Elhani* bear witness to this sacred oath and hold me to it all the days of my life."

I stared at him, my breath caught in my chest, too overcome to speak.

Caesiem stood, clasping my face in his hands. "They no longer have my loyalty. It is yours, and yours alone."

This time, our kiss was a vow, a promise of a shared future no matter what obstacles we faced along the way. We took our time, clinging to one another as if we feared this moment would be stolen from us too soon. And when I shivered in his arms, the chill of my wet skin contrasting to the heat in my blood, Caesiem laughed against my lips and lifted me, wrapping my legs around his waist, carrying and kissing me the whole way back to our cabin. He reached around me to tug open the door, and kicked it closed behind him so he could kiss my jaw, my neck.

I swallowed my laughter when he set me down and I realized, pulse pounding, that this was it. I'd made my choice. *We'd* made our choice.

He loved me.

My clothes dripped until a puddle formed around my feet, but I couldn't tear my gaze from Caesiem as he pulled off his soaked shirt, mussing his hair as he went, squeezing out the excess water.

"Here," I murmured, stepping forward and pressing my palm against the mark over Caesiem's heart, feeling his pulse thrumming beneath my hand. "This is Elhani's mark. I've heard stories. Supposedly it is his way of revealing his will and approval when…" I swallowed. "When two people are married. I thought it was a legend, but I found the same mark on me. It's meant to be…a reminder."

Caesiem lifted a brow, studying me silently. There was an intensity to his gaze that both unnerved and emboldened me in a contradictory whirlwind of emotions. I was hot and cold, terrified and confident, sure and doubtful. "A reminder of what?" he asked at last.

"That they are bound together forever."

He grinned. "I like that," he whispered, pulling me against him. I basked in his warmth as he kissed me, but just as suddenly, he drew away. "I'm sorry. You're shivering. I should let you change."

Caesiem backed toward the door.

I frowned. "We're *married*. We just promised—"

"That…doesn't mean…" He shrugged. "I didn't want to assume…"

But I shook my head, once again swallowing the distance between us. "Stay."

Caesiem's eyes were bright in the dim room, reflecting traces of the golden sunlight. He inhaled sharply.

"And before you ask, I'm sure," I cut in when he opened his mouth again. "Your vows are my vows. You are my future, too, Caesiem Xalenos."

Caesiem's mouth twitched, revealing his dimple. "Adriatus. Call me Caesiem Adriatus now." He cupped my face in his hands as he kissed me again, long and slow, stroking the ever-growing number of curls that had escaped my braid away from my face. When he deepened our kiss, he filled me with a fire that made every ounce of the cold I'd felt a thing of the past. He trailed kisses along my jaw as he helped me out of my dripping clothes, as he took me in his arms and carried me toward the bed.

"You are more than I ever dreamed or hoped for, Lo'laeni Nolanhou," he murmured against my lips.

CHAPTER THIRTY-THREE

Caesiem

I WOKE WITH THE WOMAN I loved in my arms, but dread chiseling at my heart. The sun streaming through our window painted Lo in golden light as she slept, her braid draped across one shoulder while loose, frizzy curls framed her face. With her head tucked under mine, her cheek pressed against my chest right where Elhani's mark traced my skin, I couldn't see her expression. But the steady rhythm of her breathing told me she was still asleep, dreaming peacefully.

Brushing a kiss to her forehead, I gave myself a few seconds to soak in the scene, to memorize her warmth and the way my heart swelled in this moment. *Home.* I wanted to spend forever in this cabin, stealing thousands of moments just like this one. Committing everything about Lo to memory. The exact notes of her laughter when she was truly, completely happy, her burdens of grief and fear forgotten. The taste of her mouth on mine, the softness of her skin. Every shade of green and brown in the depths of her eyes, and the way they brightened each time I told her I loved her. The music of her voice when she whispered my name as she gave herself wholly to me. When she told me she loved me.

She *loved* me.

Being with Lo wasn't like being with other women, back when it had only been about escaping. Forgetting. With her, every moment was about building our future together. It was finding home and refuge in one another's arms; it was embracing life rather than fleeing it.

But staying here would be selfish. We'd spent most of yesterday training with her water magic and then lost in one another. We'd made dinner here, avoiding the rest of the island entirely, refusing to contemplate what tomorrow would bring. We'd slept as if the war wasn't on our doorstep, as if we were just any other married couple celebrating our new union.

In the morning light, I couldn't pretend any longer. When I closed my eyes, I saw the hybrid nymphs attacking, felt them draining me of my magic.

Slowly, carefully, I slipped Lo from my arms and reluctantly left our bed. It felt all wrong, dressing as if for war when I went only to face my guardian. But after seeing the truth of my past, after witnessing the bodies lined up in the marketplace on Revaed's orders, after fighting nymph crossbreeds that had hunted us down on Nesrelle's and his command...I didn't know what to expect anymore. I wanted to trust that Revaed would never hurt me, but if he knew I'd chosen Lo's side, that I would fight against my own army for her and her people—what would he do then? Would he choose Teramyl and his people over me?

Sometimes a few have to die to save many. Choose survival above all else. Leaders must make the difficult decisions, Caes. Everything he'd ever taught me to believe in warned me that my betrayal might go unforgiven. That maybe the love of the only father I'd ever known was lost forever, and I was walking into danger.

That this war wouldn't end without one of us dead.

The Elha'tonu Forwyn had generously offered us extra leathers, like the ones their warriors dressed in to defend their island. Mine formed a neutral outfit—all black like I was used to, but not bearing the sigil or colors of any kingdom or empire. The pants and jacket were surprisingly comfortable and light, even in the island's humidity, and the boots were supple and worn, a little large but not so much that I wouldn't be able to make do. Leaving Lo with a final kiss on her cheek, I slipped out into the morning, only to find myself face to face with Nesrelle.

"No weapons, I see. Planning to just drown him?"

I lifted a hand to block the sharp angle of the sun and glared at her. "Don't you have souls to lead into the afterlife, Queen of Death?"

Her smile was smug. "I have my followers call me the Empress of Death for now. Considering the Alrenian throne was vacant, I thought someone might as well warm the seat."

"In Teramyl, we're taught the gods are uninterested in mortal kingdoms and thrones. Claiming one of our thrones doesn't seem like it would grant you any more power."

"It doesn't. I just take pleasure in how my new title troubles you mortals." Nesrelle flicked her gaze over my shoulder, toward the cabin in which Lo slept. "Don't you want to give your new wife a proper goodbye?" Her grin was sharp. "What if you don't come back? Oh, or is that the point?"

"Shut up," I growled. "Did you honestly come here only to taunt me?"

"Wait." Nesrelle's eyes widened in mock surprise. "Are you playing the deceiver again? You finally took what you wanted from her, didn't you? So now you're going to sneak away like the thief you are, and…"

I slammed my fist into her face.

Nesrelle stepped back, laughing and licking the blood off her lips, before it vanished, leaving her face as perfect as before, without a trace of scarlet on her mouth or bruising on her creamy complexion. "You do realize you cannot injure an immortal, don't you, boy?"

Shaking out my hand, I shrugged. "It felt good."

"Caesiem?"

The sound of my name on Lo's lips still stole my breath, even now, distracted and upset as I was. I turned in time to see the door creak open to reveal my wife, clothed in a loose red and gold tunic and a pair of leggings. Her hair was freshly braided, but loose curls already framed her face like a halo. A question hung on her lips as she scanned me, brow scrunched in hurt while she took in my outfit, a clear sign I'd meant to leave without a goodbye. When her gaze snagged on Nesrelle, she froze, but only long enough for her surprise to melt into anger.

She was out of the cabin and at my side in moments. "What do you want?" she snapped, meeting the Empress of Death's stare without an ounce of fear.

"I go where despair and loss are greatest," Nesrelle murmured, her voice eerily musical, raising the hairs on the back of my neck. Extending her arms, she clapped a hand on each of us, digging her nails into our skin.

Confusion and hurt flashed across Lo's face, making my heart feel like it was shattering. Her eyes darted to me before turning back toward Nesrelle, but it was enough for me to know. Her confidence was shaken, making her doubt everything I'd said and done last night. My love, my vows, every kiss and tender moment we'd shared. All of it. "There isn't despair here," Lo protested.

My fingers curled into a fist as I met Nesrelle's piercing gaze. "She can't stand our joy and wants to rip it away."

With a nasty smirk, the immortal leaned forward to whisper in our ears, her breath icy against my skin. "Your joy means you have more to lose. And the more you have to lose, the more you will suffer."

The golden light, the birdsong, the distant crashing sea—all of it vanished into blackness as Nesrelle's nails dug deeper, deeper, until I was sure she was drawing blood. Before my mind could fully grasp what was happening, before I could even open my eyes again, I smelled the ocean, heard the thunder of its waves. And then the sounds and scents of the Terebrys were swallowed up in chaos.

We were in Vicidor, and it was burning. My people were screaming, weeping. Just ahead, a woman cradled a child's body as she rocked back and forth, her voice wild and hoarse as she shouted for him to wake up. Licking her lips, Nesrelle slithered forward to brush a falsely gentle hand over the limp boy's brow—and then I saw the final breath heave from his body.

My mouth went dry. At my side, Lo seized my hand, her eyes wet with tears.

The earth shuddered, and a familiar roar tore apart the sky as a massive shadow enveloped the street.

I shoved Lo to the road, covering her with my body when a crack erupted, the one warning that the dragon had struck a nearby house before it collapsed, crumbling forward. Dust and debris spilled onto the street and mingled in the air with clouds of smoke and ash.

As I helped her up, coughing and wiping at the ash dusting her skin, Lo met my gaze with a look of understanding—and fierce determination. Before she even spoke the words, I knew what she was thinking, and it filled me with icy dread. "We can stop the dragon," she declared.

But Nesrelle interrupted us. "The dragon is already gone, its damage done." She gestured to the smoky sky, where the beast's silhouette was vanishing on the distant horizon. "See, Caesiem?" Nesrelle crooned, stalking toward us, leaving the bereaved mother sobbing on the ground, cradling her lifeless son. The sight made my insides clench. "This is what you leave your people to. Endless suffering. All your failures in Alrenor have led to this. More dragon attacks. More deaths. More destruction." She smirked. "And if you stay with your lovely new wife? You abandon them to this. And soon…Alrenor will be the same." She gestured to the emptying streets as citizens fled to the jungle on the edge of the capital. As more homes crumbled or burst into flames. As the city I'd once called home burned, lost in a ruin of ash and flame and smoke, just like Inalgoth.

Lo squeezed my hand, and I couldn't tell if it was out of fear or in an attempt to comfort me.

"I'm not abandoning them," I said. "And it's not my fault—it's never been my fault." My voice pitched low with anger, full of threatening promise. "Take me to the High Imperator. Let me see what *he* is doing."

Nesrelle rolled her eyes and seized Lo and me once more in her grasp. The street vanished; the chaos quieted. When I opened my eyes, I was surprised to find that we weren't in the capital any longer. I blinked at a pale, cloudless sky, before lowering my gaze to find a vast, ancient forest towering ahead. A cool breeze raked through my hair, smelling like earth, and rustled through the leaves, all painted in shades of gold and crimson. Further in the distance, I could make out purple and grey smudges on the horizon. The Silondrian Mountains, marking the northern border of Teramyl. We were at a high enough altitude to have left the heat and humidity behind, and we were standing at the foot of a woods I knew only from myths and fireside stories.

I repressed a shiver when I heard the voices wafting toward us from amongst the trees. With a backward glance at Nesrelle, who lingered behind, picking casually at her nails, I took Lo's hand in mine and pressed into the cool shade of the trees. The Nameless Forest, the Forgotten Forest, the Forbidden Forest. Each tale gave it a foreboding name, depending on the tone of the story. Some were meant to instill fear of the dangerous forest nymphs said to reside within, sleeping until unsuspecting travelers stumbled toward their trees and became their next victim. Others focused on the ways in which nymphs loved to strike tricky bargains, some ending in disaster and others in great fortune.

Until I'd discovered my magic and found that water nymphs were real, I had believed the stories of wood nymphs existed to keep the Teramese from crossing the border and trying to make a new life for themselves in the wilderness.

Now I knew better.

The trees creaked and groaned as we followed the words echoing off the trunks, coming from a group just ahead. Lo's fingers tightened around mine. Our breaths seemed unnaturally loud here, and the air was cold enough to make her shiver.

"Listen to me." The High Imperator's voice was unmistakable. "You will take this offering, and then you will travel to Alrenor. Leave the Teramese alone, but the Alrenians and Forwyn—they're all yours. Drain their magic. You can have your fill, so long as the Teramese remain unharmed."

A laugh rang out, as high and light as birdsong. "Your offering is a fine gesture, but not enough to gain our loyalty."

"The fool," I muttered, pausing in the shadow of a tree and ducking low, pulling Lo close to my side. Peering around the trunk, I found myself studying a clearing. On one side, Teramese guards clustered around the High Imperator, their blades raised high and their faces stern—though I could see the fear in their eyes. The imperator himself looked older than I remembered, slouched and weary, but his eyes were as pitiless as ever, even if they were lined with far more wrinkles than he'd borne even a year ago. Before him and his posse, a group of men, women, and children knelt on the ground, some shaking, some weeping, and others glaring in defiance. Their arms were bound behind them.

I scanned their faces, recognizing some from my years in the palace. Mages.

On the opposite side stood a row of nymphs. One had white hair like Sephrode's, but the others had locks in shades of vivid blue and green, colors of earth and water. Some had leaves and twigs tangled in their hair or springing up from their skin, alongside scales and webbed fingers that marked them as tied to the water.

Not far away, I could hear the bubbling of a stream carving a path through the forest, likely fed by the Xelrios River itself. It was both a reassuring and chilling sound, reminding me that there was water nearby for both myself and the nymphs to use.

Lo's fingers tightened in mine. Her whispered words were frantic. "We have to help those people."

I hadn't believed it was possible to love her more until that moment, looking at the compassion and concern in her eyes, the firm set of her jaw. She had every reason to hate my people and our cruel ways, a people who had gladly invaded her land, shedding innocent blood and stealing freedom. But she loved as fiercely as she despised seeing others suffer. When I met her gaze, I knew she wouldn't hesitate to throw herself headlong into danger to protect these strangers.

"Wait," I murmured, scanning the crowd. My heart pulsed dully in my ears, but the ever-present call of the water was stronger. Once the hybrid nymphs noticed Lo and me, they would be able to drain our magic without a single touch, in the eerily powerful way their sisters had on Elha'tonu Island. And without a weapon or magic, we would be attacked alongside those mages.

As if reading my thoughts, one of the nymphs stood taller, sniffing the air and tossing her turquoise hair over one shoulder. Her giggle was musical and uncanny. "We have more visitors."

When she narrowed her bright green eyes at the High Imperator himself, he stepped back. For half a moment, I relished the look of naked fear that darted across his face. Then it was gone, lost in that chiseled mask of stone he wore so well.

"They're not mine."

The nymph breathed deeply. "I smell water, sisters. Salt and sea and something else…something bright and burning." Her nose wrinkled in distaste.

My body tensed as I reached for the water on instinct, desperate for its protection, but it was too late. A tree root twisted from the ground, scattering dirt and pebbles as it writhed, snake-like, through the air. It moved with lightning-quick speed, lashing around Lo and me in a tight embrace and tugging us forward, into the clearing. At my side, Lo thrashed against the root binding her in place, swinging her legs and beating her fists against the wood. But I kept my body still, my breaths thundering in my ears.

The High Imperator's eyes flashed as his gaze seared into mine. I glared right back at him.

"Caesiem Xalenos," he snarled, stepping forward. "You little rat. Revaed requested assistance in securing the Alrenian Empire and feared for your safety. And here I see you've fled and are cowering back in Teramyl?" His eyes flicked between Lo and me, confusion crinkling his brow.

"No," I said smoothly, feeling strangely calm despite the root coiled around my midsection. "I'm here to see what new evils you're committing against our own people." I glanced toward the mages. "You sent Revaed and me to Alrenor to rescue Teramyl. And now you're going to sacrifice Teramese mages for the Alrenian war? Are you mad?"

The imperator's eyes narrowed. "Sometimes a few must be sacrificed for the good of the many. You, little orphan and thief, should know that all too well. You survived off others for half your life."

Before I could protest, Nesrelle materialized as if from the shadows themselves, slipping out from beneath the forest shade and stepping within the clearing. An unnatural stillness fell. The root loosened and dropped Lo and me to the ground, spilling us in a crumpled heap.

"I brought the visitors," Nesrelle announced smoothly, her eyes cutting toward the row of nymphs. "They don't pose any threat to you—you could drain their magic easily enough." She winked, her expression wicked. "I wanted them to see that soon, the same destruction and misery overtaking Teramyl would overcome Alrenor too. It's inevitable."

"Liar!" Lo screamed, launching to her feet and lunging for the Immortal with reckless ferocity.

I inhaled sharply, taking advantage of the nymphs' distraction to call upon the water. A wave answered, plunging nymph, mage, and guard alike in a rush of water. It shoved the High Imperator off his feet, putting that arrogant, cruel man on the ground.

But Nesrelle laughed lightly, lifting an arm to brush the oncoming water aside gently, like it was a bothersome insect. I'd known I couldn't hurt her, but the sight was still discouraging. Her eyes darted to the nearest nymph, and the lovely blue shade that had filled her irises only moments ago was gone. In their place were dark pupils, empty pits into death, into nothing.

"Feed," she commanded.

The nymphs leapt forward, snarling like feral animals, all traces of their humanoid features gone in an instant. Hunger gave their faces a sharp look, and their luminous eyes—yellow and green and silver— glowed with greed. Webbed fingers combed over their victims' skin, tugging on their magic, but even without a single touch, they were able to lay the mages low. To use their awful power and drain their magic.

I collapsed along with them, grimacing in pain as I felt the nymphs' influence tap into me. It was pure agony, like losing a dear friend. Like watching a part of my soul be rent from me. Like feeling every ounce of strength, of comfort, of peace, pulled away ruthlessly.

When I tried, instinctively, to call to the water, there was nothing.

Silence.

Emptiness.

Even knowing the sensation was temporary, that a nymph wasn't close enough to steal my magic permanently, couldn't eliminate my misery.

After all, my magic was in my blood, a part of me. I wondered dully if tearing it from within would spell my own ending. Could mages survive having their power ripped away completely?

"Caesiem," Lo called out, rushing to me. Did her magic work like mine? If the nymphs drained her of Elhani's power, or if, as connected as she was to her magic—magic that swirled around her, a part of the very earth and air, she couldn't lose it. Maybe it was an unbreakable bind. I envied her.

A boy mage—so young he couldn't be more than twelve—shrieked and clutched at his head, weeping. The sound drew my gaze, just in time to see one of the nymphs fall upon him, cradling his head almost gently. But as soon as she touched him, her power increased, and so did his pain. Blood leaked from his nose, his ears, his eyes. His whole body spasmed and dropped to the earth. Stomach churning, I wrenched my eyes away.

"We have to save them," I choked out, meeting Lo's concerned expression. She set her warm hand in mine, lending me strength when mine had vanished. I leaned on her heavily as she helped me to my feet. "We have to…"

My voice trailed off as I took in the chaos before us. Tree limbs trapped or skewered the Teramese without discriminating between mage or guard. I couldn't find the High Imperator, but I didn't dare hope that he'd been killed. Most likely, he'd managed to flee with some of his guards. Or maybe Nesrelle and the nymphs had let him escape.

But the mages…

The nymphs had left no one alive. Only Lo and me and Nesrelle, who studied the feeding nymphs with an expression that reminded me of a proud mother. I resisted a shudder.

My only relief was the pulsing warmth of my magic, no longer being siphoned away. I could sense the nearby stream like it was part of my own body; I could hear its comforting, familiar call. My pain vanished.

One of the nymphs blinked at the body lying at her feet, her eyes dulling, her greed melting away. Her blue hair clung damply to her scaled face, as if she had exerted herself to the point of sweating. "The magic is gone," she muttered dully. She stared at the mage. "Dead."

The white-haired nymph beside her sighed. "Why do they always die? I would have loved to have this handsome one to play with." She clutched her own corpse like a lover.

I averted my eyes from the disgusting sight.

Nesrelle crept forward, taking Lo and me both by our hands. Her skin was ice-cold and made my own crawl with revulsion, but her grasp was too firm to pull away. "They're coming for Alrenor next." She licked her lips. "It's wonderful to know, dear prince, that your story has always been destined to end in tragedy." She glanced toward Lo. "And don't you feel awful for choosing *her* instead of your people?"

I gritted my teeth. "I can help my people too. This isn't the end."

Nesrelle shrugged. "Don't be greedy, my beautiful, sad thief. You can't have everything."

With an almost tender smile, she pulled us forward, into darkness.

CHAPTER THIRTY-FOUR

Revaed

MY STOMACH TWISTED INTO A knot as I watched the hawk swoop low over Hemlaen. I already knew the sort of message it would bear on its leg, already dreaded tearing it open and imagining the imperator's searing voice. His venomous disapproval would only add insult to the blood-curdling failure of losing Inalgoth and then being forced to ally with the cunning immortal who had ripped it from my hands.

I wasn't shocked that my father had already discovered these new developments. He didn't have any water mages as powerful as Caesiem in Vicidor, but he had air mages he used to direct hawks like this one and send messages. I wouldn't even have been surprised if he had a wind mage hidden in plain sight among my ranks, a spy reporting on my every movement, my every failure.

Or maybe Nesrelle herself had told him. With her love of meddling in human affairs and stirring up misery, that wouldn't shock me either.

Squinting against the bright morning light, Zalec held up a hand to block it as he watched the hawk descend into the street we were in. We'd been walking back from my daily visit to the infirmary, where countless wounded soldiers welcomed the encouragement of their own emperor reminding them that there was hope for our war. With our new alliance, we would stamp out the Forwyn and Alrenian rebels, and know peace at last.

Even if my officers were rightfully skeptical and terrified about the prospect of trusting Nesrelle and her army, they understood our predicament and the value of having such powerful warriors—and nymphs—on our side.

The hawk landed on the cobblestones before us, holding out one leg for me to untie its message. Sighing, I tugged it off the bird and watched as the animal cocked its head to study me with one beady eye and then soared off, back to Teramyl. Father must not have wanted a response, then. Unrolling the paper, I scowled at its contents.

Reclaim the empire, or there will be consequences.

It was insulting, like I was a spoiled child acting out. There was no concern expressed for our losses, no questions about the casualties we'd sustained, no condolences or reassurances that he'd provide for the bereaved families back in Teramyl. Nothing but a heartless threat.

"Your Majesty?" Zalec asked, brow scrunched as he doubtless worried I'd received bad news.

Crumpling the message in my fist, I shoved it into my pocket. "Summon the officers for another meeting," I ordered.

The imperator's message was just another reminder of what I'd already known: failure was not an option. I already had enough of my people's blood on my hands. I wouldn't lose more.

CHAPTER THIRTY-FIVE

Kovi

THE ELHA'TONU ELDERS WERE DISCUSSING the value of Jalie's life as callously as if they were debating the cost of livestock.

"If her choice to spare Kovi's life means she'll be open to an alliance, imagine the Alrenians she could persuade to join our cause," Elder Yelaia spoke up. She was the only one who seemed to care, who spoke about Jalie as if she were human and not a deadly curse.

Elder Olahni tugged on a braid and studied Yelaia carefully. "What has your Sight shown you about her? *Is* she on our side? Can she be trusted?"

"The dangerous powers she carried from the Dark Immortal are gone," Elder Yelaia explained, lifting her chin confidently. "But for the rest...I cannot say for sure. There are too many paths, too many variables. Nothing is clear."

Elder No'haleo growled, shuffling restlessly on his feet. He'd refused to sit in a chair for the entire meeting and was the only other person aside from me who remained standing. But, while I stood with arms crossed, leaning against one of the wood beams and keeping myself still and unnoticed, Elder No'haleo paced and moved constantly. His agitation was clear.

Yesterday's attack had frazzled him—had shaken all of them. Their peaceful life was under a greater threat than they'd ever known.

They didn't realize their guests had never known such privilege, had never had peace to lose.

"Perhaps," Elder No'haleo muttered, "if you think she's so *valuable*, enough to risk innocent lives by sparing her, then we should find a way to ensure she'll be…obedient."

This time, I couldn't remain silent. His words reminded me too much of something my father would have said. *Control her.* I stepped forward, barely suppressing the fury lacing my voice. Barely concealing my climbing anger. "Did you not just hear Elder Yelaia? She's powerless. You're talking about controlling a young woman who has been fighting for her life, not a soulless snake. Are you a coward, that you would fear her when you wield magic? Or do you find some twisted sense of enjoyment in lording power over others?"

The Elder scowled.

"Are we absolutely certain she's powerless?" a quiet voice asked. A small elderly woman lifted her chin from her chest. Earlier, I'd thought she'd fallen asleep, but she must have been listening the entire time. Now, her soft tone sliced through the tension emanating between Elder No'haleo and me. "Is her connection with the Dark Immortal completely severed?"

Elder Yelaia dipped her head in confirmation.

"Then, if she's willing to work with us, we can come to a compromise," the woman went on. "As your allies, I think it's important we make it clear that we won't tolerate Empress Jaliana reclaiming her throne if our fight against the Teramese ends successfully." She settled her hands into her lap. "However, she *could* retain her title if she agreed to a marriage alliance with a Forwyn, one who would be the *true* ruler of Alrenor."

My body stilled, along with my mind. My churning emotions and thoughts quieted, and a chill settled in my bones. It all became horribly, overwhelmingly clear to me.

They were willing to let Jalie live, because, like others before them, they wanted to use and control her. They wanted to return her to a cage, to a life where all her decisions were stripped from her. Where her freedom was nothing but an illusion.

My eyes latched onto Elder Yelaia's, and I had a strong suspicion she knew, or at least guessed, what I was thinking. Jalie would rather die than become a pawn or a prisoner again.

And I couldn't—I *wouldn't*—let that happen to her.

I refused to choose my people over her ever again. If I couldn't choose and protect her above strangers, then I was worthless.

A soldier is only as strong as the ones he fights for, General Ilowhe had once told me. And though I knew the greater good of our people needed to be calculated in decisions; other times, the best way to become what our people needed was to put our own loved ones first. Above all else.

Before another Elder could say a word, I cut in. "That's not going to happen."

"Excuse me?" Elder No'haleo demanded.

I raised my voice, but I kept my tone level. "I think I was already clear. You are *not* using her. You are *not* dictating her life."

Without another word, I swept past them, deeper into the temple, toward the room where Jalie was recovering. If I had to carry her out of here to my own rooms and tend to her myself until she was well enough to leave this Elhani-forsaken island, I would. I wasn't going to watch a repeat of what our own Elders had done to Jalie.

I refused to see the light die in her eyes again, refused to watch her fear as another disgusting man terrorized her.

She was strong enough to face anything, even without the abilities or the curse Nesrelle had given her. She'd always been strong. But that knowledge didn't change my need to protect her.

I loathed the fact that I hadn't been there for her sooner, not when my father was leaving hidden bruises on her skin, and not when Daedra had betrayed and nearly murdered her.

You won't face your demons alone, I thought. *Not ever again.*

But when I paused in the doorway, the room was empty. Jalie was gone.

CHAPTER THIRTY-SIX

Jalie

PAIN LINGERED IN MY SIDE, but it was greatly diminished, and my strength had returned. With the island Elder's words echoing in my ears—*we should find a way to ensure that she'll be…obedient*—I slipped out the back door of the temple. Fresh air kissed my face, full of the scents of the sea and the tropical flowers that overhung the path. The rush of a nearby waterfall was a steady rhythm in my ears.

I didn't know where they were keeping Ryke, but the island wasn't that large, and I knew it wouldn't be hard to find him. If I could reach him before the Forwyn noticed I was missing, I would be safe. Free.

As I walked, I combed my fingers through my hair, wishing I had a leather cord to tie it back. Thankfully, Lo had replaced my dragon scale armor after she had healed me, so I'd already been dressed, ready for a swift escape. It had taken mere moments to find and slip into the boots beside my bed.

The only problem was that my sword was nowhere to be found, likely hidden by the Elha'tonu residents. Without any sort of gift or magic, without a single weapon, I felt more vulnerable than I had in weeks. And yet, I also felt more like myself. Nesrelle wasn't influencing my actions or thoughts anymore. My mind was clear.

After years of training, I knew how to defend myself, how to fight with my own body. I'd been trained to be a weapon all my life, no matter what circumstances I found myself in.

I was not weak, and I was not defenseless.

My blood thrummed in my ears as I turned a bend in the path, finding that it opened onto a waterfall plunging and misting into a large pool, larger than the one Kovi and I had fought beside.

The memory made my insides ache.

I had to find Ryke and get out of here, before the Forwyn decided to finish their failed execution—or worse, decided to force me into an alliance where I was powerless. My hands shook as I considered my options. Did I try to return to Alrenor, to see what burnt husk Nesrelle had made of my beautiful land? Should I search for allies who would fight with me to expel the Teramese?

Or did I accept that my cause was hopeless? I didn't want to assemble an Alrenian army that would slaughter the Forwyn. There was no place for me in this new world. The Forwyn distrusted me— rightfully so—and the Teramese longed to kill me. Any Alrenians who still wanted me as a leader hoped for an empress as cold and vicious as Mother had been.

A tear slipped down my cheek before I could dash it away.

I didn't need to belong anywhere, I reminded myself—not if I had Ryke. Stepping off the path, I scanned the open grass surrounding the pool and my heart leapt. There wasn't another person in sight, but there were dragons. Three hatchlings tumbled playfully together, fluttering their wings and snarling in a mock battle. Karos was nearby, half-heartedly batting at them when they rolled too close, though I could tell he was more interested in the prospect of a nap than entertaining the young ones. My heart swelled at the sight of the hatchlings. I'd heard passing comments from Forwyn outside my brig while aboard the ship, but the talk of young dragons had sounded too good to be true. I'd been afraid to believe it until now, when the glorious sight gave me hope.

As for the Misrothians' dragons I'd seen a few times from a distance, they were nowhere in sight, perhaps out hunting.

But curled up peacefully on the pool's bank, enjoying the cool mist swirling in the air and flicking his tail like a lazy, contented cat, was Ryke. He studied the hatchlings with half-lidded eyes.

"Ryke," I breathed, overcome with joy. An ache that had been building within me ever since I'd been thrown into the ship's brig and separated from my dragon eased, and I laughed with abandon. A stab of pain lanced my side, reminding me of the wound I'd borne, but it wasn't enough to stop me, wasn't enough to slow my pace as I jogged forward.

My dragon lifted his head at the motion, cocking it to focus one silver eye on me. With a snort that sent a plume of smoke into the air, mingling with the mist, Ryke leapt onto all fours and charged, swishing his tail and smashing grass as he came. He slowed only to give Karos and the hatchlings a wide berth. The young dragons stopped their play to watch us both with bright-eyed curiosity, but Karos chuffed, smoke twisting around his nostrils, before closing his eyes and curling his tail over his body, tucking himself in for sleep.

As soon as I was within range, I threw my arms around Ryke, this time crying in earnest. I ran my palm over the smooth scales of his snout while he snorted again and then emitted a sound of pure joy—a low rumbling that, as a child, I'd called a dragon's purr.

"I've missed you," I said, and as he nuzzled my shoulder, I was sure he was telling me the same, in the best way he knew how.

He stepped back and fluttered his wings, making the grass ripple around him and lashing strands of hair into my face. In the sunlight, each movement caused his emerald scales to flash painfully bright.

With a grin, I settled a hand on my hip. "I'm glad you're as ready to go as I am." I hesitated, my gaze drifting toward the hatchlings. A new ache formed, creating a lump in my throat. Where would I go? If I ran, I would never see the golden sands of Alrenor again, never walk the halls of my palace. I'd be bidding these young dragons—the hope of Alrenor's future—goodbye forever.

I would never see Kovi again.

You almost killed him, I told myself. *He risked his life in that duel—he trusted you to spare him, the way he spared you. And you raised your blade against him. Does it matter that you turned it away at the last moment? It was still too close. You were too far gone. You've done unspeakable things. Why would he ever want to see you again? He has every reason to hate you. It's better to leave now than face him, to have to see the betrayal and disgust in his eyes.*

My heart was shattered into pieces, but it would crumble into dust if I lingered. And if I let the Elha'tonu and Alrenian Forwyn have their way? They would surely break me.

"We will fly through the open sky," I murmured to Ryke, stroking his snout, "and we'll keep flying until we find somewhere so distant, they don't even know who *Amara* Jaliana is. Or somewhere so far away, there are no people at all. Just you and me."

Soft footsteps made me still. The pattern of his gait gave him away, sending a chill down my spine as I squeezed my eyes shut, refusing to turn from Ryke. I had a sudden sense that no time had passed at all since those first days of being trapped in the palace with him, when any time I strayed from sight, he was not far behind. Protecting his people from me.

I couldn't turn and look at him now. Instead, I gritted my teeth and waited for him to come to a stop behind me. Beneath my hand, Ryke's muscles went taut. *It's all right,* I thought, willing him to understand, to be at peace.

"Are you here to take me back to the temple?" I asked. My voice rang out strong and clear, without wavering. Without betraying my pain.

Kovi stepped closer. "I didn't think you'd be well enough to walk this soon."

I tensed. "I'm well enough to walk, to run, to fight, or to fly a dragon," I insisted.

"You heard the Elders talking." It wasn't a question.

In response, I finally dared to turn, lifting my chin defiantly when I met his gaze. "You'd have to command me with your magic to force me back there, and even that wouldn't work. Ryke would stop you first."

Kovi's mask dropped, the calm expression on his face giving way to…something soft. His eyes were molten again, studying me the way he had the night of the Autumn Ball. *Fierce and clever and stunning.* That's what he'd called me then.

Now, I bore an ugly rune marring my cheek, jagged and rough from nestred claws. I had a new scar on my side, the skin no longer smooth and perfect like it had been when Nesrelle had healed me. And my scars within—they were countless. I'd caused so much chaos and pain. I'd endangered and killed my own people in my quest for my throne and my revenge. I'd betrayed Kovi in the deepest of ways.

I was monstrous and broken.

"I'm not taking you back there." Kovi's eyes flicked over my shoulder to Ryke, before fastening once more on my face. "They're not going to control you. No one will. Not ever again."

I frowned skeptically. "I can't very well take my throne. If I go back to Alrenor—if I'm not killed by the Forwyn or Teramese or my own people first—there are so many people against my rule. Even Alrenians. I've failed them." My voice broke. "My city burned and my dragons died, and I didn't stop it. I couldn't save them. And…I'm not Chosen. I never was. The Life-Giver, or Elhani—our two gods seem to have been the same all along—made that clear. Maybe it's better this way."

Kovi framed my face with his hands, and I was too startled to step back. To even breathe. I froze. His touch was gentle, and his eyes were soft. He should have hated me, but he looked at me like…

Like I was an empress.

"Maybe you weren't Chosen, not then. But you're different now. You've learned and grown. You've withstood indescribable pain and loss, and you've come out stronger. I don't know another person more passionate or courageous than you," he murmured.

"The Forwyn will never trust me," I protested, but my voice sounded weak. It was difficult to focus on anything but the warmth of his touch, the look in his eyes.

"You'll earn their trust." The confidence in his words made tears prick my eyes. For the longest time, after Mother, I'd thought the only person who believed in me was Nesrelle. And of course, I'd only been her pawn. When following her, I'd thought I'd escaped a prison, only to enter a worse one, half of my own making.

"How will the Forwyn—here on the island and in Alrenor—accept an alliance with me, without some way to control me? They'll want leverage. Everyone always does. It's the way of the world." My lips twitched, fighting a bitter smile. In order to gain my throne, in order to ensure peace in my empire, I'd have to lose something. Politics were never easy.

Kovi grinned outright. "I know someone who can remind them to stay in line, under threat of being controlled by magic."

I bit my lip to hold back my smile.

"Anyone who threatens to take your freedom will lose theirs." His face turned serious. "That is, if you'll let me serve you. As your bodyguard—your true bodyguard now. I'll help you take back your throne, Jalie. I vow it. I know you'll fight for my people as well as yours."

I arched an eyebrow. "You're not afraid of how I almost killed you? Or what Nesrelle helped me do?"

Kovi pulled back and shrugged. "You didn't kill me." His smile was crooked. "I always knew you wouldn't hurt me. You couldn't live with yourself if you did."

I smirked. "That sounds awfully arrogant for a righteous Forwyn." But then my face crumpled. "I'm so sorry, Kovi," I said. "I'm sorry that—that I…"

He interrupted me by looping his arms around my waist and tugging me to him. I relaxed into his embrace, settling my head on his chest. Under my ear, his heartbeat was steady and reassuring. His stable breaths grounded and settled me. He pressed a kiss to my forehead, and

I inhaled deeply, closing my eyes.

"I love you, Jalie," he whispered, and I wanted to live in this moment forever, to listen to his words on an endless loop. His love wasn't a cruel trick to rip away my choices, like Nesrelle's supposed affection had been. It wasn't borne of forced devotion and respect for my heritage, as my people's was. And it wasn't coddling and restrictive, training me up with expectations that I couldn't stray from, filling my head with poisonous hatred, as my mother's had been.

His love was pure and unconditional and freeing.

In my mind's eye, I saw him throw down his sword and kneel before me, prepared to die rather than be forced to take my life, to be my enemy. Even when Kovi was supposed to hate me, he'd always been defending and comforting me.

"You love me," I repeated dazedly. It was almost more than I could comprehend, when everyone else had always loved me with the anticipation of getting something in return. But Kovi had always given freely, without expecting anything. I pulled back, not far enough to step out of his embrace, but enough that I could see his face. "You love me, even after—"

He didn't wait for me to finish my question, didn't need to. "Yes." There was no doubt, no trace of hesitation in those gold-flecked eyes.

I threw myself at him, and he caught me, lifting me into the air as I wrapped my arms around his neck. His mouth met mine, and this wasn't like any other kiss we'd shared. There wasn't fear or doubt in this one, no pain of an impending goodbye or impossible choice. It wasn't part of a game of manipulation, and it wasn't a futile way to resist our feelings.

This kiss—each brush of our lips, each caress of his fingers down my back while he held me—was a new promise, a new dream. And this time, they were vows we could keep, and dreams we could dare to trust in. *I love you. I'll fight for you. I choose you.*

At last, Kovi set me down, laughing breathlessly. "I'm glad to know you feel the same."

Despite my threatening tears, I laughed along with him. I didn't want him to see the liquid brimming in my eyes, even if they were from joy. But when I lifted a hand to brush an errant tear away, he clasped my hand gently. With his free one, he wiped the tear away himself, his calloused fingers whisper-soft against my scarred cheek. It was his silent reminder that he saw the strength inside me, the very best of me, even when I felt like I was at my worst.

Behind us, Ryke snorted and flicked his tail, as if alerting us to his presence. I bit back a laugh and tossed him a mock frown of annoyance. "Well, you don't have to stand there and watch, if you're sick of us," I scolded.

Ryke huffed.

"No flight just yet, I'm afraid," I added, more gently. "I won't run," I told Kovi. "You can tell the Forwyn that I'll fight alongside them, but that I'm also fighting for my throne. They can join us and help usher in true peace and unity, or they can oppose us and fail. But something tells me they won't refuse you…magic or not." An unfamiliar jolt of shyness filled me when I reached out, running my fingers along his cheek and tracing his jaw. "You're a good man, Kovi. I would be honored to have you at my side. But not just as my bodyguard. I think…I want you to consider helping me rule, someday." I swallowed thickly. "It doesn't have to be right away. We can wait until there's peace. Until we're ready. But if we win this war, I want your advice and wisdom. And I want your people to see a true joint leadership, of Forwyn and Alrenians."

Stepping back abruptly, I let the rest of my words tumble out before he could say anything, before I could lose my nerve. "I want an equal," I explained. "I know you were willing to die for me, but could you consider…living for me? As a partner? You would still defend and lead your people—*our* people—just as you always have." I paused, suddenly out of words. Suddenly feeling ridiculous. This wasn't how an empress was supposed to feel. I was giddy and nervous and unsure.

Slowly, Kovi smiled, his expression playful. "Are you…proposing to me?"

I blushed. "Well, I don't want to be forced into some marriage those Forwyn pick for me. You seemed like a better option. And I'm not saying it's something that would happen too soon—I just want you to consider it. If we win this war, and we can spend more time together, getting to know one another when we aren't fighting for our lives or being enemies…then maybe, someday, when we're ready…we could make that choice and rule together."

Kovi crossed his arms as his grin broadened. "Oh, so you're using me to get out of an arranged marriage."

I rolled my eyes. "You're making this difficult."

He laughed, tugging me back toward him and kissing my cheek. "So someday, if you don't tire of me, I could become emperor? Are you sure?"

I shrugged. "Well, if it's going to go to your head, I change my mind."

He laughed again. "I accept your proposal. Or non-proposal," he teased. But then his expression turned solemn, his eyes becoming distant, and I understood his wash of concern and sadness.

"I just hope, when all this is over, there's still an empire to lead," I whispered.

CHAPTER THIRTY-SEVEN

Lo

THE INSTANT NESRELLE RELEASED US, she vanished. I blinked dazedly, scanning the swaying palms and colorful birds flitting from branch to branch. For a moment, I was too dizzy and disoriented to register that we were back on Elha'tonu, outside of our cabin.

I turned to Caesiem, noting the hard set of his jaw and the distant, haunted look in his eyes.

"I'm so sorry," I murmured, reaching for him. His body was rigid, but when I pulled him into an embrace, I felt his muscles relax ever so slightly, his arms wrapping around me.

"I have to go," he said firmly. "I have to speak with Revaed. Maybe if I tell him what his father is doing, how he's causing even more suffering in Teramyl for this war, he'll listen to reason. We can stop this before Alrenor looks like Vicidor."

But even as he said it, even as he stepped back and I examined his expression, sorrow flitted across his face. His eyes turned regretful. I knew he was seeing the ashy ruins of Inalgoth again, just as I was. "Before it gets worse," he amended. "Can you take me to Karos? Ensure he will let me ride?"

"Yes, but I don't know why you didn't just wake me up before," I said reproachfully, slipping my hand into his. I led him away from our cabin and toward the open grasslands where I knew, at this time of day, Karos would be resting. After his morning hunt, he liked to enjoy his food and then curl up for a nap.

But as we rounded a bend curving toward one of the island's waterfalls, mist wafting on the breeze, gooseflesh rose along my skin. Something felt *wrong*. I blinked, taking in the sight of the dragons near the pool. Ryke and Karos stood side-by-side, tense and alert, while the three hatchlings hid behind their bulky forms. Nearby, Kovi brandished a sword. Jalie was beside him, weaponless and still wearing her dirt-smeared dragon scale armor.

"What—" Caesiem started, but a spray of arrows screaming from a cluster of trees to the west cut him short. We slammed to the earth together, the projectiles whistling overhead.

It already felt instinctive to call out to the water, with my hand pressed to the cold pendant at my collarbone. But I couldn't summon as impressive of a wave as Caesiem could, and as soon as the water churned forward, rushing through the trees, it slammed into a huge burst of flame, one that seared at the tree trunks and turned my trickle of water into steam.

Even though I couldn't see our attackers, that's when I knew. The sense of foreboding, the control of the flames—they were the citizens of Wenu, invading the lush land they envied so much. Somehow, they'd broken past the warriors guarding the coast.

Caesiem tensed, and I knew he was calling on the water himself. But before the sea could answer, another flurry of arrows soared from the forest, these ones tipped in flame.

"We have to move!" I shouted. Nudging Caesiem so he'd follow me, I crawled through the grass, keeping my body low as more arrows zipped toward us. Just ahead, Kovi knocked one from the air when it strayed too close. It dropped to the grass, sparking, and he stomped out the fire with his boot. His hand clasped Jalie's arm, holding her behind him, though from the look on her face, I could tell she didn't want to be protected—she wanted to fight.

But, despite her fierce expression, she didn't push forward. She had no weapons, no way to block the incoming arrows, and though she looked healthy and strong, I knew she wasn't fully healed. Not yet. Elhani's power had been easy to tap into here on the island, and I'd learned much about listening to his voice, but I wasn't as adept as Naina had been.

Ryke and Karos snarled, leaping forward to snap at the arrows and swish their tails in front of us, using their scaled bodies to protect their humans. They leapt at the fires sprouting throughout the grass, trampling each one before it could grow into a larger threat. Smoke swirled, and they snorted indignantly, as if furious that our enemies were using *their* element against us. Or perhaps angry that their fire would be useless against this threat.

In moments, Caesiem and I reached Karos's shadow, ducking low beside Kovi and Jalie. Behind us, the hatchlings shivered, cuddled together so closely that they appeared like one lump rather than three separate dragons.

I extended an arm until my fingers brushed a smooth snout. "It's all right," I murmured, trying to soothe their fear. The creatures quivered beneath my touch.

Caesiem launched more water at our attackers with a vengeance, pulling from the waterfall, sending the element swirling and cascading with a roar that rivaled the crackling flames eating at the forest. Exhilarated, I grasped Caesiem's hand and joined him. I felt the pulsing of the water's power course through my veins and rush through my chest. An entire wall of it immersed the trees, the flames, and the figures at the wood's edge. Cries of shock and rage drowned in the fury of the water. Mist and steam and smoke swirled in a strange, acrid mixture that dampened my skin.

At my side, where he knelt in the grass with his sword at the ready, Kovi tensed. "You encountered warriors like these before, on Wenu?"

he asked, his eyes scanning the area. The flames were extinguished, and the forest had gone eerily quiet.

But I knew our enemy wouldn't be defeated so easily.

"Yes," I said, grimacing at the memory. "And with their magic, they're like Nesrelle's army. If they get too close, they can incapacitate us with a single touch."

Jalie arched an eyebrow. "With pain?" There was a knowing look in her eyes, something haunted that made me suspect she'd experienced such a touch before.

I nodded.

Before we could say another word, countless warriors sprang from the trees, spears poised. Karos snarled and charged, seizing a warrior in a single bite. Blood flowed down his snout and stained the grass as the man's companions continued without pause, without fear. One woman slammed her hand against Karos's side.

Instantly, the dragon shuddered, a groan emanating from deep in his throat. He writhed, suffering from the same bone-deep agony these people had inflicted upon Caesiem and me. He cried out in a hair-raising wail, shoulders stooping, great black wings unfurling and spilling limply at his sides. His head dipped low, and he shook it side to side, as if he could dismiss the pain racking his body.

My stomach churned at the sight of his suffering. Before I could think it through, I was pushing toward our attackers.

"Lo!" Caesiem's voice was ragged. His hand slipped on my arm, failing to grab me. Failing to stop me.

Wait, I reminded myself, letting my anger clear my head, like it always had. *Think.* Enraged, I forced myself to pause and lean into Elhani's magic. Warmth seeped into my veins. His song was on the breeze, fluttering past my ear.

Elhani's magic was in the very earth of this island, thriving. Protecting.

I latched onto the sensation, concentrating with all my will on his song. Drawing a deep breath, I injected as much strength as I could into my word. "Stop!" I screamed.

The warriors stumbled, visibly shaken.

But my influence didn't affect more than the first row of warriors. At least two dozen had rushed us, and more were coming from the trees at our backs, trying to surround us. Ryke snarled, creating a living barrier between these new enemies and us, but I knew it was only a matter of time before a warrior incapacitated him with a touch.

The hatchlings huddled so low in the grass they were nearly invisible. A fiery need to protect them from this violence filled me. They were young and timid, still far from the majestic, muscled creatures Ryke and Karos were.

While Caesiem and I spun toward Karos to fend off our attackers on one side, Kovi and Jalie turned to Ryke to face our other enemies.

Caesiem and I launched another wave of water toward the warriors, knocking some off balance, holding them down in a brutal whirlpool. Bubbles danced and limbs thrashed. It was equal parts entrancing and horrifying, but Caesiem didn't relent, so neither did I. These people had dedicated themselves to Nesrelle and destroying the people of Elha'tonu, and if we didn't stop them, they'd kill everyone on this island.

Heart throbbing in my throat, I glanced to Caesiem. My focus on my water magic threatened to crumble, the effort it took to hold the liquid in the air for this long causing sweat to bead along my forehead. But Caesiem didn't seem exhausted, only invigorated…and angry. His fists shook at his sides and locks of his dark waves were plastered to his brow from the mist eddying through the air.

The wall of water trapped other fighters behind the struggling warriors, fending them off until the drowned ones crashed to the earth, and Caesiem finally let the water plunge back toward the pool. It splashed through the air, soaking us all, keeping our enemies from calling upon more fire.

But even the corpses of our enemies' fellow warriors didn't make them pause. A frenetic look in their dark eyes, they charged again. Caesiem rushed to meet them, seizing a spear from one of the bodies. It was a bit unwieldy in his hands, clearly a weapon he was unused to, yet he brandished it with confidence all the same, holding back the onslaught.

With a fierce cry, I raced to Caesiem's side and forced more enemies back with another terror-inducing command. A woman stumbled, eyes wide behind the white markings painted across her face. They were symbols of fire and bones and others with meanings I was sure would make guidespirits quake with rage and disgust at their blasphemy. They felt like the antithesis to my ribbons, and the very sight of them made me nauseous.

"This is Elhani's island, and you are not welcome here, follower of death," I snapped.

She dropped her twin daggers and ran as if her life depended on it.

I took up her blades and joined the battle.

Jalie

Kovi swept forward, the picture of a disciplined yet fearless soldier as he strode past Ryke. Smoke from the creature's failed attempts at drawing on his fire coiled about him. Ryke tipped his head as Kovi passed, his silver eye scanning the soldier uncertainly, before he seemed to recognize his scent and remember he was on our side now. As if to urge him back, my dragon nudged Kovi's shoulder, but Kovi settled a hand on the beast's snout. Ryke seemed to understand, and he shuffled back.

"You will stop, and you will not harm any of us," Kovi called to our opponents, his voice a low rumble. It would have been almost soothing, but for the clear threat emanating from it. The powerful, knee-weakening command.

The warriors took a couple cautious steps forward, rigidly lowering their spears, bows, and blades. But Kovi couldn't control them all. There were easily two dozen, with more at our backs where Caesiem and Lo fought, and Kovi could only force six at a time to bend to his will.

I joined him, blonde strands of hair flying about my face. Caesiem's water magic roared and crashed behind us, coating us in mist, soaking us both. It made Kovi's uniform cling to his body, but that only served to make him more intimidating, highlighting his every muscle and his confident, unyielding stance.

"Fight them." Kovi said simply, nodding to the approaching warriors behind the ones he'd gained control of.

Like puppets, the warriors he controlled turned as one, raising spears and blades and bows to attack their own allies.

Then I blinked, and Daedra was among the approaching warriors, her hair whipping about a face that was almost entirely covered in dark scales, and her eyes fully black, nothing but emotionless voids. I scanned the ground for a weapon—any weapon. A discarded blade, a rock, a stick. Anything at all.

Daedra sauntered forward, her lithe body unnaturally fast. Her leathers dripped with blood. In one hand, she wielded a sword, finely gilt with the old Alrenian Keepers' motto wrought on its blade: *O j'eh y'vonu.* It was an insult, a crime, one that made my blood boil. She was a traitor to the crown, and yet she bore a beautiful weapon worthy only of those who served it faithfully.

In her other hand, she clutched a dragon claw. The claw Ryke had shed, the one she had stolen from me on the Aramith battlefield. The weapon she'd used to try to murder me.

She laughed. "How does it feel, knowing you are weak? That you are *nothing* now?" As if to prove her point, she flicked her wrist, conjuring fire from thin air. The flames licked around her hand in a mesmerizing dance, tinting the dragon claw an ominous shade of orange.

Before I could retort, she twisted behind Kovi, who couldn't move swiftly enough. She plunged the dragon claw straight through his chest, blood bursting from the wound and drenching his pristine uniform. His eyes widened as his grip on his sword weakened, dropping harmlessly to the grass.

My screams were incoherent nonsense, my mind too blank to make sense of what was happening. I charged, not caring that Daedra towered over Kovi while he collapsed to his knees, not caring that I was unarmed, helpless against her. Tears streamed down my cheeks as I caught Kovi in my shaking arms. His blood made my hands slick when I tried in vain to staunch the wound, to do something, anything, to make it stop.

Daedra's laughter was unending in my ears, the only sound I could hear beyond the roaring of my own blood. Wind and mist bit at my face, suddenly chilly despite the humid air, and the sky darkened. I tried to cradle Kovi's body against me, tried to protect him from the inevitable, but as he coughed up blood, struggling and failing to speak to me, his eyes glazed over. His body stilled. When I splayed my hand over his ruined chest, there was no pulse beneath my fingers. No hint of breath or movement.

"Kovi." My voice was weak, a mere whimper. My hands were sticky with his blood. His body had already cooled against mine.

Gone.

I blinked at burning tears, glancing up when movement caught my eye. Mother stood over me, her wounded neck too close when she leaned in to whisper. Her breath stank with the tang of blood. "You shame your ancestors, Jalie. You aren't fit to rule." She raised a bloody dagger toward my throat.

This isn't real. I tried to scream the words into my mind, to fend off the awful visions. *This is the warriors' power, showing you your worst fears to incapacitate you. You can fight it.*

But the vision was chillingly convincing. I could smell Mother's dead flesh. I could feel Kovi's blood. My body shook as I squeezed my eyes shut. *Not real. Life-Giver…Elhani. You're both, aren't you? Will you listen to me now that I'm not following Nesrelle?*

At first, I thought I might have been imagining it: the faintest vibration through the earth where I knelt in the grass. When I strained my ears, I was sure I heard something, like distant notes of a sweet song, full of countless souls raising their voices, sharing lyrics in some nameless language. I didn't know the meaning of the words, didn't understand the song or the way it wrapped me in an embrace, filling me with warmth and power and courage, reminiscent of the security I experienced with Ryke curled protectively about me, or the comforting sense of home I knew in Kovi's arms.

I licked my lips, tasting it. Power. Strength. My words from what now felt like ages ago rang through my mind: *I'll never be weak again.*

As I concentrated, the song thrummed through me. *Magic,* I thought, and my body seemed electric, goosebumps rising along my skin and a rush of breathlessness and anticipation filling me in the same way an approaching storm did. I thought the magic tied to this island was meant only for the Forwyn, for those who followed Elhani and claimed they were his first, his Chosen. But now I knew that Elhani and the Life-Giver were one and the same. Maybe that meant he was my god, too…that this magic also belonged to me.

A shiver coursed through me, but not one of dread.

I opened my eyes, and the man I'd once met in the Alrenian temple was standing at my side, his sword drawn. He was clothed in a simple tunic and pants. Even his blade wasn't of remarkable quality. There was nothing that would have set him apart from any other mortal on this earth, but for the sense of power that radiated from his presence.

I gaped at him as he scanned the warriors ahead. And Kovi, who was *alive.* The visions had lied to me.

Some of our enemies were still fighting each other, caught in Kovi's persistent grip, though I knew he must have been tiring, must have been struggling to concentrate on his connection with them each time he experienced their emotions when one was slain. Others were facing off against Ryke and Kovi. My dragon was vicious, snapping men and women in two with a single bite, until most of the warriors gave him a wide berth and focused their efforts on surrounding Kovi.

One warrior managed to slip past Kovi and Ryke's wall of defense, spear pointed at me. Her eyes didn't stray toward the Life-Giver, making me wonder if she could see him at all. Not until the Life-Giver's blade slammed upward, blocking the fatal strike meant for me. As soon as the woman's weapon struck his steel, she met his gaze, and her eyes widened in terror. Trembling, she shrieked and stumbled back, muttering incoherently in the Forwyn language. She dropped to her knees, writhing in agony.

"Stand," the Life-Giver commanded me, his tone gentle yet firm. So different from the angry voice I remembered from our first encounter. "Fight." His voice echoed with the strength of his magic.

I stood on shaking feet. "What is this?" I asked, bewildered, tapping my chest. I didn't understand the feeling overtaking me.

It was a vague question, but the man smiled in comprehension, his dark eyes twinkling. "The gift you were meant to wield all along, magnified by your connection to the magic of this island. Because of your openness to listen to my song."

My heart thrummed with an overwhelming emotion. One I'd thought should have come naturally to me all along, merely because of the blood in my veins. Courage.

"The courage gift—the one that had disappeared, but has started to return," I murmured in awe.

The man dipped his head, as if in goodbye. "It's returning as more of your people remember me. Use it well."

And then he was gone.

Courage. The word coursed through me, bright and beautiful, filling me with comfort and bravery like I hadn't felt since I was a child, thinking I was untouchable as long as I was in my mother's arms. And with this bravery, every nightmarish vision the warriors tried to confuse me with melted away. Kovi was alive and fighting alongside Ryke, despite multiple attacks from warriors pressing pain into them with a single touch, or the fear that clearly oppressed them both, doubtless from other visions only they could see.

But with courage…with the Life-Giver's power…I truly was untouchable. I threw myself forward, claiming a sword from a fallen warrior and racing to enter the fray.

Caesiem

The nightmarish visions wouldn't stop coming. Revaed, storming toward me with a troop of Teramese soldiers, his blade already bloodied and his violet eyes a whirlwind of pain and fury, betrayal and hatred. Lo, collapsing in a pool of her own blood, dying before I could reach her.

I tried to blink the sights away, tried to tell my mind all this wasn't real. Just a part of the warriors' dark magic. But I could smell the blood, could hear Revaed's voice.

I couldn't focus on my magic, couldn't hear the water's call, even when the pool was mere feet from me.

Fight it, I thought.

Then I blinked and Lo was alive and at my side, wielding two daggers to parry a strike from an enemy blade. She ducked and plunged one of her weapons into his thigh, eliciting a scream of agony and rage. Loose curls clung to her sweaty face as she turned her gaze on me, the green flecks in her eyes full of a determined fire. "It's not real, Caesiem!"

she panted, leaping between a warrior and me, saving me from being speared in the chest.

I wondered if her connection to Elhani's magic, so powerful here on the island, helped her dispel the visions, or if she was simply better at ignoring them.

Hands shaking with effort, I summoned another wave of water, forcing it toward the warriors that encircled Karos. If we could prevent them from incapacitating both dragons, our enemies wouldn't stand a chance.

"This is for the greater good," Revaed's voice snarled, low in my ear. He was so close I could feel his breath on my neck, and I shivered, trying to spin around and save myself. Too late. His blade plunged into my back, piercing organs. Blood and bile filled my mouth, and searing pain ripped through my body.

Not. Real, I thought, but the betrayal slammed into me anyway. I turned in time to see Revaed's violet eyes blinking at me, eerily emotionless. My blood dripped from his knife.

Not. Real.

And yet…it was so close to the future I feared. According to Revaed, I'd chosen our enemies over our people. I'd abandoned him. I wasn't sure he would ever forgive me.

He loved our people fiercely, had killed and fought ruthlessly to protect them and ensure they could have a better life. I wasn't sure he'd understand or see my side.

My mind whirled. *Focus,* I thought. Lo wouldn't be able to protect me forever, and if I continued to allow these visions to take hold, I'd be killed without even having a chance to defend myself.

Staggering to my feet, I blinked, until the pain in my body dulled and the bloody taste in my mouth vanished. It had been a convincing vision, nothing more.

I parried a swing from a woman, who snarled in frustration as I deflected blow after blow. Nearby, Lo fended off another warrior. More were coming, having abandoned the arrows that Karos was blocking to move in for the kill.

But that meant they'd left Karos alone, and he was fighting furiously. A single swing from his tail knocked two warriors off their feet. He slammed his forepaw into another man's chest, piercing it with sharp claws and shoving him to the earth, crushing him beneath his weight. A fourth leapt forward with a spear, driving it toward Karos's soft underbelly, but Karos was faster, swinging around and seizing the man in his jaw.

Warmth flooded me, chased quickly by an overwhelming sense of courage like I'd never felt before. It coursed through me with the same giddy rush as magic, powerful and clarifying. Reaching for the water became effortless. The notes to a foreign song drifted faintly on the breeze, and though I didn't know the words, somehow I was comforted and strengthened by them.

Lo seemed to feel it too, and even Karos.

When I defeated the woman and tossed a glance over my shoulder, I found Kovi, Jalie, and Ryke fighting with the same ferocity and freedom, as if they too sensed that song. No visions could stop us, not anymore.

With our magic unrestrained and the dragons at our sides, the fight ended in mere minutes. When I glanced up from my final kill, I found nothing but bodies—at least four dozen. Dozens of warriors who had made it past the guards on Elha'tonu's coast to invade the island.

And the four of us and our dragons had stopped them all.

Karos snorted and ran to Lo, nuzzling her body as if to check that she was all right. She wrapped her arms around his neck. "Thank you," she breathed. With a flick of his tail, the dragon left Lo to inspect the three hatchlings. Ryke joined him, his emerald scales flashing as he swept his tail around the young dragons. Flapping their wings and emitting high-pitched chirps, the hatchlings cuddled against Ryke and Karos, who, together, formed a protective barrier with their bodies.

"Are you all right?" I asked, striding to Lo's side and pulling her into my arms.

She leaned back just enough to look into my eyes, her smile grim and her eyes distant. "Yes, but…" She shook her head. "I think the Dark Immortal sent those warriors, just like she is helping the Teramese imperator gather those nymphs." She shivered. "We've endangered the people of Elha'tonu, just by being here."

I brushed a wet curl behind her ear. "And we also protected them. You were fierce," I said, unable to conceal a smile.

"Do you really think now is the time for this?" The empress's voice was sharp as she strode toward us, Kovi at her side.

I scoffed and pressed a quick kiss against Lo's mouth anyway, just to spite Jalie. Lo laughed, and Jalie scowled.

"Is everyone all right?" Lo asked as she stepped away from me. Her eyes lingered on Jalie. "You almost bled out a day ago," she added pointedly.

Jalie blinked, her gaze turning abruptly distant. "Yes, I'm…" She set a hand against her side. "There's no pain left at all," she finished, eyes widening in awe.

"Was that your magic?" Lo asked.

I glanced at Lo sharply. Alrenians didn't wield magic; they had gifts granted by their Life-Giver, or so they claimed.

Jalie lifted her chin, pride flashing in her blue and gold gaze. "Yes, you felt my courage gift, shared with all of you. The Life-Giver…your Elhani…he said my gift is courage."

Kovi laid a hand on Jalie's shoulder. His lips twisted in a half-smirk, which was more emotion than I'd ever seen from him before. "As much as any other invaders have to fear from us," he said, gesturing toward the scattered bodies, "it's not wise to linger here unprepared. We need to ensure there aren't others landing elsewhere on the island, and to warn the residents."

I glanced toward the tree line blocking our view of the city. Perhaps it was far enough away that the people hadn't heard our fight or had attributed the dragons' roars to a playful scuffle. Or maybe they were preoccupied with other attackers.

"Lead the way," I told him. Despite our tense beginning, I was growing to respect Kovi. He had a calm, reassuring presence, and he had a sharp mind in a fight. Most of all, I'd noticed the way he looked out for Lo. Any friend of hers was a friend of mine.

All of us but Kovi had stolen weapons, which we wiped off hurriedly in the grass and kept unsheathed on our walk back. Scanning the trees for danger, I strained my ears to catch any sounds over the churning of waterfalls and streams, over the steady pulse of the sea, but I heard nothing. I hoped that was a good omen.

And then the screams erupted.

Kovi

As soon as we rounded the final trees, we found nothing but chaos. Countless more warriors had infiltrated the island, wreaking havoc upon homes as citizens struggled to defend themselves against the surprise attack. Flames licked at buildings lining the streets, sending families running for cover, desperately trying to flee the chanting warriors. Mothers held their shrieking babies closely while other children scurried in their wakes, but there was nowhere to run. The warriors were coming from every direction, emerging from the trees and spilling over the lip of the valley, setting fire to fields and farms and homes as they converged on the city proper.

Everywhere, Forwyn collapsed, clapping their hands over their ears and eyes, shouting and crying out in raw terror. They were trapped in whatever awful visions the invaders were inflicting, unable to fight back when they couldn't even see the real threats approaching them.

Jalie tensed, and I could practically feel the rage slamming into her. When she screamed, her voice was full of commanding power. "Ryke!"

The dragon was soaring overhead in an instant, Karos directly behind him. Even Kova and Jozek, returning from their hunts and drawn by the noise, followed. Kova's green and black form reminded me of a wraith behind the blindingly bright ivory and sapphire scales Jozek possessed. Four huge dragon shadows darkened the city, and for an instant, even the hellish fighters froze. Fear rippled through them.

I scanned the battle for General Ilowhe and our soldiers, picking them out easily in the crowd. Meli was there too with her rebels. All rushing to defend, to save a peaceful city already aflame, to stop the slaughter even as corpses piled up in the streets. I glanced over my shoulder, noting the fire in Jalie's eyes, the pain in Lo's, and the dark fury in Caesiem's.

"Follow me," I ordered, and they obeyed without question, flanking me to run straight into the heart of the fighting.

Jalie remained on my right, her shorter legs somehow keeping stride with me, propelled onward by the magic flowing through her veins. I could feel its power swelling in the air I breathed, bursting in my chest with strength and warmth. Her courage filled me just as it had in our earlier battle, clearing my mind and helping me focus on Elhani's song.

As we slammed into the first row of warriors, I sensed the way their eyes widened, the way their chanting words faltered at our approach. They'd realized their attempts to trap us in visions weren't working. Jalie's courage gift shielded us all.

One man snarled, baring his teeth and spinning his daggers as if hoping the display would intimidate us. I didn't falter in my stride, charging straight for him, slicing my sword low. My strike was precise, cutting into his thigh.

A rushing sound swirled through the air as Caesiem and Lo called upon more water, and a huge wave flowed through the city, extinguishing flame and sending up clouds of mist. The dragons swirled and dove, crushing whole clusters of warriors under their feet while snapping others in their powerful jaws.

At my side, Jalie fought gracefully, dodging a spear-wielding woman effortlessly before felling two other attackers. The courage thrumming through her seemed to heighten her abilities.

It was the same for me. The dance of battle came naturally. Every step, every strike, every parry—they were fluid and strong and sure.

We fought our way into Corapaxu, stepping between enemies and fleeing citizens wherever we could. Somewhere along the way, I found Mhel at my side, and then General Ilowhe himself. A warrior charged us, war paint flashing as he narrowed his eyes and leapt forward agilely, wielding two wicked blades.

Jalie whirled in front of me, taking the first strike. She grunted from the effort as one blade and then another slammed into her sword, but she didn't back down. Instead, she twisted on her feet, pulling away unexpectedly and forcing the man to lose his balance. Her golden hair swirled around her as she moved, and when I met her eyes, I noticed she wasn't afraid or even angry anymore. She was *laughing*. Her courage swelled inside me, and I wondered if I only felt a portion of what she was experiencing.

These enemies posed no threat to us, not in the face of the magic coursing through the very land beneath our feet, the very air we breathed. I laughed along with her.

General Ilowhe's eyes cut to me. Without a single word, his expression demanded an answer. *Can we trust her?*

"She's on our side," I said firmly, ignoring Mhel's gaze when I felt it latch onto me as well.

But neither of them questioned me. General Ilowhe rushed forward to join Lo and Caesiem where they were directing another wave of water into a burning building. I stalked through the smoke and steam, weaving my way around bodies, joining Jalie as she ran deeper into the streets. The scents of blood and ash and smoke burned my nose, but the heat of fire was melting away, lost to Caesiem and Lo's magic. Even the screams and groans of the dying had diminished, though I couldn't tell if that was because the roaring of the water and our dragons was louder, or if the fighting was nearly over.

A quiet wail interrupted my thoughts, and I stiffened. Ahead, Jalie froze in her tracks, scanning the mist-enshrouded street. I could see nothing but bodies and empty homes.

Jalie turned to me. "In there," she said, nodding toward the home on our left. Its windows were shattered, and its front door hung crookedly on its hinges. As we approached and I discerned the wailing more clearly, my stomach twisted. It was a child.

Without hesitating, Jalie threw open the door and dashed inside, weaving her way around toppled furniture and past bodies lying in their own blood. Toward a table at the far end of the room, turned on its side. She knelt carefully, extending a hand and murmuring gently.

"You're safe," she said, though I suspected the Forwyn child didn't know the merchant language.

I hesitated a few feet away, glancing down at the blood darkening my blade, at the gore splattered on my uniform.

Elhani's song whispered through the air, as sweet and soothing as a lullaby, and then Jalie stood, holding a boy no more than two years old. His trembling arms threaded around her neck, and she carefully pressed his head into her shoulder to shield him from the sight of his dead parents.

For a moment, I was speechless, watching the woman who'd once declared so confidently that she hated all Forwyn now cradling a Forwyn boy. Ash and dirt and blood were splattered across her gold skin, and the white scar on her cheek—Nesrelle's own rune—stood out starkly. When she glanced at me, she quirked an eyebrow.

"What are you doing?"

Shaking my head, I followed her as she exited the house, emerging into the misty street.

The child emitted a pitiful whimper, stirring fitfully in Jalie's arms.

Distracted, neither Jalie nor I noticed the blades until they were inches from our faces, the Forwyn warriors of Elha'tonu glowering at us.

"Drop your weapon," one of the women said, her eyes flicking distastefully over me. Her own leathers were smeared with blood, and I couldn't tell if it was from others, or if she'd been wounded in battle.

I tightened my grasp on my sword, the temptation to use Elhani's magic and command these warriors to drop their own weapons dancing along my tongue.

"Give us the child," a man demanded, his voice raspy, either from inhaling smoke or shouting throughout the fighting.

Jalie was motionless at my side. The child started crying in earnest again, his small body clinging to her with all his might. I realized that in this moment, the boy only saw terrifying, weapon-wielding strangers, while Jalie could at least offer him the sensations of courage and comfort through her gift.

"We mean no harm," I bit out. "We heard him crying and went to find him. She won't—"

"Are you a traitor now? Did you pick her over us?" The man stepped closer, until the tip of his blade rested beneath my chin.

Scowling, I dropped my sword and lifted my arms. "I am no traitor, and she is on *our* side. She fought with us. She is soothing that boy with Elhani's magic."

"Blasphemy!"

Jalie interrupted the man before he could launch into another tirade. "If this is the sort of alliance you plan to form, we will never win the war against the Teramese or Nesrelle," she said. "And I know you can feel my gift. It's what's comforting this boy, after all he's lost." Her words trembled, only for a moment, and though I no longer felt her emotions as I once did, I imagined the grief from losing a parent was striking her fresh, all over again. She laid a hand on his head. "I'm not here to hurt him. I'm trying to help him. Of course you may take him from me. See if he's all right. See if he has any living family. But for the Life-Giver's sake, lay down your weapons and stop pointing them at a child." Those last words were given with all the command of an empress, her sapphire and gold eyes burning into the Forwyn with an intensity that clearly unnerved them.

Chastened, the warriors glanced at one another before drawing back and lowering their blades and spears. I swallowed my urge to grin as more soldiers flooded the area—from General Ilowhe and our Aerekni group, to Meli's men and women, to the Elha'tonu Elders themselves. All were weary, some sporting cuts and bruises or other minor injuries. At the general's side, Lo and Caesiem scanned the street as if searching for any last fire to put out.

But when Lo caught sight of us, she launched forward, pressing in between the warriors and Jalie. "What are you doing?" she snapped, hands on her hips. "I spent *hours* fighting to save her life, and you're trying to rip her open again?"

Jalie laughed aloud, studying Lo with newfound respect.

Overhead, the dragons circled, watching for any remaining enemies. Their wing beats were a reassuring rhythm, a reminder that they were on high alert to protect us.

"Can we trust her?" Elder Olahni demanded, nodding to Jalie while her brow bunched in suspicion. Even she, the most ancient of the Elders, was carrying a dagger. All had left the safety of their temple to defend their people. It warmed me, knowing they, unliked Elder Ettonou and those who'd served with him in Alrenor, were prepared to sacrifice and lead as true rulers should.

Before I could open my mouth, Lo spoke up. "You can trust her." She waved her arm toward the battle we'd come from. "She just fought alongside Caesiem and Kovi and me, killing another few dozen of these warriors. We don't have time for fighting against each other, as this attack has made clear. I don't know how these warriors broke through your defenses, but this is the second battle on Elha'tonu in as many days, and I can guarantee Nesrelle is to blame. The war you were so reluctant to join? It's already started, and it's here, on your own land. This was only the beginning. We have to make plans to strike back, and we can't delay another moment."

"She's right," General Ilowhe added, joining us to stand at his daughter's side. Lo glanced at him, visibly softening under his grin.

Elder Yelaia pushed through the other Elders, nodding. "I've seen it. If we don't act, they will." Her eyes scanned the crowd until they landed on Caesiem. "I know what you want to do, and unfortunately, I can't see clearly if you will succeed or not. But I do know it's time. If you're leaving, you must do so soon. And you shouldn't go alone."

CHAPTER THIRTY-EIGHT

Lo

"YOU REMIND ME SO MUCH of your mother," Father said as he sat in the grass beside me. His face was fatigued, lined with sorrow. Thankfully, we hadn't lost many in the fight, but seeing the destruction and terror wrought on this peaceful town, watching the bereaved bid their loved ones goodbye, had made today utterly exhausting.

I stared into the bonfire before us, its flames licking at the air and casting dancing light over the gathered people. Forwyn, Alrenian, Teramese. All united in tending to the wounded, comforting the grieving, and preparing for war.

I'd been surprised at how easily everyone, from the Elha'tonu Elders to my own father—had agreed when I'd proposed that Jalie, Kovi, and I all accompany Caesiem to Alrenor. Most likely Elder Yelaia's insistence that now was the time for us to gather forces back in Alrenor had helped. They'd agreed that we were the best representatives to try to convince a force of both Alrenians and Forwyn to fight together and take back the empire.

However, they'd also insisted on additional companions joining us, as we had Jozek and Kova as well as Karos and Ryke. After much debate, they'd selected Mio'e, for as a more recently freed slave, she was especially passionate for the cause; Pauni'a, probably because she refused to remain behind when I was going; Mhel, as another Aerekni soldier and friend of Kovi's; and Vander, since he bore his own powerful magic and could further represent the Teramese. Perhaps between him and Caesiem, if Revaed refused to pull his troops from the empire, we could at least amass more Teramese soldiers to our side.

Now, wrapping my arms around my legs and resting my head on my knees, I glanced toward Caesiem, standing outside the temple with his friends and speaking in hushed voices. I knew his friends were worried about him and how Revaed would respond when Caesiem confronted him. But Caesiem, despite his doubts and lingering sense of betrayal, had seemed optimistic. "He'll listen to me," he'd murmured earlier as we'd retreated to our cabin, only long enough to bathe and pack for the upcoming trip. The Elders, General Ilowhe, and Meli had agreed that we should leave first thing in the morning.

I could only pray Caesiem was right.

Sensing my eyes on him, Caesiem turned away from Vander, flashing me a quick smile. It was a little too easy, a little too assured. Just like that charming smile he'd given me at The Broken Crown, when he'd first tried to win my trust as a thief and vigilante. He might try to hide it, but I knew he was afraid.

I sighed, turning to my father. "How am I like Mother?" My memories of her were foggy, focused more on feelings or tiny moments than a solid idea of who she had been.

Father laughed softly, the sound wistful. His eyes turned distant as he studied the stars in the velvet sky, and when he spoke, he was caught up in his own memories, lost in the past. His words painted a vivid picture that I let myself fall into, trying to cling to this one chance I had to feel like Mother was here and alive again.

"She loved as fiercely as you do, and when she wanted to defend those she loved, nothing could stop her. She was fearless that way. In fact, that's how we met—how we fell in love. As palace slaves, neither of us wanted to grow close to anyone when we knew the risk of loss attachments would bring. Karye could notice and separate or kill one of us for it. Not that she didn't want her slaves to…well, create more slaves for her. But Karye always took advantage of actual love, always delighting in tearing families and loved ones apart."

I repressed a shudder, knowing all too well that this was true.

"I caught your mother stealing one day, taking supplies from the infirmary for some sick slaves. She was terrified—she didn't trust the other slaves, and she didn't know me, so she thought I might turn her in to gain favor with Karye." A smile tugged at Father's lips. "Instead, I helped her. I was impressed with her bravery, her determination to help others no matter the risk. It was impossible not to fall in love with that—a heart full of such goodness and courage and strength. You have that same fire inside you, Lo."

Tears burning my eyes, I rested my head on Father's shoulder. He wrapped his arm around me, pulling me closer, his own body trembling from grief. "Not a single day has passed without me thinking of her, missing her. And for so long…" He drew a deep, shuddering breath, and in response, one of my own tears slipped free. "For so long I grieved you and Edi too. From the beginning, we had to keep our relationship or the fact that I was your father as secretive as possible, so Karye wouldn't do her worst. We exchanged vows as best we knew how, committing our love to Elhani. It wasn't the official marriage we dreamed of, no grand celebration, no chance for a home of our own. We had nothing but stolen moments, yet Elhani blessed our union with his mark on our skin. When your mother found out she was pregnant with you, we were terrified. We could conceal the fact that I was the father, but Karye still enjoyed tormenting mothers and their children. It seemed like a miracle when she didn't send your mother or you away from the palace after you were old enough to walk, to serve as a slave yourself. And even more miraculous when Edi was born too, and we all remained together…or as together as we could be.

"Of course, she sent me away to a different family anyway, not long afterward. I only had a few months with your little brother." His voice broke, and his hand tightened on my shoulder. "And the fact that she killed him…it haunts me that I wasn't there to protect both of you. To stop her."

I blinked, more tears threatening. "I was there," I whispered, "and I didn't stop her." Slowly, haltingly, I explained what had happened. It was the first time I'd shared the story aloud, because it was the first time I felt strong enough to do so. The memory of Edi appearing to me alongside other guidespirits in the battle of Inalgoth was seared in my mind. He'd said he didn't blame me, and that he was always with me.

And so, I told Father about that moment as well, about Edi's message to us from the Golden After. While he listened, tears sparkled in Father's eyes, shimmering in the firelight. "He's right. It wasn't your fault, Lo." He pulled me to his chest, and we both cried together. Tears of grief for the family we'd lost and the years we'd been apart, thinking we were alone. And tears of joy for knowing our loved ones waited for us in the Golden After, that they watched over us even now, when Father and I were finally reunited.

At last, he pulled back. "I want you to know that I trust you and your strength. I know you can rally the Forwyn. You'll lead us to victory." He brushed one of my curls back, away from my tear-streaked face.

"I hope you're right," I murmured.

There was a beat of hesitation in which I mulled over Father's words, thinking about how he and Mother had found Elhani's mark after promising themselves to one another. I was about to explain that Caesiem and I had the same marks on our own skin, when Father broke our silence first. "You love him, don't you?" He nodded toward Caesiem, his voice low, but not upset.

"I do," I whispered.

"He seems…" Father shook his head, as if at a loss for words. "He's not what I expected. I saw the way he fought at your side today—

how protective he is of you. The way he looks at you. He really does seem to love you."

"He does," I said adamantly. "He…" I searched for the words. "Father, I found Elhani's mark after our wedding."

Reflexively, Father's fingers brushed his jacket, right over his heart.

"We made our own vows to each other," I went on. "I hope…I hope you can understand. I hope you'll even learn to like him."

Blinking back more tears, Father pulled me into another fierce embrace. "I understand. All I want is for you to be safe and happy. And if he brings you this much joy…then I do like him."

Warmth flooded me as I soaked in this moment. It seemed unbelievable that I finally had a family, that I was no longer alone.

Just then, Elder Yelaia stepped forward, Pauni'a at her side. "Lo?" she asked, a smile tugging at her lips. "I wanted to give you a proper sendoff, before you go." Her eyes flicked to my hair. "We might not have dragon scale armor, but we have those leathers we left for you in your cabin, and…your friend told me about how you discarded your ribbons. Don't you think you should return to Alrenor wearing some again?"

Flashing a grateful grin at Pauni'a, I met Elder Yelaia's steady gaze. My fingers strayed to my neck, to my braided ribbons. "There's only one color I need to wear into battle."

"One gold ribbon?" Caesiem's smile revealed his dimples as he slipped my single braid over my shoulder and brushed a lone curl behind my ear. Back in our cabin, with our packs and the leathers the Elha'tonu residents had gifted us laying out, ready for us to leave in the morning, it was difficult to dispel my jitters. I'd stood staring at my things, wondering if I needed anything else.

Now, Caesiem's gentle touch sent warmth and electricity through my body, a pleasant distraction.

"That's all I need right now," I murmured. "To remember Edi and Naina and everyone else lost to us. To remember I fight for them, and I fight to prevent more from joining them before their time."

Caesiem sighed, leaning forward until his forehead met mine and our breaths mingled. "If I fail…"

"Don't think about that right now," I interjected. "Revaed might listen to you."

"But if he doesn't," Caesiem went on, voice firm, "and we must fight him, I know you'll succeed in uniting the Alrenians and Forwyn. How could anyone see your heart and conviction and *not* be persuaded?" His smile turned crooked. "You persuaded me."

I laughed, wrapping my arms around him and laying my head against his chest, relishing the sound of his heartbeat. "I hope you're right."

He pressed a kiss to the top of my head. "And," he added, his arms tightening around me, "if something happens to me…"

Jerking my head up, I met his eyes, studying the darkness lurking in those blue irises. "It's entirely too soon to worry about that."

Caesiem's brow furrowed, but he didn't say another word, just drew me closer, kissing me slowly, fervently, as if memorizing this moment. I ran my fingers through his hair, deepening our kiss, concentrating only on the joy of having him here, now. Of knowing he loved me. Of trusting in our forever.

Jalie

One of the Elders delivered my breakfast to my room in the temple— which they'd insisted I stay in for one more night, likely so they could keep an eye on me—first thing that morning. Seeing the plate of fresh fruit, bread, and eggs, I relished how familiar it was after living off gamey meat while with my army and then jerky aboard the Forwyn ship.

Just as I'd finished the last of my food, Kovi appeared in my entryway.

"You look…different," he said, scanning me up and down, taking in the black leathers the Elha'tonu Elders had brought to my room last night. They were supple and surprisingly light—not as comfortable and cool as dragon scale armor, but not as heavy as I'd expected. The sleek black was accented with a hints of gold, reminding me of the gold scales the Dragon Keepers had loved to wear back home.

Standing, I crossed my arms. "What does that mean?" I asked coolly.

He laughed and stepped inside, taking my hands and pulling me closer. "It means," he murmured, his voice so soft as he leaned in that his words were a caress against my skin, "that you look happy, and your joy is breathtaking. And I wish we didn't have company right now."

I bit my lip, half-tempted to kiss him anyway, but when I looked over his shoulder, I noticed the woman waiting in the doorway. Her dark skin shone with a golden tint, and her brown eyes flashed with gold flecks. She was clothed in brown leathers similar to what Alrenian guards or soldiers who didn't have coveted dragon scale armor wore— and her curls were pulled into a simple bun.

But I would have recognized her anywhere, understated appearance or not.

Kovi stepped back, still cradling one of my hands in his own as he nodded toward the woman. "This is Meli."

"I know," I said slowly. "She used to be my mother's truth-gifted advisor."

Meli's smile tightened. "Until she threatened my life for speaking the Life-Giver's truth about slavery, exposing how much he hated it."

I swallowed hard. "I didn't know," I murmured. "Mother didn't say exactly why you vanished."

Meli waved my excuse away as she strode forward. The small space suddenly felt much smaller with three of us gathered within. "You were young then, and that's not why I'm here anyway. I know you're on our side." Her eyes flicked to Kovi's and my interlaced hands. "I wanted you to meet some of my Alrenian fighters before you go."

My chest warmed at the thought, and I straightened. After the battle yesterday, I'd been trapped in a meeting with the Elders, General Ilowhe, Kovi, Lo, and Caesiem. Once it had been decided that we would fly to Alrenor, the Elders had offered me a bath and food. It had quickly become clear that they'd wanted to keep me under close watch while the city recovered and prepared for war. They didn't fully trust me.

With Nesrelle's mark still burning on my cheek, I couldn't exactly blame them.

Gathering my pack, I followed Kovi and Meli outside to the grounds, where a handful of Alrenians were gathered. The eldest of the group, a woman with a brutal scar carved across her temple and through one eyebrow, stepped forward, studying me curiously, before dropping to her knees and holding her hands palms up.

I stopped dead in my tracks, overwhelmed by the gesture. The others followed suit.

"Empress," the woman said. Her braid, blonde tinted with grey, slipped over one shoulder when she bowed her head. "We are honored to see that you've joined our alliance, and we are happy to serve you."

I swallowed thickly, and Kovi squeezed my hand in response. Drawing a deep breath, I tossed him a smile before releasing his hand and approaching the group. Meli remained beside Kovi, grinning proudly.

"You may rise," I told them. "It's my honor to meet you. I wish…" My voice trailed off. "I wish I'd seen the wisdom in this Forwyn-Alrenian alliance much sooner."

The woman stood first, meeting my gaze confidently yet reverently.

"We wanted to tell you that we have faith in you and your ability to lead our empire into peace and unity."

One of the men stepped up beside the woman. Though he didn't appear to be any younger than Kovi or me, his face was rather boyish. He dipped his head. "We also wanted to wish you safe travels. When the time to fight comes, we will follow you."

"Thank you," I said.

As Kovi and I bid them goodbye, my mind whirled. If we won this war, I'd have everything I'd ever wanted. Ironically, it had only taken me losing everything to get here.

CHAPTER THIRTY-NINE

UNDER THE STEELY GREY SKY, the scent of the sea was different here, carrying a bite of autumn's chill. As my eyes swept over the small city of Vernae, following the curve of the coast, I watched countless gulls streaming in off the choppy Alrenian. The restless breeze and building clouds promised a storm.

I also noted with relief that Sephrode had told me the truth when I'd sought her out last night, offering her a shiny bead the Elha'tonu Elders had given me. The Teramese didn't occupy this city, not any longer. Only Forwyn and Alrenians walked the streets, though many appeared to be seeking shelter, watching the sky warily as they ducked indoors. A few saw our dragons and gaped in fear, likely wondering if the Teramese had gained control of the creatures and were coming to attack.

Revaed must have decided fighting over this small fishing city wasn't worth it, not when he needed as many of his forces as he could gather in Hemlaen. But that meant Hemlaen would be overflowing with troops, and that my mission would be all the more uncertain.

What if his soldiers took me prisoner before Revaed even saw me? What if Revaed declared me a traitor to the crown, and had me executed?

Karos landed alongside Ryke, Jozek, and Kova on the outskirts of the city, tucking his black wings against his sides and sniffing the wind restlessly.

"He's hungry," Lo laughed, when she saw me studying the dragon.

"So am I," Vander announced cheerfully, sliding off Jozek's back and retrieving the pack he'd strapped to his saddle.

Mio'e followed him, her expression unreadable. She ran a hand through her shorn curls, studying the city. None of the buildings were tall or impressive, and Vernae didn't even have a gate encircling it. It was simply a sprawling mass following the sea, full of quiet merchants and fishermen. A world away from the opulence and arrogance of the Alrenian capital.

Vander tossed me a look as Lo dismounted and I did not, his silver eyes searching.

"I'm not hungry," I said, "and there's no time to waste. Speak to the people of Vernae as we planned, and I'll return with Revaed's answer."

Lo reached up and squeezed my hand. She didn't say anything else. We'd already decided last night that we wouldn't let our thoughts linger on the possible negative outcomes. I carried enough weight thinking about facing Revaed as it was.

"We'll have the people rallied and ready to fight," Jalie said confidently from her spot beside Ryke, stroking his emerald scales. The dragon leaned his snout into her shoulder, snuffling playfully.

With a nod, I murmured in Alrenian to Karos, and the dragon launched into the air. Though Lo had insisted the dragons had all learned commands in Alrenor's tongue, I suspected from the way he listened and interacted with her that he'd long ago learned the merchant language too. Wind howled in my ears, and I patted the dragon's side reassuringly as I urged him to turn back toward Hemlaen.

"Drop me outside the city," I shouted, "and then you can find your dinner."

With an eager snort that told me he really did understand, Karos flapped his wings and propelled us toward Hemlaen. Toward Revaed.

I approached the city gates warily, scanning the patrolling guards, waiting to see their reaction. A Teramese flag snapped proudly in the breeze. Though Hemlaen wasn't much larger than Vernae, it drew in more travelers and business, which meant it was surrounded by high walls on three sides. The fourth backed up to an ancient forest leading to the coast.

It was clear why Revaed had chosen this city: it was easily defensible, it possessed a harbor large enough for Teramese ships needed to ferry troops and cargo, and with the surrounding countryside of farmland and rolling hills, the guards posted on the wall could spot anyone approaching from miles away.

When I was within shouting distance, the guards called to me.

"Who are you, and what is your business?" the man demanded, narrowing his golden eyes and resting his hand on one of the arrows in his quiver.

Acknowledging his unspoken threat, I stopped and lifted my head, wondering if the men would recognize me. For half a moment, I considered using my true name, but I discarded that notion. I wasn't here to hurl insults in Revaed's face, even if I wasn't sure I wanted to bear his name any longer. "Caesiem Xalenos," I said steadily, "and I'm here to speak with Revaed."

The first man stiffened, drawing his arrow and stringing it to his bow in a single smooth motion. His companion, a stocky man with sharp, pale green eyes, was slower to ready his weapon.

"Traitor," the first man snarled, aiming his bow at me with a murderous glare. "Where have you been?"

The sea's current pulsed in my head, steady and strong, drowning out my worries and fears. It sang in my blood, begging me to call on it, to remind these men who they threatened. But that would be counterintuitive to my purpose, so I stood my ground and lifted my hands, showing that I was unarmed. My sword was still strapped to Karos's saddle, probably miles from here by now as he circled the countryside, searching for his next meal.

"I mean no harm. I'm here to speak *peaceably* with my guardian."

The first man scoffed, but the second cast him a sidelong glance. "He's a Xalenos; we shouldn't be threatening him…"

"Shut up," the first guard said, rolling his eyes. He fastened his gaze on me again, grinning maliciously. "All right, I'll have you escorted to Revaed."

He snapped his fingers, and the gates groaned open, their cranks operated by unseen hands behind the wall. I waited, my chest feeling empty when I realized I was mere minutes away from seeing my guardian again. I wasn't sure what I feared more: finding betrayal in his eyes when he heard of my new alliance, or learning he didn't regret how he'd used and manipulated me from the moment he'd adopted me into his family.

It was already disconcerting enough to need an escort to approach Revaed—a clear sign that things had shifted between us.

But the figures that stepped through the gates weren't guards at all. They were hybrid nymphs, their skin coated in a blend of glistening scales and wrinkled bark, their green hair like a mixture of moss and seaweed. When they smiled, their teeth were as sharp as needles, and their luminous eyes gleamed in shades of pearl white and earthy brown.

A chill swept through me at this confirmation that Nesrelle had been speaking the truth. Revaed had allied with her, and with these creatures.

The earth itself dipped and rolled where I stood, nearly shaking me off balance. There was a shuddering, rumbling sound as the dirt cracked open and two huge boulders rose from the ground, trapping me in place.

Not that I had anywhere to go. There was no retreating from this meeting, as much as I dreaded it.

The pair of nymphs giggled as they approached, one reaching out with a webbed hand to stroke my cheek. Her fingers were cold and clammy, and I ground my teeth at the lecherous way her eyes raked over my body. "Could we drain a little of his magic?" she asked in a sing-song voice, and I could have sworn my blood was freezing over.

"No, sister," the other snapped, her tone richer, deeper. "We must wait to see what Emperor Revaed wants to do with him first."

Despair knifed through my chest, raw and startling. As much as I had dreaded and prepared myself for Revaed turning me away, I hadn't expected *this*. This was a fresh betrayal, setting his nymphs on me, a not-so-subtle threaten to both me and my magic.

My eyes burned, but my anger over yet one more treacherous act was stronger. As the nymphs yanked my arms and led me roughly into the city, I lifted my chin and straightened my spine. I would walk in as a prince, even if I was about to be cast out as an unwanted son.

CHAPTER FORTY

Revaed

A CHILL OF FOREBODING STRUCK me before Nesrelle's voice did. "He's here."

She didn't need to say who she meant; I knew immediately, my heart somehow simultaneously expanding and cracking within my chest. Before I could turn around and fully register her presence, she was gone again, vanishing as quickly as she'd appeared.

I stiffened, pulling back from the table upon which multiple maps were scattered, along with another missive from my father. General Xelia's piercing blue eyes widened almost imperceptibly at my sudden motion, and across the table, I sensed more than saw some of the other officers shift uneasily. Despite their knowledge of our alliance with Nesrelle, none of them had seen the Empress of Death, and any time I glanced toward the fiery-haired goddess, listening to her words, they seemed to think I was preoccupied…or listening to voices. I had the distinct impression that they were talking behind my back, thinking I was going mad, but too terrified of my family's reputation—of *my* reputation—to say it to my face.

Maybe I was. Maybe Nesrelle's visits, her whisperings in my ear, her calculating gaze filling my soul with ice…maybe it was all in my head.

I'd never been visited by a Teramese god before, and what reasoning did I have to believe an Alrenian one, even a cruel and cunning goddess, would take an interest in me?

But unfortunately, her power and chilling presence did feel all too real. I knew she took joy in my misery and the suffering of those around me.

And besides, the nymphs she'd sent were most definitely real.

"Your Imperial Highness?" General Thelos ventured, trying to bring my mind back to the subject at hand. "My troops are prepared to move again, but I'm not convinced we should cut a direct route to the capital without ensuring some of the smaller cities and towns along the way are secured first. The citizens have been restless and rebellious. We want total control of the empire. A fractured land will only give rebels a better foothold. What if those citizens choose to march on the capital and join the forces you say are sailing from Forwyth?"

I shook my head, skin prickling. *Those cities are burnt to ashes.* Nesrelle had shown me what her army had done in a chilling vision, and I believed her. She'd shown me the ruins of Aramith, the bones and the cinders and the desolation. The same destruction had been wrought on the town of Wenlaen, on her army's way toward the capital. There weren't enough living to fight back, not from those locations.

But before I was forced to try to explain myself and my knowledge without sounding as mad as they suspected I was, the messenger I'd been anticipating darted into the room, dipping into a hasty bow. "Your Majesty," he said breathlessly, "forgive the interruption, but…"

"Prince Xalenos is here," I finished for him, my tone level despite the whirlwind of emotions I was experiencing.

General Thelos glanced up sharply, rubbing at his beard as he processed this information—and wondered how I'd already known it.

"I'm afraid we will need to reconvene later," I announced, scanning the room coolly. Mixed expressions returned my stare, ranging from shock and hope to outright frustration or anger. Mentally, I took note of the ones that seemed the most furious. They'd be the ones to watch, the ones who wouldn't be so amenable to forgiving Caesiem's absence. They were the ones who believed he was a traitor and nothing more.

Still, they shuffled out without protest, and the messenger followed, making way for two nymphs to press into the room. My officers were too disciplined to let their discomfort show, but the messenger visibly shuddered as he passed the creatures, darting hurriedly out of sight.

"Leave us," I ordered the nymphs, not even sparing them a glance. My eyes were fastened on Caesiem, whose vivid blue gaze was churning and dark, as restless and unpredictable as the Terebrys. I couldn't read him, and that terrified me.

He wouldn't betray you.

"I think," one of the nymphs hissed, "you should allow us a bit of a reward for bringing him to you."

My gaze flew to her, and my eyes narrowed. "I think not. *Out.*"

The nymphs simpered, but to my relief, they released Caesiem's arms and obeyed without further dissent. The creatures were positively terrifying sometimes, but without magic, I wasn't their ideal prey…and their path to obtaining it was through following me. At least, for now. I knew better than to trust that Nesrelle wouldn't backstab me the instant she found something or someone that better suited her mission.

For a breathless, tense moment, neither Caesiem nor I spoke. We simply stared at one another, trying to read each other's expressions. He was dressed in unfamiliar black leathers, but he wore no weapons. Of course, with his magic, he'd never been one to worry about facing his enemies without a blade. He had something far better, never more than a thought away.

My stomach dipped to imagine him thinking of us—of me—as his enemy.

I'd prayed Nesrelle wasn't right about this, but…

I repressed a shiver and pulled my arms behind my back, clenching my fingers together. "You're alive," I said, nodding to his outfit. "And not wounded this time, I see." Another beat, before I forced out the question that I wasn't sure I wanted answered. That I *needed* answered. "Where were you? I was worried."

I wanted to rush forward and pull him into my arms, but something in his eyes held me back.

"You were worried?" Caesiem repeated slowly, stepping forward with his hands hanging loosely at his sides. He was uncharacteristically still. That had been my first warning that nothing was right, and everything was wrong. Even if I wanted to deny it. "You were so worried you had your guards threaten and set your nymphs on me?"

A muscle in my jaw ticked, anger flaring. "That was not on my orders, and they'll be duly punished for that." I swallowed thickly. "You know I'd never threaten you."

Caesiem's eyes were cold, assessing. He studied me warily, like I wasn't his guardian, but a stranger. "I'm not sure I know anything for certain anymore," he muttered. Raising his voice, he took another step closer. "Did you ever plan to tell me about my parents?"

Panic swelled in my chest. *You are calm. You are poised.* The serene aura I'd mastered during my time in my father's court slipped into place, despite my rising fear and anger and hurt.

"Well?" Caesiem pressed, and this time, his voice trembled.

"What about them?" I asked, shoving my hands into my pockets, trying to look casual.

"*Everything!* How dare you stand there and pretend that you never knew who they were, never knew their fate? It would have been one thing if you had confessed it all to me, because I know everything that happened to them was under your father's orders, but you *lied*. You told me you didn't know who I was. All along, you knew they died on the run, fleeing from your father, to protect me from *your family*."

My mouth wouldn't move. The words wouldn't come. The pain on Caesiem's face was unbearable, but I would have been a coward to look away, so I forced myself to meet his gaze.

He gestured to me fiercely. "And now you're still silent. How many more lies did you tell me? How many other secrets have you kept?" Caesiem's voice broke. "And I know you threatened Lo, and you killed some of her sisters. You *used* her to attack her own people." He blinked, trying to hold back tears.

"I wanted to protect you from the evils of this world," I whispered. My whole body was numb. I had the sickening sensation that something vital was being carved from my chest, but I was helpless to defend myself, unable to even feel the pain anymore. I was a terrified boy again, facing my father's wrath and punishments. I was a lost prince again, thinking naively that I could shield this young orphan, this new family I'd found, from everything brutal and awful and difficult by making all the hard choices for him and covering them all up. I was the man who'd murdered mages in cold blood to prevent them from laying a hand on Caesiem one more time.

"Maybe you should have been more concerned with protecting me from *you*," Caesiem snapped. "I saw the rows of corpses you left in the market square. I thought we came to Alrenor to get away from your father's violence, to give our people hope and peace."

"We did!" I protested. "But sometimes the price of peace is war."

Caesiem's fist clenched at his side, and a pitcher of water left on the side table churned, the water inside bubbling and rising like a miniature ocean before a storm. Energy from his magic pulsed in the air, heavy and oppressive. For the first time, his magic instilled fear in me. Would the man I'd watched drown his enemies on land do the same to me?

"This isn't war," he said, his voice low and ominous. He was trying to keep himself under control, but I could see how his magic responded to him naturally, how it was prepared to protect him from a perceived threat—from *me*. "We invaded Alrenor, and then we murdered its citizens when they didn't like our violent acts. We forced them into obedience or death."

The numbness spread, and I had the disconcerting impression that it wasn't me standing in that room anymore. No, I was nothing but a witness, studying the moment another man broke apart. The moment his world collapsed in on itself.

"Who does that sound like, Revaed?" Caesiem pressed. "Who else would do such a thing?"

My head was spinning, my thoughts foggy. The water swirled around the pitcher now, glistening and beautiful. It wasn't much, but it was enough. I'd seen Caesiem kill with less.

"*Who?*" he demanded.

My lungs burned, and I realized all this time I'd been holding my breath, already imagining the moment I drowned. I inhaled, my body shuddering, and when I spoke, my voice was a raspy whisper. "The High Imperator."

Caesiem

I'd thought Revaed's confession would be the final push to make my anger overflow. I'd thought hearing him say those three simple words would have been enough to make me scream at him, to tell him that he was a traitor and a liar, and no guardian of mine.

But instead, I deflated. The swirling water splashed sloppily toward the pitcher, most of it missing the glass and spilling over the table and onto the floor.

Revaed didn't seem to notice. He looked lost, his violet eyes shadowed and haunted, his body trembling and hunched. The calm, confident man I'd known had disappeared.

"You let your father turn you into him." This time, my words weren't full of vitriol, only despair.

Bitterness twisted Revaed's expression. "And *you* let a pretty face turn you against your own people." His eyes scanned me again, as if from a simple look he could tell where my leathers had been crafted. "That's where you've been, hasn't it? With her? With *them*. You've chosen to side with the Forwyn, against Teramyl. You've as good as said it…that we were wrong to come here."

"Weren't we?"

Anger flashed in Revaed's eyes, the first spark since I'd pushed him to confess that his actions mirrored those of the father he despised so much. "What was the right choice, Caes? To let our people *starve*?"

I scrubbed a weary hand through my hair. "You pretend that was our only option."

"You agreed with me until you met her."

I gritted my teeth. "I agreed with you until she showed me what is good and right, and how much her own people have been suffering too. Until she showed me that continuing the cycle of hurting more innocent citizens won't end our pain. All it's done is cause war and death, for them and us. How many of our soldiers have we laid to rest since we came here?"

Revaed spun away, pacing the floor restlessly. "You saw the letters. The Elders ignored our pleas. The Alrenians are vicious, and the only way to communicate with them is in the language they understand: war." His head snapped up. "As for the Forwyn, and Lo herself, I gave them a choice. I gave her a choice. But she decided to defy me at every turn, threatening *my* people." He pressed a hand to his chest. "My only purpose is to protect the Teramese. And might I remind you, that's yours too. How dare you put foreigners over your own people! You saw how our citizens depend on us, how they suffer. If not you, who will defend them? How could you choose the Forwyn and leave the Teramese to *rot*?"

"I'm not choosing the Forwyn over our people. I choose *both*."

Revaed paused, sneering. "It doesn't seem like it."

"It's time we pulled our troops out of Alrenor and stop this war," I went on. "We'll save countless lives—"

This time, Revaed's expression bordered on frantic. "No! Do you know what will happen to our soldiers if they return to Teramyl defeated? Do you have any idea what the imperator will do to them? We'll condemn our soldiers to *death*. And those who do manage to escape my father's wrath will have the glorious, peaceful opportunity to starve or burn to death alongside the rest of our citizens. How is that saving lives?"

My pulse pounded in my temples. "If you would just stop and listen—"

"No." Revaed spun toward me, suddenly deadly calm, his voice cold. I repressed a shudder. "You need to leave now, before I call the nymphs and declare you a traitor to our people. Get out of my sight, and never threaten our people—*my* people—again."

I forced myself to straighten, to mask my pain. "Or what?"

Revaed swallowed, and his eyes shuttered. There was no anger or grief left in his expression—there was nothing at all. "Or I'll be forced to keep the vows I made to defend the Teramese to the death. No matter who you are…or were."

CHAPTER FORTY-ONE

Lo

HOW DOES IT FEEL TO be a married woman?" Pauni'a's eyes glinted mischievously as she settled onto the grass beside me and nudged me with her elbow.

I paused mid-bite, despite how my stomach grumbled or how delicious the fresh bread layered with creamy cheese was. The Elha'tonu residents had been generous when offering us supplies for our trip. "You should never travel without something to eat," Elder Yelaia had told me matter-of-factly when she'd added some of the food to my pack. "Besides, even my Sight hasn't shown me exactly what you'll find there. Better to go prepared. Every vision I've seen has been full of hurting, suspicious people on either side. They might as soon run you out of town as feed you."

Now, I glanced at my friend thoughtfully. "How do you know?"

Pauni'a rolled her eyes. "I was *there* when you were married."

For some reason, her raised voice embarrassed me, and I glanced around the circle our group had formed to make sure no one else was paying attention. Kovi and Jalie were seated close together, speaking in low voices, Vander was casually using his magic to send a few leaves twirling through the air, and Mhel was attempting—and failing—to engage a standoffish Mio'e in conversation. Turning back to Pauni'a, I pointedly dipped my voice lower. "I meant, how did you know Caesiem and I finally…worked things out?"

Pauni'a rested her chin in her hand. "I gathered it from all those steamy glances between you two. I would have preferred to hear the news from you, but…" She shrugged. "I figured you were busy." She waggled her eyebrows.

"*Nia*," I snapped. Heat flushed through my entire body, and this time I was sure Vander must have heard something. He'd abruptly lost control of one of the leaves he'd been playing with. We were discussing his friend. Maybe he didn't know what had happened between Caesiem and me either. Maybe he'd be furious and feel like his friend, his prince, was choosing me over Teramyl.

Despite my scandalized tone, my sister rolled her eyes. "I'm sure everyone else here figured it out too." She hesitated. "So how is it?"

I nudged her with my elbow, trying to look serious despite the dreamy grin pulling on my lips.

"Oooh." She giggled. "I'm glad you're happy," she finished, her expression turning solemn. "Anyway, I mostly knew you'd finally both accepted your marriage because of a dream," she went on. "I saw two of Elhani's marks overlapping, and I had the sense it was the two of you, finally and truly together. I've had a lot of dreams lately." Her eyes turned thoughtful.

"Do your dreams tell you the future?" Once, Pauni'a had explained that she'd known I'd never been meant to be a nun, all because of some dreams she was convinced Elhani had sent to her. She hadn't mentioned having any others since then, and in the midst of the building war and my confusing relationship with Caesiem, I'd all but forgotten about my sister's dreams.

She shook her head, her braids—adorned with fresh ribbons thanks to the Elha'tonu people—swishing over her shoulders. Next to the black leathers that matched my own, they were a riot of beautiful colors. "I think they're more like the Alrenian truth gift, showing me current events in the world. I've had many dreams about the destruction in Alrenor." She swallowed. "The Dark Immortal's army left Wenlaen and Aramith looking like wastelands. And Inalgoth?" Her eyes sparkled with unshed tears. "It's barely recognizable."

I reached out, taking her hand. "We're going to stop her. Her, and Revaed." My thoughts turned to Caesiem, and I sent my hundredth prayer of the day to Elhani, pleading with him to keep the man I loved safe.

Across our circle, Kovi stood, brushing the dirt from his pants. Unlike the rest of us, he and Mhel were clothed in fresh Aerekni uniforms, their red and gold attire standing out against the black everyone else wore. "Are you ready?" he asked me.

A pit formed in my stomach and my eyes darted to Jalie, who gave me a single nod in return.

"Yes," I said, standing. The others followed suit as I scanned the sky. Our dragons were out of sight, and suddenly I questioned if I'd made the right decision. Maybe the citizens would have been more likely to listen to us if they'd watched us fly into Vernae on dragons. *Whoever controls the dragons controls Alrenor,* I thought.

But right now, everyone was on edge, and the sight of dragons was as likely to inspire fear as courage. After all, they had every reason to believe the Teramese controlled the dragons.

To my surprise, Jalie approached me. "You know how to interact with the citizens, whereas I've had the pleasure of spending most of my life in a palace." The trace of bitter sarcasm in her tone wasn't lost on me, and not for the first time, I wondered how the Elders had treated her, all the while claiming a unified front. "So where in the town should we go first?" she asked, arching a brow.

It was obvious she didn't like following someone else's lead, but her eyes didn't hold any hostility, not anymore. I might have even dared to call the relationship growing between us a tentative friendship.

I shrugged, at a loss. "When I wasn't visiting homes, the people came to me at the abbey," I said sheepishly.

"What do you think, Elha'tonu?" Mhel asked brightly, turning to Kovi.

The young soldier didn't hesitate, his lips forming a crooked smile. "Follow me," he said.

Jalie

"Elha'tonu?" I whispered to Kovi as we neared the city. The dirt road we followed was narrow and unassuming, without a guard in sight to stop or question us. "I thought that was the name of the Forwyn island."

Something like embarrassment darted across Kovi's features. "It is…but that's also what they called me at the academy. It means Elhani-blessed."

I smirked, and he sighed, knowing I wouldn't relent until I had more than that.

But before he could explain, his friend Mhel, who'd clearly been eavesdropping on our conversation, spoke up. "That's his nickname because he was always the best. Disciplined, strong, dedicated…the perfect soldier. It was practically eerie, the way he never made a mistake."

Kovi shook his head, and though he tried to conceal it, I could see the darkness lurking in his gold-flecked eyes. "I've made many mistakes."

Everyone fell silent as we entered Vernae, everything about it quiet and oppressive. Fear practically emanated from the buildings, making air already heavy from the tension of an oncoming storm feel even thicker. Businesses and homes had shuttered windows to protect against the imminent foul weather. A few citizens—both Alrenian and Forwyn—

paused at the sight of us, gaping openly or hurrying away while darting suspicious glances over their shoulders. One Forwyn woman met my gaze and openly scowled, muttering what I assumed were curses under her breath as she stormed away.

No one in our group spoke, and I wondered if everyone else was experiencing the same doubt I was. All my hopes, so alive in the sunshine on Elha'tonu or in Kovi's arms, seemed foolish here with the angry, broken citizens before us.

But Kovi didn't falter in his long strides, forcing me to stretch my legs to keep up. He stopped outside a long, low building with warm light and cheerful conversation spilling into the street each time the rickety door creaked open. The sign was in bad need of a fresh coat of paint, but I made out the words *Hungry Kraken* before Kovi pushed open the door. The first cluster of patrons at the nearest table were all Forwyn, and I froze instinctively.

For an embarrassingly long moment, I hesitated on the threshold, pulse pounding in my ears, eyes scanning the room. There were a few Alrenians in the shadowy corners of the space, clearly keeping to themselves, but everywhere else there were only Forwyn. Forwyn dressed like guards—a clear sign they had the upper hand in this town— and a Forwyn barkeep wiping the counter. I was willingly walking into an enclosed space full of my enemies.

They might tolerate the presence of other Alrenians here, but the Alrenian empress? They had every reason to want to kill me.

Kovi's eyes flashed as they met mine. "You're safe," he murmured.

"He's right," another voice said, a warm hand resting on my arm. I turned to meet Lo's gaze, confident and unyielding. "We won't let them touch you."

Courage, I thought, lifting my chin and shaking off Lo's hand. "I'm not afraid," I snapped. "I just…hate stepping into filthy pubs."

It was a ridiculous excuse, one I was sure even Lo knew was a lie. I shuffled forward anyway, setting my hands on my hips while I surveyed the room.

The Forwyn guards stiffened, some standing and setting hands on sword hilts. One, a burly middle-aged man with flecks of white in his beard and a receding hairline, pushed forward as the rest of our group entered and Kovi let the door close.

"What's your business here?" the man asked, addressing Kovi. The guard's tone held begrudging respect at the sight of Kovi's Aerekni uniform. His eyes shot to Vander and then to me. "Who are you, and who are *they*?"

Kovi's stance was calm and assured. "We didn't come to cause trouble. Everyone with me is a friend." The subtle emphasis of the word rumbled low in his voice, like an unspoken threat: touch them and face the consequences. His eyes flicked to the barkeep, who was scowling openly. "We've been traveling and would like a few drinks and friendly conversation."

"That looks like the Alrenian empress," another patron said, this one an unarmed woman who'd abandoned her bowl of stew to stand and point accusingly. "She's the spitting image of her bloody mother, and you have the gall to bring her into our town?"

I leveled an angry stare right back at her. All fear vanished as spots danced across my vision, and I stalked toward the bar, slamming down a single drae, one of the few coins General Ilowhe had been able to supply us with. "Yes," I seethed, "it's awful that I'm here, in your town, paying for a drink."

Kovi was at my side immediately, setting a gentle but firm hand on my arm and shooting me a warning look before turning back to the room. Everyone had gone utterly still and silent at my proclamation. One of the guards broke the quiet by drawing his blade, the shriek of steel infinitely loud.

"No one is in danger," Kovi said calmly, lifting his hands.

"We're here to help you," Lo added, conviction filling her voice. In the flickering firelight cast from the hearth across the room, the shades of green in her eyes were especially bright. Somehow, she was as calm as Kovi, despite the fact that everyone in the room was glaring at us.

The first guard scoffed. "*Help* us?"

"Yes," I interjected firmly. "Help you take back Alrenor from Teramyl and Nesrelle's foul army." My eyes scanned the room, settling pointedly on the handful of Alrenians at its far reaches. "*All* of you."

"Then why is *he* here?" another man sneered, studying Vander.

Next to Vander, the Forwyn girl with the shorn hair—Mio'e, Lo had called her—crossed her scarred arms over her chest and rolled her eyes. "Stop being dense. Your own people are here with Alrenians and Teramese, saying they've come on friendly terms and want to help when you're all clearly terrified Teramyl's army will return any moment, and you're too suspicious to even listen?"

All across the room, men and women shuffled uneasily on their feet, turning to one another.

"Just give us a chance to explain everything," Kovi said, taking my hand and cradling it gently, reassuringly. He nodded to the two nearest empty tables. "We'll sit and talk."

Kovi

A heavy silence filled the pub. Lo, Jalie, and I had done most of the talking, explaining how our alliance with a ragtag band of Alrenian and Forwyn rebels, and then Caesiem and his friends, had begun. How Inalgoth had fallen and Nesrelle's army currently occupied it, and how we'd managed to secure the help of the Elha'tonu residents. How the nymphs had been attacking even Forwyth, and how Nesrelle and the Teramese were now working together.

"They've been attacking here, too," the barkeep revealed, his eyes darting to the windows, where rain was pounding against the glass. It was only the start of the storm that had been building. "It began with fishermen disappearing, not long after the Teramese retreated and left Vernae alone."

One of the Alrenians in the back gained confidence and spoke up. "And then some homes were broken into in the night." Her voice trembled. "They took my sister."

A pit formed in my stomach. Sephrode, the water nymph who'd pretended to be Jalie, who'd taunted me with ominous words about the future, had been drawn to my magic. And the hybrid nymphs who'd attacked Elha'tonu had sought victims with magic too, draining them. I imagined that each new kill was making them stronger, deadlier, as they gained more and more magical power.

"This is why no corner of Alrenor is safe," Jalie announced, pushing back her chair and standing. I sensed her courage gift immediately, Elhani's song whispering through the air. I wondered if her gift was strong enough to reach every person in this room, because something in the atmosphere changed. Every eye turned to her, and there was respect rather than hostility or fear in their gazes. "For too long, Alrenians and Forwyn have weakened our empire and one another by fighting. I know my mother and all my forebears committed unspeakable crimes against you." She swallowed, her eyes lingering on each Forwyn man and woman. "The Teramese and Nesrelle herself have taken advantage of our weakness. They think they can rip our empire away from us, steal our lives and our gifts and magic, and leave us cowering and afraid." Her eyes flashed. "They're wrong. Now is our chance to show them how strong we are, together. It's time to put aside our differences and build a unified, peaceful empire."

"How can we trust you?" a Forwyn woman demanded, lifting her chin. Her dark eyes flashed with doubt. "How do we know this alliance won't end as soon as you take back your throne?"

"Because we stand with her," Lo said from Jalie's other side, rising to her feet. I stood too, once again taking Jalie's hand. Lo tossed a pointed glance at our companions, who joined us.

"And because some of the Teramese, like me, have realized this war has done nothing but harm and kill our own people," Vander added. "We want to right the wrongs we committed by invading."

"I vow to you, here and now, that I will begin my reign with instating Forwyn advisors. There will be a new council, to lead alongside me," Jalie said.

Many gazes lingered on Jalie's and my interlaced fingers, and the sight seemed to appease them. My uniform brought a sense of security, and they seemed to believe that if I trusted Jalie, they could trust her too.

"The Teramese overpowered our land in mere days. Took our capital, held our dragons hostage. And now you say most of our dragons are dead, and the Dark Immortal herself has an army?" It was the barkeep again, shaking his head and fidgeting with the ribbons around his neck. "How can we hope to win against that? Against those unnatural creatures attacking us from the sea, or the Dark Immortal herself?"

Fear rippled through the pub, despite Jalie's best efforts with her gift. I could taste it on my tongue, thick and potent, alongside the warm courage humming through my veins. "Because," I said, "if even the citizens have had enough, if you arm yourselves and fight back…we will be a larger force. Because we have Forwyth and their years of honing their magic on our side. And we have the only living dragons left. When the storm ends, we'll show you."

A guard scoffed. "What will the citizens arm themselves with? Sticks and clubs? Weapons have been illegal since back when the Alrenians were in power." His eyes darted to Jalie, as if regretting his words, but Jalie didn't react.

"Share the weapons you have in the guardhouse. And I'm sure there are illegal weapons hidden away, in every city. How else did the

Alrenian rebellions form?" I turned toward the few gathered in this pub, who shifted uneasily, guiltily. "Ask your smithies to begin crafting more immediately. The only alternative is to sit back and let the nymphs continue to attack, until Nesrelle and Revaed bring their armies to your doorstep. They won't rest until the entire empire is under their command."

"Don't be afraid of arming yourselves," Jalie added. "I will alter the law so that citizens who possess weapons for the purpose of defending themselves and their empire will not be punished."

"Your choice is to live in peace or fear," Lo chimed in. "We've seen the corpses Revaed has left as messages to us within the capital. We've seen the terrors Nesrelle's army wages. Do you want to sit by, or do you want to defend your families and your land? Your future?"

Quiet descended as the pub's occupants mulled over our words. The only sound was the drumming of the rain on the roof.

Slowly, the burly guard stood. "If the soldiers of Aerekni side with the empress and this alliance, I will fight with you."

"And me," another guard added.

One by one, more joined in, until even the Alrenians were standing.

I couldn't hold back my grin. It was time to do what I did best: form a plan.

CHAPTER FORTY-TWO

Nesrelle

THESE ONES WERE HIDING IN the sewers," Daedra crowed, shoving two trembling Alrenians to their knees before my throne. Unlike others of their race who were so foolishly and naively proud, these two had finally recognized their mortality, and how fruitless it was to resist death.

Now or later, it was coming for them, inevitably.

If only their terror wasn't drowned out by the stink of sewer water dripping from their filthy clothes.

I scrunched my nose at the stench. "So you brought them here to sully the throne room?"

Daedra hesitated, blinking at her companions as if they held the answers. I resisted the urge to roll my eyes. She and the rest of the Alrenians were beginning to resemble my beautiful nestrae more and more, but they still had many irritating human qualities. Uncertainty. Doubt. Fear. The last was delicious to feed on, but frustrating when it held them back. They were so close to being unstoppable.

"We thought," Merev began quietly, dipping his head, "that you might want to…feed on their fear, Your Imperial Majesty."

Rising from the throne and brushing my blood-red skirts out of my way, I waved a hand at the cowering pair. "Put them with the others. I can feed on the entire city's fear well enough from here. *Without* having to smell my victims."

My eyes darted pointedly to his, taking in their infinite blackness. His shoulders slumped with lingering mortal fear. It assured me that my point had not been missed: I was feeding on his fear as well as that of the citizens still hiding and struggling to survive within the capital.

I relished the terror and pain emanating from this city, the way the citizens were forced to hide in the underground tunnels and sewers weaving under the streets. The way the surviving remnant of my army grew more devoted to me each day, slipping into their worshipful roles as eagerly as my nestrae had.

But most of all, I was eager for the coming battle, to once again experience the thrill of mortals dying and grieving.

For the past week, Lo, Jalie, and their allies had planned and prepared, as if they believed they could outmaneuver *me*. They'd left the city of Vernae to visit the towns following the Layvok River, and then they'd entered Brema Wood. They'd even convinced another soldiers' academy to join their cause. Everywhere, they rallied citizens and spoke of lofty plans for unity and peace.

Meanwhile, the Aerekni academy survivors, Meli's resistance fighters, and the Elha'tonu warriors had brought forces to the Aramith Mountains, settling in the valley Jalie's army had once occupied. It was there that newly recruited citizens, guards, and academy soldiers began to flood in, adding to their numbers.

It was amusing to see their efforts, and I took great pleasure in knowing that the more people who joined them, meant more who would experience the pain and misery of battle. I welcomed their growing numbers. Relished them. All it meant for me was more sorrow I could feed on, more souls I could watch drift into the afterlife.

Meanwhile, my urging had finally paid off, and Revaed and his troops were on their way to the capital.

"We'll gather our strength and then wait for them to come to us," I'd crooned to him over a game of chess, which had become a nightly habit.

Ever since Revaed's meeting with Caesiem, he'd been even more taciturn and moody. I'd found myself visiting more and more often, his presence delightfully intoxicating.

When I'd pushed him to prepare and move his soldiers, he hadn't resisted. Over the past several days, I'd tracked his progress, some of his forces coming by ship and others by land. Most of them would reach Inalgoth, or what was left of it, by tonight.

Soon, we'd be ready.

I couldn't resist a gleeful smile as I thought of the nymphs residing in the river and in Brema Wood. The High Imperator had been all too eager to supply me with this plentiful army. And with the Alrenian gifts having returned and more Forwyn having learned to connect with their magic, my nymphs would have plenty of humans to feed upon.

"Daedra?" I asked, before she could follow the other soldiers out. "Are you bored?"

She bowed. "No, not when the Goddess of Death has given me so many of these mortals to...*play* with." She smirked around her words.

I shrugged. "Well, I am. I'm ready for more blood." I tapped my fingernails on the throne's armrest, thinking not for the first time that it was a shame Empress Karye was dead. She'd fed me with so much misery, so much death. My eyes snapped again to Daedra's. "Be prepared for battle. I'm going to send a message. It's almost time."

CHAPTER FORTY-THREE

Lo

"L O!" PAUNI'A'S VOICE SPLIT THE stillness of the night, wrenching me from sleep and Caesiem's arms. I was out of my bedroll in an instant, Caesiem on my heels.

"Nia?" Despite the coolness of the autumn night in the army encampment, where we were surrounded by the Aramith Mountains, I didn't pause to grab a cloak. My loose tunic let the air bite at my skin, but I was too worried to care. Pushing open the tent flap, I met my friend's wide brown eyes. Frizzy curls framed her face and one of her ribbons hung loose from a braid. She looked like she'd just awoken.

"I had a dream," Pauni'a announced, her eyes darting between Caesiem and me. "Nesrelle ordered her nymphs to attack every city and town we've visited. She's slaughtering the citizens."

Father paced the interior of the tent restlessly, lanternlight flickering wildly off the canvas. Everyone else was tense and still, trying to process. As soon as Pauni'a had told me of her dream, I'd found Father and he'd ordered this meeting, asking Pauni'a to share the grisly details. Innocent citizens, young and old, were being brutally attacked and drained of their magic and gifts to the point of death. Others were carelessly toyed with, accidental kills as the nymphs laughed and played with their prey, weaving tight roots and branches around bodies or simply drawing them too deep into water and letting them drown.

"Maybe her dreams are just…dreams?" one of the gathered Aerekni soldiers said, a man whose name I didn't remember. His tone was doubtful.

Across the tent, Meli's gaze was distant and unfocused as she shook her head. "I see it too," she whispered.

"Then the next stage of the war has begun sooner than we expected, and we have less time than we hoped to prepare out forces," my father said, keeping his voice level to dispel the atmosphere of fear thickening the air. "But that doesn't mean we can't rally and strike back."

Meli raised her hand, brow scrunched with concern as her eyes remained glazed, like she was still witnessing events occurring miles away. "Wait," she breathed. "Nesrelle…she knows I can see what she's doing in this moment. She's…sharing a message. A message for all of us."

At my side, Caesiem stiffened. I shot him a sideways glance, noting the way a muscle in his jaw jumped and his gaze turned stormy and dark. The Dark Immortal had been taunting him ever since we'd arrived in Elha'tonu, if not before. Just at the mention of her name, I saw the bodies of those Teramese mages strewn across the clearing all over again. I slipped my hand into his, threading our fingers together.

I couldn't help but notice how, from her position on my other side, Jalie's hands curled into fists, or the way Kovi took a protective step toward her, as if he could shield her from the mere memory of the Dark Immortal and all the ways she had tormented Jalie.

Father stopped in his tracks, nostrils flaring. "A message?"

"She will call off the nymphs' attacks and give us a chance to save the citizens she's imprisoned in Inalgoth." Meli swallowed, lowering her hand slowly and blinking, returning to the present. Her eyes focused on the room, sweeping from the general to Caesiem and me, then Kovi and Jalie. "She said if we want to stop the killing, we must leave for the capital immediately and face her. Face the army you created." Her eyes darted to Jalie. "Face your past." She turned to Caesiem and me. Meli drew a shuddering breath and closed her eyes. "If we refuse…she'll kill every last one of the survivors in Inalgoth, and she will let the nymphs continue to feed until every town, every city is drained of citizens, and there is no empire left to defend."

A chill swept through me, and I shuddered so much that Caesiem released my hand to wrap a comforting arm around my waist. "This is just a game to her," I said. "She's luring us into a trap. Why?"

"It's madness," Father said, shaking his head furiously and turning to me. But it wasn't anger in his expression—it was raw fear. His deep eyes, those eyes that reminded me so much of Edi, were terrified and pleading. He knew what I was thinking, what I had already decided as soon as Meli had finished speaking. "We can't do this. Rushing into battle before we've had time to prepare, to plan, to amass the citizens who have agreed to join us…we'll be horribly outnumbered. No matter the dragons and the magic we have, with Nesrelle and those nymphs…it could very well be suicide."

"We have to." It was Jalie's voice. I glanced toward her, taking in the dark circles gathered under her eyes and the tangles in her long, blonde hair. I wondered if she'd been haunted by nightmares of her time working with Nesrelle before she'd been summoned to this meeting. I wondered what her guilt was like, knowing she'd helped Nesrelle build the army now possessing the capital.

"It's true that the Dark Immortal likes…to play games," Kovi said, his voice a soothing baritone despite the tense topic. Like my father, he knew how to assuage panic. He knew how to lead. He turned to his general. "But the truth is, she's already forced our choice. Even if we considered the citizens of Inalgoth a lost cause, which I don't think any of us are prepared to do, those who would have joined us from around the empire are already fighting their own battles against these nymphs. They won't be coming to us any time soon. Nesrelle wants this to end in the capital, where I'm sure the Teramese forces are also already gathered, waiting for us."

"And Revaed," Caesiem muttered darkly. I could practically feel the sorrow and betrayal emanating off him. I couldn't imagine how difficult it was for him, knowing he was about to face his own soldiers in battle. His own guardian. The expression on his face when he'd told me his meeting with Revaed had failed…I never wanted to witness him suffering that much heartbreak again. And yet, I knew his grief was far from over.

"So we play right into the Dark Immortal's hands?" Father spat, running a hand through his hair in frustration. "I don't like this. If we wait, we can plan, come up with a new strategy for our smaller numbers. Even with the dragons, besieging the capital will put us at a disadvantage."

"We can't wait," I said. "If there's a chance she's speaking the truth, we have to save the survivors. I can't live with their blood on my hands."

"And what good is her word?" Father asked. The anger in his eyes had again melted into panic. Sorrow. "She's the *Dark Immortal.* She's known for her cunning, her brutality, her treachery."

"And yet," Jalie murmured, her face carefully blank, "she *was* always true to her word, in every deal she and I struck. Even if the agreements she made were for her own benefit, she fulfilled them all, until…I broke my own end of our bargain."

I nodded in understanding. "Just like the moment you turned on Nesrelle, the healing she'd used on you was undone, and you nearly bled out all over again."

Jalie's mouth twisted in a wry smile. "Yes, going against Nesrelle isn't pleasant."

Silence stretched over us all.

"Again," I repeated, "we don't have a choice."

Kovi gave a sharp nod.

Meli, visibly shaken from her vision of Nesrelle, blinked back tears and sighed. "No, I don't think we do. She knows what this will cost us—every one of us. She knows the sacrifices we are willing to make—and have already made—for our people. That's exactly why she's doing this."

"Elder Yelaia," Father asked. "What do you see?"

The Elder stepped forward, her mouth pursed in concentration. Slowly, she shook her head. "Every future, every path, every choice I see…they all result in death. Much death."

Father's officers and the Elha'tonu Elders burst into conversation, some arguing to fight for those we'd vowed to protect while others insisted leaving now would be suicide.

"Is there any hope, if all you see is death?" Elder Olahni asked Yelaia quietly. The voices around them died down, everyone eager to hear Yelaia's answer.

"I see hope too," Elder Yelaia said, frowning. "I see images of both victory and defeat, but I can't find a clear path to either. There are so many individual choices to be made upon the battlefield. But I do see victory as a possible outcome, even if it comes at great cost. We *must* fight for that."

Again, most of the occupants of the tent began talking at once, while I turned to Caesiem, studying his pained expression. "Don't worry about me," he murmured when I squeezed his hand, trying to offer comfort. "Revaed will make his choice. And I…I have made mine. It's *you*."

At last, my father's voice quieted the tent, settling everyone into silence. "All right! We have made our points." Father deflated, his expression etched in wrinkles that indicated his resignation. "Let's take a vote. All in favor of leaving tomorrow for the capital?"

The chorus of affirmatives made it clear my point had won, even before Father took the vote for those opposed.

"Then it's decided. Spread the word—we depart first thing in the morning. May Elhani hold our hands," Father sighed, taking our traditional farewell blessing and making it a prayer.

"And the guidespirits lead us home," I murmured.

CHAPTER FORTY-FOUR

Caesiem

THE NIGHT AIR BIT AT my skin as I headed toward the tent Lo and I shared. Everyone else had already separated to prepare for departure in the morning—all except Lo and her father, who'd requested a few minutes alone. I didn't blame them. To live their whole lives thinking their entire family was dead, only to find one another on the brink of war, made their relationship all the more precious. They were trying to steal every moment they could get, sharing stories of their pasts, making up for lost time. They were terrified of losing one another, the same way I'd once feared losing Revaed.

And now, you have *lost him.* That thought left me feeling hollow and cold. I paused outside my tent entrance, sighing and squeezing my eyes shut. Trying to banish the searing memory of Revaed's expression. The betrayal and anger and pain. And his final words: *No matter who you are…or were.* Words that effectively proclaimed I was no longer his heir. That I was as good as dead to him. Worse than dead, because he saw me as an enemy to our people, and that meant we were on opposite sides of this battle.

I just wasn't sure what I'd do if I came face to face with him in the midst of it.

Kovi

Preparing to set off the next morning was a solemn affair, everyone weighed down with uncertainty. Only a handful of soldiers remained behind with the three hatchling dragons, to keep them far from battle and to protect them at all costs. They represented hope for the future of the empire, hope that one day, there would be a strong and proud line of dragons once more.

"Whoever controls the dragons, controls Alrenor," Jalie had murmured as she'd cradled the black hatchling in her arms, blinking fiercely as she bid him goodbye. She'd looked into the eyes of the soldiers standing by. "Protect them with your lives. Someday, they will be the might of our empire. And if we fail, they'll be your hope to fight back again."

Lo smiled at Jalie reassuringly. "We won't fail," she told the soldiers firmly. "May Elhani's strength and song be with you."

They nodded reverently to both women, and Jalie returned Lo's smile hesitantly. "You make a good leader," she murmured as they approached the line where Caesiem and I awaited them. "Maybe, when all this is over, you'd consider being on my council?"

Lo swept her braid over her shoulder and sighed, her eyes growing distant. "I'll think about it."

I couldn't help my grin as Jalie neared me. Pulling her close, I pressed my mouth to her ear and whispered, "I knew you two would become friends."

Jalie stepped back, biting her bottom lip to keep from grinning and shaking her head. But her eyes strayed back to where Lo stood next to Caesiem, deep in conversation. Ever since Caesiem had returned from his failed meeting with Revaed, he'd been somber. I couldn't blame him—I couldn't fathom fighting against someone like General Ilowhe, couldn't begin to comprehend how I'd feel if I had to betray him.

Behind us, Karos watched over Lo and Caesiem warily. He'd

refused to let anyone but those two approach him since we'd arrived at camp. With his wild, unpredictable nature, the soldiers had given him a wide berth. But Ryke had wormed his way into many hearts, and he was already pushing past Jalie and me to greet the approaching general. Ryke tilted his head, as if expecting a greeting—or a treat.

"Nothing this time, I'm afraid," the general said, holding up his empty hands apologetically.

Huffing, Ryke turned away to nuzzle Jalie's shoulder. While Jalie stroked his scales and spoke quietly to him, General Ilowhe pulled me aside. "None of the dragons will listen to our commanding officers, but at least one of them will obey you." His eyes flicked toward Ryke. "And I know Mhel, Lo, Jalie, and Pauni'a trust you—maybe Caesiem and his friend do too. I need you to be the strategist for our dragons. Guide them and their riders where they are most needed in battle."

"Of course, sir," I answered.

"And…" He hesitated. "Keep my daughter safe."

I dipped my head in understanding. I knew the general trusted Caesiem to protect Lo, but I also knew he wanted as many defending her as possible. Lo was his whole world. "I'll do everything in my power."

"Thank you, Kovi," he murmured, dropping his formal tone. "May Elhani be with you." Before I could react, General Ilowhe pulled me into an embrace.

"And you," I replied, swallowing against the burning tears building in my throat as I hugged him back.

Lo

The days passed too quickly and too slowly all at once. We set a hard pace, our dragons walking alongside us except to occasionally fly off and hunt. I suspected they were also scouting the path ahead, even when Jalie, Pauni'a, and me weren't on their backs doing our own reconnaissance.

By the time we set up camp the first night, my feet were sore, and my legs ached. My nightly running outings hadn't come close to covering the miles we had traveled that day.

After our meal, Caesiem made it his mission to seek out a jiadro to borrow from one of the soldiers. Perched on a rock near one of the countless fires lighting our camp, he strummed a jaunty tune. "For Noa'him," he said, and the solemn look in his bright eyes told me everything. He'd seen the man's body in the Akytha square—a man who had offered him a room at his pub in exchange for entertaining his patrons. A man who, I suspected, had also become a friend.

The song was normally one sung in Forwyn, but someone must have translated it for Caesiem into the merchant tongue, maybe Noa'him himself. As he started to sing, the rich notes weaving over us in a mesmerizing melody, Mhel and Oru and Huvoki joined in. One by one, other soldiers added their voices to the song. Even my father chimed in, winking at me when I caught him hitting one of the notes off-key.

As the song ended and Caesiem led into the next, my spirits lightened. I glanced at Jalie and Kovi, sitting across from me, caught up in a quiet conversation. It felt like an intimate moment, like they were in their own world, and not for the first time, I marveled at the connection these two had found, against all odds. Surely, if an Aerekni soldier and the daughter of Karye herself could overcome the hurt and pain our peoples had caused one another, then that healing and unity could spread throughout the empire.

We just had to win it back first.

Jalie

By the second day of our march back to the capital, I found myself falling into a rhythm. Perhaps because of Lo's acceptance, her friend Pauni'a treated me with kindness, even if she did seem a bit wary of me. But what the three of us lacked in trust, we made up for with our ties to the dragons. Pauni'a had bonded with Kova on our flights around the empire, and so we were regularly asked to scout ahead of the army's path, ensuring our way was clear. Each town we passed was eerily empty of any sign of the Teramese, save for the marks of war they'd left in their wake.

That first night, I shared a tent with Pauni'a, and the next morning, I woke to the same whispers and darting glances I'd received from soldiers throughout our travels yesterday. Despite their suspicion or outright anger, I kept my head held high and refused to be afraid. These soldiers were not the Elders who had controlled my life, harmed me bodily, and threatened me with execution. And I was not the scared little empress I'd been before, anxious to please her mother's memory. I wouldn't let them frighten me.

Still, I was relieved to see Kovi approaching, two mugs in hand. As always, he was dressed impeccably, his uniform pristine despite the fact that we had slept in hastily erected tents last night. Mischief twinkled in his dark eyes when he handed me one of the steaming mugs. "Tea for you, and coffee *without* cinnamon for me."

I stifled a laugh and smirked. "What about a kiss *without* poison in thanks?"

Kovi happily obliged, nearly spilling both our mugs when he wrapped his free arm around my waist and pulled me against him.

I wasn't surprised by the muttered "bloody empress" when a Forwyn soldier walked by, but I felt Kovi tense. His expression was murderous as he glanced over my shoulder at the passing man. "You shouldn't have to deal with that," he muttered. "I'll talk to General Ilowhe and have him…issue some warnings."

I wasn't as angry as I'd expected. I hadn't been yesterday when I'd seen the doubt and hatred on faces, and I wasn't now. Instead, I was realizing just how much pain my mother had caused. To the Forwyn, I was a constant reminder of Karye's cruelty, both in my appearance and my past actions. Could I blame them for doubting my loyalty? Still, I appreciated Kovi's defensiveness and nodded before turning my attention to my tea.

Sighing with pleasure, I inhaled the steam rising from my mug before savoring the first sip. To my delight, I discovered that Kovi had scrounged up some sugar and added the perfect amount to my drink.

The rest of the day was another bone-wearying trek, though this time Caesiem seemed determined to mask his brevity with charm and songs, leading soldiers in pub tunes. Kovi and Ryke were steadying presences at my side, keeping any especially hateful soldiers far away.

On our scouting flights, there was nothing to be found but Forwyn and Alrenian citizens—not a single Teramese soldier had been left behind on the path to the capital.

My scar prickled with a faint pain each time I thought of Nesrelle and her ability to discern thoughts. She knew every one of our plans, and had, in her usual taunting fashion, made this war into her own game. She was a spider waiting amidst a trap, luring us in with our refusal to abandon our people.

That second night, the mood turned more somber after dinner.

"Rhi'il would have had a mad plan to go along with our battle strategy," Kovi's friend Oru said softly. He, Mhel, and Huvoki hadn't said anything negative to me or cast me any nasty glances, but they hadn't exactly made a point of trying to get to know me, either. I had a feeling they disapproved of Kovi's association with me and believed I would break his heart.

They watched you try to kill him. Twice, a wry voice in my head reminded me each time I felt a sting of disappointment. *If you were in their place, you would do a lot worse than simply ignore them.*

Kovi turned to his friend, a wistful smile on his lips. "And it would have succeeded."

I wanted to hold Kovi's hand, or pull him into an embrace, but his grief for his friend felt like something to be shared only with his fellow soldiers. I hadn't known Rhi'il other than as the man who'd helped free Kovi and me from our shackles before the battle for the capital. Rhi'il hadn't trusted me, and I, caught up in my lust for revenge and the sound of Nesrelle's voice, had hardly acknowledged him.

I didn't have the right to comfort Kovi.

"We fight for him," General Ilowhe said firmly. "And for all our fallen soldiers."

"And Naina and Jo'elli and Eloiyah," Pauni'a murmured.

"We fight for the ones we lost years ago, too," Lo added, lifting her chin. The green flecks in her eyes sparkled in the firelight. "Mother and Edi." Her eyes darted to her father's, and his expression twisted into something bittersweet, the echo of a smile touching his face. "Everyone who died in our endless hatred of one another. That ends now, here, with this alliance we've started."

She glanced around our fire at our companions—Caesiem and his friends; General Ilowhe, Kovi and other Aerekni soldiers; Meli and a couple of her Alrenian rebels; and me. Then her eyes strayed further, scanning the camp full of Forwyn and Alrenians.

"We fight for my mother too," Kovi said, his voice low. "She would have wanted this."

"And my cousin," Huvoki added, "who was murdered during his enslavement at the palace."

The list of names continued to grow, lost family members killed while enslaved. Many by my mother's hand. As the soldiers around the fire recounted gruesome and aching stories of loss, my chest became tighter and tighter.

At last, I crept away, out to the edge of camp where Ryke was curled up, asleep. Here the conversations and songs were just a low backdrop, a gentle and soothing hum beneath the churring of insects and the whisper of the breeze through the grass. I sank beside my dragon and leaned into his warmth. He shifted and opened his eye, peering at me curiously before sighing and nudging me gently. Tears burned my throat and stung my eyes, threatening to spill over.

I wasn't surprised to hear Kovi's footsteps, but I couldn't turn away from Ryke, couldn't look the man in the eyes and let him see the pain in my expression. Even for him, I desperately didn't want to appear vulnerable or weak.

"How can you stand to look at me?" I asked bitterly. "Do you see what they see? A likeness of Karye, the woman who murdered their loved ones?" I blinked away the tears blurring my vision and finally turned, leaning against Ryke's body.

Kovi's eyes weren't pitying, as I'd feared they would be. He studied me as he always did, like he respected and valued me. Like I was strong and kind, a worthy empress. Not a weakling. Not a monster.

"I see Empress Jaliana, who has fought and bled for her people, and who dreams of peace." He stepped closer, cupping my face in his calloused hands. His touch was achingly gentle. "I see a courageous woman who loves and fights fiercely for everything she believes in."

I inhaled sharply. "But there isn't even a small piece of you that…doubts? That still sees me as your enemy?"

Kovi leaned forward until our noses brushed. "Not at all. There isn't a piece of me that doubts, because every piece of me belongs to you."

Once again, my eyes burned. "Kovi…I killed your father," I whispered, and immediately hated myself for the confession. Why was I intent on pushing Kovi away in this moment, when he was offering me the comfort and love my heart longed for?

But I'd hate myself even more if I kept that secret to myself.

Kovi didn't stiffen or jerk away. He didn't even hesitate. "I know."

It was me who pulled back, blinking at him in confusion.

"He chose his path," Kovi went on, before I could formulate words. "He chose violence and revenge, and maybe in that moment, with Nesrelle controlling you, you did too. But he would have murdered you if you'd given him the chance, if you hadn't killed him first. So no, I don't hate you for that. You are *not* my enemy, and you are *not* your mother."

Wrapping my arms around myself, I stared at the sky, studying the stars. "A part of you has to grieve him, though." I swallowed. "I…I am still grieving my mother, and maybe that makes me a horrible person, knowing what she was."

"It makes you human," Kovi said. "And maybe there's a part of me that grieves who I thought my father was, who I wished he had chosen to be. But he wasn't a true father to me. Your mother? It sounds like she truly did love you. That's more than I can say about Elder Ettonou."

Maybe Kovi let his mask drop then, allowing the pain to leak into his gold-flecked eyes, or maybe I was becoming adept at reading him. I reached for him, pulling him into my arms. "Can you…tell me about Rhi'il?" I prodded, hoping it was what he needed. It was what I would have wanted in those early days after losing Mother—someone willing to hold me and listen.

And so Kovi did, sharing stories that made me laugh along with him, that made me wish I'd known this friend who'd been like a brother to the man I loved. When Kovi asked me in turn about my mother, I haltingly told him about our dragon stories, about our rides on Reyva, and about the way she'd spoiled me, singing me lullabies and treating me like I was the center of her world.

When I finally succumbed to tears, Kovi held me as I cried, and for once, I didn't feel weak at all.

CHAPTER FORTY-FIVE

Lo

EVERY NIGHT WE'D STRATEGIZED AND conjectured what we would find when we arrived at the capital, and every night we'd come to the same conclusion: Nesrelle would already know whatever we planned. In spite of that, we'd decided Meli and her forces would infiltrate the underground tunnels, since her rebels were familiar with their layout and could bypass the city walls that way, pushing into the heart of the capital. With her truth gift, Meli was also confident she could share her gift to combat Nesrelle's army's ability to force visions upon their victims. Meanwhile, those of us who could ride on dragonback were to concentrate on taking out any enemies fortifying the walls, and then opening the gates to allow the rest of our soldiers entrance.

Of course, we didn't know where Nesrelle would place the survivors she claimed we could save. We also didn't know how we could defend against the nymphs and their power to drain magic. All we could do was pray that our own powers would be enough.

Whenever I'd considered what we'd find once we reached Inalgoth, I'd imagined Nesrelle herself waiting on the ramparts with her soldiers, an eager witness to the coming slaughter. I'd pictured a heavily fortified city prepared for a siege, bristling with angry soldiers and weapons.

Instead, when Inalgoth's silhouette appeared on the horizon, late on the afternoon of the fourth day, everything was unnaturally still. Even from a distance, I could tell there weren't any archers on the walls, no watchers looking out for us.

At least, not that we could see.

"She'll enjoy making us squirm," Jalie said. She and I were near the front lines with my father and our dragons.

On my other side, Caesiem went utterly silent, watching the city with dark eyes. Was he thinking about Revaed holed up in there somewhere, prepared to side against the boy he'd adopted as his own son? For the thousandth time, I wished I could take Caesiem's pain.

"After Karye killed Edi," I murmured, my voice loud enough for Kovi, Jalie, and Caesiem to hear, "she thought she'd destroyed me by forcing me to watch him bleed out." I fisted my hands, refusing to let my words tremble or the tears fall. Not this time. "She was sure she'd created a broken, obedient, terrified little slave out of me. But instead? She made me angry. She made me want to strike back, to fight rather than bow down. And that made me brave enough to retaliate."

When I met Jalie's eyes, there was no accusation or fury in her gaze. Only a hardened determination, an understanding. "The Dark Immortal tried to do the same to you, Jalie." My eyes flicked to Caesiem. "And the High Imperator…perhaps even now Revaed himself…they think they can force you into fear and despair.

"They've all tried to break us, but instead, they forced us to be strong, to survive, to fight back and overcome. They helped create us." I smiled, just a little. "So let's show them exactly what we are. Let's be the weapons they forged us into."

Jalie nodded. "Nesrelle said I was her executioner, her weapon." Her grin was deadly. "So be it. I'll be the weapon that stops her."

"Revaed raised me to be a deadly mage," Caesiem added, his eyes studying Inalgoth intently, "and that's exactly what I will be."

Ahead, Father spoke to his officers, breaking our army into ranks and organizing Meli and her fighters so they could approach the hidden entrances leading into the city. When he turned to his army, his speech was simple. "For our dead. For peace. For mercy. For freedom!"

The cry became a chant amongst the soldiers, until the shouts roared so loudly they reverberated in my chest. *For freedom!*

It was our way of announcing our presence as we surged forward, our masses spreading out to encircle the city walls. Caesiem sprang into Karos's saddle, wrapping his arms around my waist and enveloping me in his warmth.

"Nesrelle will hear us. She'll come," Jalie called from Ryke's back, as Kovi buckled himself into the saddle with her.

From her spot on Kova's back, Pauni'a flashed me a confident grin. Mio'e settled into the saddle's second seat, her expression full of grim determination. When she felt my stare, she gave me a single, respectful nod for good luck—her acknowledgment that we were allies now, fighting for the same thing. Vander, with his wind magic that helped him fly Jozek as if he'd been doing so all his life, pressed a hand to his chest. Behind him, Mhel smiled. "May Elhani go with us," he said.

Before we could launch into the sky, a groan split the air. I whipped my head toward Inalgoth's gates so swiftly my neck ached. They were opening.

In the gathering dark, the figures pouring from the entrance were mere shadows at first, difficult to discern. Then my eyes landed on the first too-small form, and then another. *Children.*

There were Forwyn and Alrenians, men and women and boys and girls of all ages, dressed in dirtied clothes and armed with weapons ranging from rusty swords to mere rocks. And they were charging right for us.

Nesrelle had sent the citizens we'd come to save into the battle.

CHAPTER FORTY-SIX

Kovi

"NESRELLE'S ARMY," JALIE BREATHED, HER eyes flashing as they landed on leather-clad forms lingering in the gateway, behind the oncoming citizens. "There they are, hiding behind their victims. They must be controlling these survivors with visions, making them think we are their enemies."

Fury pulsed through me, so powerful that for an awful moment, all my training and discipline fell away. There hadn't been any lessons on how to face an attacking horde of your own people, no advice regarding what to do when armed children charged you, their eyes alight with murderous intent. As our own army faltered, soldiers stopping their advance altogether and casting horrified glances at their fellows in arms, at a loss, I realized that someone was calling my name.

My eyes snapped to Jalie, who'd twisted in the saddle to meet my gaze. "Kovi!" Most of her hair had already pulled free of her braid, whipping around her face in the autumn breeze. The wind still reeked of smoke, and bits of ash trailed in its wake. "We need your magic."

I drew a deep breath, straining my ears for the undercurrent of song beneath the otherworldly screeching of the citizens, clashing their weapons together and clamoring for our blood. But I couldn't tear my eyes from the awful sight. The front line of civilians was mere yards from our own, hurling forward recklessly.

"Hold the line!" General Ilowhe shouted. "Disarm and defend! We are here to protect them! Do not strike to kill! Do *not*—"

The first attacker slammed into him with a scream of fury and a flash of steel. Chaos erupted. Everywhere, soldiers scattered, their efforts to parry and protect themselves hindered by their hesitancy to strike back at their enemies.

A cluster of leather-clad fighters encircled Meli, shielding her so she could concentrate on her gift. In her proximity, many of the citizens froze mid-attack, glancing about with glazed eyes, confused and lost as Meli's truth gift freed them from their visions. But even when they stopped attacking, they were still in danger, caught in the frenzy of the battle where other civilians lunged for them. Many were cut down where they stood before our soldiers could ferry them to safety along the sidelines.

And our own soldiers...they were falling. Elha'tonu warriors in their black leathers with their brightly painted faces, even as they wielded Elhani's magic. Warmth crackled through the air while they tried to help Meli draw the citizens out of the visions Nesrelle's army had them trapped within, or created invisible shields that repelled several strikes before they crumbled. Meli's rebels were piling up too, alongside red-uniformed Aerekni graduates.

All slain by our own. By the people we'd come to protect...

"Kovi!" Jalie's voice turned pleading. Only seconds had passed, but those seconds were like years on a battlefield, where fate chose who lived and died in mere moments. I was losing myself to an unfamiliar fear—the fear of being out of control, of realizing there was no good strategy. I was backed into a corner.

Elhani! I thought, leaning into the warmth building around me, the whispered hint of song on the breeze. Jalie clapped her hand over mine, reassuring and strong, and a surge of her gift pulsed through me, filling my blood. It granted courage to clear my head and dispel the horrors of the battlefield.

"Stop!" I shouted, but I could only control half a dozen people at a time. Those six heeded my call, though the chaos of battle nearly drowned out my voice when I ordered them to flee and find safety.

Jalie spurred Ryke forward, lifting her voice so Lo, Pauni'a, and Vander could hear her. "We have to stop Nesrelle's army!" She nodded toward the open gates. "If we end them, the citizens will stop attacking."

Lo gave a sharp nod and commanded Karos to follow Ryke. Kova and Jozek trailed close behind. The wind screamed in our ears, drowning out the din of battle until it felt like we were in another world, full of the roar of the air and the beat of dragon wings. It seemed an inopportune moment for my heart to lurch at the sight of the ground sinking far below us, but as soon as my fear of heights came alive, Ryke was already diving for the line of Alrenian warriors. Black scales marred their skin so effectively that many of them barely looked human anymore.

The first row summoned a wall of fire, flames bursting into the air and blocking our path. Snarling, Ryke dipped to protect his human passengers and dropped to the ground, the other dragons landing around him. The earth shuddered as Jalie and I unfastened our buckles and leapt from Ryke's back, our blades singing from their sheaths. Another blast of fire greeted us, but Vander was faster, lifting his hand and sending the licking flames back in a gust of wind.

Arrows rained toward us next, but Ryke curled around Jalie and me, shielding us with his scaled body. Alrenian curses rang out, followed by retreating footsteps. I darted from behind Ryke in time to see our enemies charging down the street, deeper into the city. A warning prickled along the back of my neck. Their numbers were small, and our dragons were unfazed by their powers, but retreating hadn't been part of this army's fighting tactics in the first battle for Inalgoth. They'd attacked recklessly, not caring for their own safety as they threw themselves at their foes. And they hadn't hesitated to plunge their victims into nightmarish visions so they could easily pick them off.

This time, they hadn't even tried to use those powers against us. Perhaps they couldn't control us with visions at the same time that they tormented the civilians.

But I didn't think that was what was happening. The eight of us froze in the city's entrance, studying the ash and smoke curling up from the street in the wake of the Alrenians' flight. The fading twilight sky cast the ruins of Inalgoth—the crumbled buildings, the scorched stone, the ash—in unnatural shades of purple and blue.

Nesrelle's army was luring us in.

CHAPTER FORTY-SEVEN

Jalie

PAIN LANCED THROUGH THE SCAR on my cheek when I stepped forward, grasping my sword hilt tightly. Those retreating Alrenian soldiers, those men and women who had pushed children into battle, hoping they would be slaughtered…they had been *my* soldiers once. I had been the one to lead them into making a deal with Nesrelle, forcing them to become these monstrous creatures. They reminded me a little too much of the nestrae that had tormented me after the battle of Aramith. Dark and scaled, with soulless eyes.

For strength and revenge and glory, they had become demons. Nesrelle's pawns.

It was my fault they were here now, threatening the people I had vowed to protect. I had to stop them.

Screams followed the soldiers' retreat, and horror raked its claws down my back. There were more survivors within the city, and Nesrelle's army was attacking them. I started to spring forward when a cry from Lo jolted my attention away, back toward the battle outside the walls. To where the other half of Nesrelle's army was pouring forth, out of hidden exits within the walls, and attacking the citizens our soldiers were trying to disarm and protect.

"We have to get the people out of there or it'll be a massacre," Lo said, her expression frantic. A memory of her using her dragon, Karos, to fly Forwyn children to shelter during the last battle flitted across my mind. I'd seen it, but I'd been too caught up in Nesrelle's voice to notice or care.

I glanced at our group. "Take the dragons and fly as many citizens as you can to safety." My tone turned dark, full of hatred. "I'm going into the city to help the other survivors, and I'm not stopping until every last one of Nesrelle's soldiers is dead."

Lo pressed her lips into a firm line. "Yes, but not alone." She turned to her friend. "Nia, you and the others take all four dragons. I'm not leaving the empress."

Kovi crossed his arms over his chest. "If you think—"

Lo raised a hand. "Of course not." She flicked her gaze to Caesiem before he could voice his own protest. "The four of us stick together. I have a feeling this is what Nesrelle wanted anyway." Spinning to Karos, she placed a calming hand on his snout. "Nia is a friend, and she needs help saving other friends. Let her ride."

Karos dipped his head, stilling to let Pauni'a pull herself back into his saddle.

Ryke snorted, pawing the ground like an agitated horse and leaning against me. "The citizens come first, Ryke. Save them, and then come back to me."

Mio'e glanced sharply at Lo. "Don't get yourself killed."

Lo grinned. "And to think once that would have been just what you wanted." Her face sobered. "May Elhani go with you."

As soon as Pauni'a, Mhel, Vander, and Mio'e were buckled into their saddles, the four dragons took off, circling over the battlefield and then diving low to attack our enemies and pick up citizens.

"Hurry," I urged, charging into the capital. My boots churned up the ash and dust coating the cobblestones, each footstep thudding dully in my ears in synchronization with the beating of my heart. The screaming of my people drove me onward. Kovi easily kept pace beside me, his steady presence helping my courage gift pour through me, warm and reassuring, as simple as breathing.

A rumbling sound was the only warning before rocks tumbled and the ground quaked. A tree root burst through the cobblestones, splitting stone. Unable to stop myself in time, I collided with the root and flew through the air. As I crashed into a heap, dust clouding around me, the breath heaved from my lungs. Coughing and blinking burning eyes, I staggered to my feet and squinted through the grey haze choking out the dying daylight. My chest ached, and the ash was smothering.

"Kovi?" I shouted.

A bony hand seized my shoulder, and I whirled around to face…Mother. Her eyes were bright and piercing, her golden skin untouched by the swirling ash. But just like every other time she'd haunted me, she reeked of decay, and congealed blood clung to the wound in her neck.

"You're not real," I rasped.

"Pathetic weakling." Mother's eyes gleamed with an otherworldly light, full of hatred. Even beneath my warm leathers, the hairs rose along my skin, and I stumbled back, trying to pull away from her. "I should have smothered you as a baby rather than let you become my heir."

I didn't want to be lost in my grief, not anymore. Not when I knew this woman had caused Kovi so much pain. Not when I knew she'd ruthlessly slain innocents. She'd been tender toward me, the daughter who was her pride, her legacy, but that side of her…that had hidden the darkness rotting inside.

But…she was also my mother. Hers were the arms that had cradled me when I'd had nightmares as a child. Hers was the voice that had filled my days with dragon stories and my nights with lullabies. She was the one who had taught me to fight, to ride dragons, to be clever and cunning. To wear my outfits like armor, to never shy away from protecting my empire, and to be a leader, confident and unafraid. The memory of her words had leant me comfort in my darkest days, surrounded by my enemies. They had been the ones that had kept me sane, grounding me in who I was and who I was meant to be.

I couldn't forget that, and so, even though I wished I could be numb, pain lanced through my chest at her words.

Courage, I thought. *Use your gift and push away this vision. It's not real. This is Nesrelle's army, preying on your fears and weaknesses.*

But Mother looked and sounded and smelled horribly real as she advanced, drawing a gilded dagger from her thigh sheath, tucked beneath her short dress. Bile rose in my throat. "I'm your *daughter.* You loved—you love me. You would never hurt me."

She scowled, her beautiful face twisting with disappointment and rage. "You're no daughter of mine."

She can't hurt me, because the dagger isn't real.

The first slice of the blade was too quick for me to dodge—a blur of movement—and even then, I couldn't pick up my sword from where it had fallen, not against my own mother. Even if a part of my brain understood this wasn't truly happening. It couldn't be.

The second swipe of her blade cut through the leather on my arm, the bite of metal carving a shallow cut beneath my armor and drawing warm blood.

My stomach churned. *The dagger is real. But that would mean…*

I lifted my eyes to meet Mother's, the exact same shade of blue as mine. There was no love in her expression, no remnant of the woman I'd known.

Somehow, my mother had returned from the dead, and she was real enough to kill me.

Caesiem

As soon as the nymphs' tree root sent Jalie sprawling to the ground, the courage gift she'd been sharing with us vanished, swift as the sun disappearing behind a cloud. The world instantly turned darker, as if the nymphs' presence was leeching the last dregs of daylight. Branches wound overhead, twisting through the ruins, crumbling stone and further destroying the once shining city of Inalgoth. They blotted out the sky, immersing Kovi, Lo, and me in darkness.

Up ahead, I heard Jalie shout for Kovi, and then…

And then I was standing in a condemned home in Teramyl, half-suffocating from the stench of rotting food and bloated corpses. The body of one of the plague victims sat hunched over a table, as if he'd simply leaned forward to take a nap. But he would never move again. Flies hovered everywhere, and I forced down the urge to vomit. My stomach was aching and empty, my body weak, and if I didn't persevere through the horrors of this house and sift through the rotting food for something halfway edible, I might pass out in the street. Maybe Elyxia or Jarex or one of the other orphans I lived with would find me, or maybe I'd lie there until I died, just another casualty in this hurting city.

I trudged toward the kitchen, where a second body was curled on the floor. It was difficult to tell if it had been a man or a woman, the corpse's features were so decayed. Flies flitted at my approach, revealing the worm slithering out of what had once been a nose. I shivered despite the heat of the day.

How many nightmares haunted my sleep after desperate trips like these? How many times had I wondered if my parents had met this same gruesome fate? And despite the fact that children rarely perished from the plague, how many times had I feared contracting it anyway and wasting away, my body slowly failing me, leaving me a grisly corpse?

I blinked and I was in the palace dungeons, the High Imperator on one side and Revaed on the other. *A traitor,* the imperator was saying as I studied the shackled prisoner in the cell. Long, greasy hair hung in his eyes, and I wondered how long the man had been imprisoned. He didn't appear to be a threat anymore, but Revaed's mouth was set in a firm line. If Revaed thought this man was dangerous, then I would trust the High Imperator's words.

He has been part of the insurrectionist group harming our citizens, the imperator explained. I'd seen the damages left behind from the insurrectionists myself: the destroyed businesses, the injured people, and the bereaved families.

A bucket of water was already waiting in the corner of the cell, a thrumming presence that wouldn't be ignored. I drew on it, the water rising and swirling in a hypnotic dance before it rushed toward its victim.

I already had a reputation in the capital. I'd heard the whispered words at court: *the imperator's executioner, the mage who drowns his victims on land.* And as much as each kill churned my stomach, I knew it was all part of my responsibilities as a future leader. As a mage who had pledged himself to the royal family and his people. I had to protect Teramyl.

Just then, something broke through my visions, a firm grip eliciting sharp pain that spread throughout my body. A part of my mind recognized that I wasn't in Teramyl, that these were all memories of the past. Ugly moments and fears that haunted me.

You're in Inalgoth, and Nesrelle's army is doing this to distract you. Focus!

But all I could see was the High Imperator's piercing silver eyes, the weight of his gaze heavy and terrifying. It reminded me of another terrible memory: the spray of blood and his young mistress's severed head after the imperator had discovered her in my bed.

More pain lanced through me, and this time, a terrible, yawning emptiness.

I realized in that moment that my connection to the sea seemed…duller. It was as if the call I'd heard all my life, even before I knew about my magic, was coming from far away. That thrum of energy, that constant pulse of the waves, that rush of adrenaline when I smelled the briny air—it felt and sounded quieter in my head.

My pain was intense, growing stronger by the minute. A piece of my soul was being carved out, slowly and deliberately, in a way that was both agonizing and heartbreaking. I wanted to weep, but I was hollow. I wanted to scream, but my tongue clove to the roof of my mouth.

When I tried to call on the water, my focus was weak. My thoughts were trapped in my own head, unable to connect to the element. Panic seized me, and the coppery tang of blood pooled in my mouth.

I trembled, helpless. Terrified. I knew this feeling, and I'd never wanted to experience it again.

My magic is being drained.

CHAPTER FORTY-EIGHT

T HE INSTANT THE INFLUENCE OF Jalie's gift winked out, darkness settled over the street, cloying and impenetrable. I shifted on my feet, trying to see…anything.

"Kovi!" Her cry sent my pulse racing, and I charged, trying and failing to see through the unnatural blackness to find the root she'd tripped over, to find *her*.

Instead, my boots pounded on cobblestones I couldn't see, echoing as if I were in a tightly enclosed space. No other sounds broke through but the rhythm of my breaths and my footsteps.

"Jalie!" I shouted, but my voice reverberated, whirling around me. Mocking me. As if I were the only one left in the world, forever separated from Jalie.

A chill raked up the back of my neck, warning me of someone or something behind me.

I whirled to find that the darkness had lifted enough for me to see someone staggering along the street.

Strangest of all, I wasn't standing among the ruins of Inalgoth any longer. I was on a narrow road in Hemlaen, afternoon sunlight glinting off blades as Aerekni graduates and Alrenian rebels clashed together in the middle of the city. The earlier silence gave way to the roar of battle. My stomach clenched when I noted numerous red-clad soldiers around me—men and women I'd trained with for three years and who were no longer alive. An ache spread through my chest when my gaze snagged on Rhi'il.

This is just a memory.

"Rhi!" I called, but my friend didn't break his concentration, fighting with his familiar grace and determination.

Everything was how I remembered it from that first battle in which we, the Forwyn graduates of Aerekni, had put our skills to the test. Except…I wasn't fighting alongside them. The battle raged without me as if I were a ghost, trapped in a memory that repeated itself endlessly. I was invisible and silent to everyone.

Until the figure I'd noticed before limped forward on a bloody, wounded leg. His eyes were glassy and dead, yet they were fixed on me.

I gritted my teeth, recognition pouring over me. This man was one of my first kills, one I'd wounded and left to bleed out. I spun as more footsteps approached—the garish form of the man I'd beheaded in this same battle, followed by the green-eyed woman I'd stabbed in the heart, congealed blood coating her ruined chest.

All three encircled me, their steps slow yet assured, more graceful than the dead had any right to be. They swung their weapons as one, forcing me to dodge and duck and parry. And then they were fighting in earnest, their movements precise and deadly and strong.

This is a vision, I reminded myself. Doubtless, the soldiers surrounding me were members of Nesrelle's army, using her dark power to wear the faces of the dead. Worse were the other faces that joined these soldiers, men and women that I'd controlled with my magic before they died, the ones whose deaths I'd tasted.

Fear hung over me like a cloud, filling my head until my thoughts turned sluggish. The clarity I normally possessed in battle, helping me keep my training close, reminding me of exactly what I needed to do to win, was falling apart. Everything I knew was disintegrating into ash as oppressive as the dust coating Inalgoth.

I slammed my blade into the nearest soldier, and as blood trickled from his mouth, his face changed once more. The wide, dark eyes and betrayed expression belonged to my best friend. Horror froze my insides as he collapsed. "Rhi'il!" I cried out, unable to stop myself. My limbs went numb, my sword threatening to fall from trembling fingers.

Not real. Not real. Notrealnotreal. It was so hard to convince myself of this truth while my best friend died, while I lost him all over again. Guilt slammed into me, raw and piercing, even sharper than the first time he'd passed. I'd failed him then. I'd failed him now. It was all my fault.

I almost didn't react in time as another soldier charged, taking advantage of my distraction. My defense was weak, but the screech of steel against steel when I parried the woman's blow snapped me back to the moment. To the twisted reality this army had immersed me within. I kicked the woman away and plunged my sword into her chest, and this time…this time I expected the transformation, but it wasn't any less horrifying.

Jalie's beautiful blue and gold eyes stared back at me, her full mouth forming voiceless words as she gaped. Heartbreak shimmered in her tearful gaze, and for a moment, I was certain it was my own heart that had been pierced. That I was the one dropping to the street in a cloud of ash, choking on my last breaths.

The soldiers leered, their strikes too fast for my grief-numbed body. Something clamped down on my arm, and I didn't even have the chance to fight back before a twisting branch curled around my wrist, strong and irresistible. Vice-like, it immobilized my sword arm, forcing me to toss my blade to my left hand. My enemies continued to advance. An attack sliced through my defense, leaving a gash down my side. Blood trickled over my skin—it was a shallow wound, but enough to remind me that my flagging strength could be deadly.

Limited to my left hand and pinned in place, I was more vulnerable than I'd ever been. Something pulled on my magical abilities, silencing Elhani's song. A chill swept over me, overwhelming and devastating.

The darkness settled more thickly, and I realized with painful clarity that this was it—the moment my enemies made my worst fear come to life.

They'd drain me of magic, and immobilize me with grief even as they physically hemmed me in. They'd steal all control and power from me. I hadn't been lying when I'd told Jalie, in a time that now felt like ages ago, that I wasn't afraid of pain or death. But I *was* afraid of losing control, of not being able to face my death like a soldier in a fair fight. Of having every ability stripped from me until I was helpless.

Of failing my people by falling before the battle was won.

Of never seeing Jalie again.

Of *this*—this darkness closing in, sapping me of all strength.

Lo

When Jalie's courage gift melted away, I prayed it was only because she was distracted, and not because she was wounded. Or worse.

But I didn't have time to lose myself in fear for my companions. When I glanced around, I realized with horror that the desolate ruins of Inalgoth had transformed into the rooms in Karye's quarters. Torches ensconced on the walls cast a dancing orange glow, a shifting atmosphere of light and shadow.

My blood froze in my veins. I knew this moment, knew this night, one that haunted my nightmares, waking and sleeping. One that filled me with failure and guilt and endless, yawning pain.

Panic flared, and bile filled my mouth. I couldn't face this moment again, couldn't live this grief once more.

Unexpectedly, Naina's voice echoed in my mind, like warm sunshine breaking through dark clouds. I blinked and searched my vision, but the rooms didn't change, and there was no sign of the motherly woman anywhere. I couldn't discern her words, and the sounds quickly faded while I searched the space again, finding it just as I expected it to appear. Karye was lounging in an armchair by an unlit fire, speaking with one of her advisors. There had never been many people she trusted within her own rooms, but this man had been one of them. And she was talking casually of...*killing*.

The tray shook in my hands despite my years of forced calm and discipline. My footfalls were silent—I was a mere whisper. A ghost. I flitted through the room and deposited the tray soundlessly on the side table, refusing to glance at the empress or her advisor despite the curiosity nipping at my brain. It wasn't worth it—I knew that.

"They're like...dogs," Karye said, her sneer obvious from her tone. "Sometimes they need to be put down. It also sends a clear message to the others—one powerful enough even for *them* to understand."

"Of course, Your Majesty," the man said.

"Don't hesitate to dole out discipline. It's our duty, as the Chosen Ones, to put these infidels in line." She lifted a pastry casually from her tray, as if she were discussing the weather and not human lives.

To my growing terror, I realized that I was rooted to the spot.

Leave. The. Room. I willed my legs to move. *She'll notice you. Leave. Now.*

Movement out of the corner of my eye drew my attention, and a small measure of relief flooded me at the familiar sight of my brother Edi, dusting the room. Karye didn't care that she had an audience of Forwyn as she spoke about murdering us—she probably preferred it this way.

The monster.

I hated her. Hated her for the way she callously slew slaves and incited fear. Hated her for the way she thought she owned us and could dictate our lives, making each day a living hell, an endless torment of servitude and terror. Hated her for the fact that she had sent our father away long before Edi or me could get to know him, and that she'd recently sold our mother too. Hated that she took joy in dismantling families.

And now…now she called us dogs. Infidels. She took sick, twisted pleasure in using and hurting and killing us.

Blind rage took over, and I lifted my chin, staring straight at Karye. I studied her sharp jawline and perfectly straight nose, the dusting of freckles tracing her gold-sheened cheeks, and her long curtain of golden hair shimmering in the torchlight. She was powerful and beautiful and utterly disgusting. There was no remorse in her gaze, not even when she turned her head, sensing my stare, and met it with her own cold assessment.

For a long, soundless moment, we glared at one another, and somehow, foolishly, I wasn't afraid. I stared death in its lovely face and longed to spit at it.

Then Karye was up, drawing a dagger from the sheath at her thigh in one smooth movement. Stalking toward me. Her gilded dagger, as extravagant and deadly as her, flashed in a strike to kill…and I was still trapped in place.

There was a blur of motion as Edi shoved himself between the empress and me. A sickening sound I'd never forget as long as I lived filled the air: flesh being sliced open. Collapsing, Edi gurgled as he choked and drowned in his own blood.

Hands shaking, I dropped to my knees, cradling my brother and screaming until my throat was raw. Laughter taunted me, danced around me, echoing endlessly. Karye's remorseless eyes watched me. Blood slicked my leathers.

My leathers.

This wasn't real. This was a vision, a memory.

Elhani, I prayed.

Courage fired in my veins. Naina's voice grew stronger, and this time, I could hear her clearly. *The darkness of your past can no longer hold power over you, because you are stronger now than you were in that moment. What once overcame you is exactly what you are capable of overcoming now.*

Edi's words from when he'd appeared alongside other guidespirits after my wedding ceremony echoed in my head. *We're always near, Lo.*

And then Elhani's declaration: *You are a world-changer.*

Determination flooded me, warming me from the inside out. The branches twining overhead shook, and the body I'd been cradling vanished, a mere figment of a false vision. When I lifted my eyes, it was one of Nesrelle's twisted Alrenian soldiers leering over me, not Karye. Dark scales snaked up his neck and along his cheeks, and his eyes were empty and soulless. I lifted my sword from the street, where I must have dropped it when I'd reached for my brother's imaginary body. Standing, I met the soldier's stare without fear. Elhani's song was louder than the pounding of my heart, the anguish of my grief, and the mocking laughter of the soldiers and nymphs scattered in the street.

I channeled his strength, letting it lace my words with power and magic. "Leave," I snapped. "Leave this city, crawl into a dark corner of this earth where you belong, and never torment me or my people again."

Several soldiers froze, including the man who'd been tormenting me, waiting until he'd drawn as much misery from me as he could before landing his killing blow. Their mouths went slack, and their weapons fell from their hands. Trembling, they stared at me like I was *their* greatest nightmare.

I took a step forward.

I am not afraid, and your darkness no longer holds power over me, I thought.

With cries that sounded more animal than human, the soldiers fled, racing out of the city, straight toward the army flooding through the open gate. *Our* army. Our dragons flew at the head, leading the charge. Pauni'a whooped and lifted a victorious fist as she dove low, knocking enemy soldiers off their feet. Behind the dragons, Father ran with Meli at his side. Meli's brow furrowed while she focused on her truth-gift, sharing it with those around her.

A groan caught my attention, and fear raked its claws down my spine. The nymphs were still closing in on my friends. Caesiem was only a few yards away, kneeling in the street, his eyes glazed over. A nymph had her webbed fingers splayed against his throat, her vicious green eyes wide with delight as she drained his magic.

I leapt forward, taking advantage of her distraction and slicing my sword in one clean arc through her neck. Her head teetered before falling from her body, rolling away in a cloud of dust. Caesiem shook himself out of his trance, shoving the body off and staggering to his feet.

My fingers shook as I dropped my bloody sword and unfastened the leather cord around my neck, draping it around his instead, letting his pendant rest close to his heart.

"Are you all right?" I demanded breathlessly, my eyes scanning his body for any sign of injury. But I knew the worst damage wasn't visible. How much magic had the nymph stolen? How much had she weakened him? I couldn't dispel the awful images of the dead mages from the forest in Teramyl, those hollowed-out corpses the nymphs had left behind.

With a feeble, crooked smile, Caesiem nodded, lifting a hand to summon the sea. It was a small wave, sparkling and twirling around us, but it was *something*.

Relief filled me, interrupted by a burst of flame from the Alrenians, and more roots and branches punching through the earth, slamming into buildings and crumbling stone. Screams rent the air as our soldiers were pummeled with flying debris or licking flames. Karos snarled and dove, tearing enemies in his powerful jaws, but our dragons couldn't protect everyone from the building fire.

My throat ached as the flames grew, the hot air making sweat bead along my forehead. The city was burning all over again. When I tried to reach for water, my connection was feeble, a tentative thread that could snap at any moment. It was Caesiem's magic that fed my own, and his well was almost depleted. Coughing against the swiftly thickening smoke, I raised my sword and, with Caesiem by my side, charged the enemies bearing down on us.

Caesiem thew a wall of water between us and our flame-wielding attackers, steam rising as the fire extinguished. I blinked against heat and smoke, water and mist, until forms emerged. Overhead, the dragons roared and dove, plowing through enemy lines. Behind, our army split the air with war cries, fending off nymphs and Alrenians, fire and earth.

There was no sign of the Teramese or of Nesrelle. Not yet.

Be the weapon, I thought, the memory of Karye slaughtering my brother lingering in my mind. Instead of weakening me, it strengthened my focus. She'd forged me into something new through pain and loss. I was different, braver. I knew I could face my worst fears, again and again, and survive.

Elhani, I thought, and his magic flowed through me, more powerful than ever. It didn't matter that my connection to the water was all but gone, not when I could feel him, could feel the guidespirits, could feel each loved one who had gone before me—Edi, Mother, Naina, Eloiyah—fighting at my side.

When I blinked, I realized I didn't just feel them. I *saw* them.

My eyes were drawn to Mother first, her form bright and strong, holding up a sword to fend off the soldiers attacking me. She glanced over her shoulder and winked. Then I found Edi, his expression confident and unafraid. Naina stood at my side as the battle raged around us, one healing hand on my shoulder and a patient, sweet smile on her lips to encourage me. Eloiyah was on my other side, her words like a song. *We fight with you, sister.*

My courage burned hotter than my enemies' flames. I sliced through them like they were nothing. Like they were mere smoke, vapors to be dismissed with a simple wave. Their attempts to taunt me with my fears were weak and insignificant, because there was nothing left for me to fear. Not today.

I am the weapon Karye created. I am the sword that Nesrelle forged.

When Caesiem turned to me, his blue eyes full of wonder, I realized that somehow, my magic was strong enough for him to see the guidespirits too. "Lo," he breathed.

The fear snaking through Nesrelle's army was a palpable thing. Their soulless eyes finally filled with something human again—raw terror. Their gazes lingered on the bright, immortal forms fending them off. Nesrelle's soldiers fed on pain and death, but the guidespirits were their antithesis. They were the souls who had faced death and won. They lived on, their spirits bright and strong, in the Golden After, untouchable by pain and loss and grief. They feared nothing, and they could not be killed.

They were everything glorious, the very spirits my army fought to honor. To remember.

And Nesrelle's army couldn't stand against them.

CHAPTER FORTY-NINE

I'D FINALLY LIFTED MY SWORD to deflect Mother's blows, but I was weakening, my body tiring. She was relentless, fueled by unnatural energy, as if somehow, in death, she had become stronger. As if a source beyond the grave powered her limbs, when death should have already devoured them with decay.

My body knew how to defend, how to duck and parry and dodge and dance. But I couldn't find the will to retaliate and strike a killing blow. Beneath my leathers, sweat snaked down my back. Warm blood trickled from where Mother had scratched me. It was a small injury, no more than a nuisance, but it was a reminder that I wasn't invincible. When Nesrelle's curse had filled my veins, when her dark powers had circled like shadows around me, I'd felt like I could stand against death and defeat it.

Now, I was fighting a corpse, and I was vulnerable.

No. You have your courage gift. The voice in my mind sounded impossibly far away, crowded out by raging pain and fear. My ragged breaths echoed in my ears; my pulse was a battering ram against my ribcage, attempting to break free. I was trapped in this fearful world where Mother glared at me, murderous and disgusted, and I knew I wasn't strong enough to defeat her. She would wear me down, and then she would kill me.

This isn't real.

Mother knocked my blade from my grasp, a harsh laugh scraping from her ruined throat. I blinked against the tears. She already thought I was weak—I wouldn't let her see me cry. I would face my death fearlessly, as she'd taught me. Even if she was the one dealing the killing blow.

Mother prowled closer, her mouth twisted in a sneer. "You've made this too easy. I can't wait to watch you bleed out, *again*."

Again. That single word nudged something in my mind, at the same moment that new magic flooded the air. Elhani's song swirled around me like a soothing embrace, a protective wall. I drew a deep breath, full and pure despite the ash drifting on the breeze, and renewed courage flooded me. The vision fell away, revealing the truth.

It was Daedra, not Mother. Daedra, with her pupilless eyes dark and gleaming coldly. Twilight had melted into night, with a sky blanketed in stars that washed my broken city in silver. It was eerie and beautiful, and it reflected off the black scales covering half of Daedra's face. Her leathers were smeared in blood, and I wondered how many citizens she'd preyed upon while stalking this city like a vengeful wraith. *My* citizens.

Rage curled low in my stomach, like a dragon coiling and preparing to strike.

"You really think you can kill me a second time?" I smirked, more confident than I should have been given the fact that she'd stripped me of my weapon. But something was making her hesitate, as if she could feel the courage emanating from me. The power and magic.

It made me feel unstoppable.

With a snarl, Daedra leapt as I ducked, slamming my shoulder into her torso. She grunted and fell back, barely managing to regain her feet. But I didn't retaliate, didn't even reach for my sword. I just shot her another cocky grin as a familiar shadow fell over us, Ryke's wing beats a sound I knew as well as my own pulse.

Before Daedra could do anything more than blink in surprise, my dragon dove low, his open maw consuming her in one powerful bite.

Glancing upward, I saw Mio'e's slender form on his back, just as Ryke settled to the ground. The young woman glanced over her shoulder, her dark eyes bright with victory, a smile on her usually grim face.

"Thank you," I said, extending a hand as Ryke stretched, leaning his side against me like a contented cat.

"Would you like a ride?" Mio'e asked.

I swallowed my smile and shook my head. "Not yet. I need to find Kovi."

"That's why you should climb on," Mio'e urged. "I saw an Aerekni soldier deeper in the city, and I'm pretty sure it was him."

Kovi

Magic collided with the darkness attempting to overtake me, washing over my body with light and warmth and power. Elhani's song was strengthening and sustaining, pulling me back to my feet.

"Let go of me," I commanded, and the air vibrated with the sheer authority of my words. The branch and the hand both fell away.

As the darkness cleared, I turned to find the battle raging around me. The nymph that had held me in her grasp stumbled back, sneering in fury and defeat.

My throat tightened at the memory of my kills, of how vivid my vision had been, but now was not the time to hesitate or let those old guilts assail me. I was a soldier, duty-bound to serve my people, no matter the cost. And the blood I shed was not innocent. My only choice was to kill, or to watch my people suffer and die.

I seized my sword and lunged, slicing straight into the nymph's chest, where her heart would be…if nymphs had hearts. Green blood poured from the wound, and she choked, flailing helplessly before collapsing in the dust.

When I assessed my surroundings, I realized that I was far deeper in the city than I'd been when I'd first been immersed in visions. Our army had poured into Inalgoth's streets, facing off against the nymphs and Nesrelle's soldiers. But we were being hemmed in by walls of flames.

A new cacophony pounded in my ears—the sound of countless boots beating against the cobblestones. The sound of more enemy soldiers approaching. A flood of dark-uniformed Teramese was charging through the capital, straight toward our bottlenecked forces. The gates slammed shut, their hinges groaning in protest.

Nesrelle and her allies had sprung their trap. They would burn and slaughter our army, and it would be a massacre.

Even with the dragons on our side, who were viciously tearing into our enemies, there would be no winning, not with the fire destroying the city all over again. The dragons could survive the fire, but they couldn't extinguish it. And despite whatever efforts Lo and Caesiem made with their water, or how Vander attempted to manipulate the fire away with gusts of wind, there was no stopping it, not completely. The greedy flames were growing, blotting out the sky with thick, overwhelming smoke.

Those who weren't burned alive would be smothered.

Time was running short.

Every part of me longed to rush into the fight, to join my brothers and sisters, to find Jalie and ensure she was all right. Instead, a nearby channel caught my eye. Even with the ash choking its waters, it sparkled under the remaining starlight that hadn't yet vanished behind layers of smoke. It shimmered, tantalizing, a reminder of the water nymph's words to me before Inalgoth had burned the first time.

All I require is a portion of your magic, she had said. *Pledge some to me, and your city doesn't have to burn to ash.*

Since then, I'd learned that the nymph's name was Sephrode, and she'd often worked as a messenger for Caesiem. He'd summoned her with shiny objects, from coins to buttons off his jacket.

I didn't know if Sephrode could be trusted, and I knew that agreeing to her deal was risky. What would happen if she drained me of *all* my magic? Did I even have enough left to give, after the hybrid nymph had already fed off it? Could this magical tie I had to Elhani and his power eventually…run out? Could it be severed forever? And what happened to me if it did?

But those questions felt inconsequential in the face of what was about to happen to my entire army. To everyone I cared about. Jalie. General Ilowhe. Mhel and Huvoki and Oru and countless other soldiers. Lo. Caesiem and Vander and Mio'e.

There was no time to wait and plan. I knew that, if he were alive, Rhi'il wouldn't have hesitated. The memory of his words rang in my mind: *All the best ideas are conceived in madness.*

Racing toward the channel, I leaned out as far as I dared. I might have been willing to risk many things, but I didn't think swimming with the nymph would be wise. Ripping a button from my jacket, I tossed it into the water, waiting, waiting.

What else had Caesiem done? Did I need a magical tether to the water to summon a nymph? My pulse throbbed in my ears, a discordant rhythm mingling with the roar of fire and the clangs and shrieks of battle.

Pulling on my magic, I tried a command. "Sephrode, come here. I need to speak with you."

Nothing.

My hands were shaking as I tore every single button off my uniform, hurling them all into the channel. My jacket hung limply off my frame, and in my impatience, I ripped it off too, tossing it to the ground.

I stood there in my undershirt, soaked in sweat from the building heat of the approaching fire—and my own desperation.

Nothing stirred in the water. Its murky, ashy depths made it impossible to discern anything at all.

"Sephrode!" I shouted.

At last, ripples traced the water's surface, and a head trailed by flowing white hair poked out. Sephrode's yellow eyes flashed as she bared her needle-sharp teeth in a smile. "I knew I'd be seeing you again," she said, splashing forward to set her webbed fingers on the edge of the channel, leaning in close enough that I could feel her chill breath on my skin. Her eyes flitted over my shoulder, toward the roaring flames.

"Your people are trapped and about to burn," she murmured.

"I know," I gritted out. "And that's why I need your water magic. I need enough to drown the flame…but *not* my people."

Sephrode's smile widened. "So you summoned me to make a deal? You'll give me some of your magic, to strengthen mine and save your army?" She settled a cold, wet hand against my cheek.

I swallowed, hating the helpless feeling crawling up my throat, hating the way it felt to hover over the water with this creature, wondering if she would pull me in and drown me. I had to remind myself that this was *my* choice, whatever happened. Sephrode wasn't in control, not when I'd accepted my fate. "What will happen to me?" I asked, keeping my voice level.

Her eyes widened. "I will try not to drain you entirely, for tearing all magic from a soul is an irreparable wound. It would kill you. It would be a shame to kill one as handsome as you." She blinked, smiling once more. "But I can't make any promises. Your magic is powerful and intoxicating." Her pupils dilated as she inhaled deeply, like she could smell the magic emanating from my skin.

Gritting my teeth, I nodded once, sharply. "Do it. But I swear, if you don't follow through on your word, if you harm any of my people, I will find my way back from the afterlife to tear you apart."

It was an empty threat, and she knew it. Caressing my cheek in a way that sent uncomfortable chills down my back, Sephrode hummed softly in the back of her throat. "I accept."

I squeezed my eyes shut and focused on Jalie. Elhani's song faded in my ears, a distant song carried on a fickle breeze. The thrumming and warmth of magic under my skin turned softer, the heat melting into cold. A numbing weakness seeped through my limbs. *This is it. She'll kill me, and I don't know if this will even work. I'll never see Jalie again. I won't even have the honor of dying in a fight on my own terms.*

A dull pounding filled my ears. Thud. Thud. Was that my slowing pulse? My chest tightened, like my heart wanted to give out, or my lungs refused to take in air.

No, I thought. *This* is *on my terms. I choose this sacrifice.*

I didn't pull away, didn't tear open my eyes. I welcomed the dark embrace. *For my people.* If this gave my loved ones a chance to live…I was at peace. *For Jalie.*

CHAPTER FIFTY

Jalie

A S SOON AS I SPOTTED Kovi's prone form on the edge of the channel, a soggy white-haired nymph hovering over him, I screamed my command. "Vorre!" Ryke didn't hesitate, plunging to the street and landing with a shudder that shook the ruins around us. Before Mio'e could unbuckle herself from the saddle, I'd already struck the ground, was already running.

I didn't pause to draw my sword. I just lashed out with pure venom, swinging my fist with all my might. It cracked against the nymph's face, sending her reeling into the water. She snarled like a cornered animal, her pale cheek already bruising as she glared at me with feral yellow eyes.

Ignoring her, I pulled Kovi's motionless form into my arms, shaking him. "Wake up," I pleaded, framing his face with trembling fingers. He was cool to the touch. "Kovi, *please.*"

"What did you do to him?" It was Mio'e voice, low and threatening. She hovered behind me with her sword drawn, studying the water nymph.

"He summoned me, and we made a deal," the nymph responded, her voice an eerie, sing-song melody. "If you want to be angry, be angry at him for risking his life for you."

Her words sounded truthful. After all, that was just like Kovi, to sacrifice for his people. For me. He was a man of his word, dedicated to protecting others. Every one of his actions since I'd met him had proven he was willing to face pain and death if it meant saving lives.

I squeezed my eyes shut and pressed my forehead to Kovi's, my mind whirling. When I laid my hand on his chest, I thought I felt it rise and fall, but I was terrified it was only my imagination, only wishful thinking. "Kovi, you *cannot* die."

Warm breath caressed my cheek, startling me into pulling back. Kovi's dark eyes stared at me, their golden flecks sparkling with mirth. "I wouldn't dare defy an order from my empress," he said, his lips curling in a crooked smile.

"Thank the Life-Giver," I breathed, throwing my arms around him.

"As touching as this is," the water nymph interjected, "unless you want to drown, you need to leave. Now."

Caesiem

The flames were closing in, the heat and smoke reaching unbearable levels. Salt stung my eyes as I met an enemy soldier blow for blow, all the while dodging attacks from a nymph. Branches tangled overhead, joining the smoke in choking out the sky, swallowing up all light until there was nothing but the orange glow of the fire, casting dancing illumination across everyone's faces.

My connection with the water wasn't gone—I could feel it still, calling faintly to me beneath the roar of the fire, but it was painfully brittle, like a frayed rope pulled taut. I wasn't sure if the nymphs' draining power would be permanent, or if, given time, I could recover my strength. Surely, the magic that lived in my blood, in my soul, couldn't be severed like this forever. Not when I still drew breath, still felt the pulsing of the waves in every beat of my heart.

Each time I pulled on the sea, only a pitiful stream of water answered my summons. Not enough to drown out the fires raging toward us. Vander circled overhead on Jozek, the dragon's silhouette casting an eerie shadow as my friend tried in vain to redirect the flames with his magic. Soon, the inferno was too great and closing in too fast. He was forced to give up, or only feed the fire's endless hunger.

Swallowing, I forced my latest opponent away and took a step back, surveying the scene. Our forces were dwindling, trapped. Lo's eyes met mine, frizzy curls escaping her braid and framing her face. Determination burned in her expression, but also fear. The magic she'd used to make those…guidespirits, as she called them…appear had melted away as exhaustion took over.

"The guidespirits are still with us," Lo whispered, as if reading my thoughts, "even when we can't see them."

My stomach clenched when I noticed a black wall advancing— more soldiers. The dark uniforms of the Teramese was a sight I'd been dreading all along. I wondered if they'd come to watch us burn to death, or if they were waiting to see if any survivors would slip past the flames.

Where is Revaed? It wasn't like him to hide behind his army. It wasn't like him to not be leading the charge.

"This isn't how it ends," I growled, seizing Lo's hand.

Smoke wove toward us, a swirling, consuming mass. The flames would be here in mere minutes, and there was nowhere to escape.

The water protects its own, I thought. *Sephrode. Someone. Help us!*

I didn't know if Lo's and my combined efforts worked. The quiet thrum of the sea didn't seem to change in any way, making me wonder if I was only imagining my tether to the element now. Maybe I was only wishing it still existed. Maybe my magic was gone forever.

But then you would be dead, a hollow husk like those mages in Teramyl.

A rushing sound broke through the roar of the flames and the shouts of battle. Churning. Frothing. My heart leapt—those sounds were as familiar to me as my own breath. A wall of water pummeled into the twisting flames, shrouding the world in mist and smoke.

Coughing, I pulled Lo behind me, charging for the nearest wreckage, a shapeless lump that had once been a stone building. Tangled roots and branches, thorny and wild, sprouted from its walls. All around us, our army was scattering, trying to flee the oncoming water.

We can't survive the fire only to drown, I thought. Determination flared to life inside me, bright and hopeful and strong. As the water crashed into nymphs and enemy Alrenians alike, sucking their forms into swirling, angry depths, I lifted a hand.

Back.

The water recognized me and heard my command. I stepped forward, Lo trailing my footsteps as I advanced, hand still lifted, mind still screaming my order. *Back. Back to the sea. Take our enemies and leave our soldiers.*

Swirling, foaming, tumbling, roaring…the water devoured flame and soldier, blackening with ash and debris. But with my command, it changed its trajectory, retreating the way it had come. Taking countless enemy soldiers with it, it crashed through the streets, dumping back into one of the city's channels. The rest wound like a wild river through the heart of the capital, twisting toward the shore, returning to the Great Sea. Beneath the night sky, it shimmered like molten silver, alive and vibrant.

Lo's fingers tangled with mine. "You did it," she breathed.

Already, our forces were recovering, charging for our enemies who had survived the onslaught. Mostly, the remnant consisted of the hybrid nymphs, whose tie to the water had helped them stand strong against it. Likely those who had been washed out to sea had lived as well, and they would swim back to renew their attack. But for now…

For now, the way was clear. My magic was back.

And the rest of the Teramese army—along with Revaed—was waiting.

CHAPTER FIFTY-ONE

Revaed

"WE SHOULD BE OUT THERE," I said, pacing the marble floor angrily. "Why hold back most of our army? Why lure our enemies to the palace when we can meet them at the gates?"

Lounging in the throne, Nesrelle brushed a fiery curl off her shoulder. "Think of it like a game of chess. We spring the traps and wait for them to come to us, where we make our final play."

I whirled on her. In the vast space of the throne room, my words echoed. Overhead, the glass ceiling permitted starlight to fill the room uninhibited, save for the growing smoke clouds snaking across the sky. The sight was ominous. "This isn't a *game*. And if you're burning the city again, my soldiers can be killed as easily as theirs." I fisted a hand and forced coolness into my tone. "Of course, you're only hoping for the greatest number of casualties. This isn't about victory for you."

Her eyes flashed brightly. *Mirthfully.* "That's what you silly mortals never understand. You fight against death, so determined to change fate and avoid losses. But no matter the outcome, I *always* win." She shrugged. "*Everyone* dies eventually. There is no defeating death."

I thought of my father and his sick desire for power and control. As long as I could remember, he'd always been that way, self-consumed and callously, terrifyingly cruel. Sometimes I'd suspected his own father had treated him poorly, that years of abuse had worn him down, chiseling him into a monster.

But what made an immortal relish chaos like this? What made Nesrelle choose to spend so much time dabbling in the affairs of mortals, living off their pain, when she had eternity? Surely we were insignificant to her. And yet…she focused on us, on our suffering. On our ends.

Nesrelle rose, her smile transforming into something hard. The brightness in her eyes froze to ice, unyielding and empty of anything resembling humanity. Her skirts flowed around her, rustling across the sleek floor while she approached, as graceful as the empress she claimed to be. "Yes, I relish your chaos. You may be insignificant, but your pain fuels my strength, and death is my gift and my curse. It is my great joy to watch mortal spirits be rent from their bodies, but also my unending torment to forever be forced to help set them free, to usher them along to the afterlife. Death is my responsibility, my *purpose*."

I stiffened. "Well, it's not mine. I'm here to save lives, to *help* Teramyl. I'm not waiting here any longer. I won't sit back and watch my soldiers fight and burn to death for me." I marched toward the doors, fury alight in my veins. I wouldn't be used by this goddess of death, wouldn't be her tool.

"And yet," she said softly, her words having the power to still my steps instantly, "you didn't argue when I first suggested you wait here. Why is that, I wonder? Is it because, deep down, your meeting with Caesiem rattled you? Because you fear meeting him in battle?"

In a blink, she was in front of me, leaning forward until her icy breath washed over my skin. "Will you choose the greater good and save your people? Will you kill him, I wonder?"

My throat tightened, all my words melting off my tongue, my breath stolen from my lungs. I had no answer. Ever since speaking with Caesiem, I'd been haunted by his accusation that I was just like my father. I'd doubted my every choice, my every move. To retreat and subject my army to the High Imperator's punishment was unthinkable.

But to fight against my own heir? My family?

That was also…impossible.

What choice did I have? I was a leader. It was *my* responsibility, *my* purpose, to defend and protect the Teramese. No matter what that entailed.

Nesrelle inhaled deeply. "And this is why your very presence is intoxicating." Her smile was twisted, disgusting. "You're fraught with misery. A walking tragedy."

She seized my arm, and in an instant, the throne room vanished. I opened my eyes to the scents of brine and smoke comingling in the air, to the sight of torrential water rushing through the city. Mist and smoke traced paths through the night sky. Nesrelle and I stood on the rooftop of one of the few buildings untouched by fire or the hybrid nymphs' destructive branches, studying the army advancing toward my soldiers…the ones that weren't being swept away in the sea that had come to shore.

My people, drowning on land. I knew whose work this was. A painful void opened in my chest.

"He didn't hesitate to kill Teramese," Nesrelle murmured. "I wonder: Does that fact make your choice easier?"

CHAPTER FIFTY-TWO

Lo

WITH CAESIEM AND ME ONCE again saddled on his back, Karos swept over the city, joining Jalie and Kovi astride Ryke. Pauni'a, Vander, Mhel, and Mio'e trailed us on Jozek and Kova.

Below, our soldiers raced through the soggy streets, churning up mud that splattered across their leathers or bright red Aerekni uniforms. Father was in the lead, blessedly uninjured and fiercely undeterred. Caesiem's magic had swept many of the Teramese away, but more met our forces in the streets. Their attempts to ambush our soldiers were thwarted every time by our dragons, who gave us a keen view of the city before diving low to attack our enemies with claw and fang.

But the greatest number of enemy forces surrounded the palace. As Karos soared high to where the air was clearer of smoke, I drank in the sight. Countless black uniforms filled the ruined grounds, littered with charred trees and rubble. The courtyard where we'd last battled was just as packed.

There was no sign of the slain dragons. Nesrelle's army must have dispatched of their corpses. I wasn't sure if that was a relief or not.

Continuing my scan, I found countless more enemies surrounding the buildings, which were blackened and crumbling, many with branches punching through them. The hybrid nymphs must have practiced their magic here to prepare for the battle. Or perhaps they'd simply taken joy in destroying the once-beautiful palace.

We were the first wave of attack against our enemies.

Karos sensed my emotions—a storm of anger and determination, fear and sorrow—and he shuddered eagerly, prepared to strike against the ones causing me this pain. Perhaps he, too, was remembering the slaughter and the dragons we had lost that terrible day.

Flicking my braid over my shoulder, I glanced at Jalie. Ryke flew abreast Karos, keeping near enough that I could be heard by the Alrenian empress. "For our dragons!" I shouted.

Caesiem's grasp around my waist tightened. I wished I could take away his pain, wished he didn't have to face his own people in a bloody battle. Or his own guardian. But he didn't hesitate to respond to my cry. "For our dragons!"

Jalie's blue eyes were alight with an inner fire: her determination and courage. "Whoever controls the dragons," she called out, the corner of her mouth curling into a smirk, "controls Alrenor! Let's remind these usurpers."

Karos unleashed an ear-splitting roar as we dropped into a dive. The wind whistled in my ears and tugged at my braid, ripping curls free to lash against my face. My heart pounded, thrilled and terrified. Karos's night-dark wings tucked tightly against his body as he fell faster, faster, letting his own weight increase his momentum. At the last moment, when I caught a glimpse of terrified sets of gold and silver eyes, Karos unfurled his wings and slammed directly into the front lines.

The noise was deafening, the sheer impact forcing me to duck low and cling to Karos with all my strength as he sent bodies flying. Screams were lost in the cacophony of landing dragons, echoed several times over as Ryke, then Kova and Jozek followed. Teramese soldiers cried out to one another in a panic, struggling to reform their lines. Archers shot wildly. Caesiem summoned a wall of water to sweep the projectiles away before they could strike their marks. More screams erupted as Karos attacked with his powerful jaws and teeth, snapping at anyone who came near enough to threaten his cargo with blade or arrow.

Soon, I was lost in the chaos. My whole world narrowed to the blood pulsing through my veins as Karos carved his way through the Teramese ranks, deflecting arrows with his scales. To the slice of my blade, falling again and again while I cut down any soldier within arm's reach. To the smell of terror and blood, death and ash, that overwhelmed everything.

When soldiers attempted to strike at his soft underbelly, Karos rose into the air. Then with a fierce cry, he dove and crashed into another cluster of enemies.

When the first cries from our own army reached my ears, I twisted in my saddle, finding my father leading his troops. My heart warmed at the sight of our mismatched ranks: Elha'tonu warriors and Elders, Aerekni soldiers, my sisters, and Alrenian and Forwyn rebels.

Ryke emitted a piercing cry and landed in the courtyard where Caesiem and I had been married, right outside the building that housed the throne room. Understanding Jalie's intention, I shouted to Karos, and we followed, dropping to Ryke's side. Clearly upset to be parted again from the woman he'd bonded so closely with, the emerald dragon swished his tail restlessly as Jalie dismounted. With a reassuring pat on Karos's side, I sprang down to join her and Kovi, with Caesiem right behind me.

"Go back and fight with the other dragons," I told Karos. "Keep our soldiers safe." I ran my hand along his snout in a quick goodbye, turning to Jalie as she urged Ryke to leave also.

The carved doors leading into the throne room were…unguarded. In fact, no enemies moved to stop us as we advanced toward them, and that fact alone sent a warning down my spine.

"Let's end this," Jalie said firmly, studying the doors with her jaw set. Her eyes flicked to me. "*Amara'rekni*, are you ready to take up your mantle again?"

I repressed a shiver when I thought of Nesrelle and her claim on the title of empress. Empress of Death. "Unfortunately, an Immortal can't be killed." I frowned at the blood darkening my sword. "But she can be stopped."

Beside me, Caesiem was unusually still. "Revaed is in there," he said, as confidently as if he could sense his guardian's presence. "Maybe he can be reasoned with," he added doubtfully.

Kovi reached the doors first, his movements graceful and deliberate, his expression calm and unruffled even with blood and ash smeared on his face. His jacket was gone, leaving him in nothing but an undershirt. I might have laughed to see him so disheveled, so unlike himself, if my mouth wasn't drying with fear.

"Let's find out," Kovi said, opening one of the doors with a creak, leading the way into the cavernous Great Hall. Unlit by torches or candles, it was immersed in shadows. Jalie followed, her proud stance revealing no hesitation, though I could only imagine how it hurt to return to her home and find it in ruins, occupied by the enemy. I stepped in next, with Caesiem taking the rear.

For one too-long moment, nothing but darkness and our own breaths echoing off the walls greeted us. Then the doors at the far end of the hallway swung open, and a line of soldiers stepped aside to welcome us into the throne room.

Jalie

The sheer audacity of the wordless invitation—as if I needed to be invited into my own throne room, sent rage pumping through my veins. Fingers curled tightly around my sword hilt, I stalked forward. My hair had come loose during flight, a tangled mane brushing past the grime- and blood-streaked leather protecting my shoulders. Every step of my boots was a drumbeat, an angry announcement of my presence.

I am here. I have come to take back my empire.

Nesrelle herself hovered by my throne, with Revaed at her side, appearing shockingly diminished, like he was merely her shadow. His violet eyes fastened on something over my shoulder—Caesiem. Before he could mask it, pain flashed across his features. *So he* does *have something to lose, after all.*

Clothed in dragon scale armor of ivory and gold, Nesrelle made a mockery of my heritage. Of *me*. "Welcome, little *amara*," she crooned. "How I've missed you." Her eyes traced the rune marring my cheek, almost lovingly.

I sneered, tightening my hand even more on my sword hilt to keep my grip from shaking. I didn't want her to see my fear, my reservations. Despite my courage gift, there was something positively eerie about finding her waiting in the throne room with only a handful of guards at the door and the Teramese usurper at her side. What new mind game was she playing?

"What do you want?" Lo spoke up before I could, joining me with Caesiem at her side. Kovi lingered protectively on my right, knowing better than to step between me and danger, but keeping close if I needed him. Always the ready bodyguard. Always my protector.

Nesrelle's mouth twitched in amusement, as if the sight of us was laughable to her. But I wasn't fooled. I could see murder gleaming in her too-bright eyes. "I can't speak for Revaed or the Teramese, of course, but…me?" She studied me thoughtfully. "I will call off my army—nymphs and mortals alike—and let you enjoy your throne if you do one simple thing for me."

I rolled my eyes. "I know better than to trust you. I'm not here to negotiate. I'm here to fight. And if you don't step away from my throne, then draw a blade and face me." I raised my chin and pulled myself up to my full height, even if the goddess of death still towered over me with her tall, lithe body.

Everyone else in the room remained terribly still. I had the sense that Caesiem and Revaed were barely even breathing.

Then there was a hint of movement—like shifting shadows within the darkness that pooled around the room's columns. Other enemies, lying in wait.

I tried to tune out all other sounds, all other senses, and focus on Elhani's song.

Nesrelle scoffed. "I'm not going to waste my time on you anymore." The disdainful way she said those words shouldn't have hurt, shouldn't have cut at my pride, but it did, and I hated her for it. Hated myself for it. She gestured to Lo and Kovi. "Think of all the lives you could have saved if you'd killed them when I asked you to. Your people wouldn't have had to suffer in Inalgoth. Your home wouldn't have had to burn and fall into ruins." She sighed with mock sorrow. "But you could still save Alrenian lives now." Her eyes darted between the two Forwyn flanking me. "You can still choose to kill them."

I gritted my teeth. "Absolutely not."

Lifting a cool brow, Nesrelle shrugged. "I expected you'd say that. Because you're weak."

She flicked her hand, and hybrid nymphs melted from the shadows, their luminescent eyes reflecting the starlight, their earthy shades of hair flowing long down their backs. They were all bark and scales and needle-sharp teeth.

The first branch slammed through the marble floor, splitting and cracking stone and blocking the double doors behind us. The next rose in the entryway leading deeper into the building, back toward halls stretching to rooms and buildings that probably didn't exist anymore. Ones that Mother and I had once walked together.

I shook off the memories and the prickling feeling running up and down my skin. We were shut in with Nesrelle, Revaed, a handful of soldiers, and some hungry nymphs. I closed my eyes to focus, letting my courage flow over me and counteract my fear.

When I opened them again, the nymphs were already racing forward on too-fast feet. And the world…the world was dark and different. Misty and grey and empty—and full of distant chanting.

Recognition struck me. This was the same place that Nesrelle had brought me when I'd nearly died. The same place where the nestrae had tormented me.

Nesrelle's world.

CHAPTER FIFTY-THREE

Caesiem

MY FIRST MOVE WAS TO step between the oncoming nymphs and Lo and put up a wall of water to fend off their attacks, but she'd already called upon the sea herself. It poured through a crack in one of the throne room walls, raining in a waterfall until it paused and hovered in mid-air, deflecting chunks of rock and the roots the nymphs drew from the earth and propelled toward us. A particularly large boulder splashed into the water, soaking us in a spray of mist, but Lo held firm.

I locked eyes with her, and I could tell by her expression exactly what she was thinking and urging me to do. *I'm fine. Go talk to Revaed.*

Turning, I barreled toward my guardian, who was frozen beside the throne, his violet eyes inscrutable. I must have missed the moment when he'd drawn his sword, but now he held it aloft uncertainly, his gaze focused on me. *Is he going to use that against me?*

Though I hadn't drawn my own weapon, I knew that didn't matter. Revaed understood—had always understood—that *I* was the weapon.

Did he think I'd come to kill him?

"Revaed!" I called over the clamor of the battle as Teramese and nymphs clashed against my allies.

As soon as I advanced, several Teramese guards rushed to block my path, determined to defend their emperor to the death. I held up my hands in surrender, but the foremost man sneered, his eyes alight with the fury of betrayal. "You traitorous coward. You will not touch the emperor." He swung his blade, prepared to cut me down, unarmed as I was.

I leapt back, sliding my sword with a hiss from its sheath and parrying his next blow. Each one of his moves was precise and forceful. While I dodged his guard's attacks, I caught glimpses of Revaed out of the corner of my eye. He wasn't coming to intervene, and he wasn't telling the guards to stop.

I sent a stream of water rushing toward my opponent and the two other guards closing in on me.

"Stop!" Revaed's voice was breathless.

I released my tether to the water, and it crashed to the floor, splashing harmlessly around our feet.

The guards stepped back uncertainly, studying their emperor as he stalked toward me, his stance rigid. "You *killed* them." His hands shook at his sides. I understood who he meant immediately, even if I wasn't sure *how* he knew. All those Teramese soldiers who had drowned when I sent the water back toward the sea.

"I didn't have a choice. We were going to *burn* to death, thanks to the army you chose to ally with," I spat.

Something flashed across Revaed's face, there and gone in an instant. "You chose the Forwyn over your own people." The raw betrayal in his expression chilled me to the core.

I wanted to scream, to remind him that we'd been over this already, that I chose *both* peoples.

The first strike of his blade came so swiftly, a flash of silver in the dim room, that I almost didn't block it in time. His sword slammed into mine with such intensity that the impact shuddered through my entire arm, rattling my bones.

Revaed's hair hung in loose waves across his brow, as if he'd run his hands through it endlessly, and there was a rage in his violet eyes almost akin to madness. Dark circles shadowed them, speaking of sleepless, haunted nights. His chest heaved as he swung again. Again. Advancing on me, the boy he'd once sworn to protect. His *family*.

With a strangled cry, I parried, joining him in this twisted, heartbreaking dance. Revaed's guards shuffled back, giving us space, understanding that this was *our* fight.

"I suppose now you're going to kill me too," Revaed said, jabbing low. I sidestepped and made my first offensive move, slicing for his torso. It was a slow, half-hearted strike, born of raw hurt more than an intent to harm. I didn't want to kill my guardian. I *couldn't*. "What will it be?" he went on. "Drowning? Or will you stab me in the back?"

His next strike was vicious, pushing me back, then back again, until I was retreating toward the far wall, the one with a huge, jagged crack splitting down its length. I met Revaed strike for strike, even if my chest was so tight I could scarcely breathe, could hardly force my words out. "I am…*not*…here to…kill you."

Revaed laughed, low and harsh. The light in his eyes was terrifying, unfamiliar. "You chose these foreigners over your own people. You want me to send our army back for the High Imperator to punish and kill."

"No—we can find another—"

"You *abandoned* us. Why would I believe anything you say?" He narrowed his eyes. "You're a liar, a trickster, a thief. I should have known from the beginning…you've only ever been on your own side."

"You're spouting nonsense!" I shouted, as Revaed swung wide. I ducked, and his sword clattered against the wall. He'd backed me into a cramped space…and now what? Would he murder me here?

I dared a glance over my shoulder, at the wide crack permitting silver light to pool on the floor. It was large enough to fit through, so I took my chance and acted swiftly.

Maybe Revaed had gotten one thing right: I *was* a thief and a spy. I could move fluidly, quickly. Before Revaed could strike again, I was leaping through the crack, landing in a wide, desolate courtyard surrounded by swirling ash and charred, broken palms.

With a grunt, Revaed joined me.

"We can stop this," I said, gesturing toward the city. The din of battle happening throughout the palace grounds and further down in the streets was duller here, letting the rush of the sea take up more space in my ears. It filled me with reassurance, even if I was tiring. I could tell my pull on the water was growing weak again, and I'd need time to replenish it.

"To retreat would be to condemn them all to death," Revaed said coldly, "but I suppose you don't care, do you? Alrenor is your home now. Who gives a damn about the starving citizens in Vicidor, or about the soldiers who will be executed if they return without this land in our grasp?"

Wind whispered, swirling ash through the air between us.

"What happened to standing up to your father?" I demanded. "What happened to building a new life for ourselves? You've become cruel and violent, justifying every choice by saying it's for the good of our people. But look where it's led them—straight to death. To this war. How many have burned in this very city? How many more are dying now, because you're too stubborn to listen to reason?"

Revaed froze, something unfathomable passing over his face. Hesitation? Regret?

"Are you going to kill me?" I demanded.

Revaed's nostrils flared, but before I could tell if it was with surprise or anger, the battle burst into the courtyard. A cluster of Teramese, Alrenians, and Forwyn were locked in a fight, circling around one another, sweat and blood dripping off them. One of the Teramese broke free when he noticed me facing off against his emperor. With a fierce cry, he crashed into me, forcing me on the defense. Two more rushed to his aid as additional soldiers charged into the courtyard. Revaed and I were pulled into the heat of the battle.

The beat of dragon wings thundered through the air, their riders guiding them to the throne room. Glass splintered and crashed as they broke through the ceiling, and my heart lightened. Reinforcements had arrived to help Lo and the others. I just had to keep fighting, had to survive long enough to join them. To ensure Lo was safe.

I fended off enemy after enemy, but more continued to spill into the courtyard. Somewhere nearby, Revaed fought off his own attackers, Forwyn and Alrenians who recognized him and hoped slaying the Teramese leader would hasten the end of this battle.

Blood stained the cracked cobblestones, and corpses piled up, adding to the debris and tree trunks I was forced to dodge and leap over. Three soldiers surrounded me, and I called on a weak stream of water, enough to envelop one of the men and drown him. When I tried to call on the sea again, my pull was too weak. Nothing came.

Gritting my teeth in frustration, I threw my energy into striking back at my enemies. But the trouble with my magic depleting was that it also taxed my physical stamina. My movements grew clumsier, my reflexes became slower.

When footsteps crunched on the ash behind me, the hairs on the back of my neck rising in warning, I couldn't react fast enough. I sensed more than saw the blow. I felt death hovering near.

I heard the blade strike home, burying deep into flesh as warm blood splattered across my face.

Lo

As soon as I deflected the nymphs' attacks with a shield of water, they focused their efforts on Jalie and Kovi. I lifted my sword to race in and help, but a chilly voice froze me to the spot.

"When I saved Jalie's pathetic life," Nesrelle muttered, "I thought my ability to claim one mortal life for an early death had been taken from me, not to return again for another full year. It's the way your precious Elhani limits me." She spat. "I can only take one mortal of my choosing early…the rest I cannot touch before their times have come. When I first met with you, I had to wait, had to let Jalie play the role of my executioner."

I spun to meet her vibrant blue eyes, assessing me with predatory intent. She wore a naked sword at her side, but she hadn't drawn it, not yet.

"But now," Nesrelle went on, stepping closer, "that power has been returned to me. Jalie broke our deal, and if not for your magic, she would be dead. My healing powers on her were undone." Her eyes narrowed. "I should have known choosing to gift life instead of death was a mistake. I should have left her to bleed out."

Nesrelle drew a gleaming dagger from a sheath at her waist and pressed nearer. I growled and swung my sword repeatedly in attacks she didn't even bother to deflect or dodge. Over and over, I sliced at nothing, my weapon singing through air instead of hitting her torso, her neck, her arms.

She was an Immortal, and an Immortal couldn't be slain.

"Halia told me she hurt you, once," I snarled.

Nesrelle's teeth gleamed. "You'd love to draw my blood, wouldn't you? Any damage she did to me wasn't lasting, as you can see." She shrugged carelessly, raising her dagger.

I stumbled back, my feet striking something solid and tripping me. I struck marble and rolled, finding myself facing Edi's body all over again. The pool of blood he rested in was expanding, scarlet staining the pure white of the floor.

"I could slit your throat like your dear brother, so you can think of how you failed to save him as you die."

The sound of beating wings was followed by the cacophony of breaking glass, so ear-splitting it sounded like the world was being torn asunder. I ducked, covering my head, as glistening shards rained from the ceiling and several huge forms landed in the throne room, making the floor shudder. When I dared to glance up, Karos lumbered forward, crushing a nymph beneath his foot. And on his back...

"Nia!" I cried, overjoyed to see my sister alive and here, helping us fight. Karos picked up his pace when his eyes landed on me, rushing to my aid.

Nesrelle only scoffed, holding up a pale, slender hand and brushing it against Karos's snout. My dragon snorted and reared back, kicking at air and roaring in pain and fury. Pauni'a slid from the saddle, crashing to the floor and just managing to catch herself on her feet at the last moment.

Fury sank its talons into me. "Don't you touch them!" I shouted.

Heaving myself to my feet, I lifted my sword and slammed it into Nesrelle's chest. Or what would have been her chest if the blade hadn't simply slid through air. I ground my teeth together and struck again. A part of me knew it was foolish, that I was wasting energy, but my vision was turning red with my rage.

And anger was better than grief or fear.

What once overcame you is exactly what you're capable of overcoming now.

Out of the corner of my eye, I saw a flash of steel and black leather as Pauni'a ran to me, her blade lifted. "Stay back!" I cried, raising a hand, praying my friend would listen. "Help the others."

I retreated as Nesrelle advanced again, near enough that when she leaned down, a stray red curl grazed my cheek. Again, my foot struck a body. Nausea danced along my tongue, but I couldn't stop the urge to glance down, to take in the vision that Nesrelle had chosen to taunt me with.

Naina, curled up and still...so still.

I bit back a scream and kicked. This time, my boot struck Nesrelle, but my feeling of elation vanished as she laughed, clearly unaffected.

My boot slipped in blood as I retreated further, and I didn't even have to turn my head to see Eloiyah's body out of the corner of my eye. My body shook and my vision blurred.

"Just as you failed to save them, you'll fail to save yourself."

Elhani, I thought, my voice sounding weak in my own head.

"Even Elhani himself cannot stop or deny me. Your life is mine to claim." Nesrelle licked her teeth, sharp as fangs, and when she darted forward, impossibly fast, I knew this was it.

"No!" Pauni'a screamed, throwing herself forward.

Between Nesrelle and me.

Between death and me, just as Edi had once done.

I didn't even have time to shout before my sister was collapsing, crumpled at my feet, blood pumping impossibly fast from her chest.

CHAPTER FIFTY-FOUR

Kovi

THE NYMPHS RUSHED FORWARD, HURLING projectiles toward Lo and me. I ducked and charged, blade at the ready, relieved to hear the rushing of water as Lo defended herself.

Ahead, Jalie cried out, wandering aimlessly through the vast throne room, away from the fighting. Even the nymphs ignored her, their luminous eyes instead pinned on me. *She's in a vision,* I thought. Nesrelle was making Jalie suffer, drawing out her misery, and the nymphs knew to wait, to attack later after the Dark Immortal had her fun.

A furious, all-consuming need to race to Jalie's side and protect her, to destroy anything in my path, burned through me. Though my magic was weak and Elhani's song still distant after Sephrode had drained so much, my mind knew what to do. I was a soldier honed for battle, after all.

When a thorny branch flew at me, I sliced it in half. When a nymph split the very floor at her feet and hurled a chunk toward me, I dove and rolled forward, dodging the crack in the floor. When another nymph hissed, launching at me with fangs and teeth and flying blue hair, I severed her arm before she could claim more of my magic. She stumbled back, and my next strike punched through her gut.

I was moving again before her body struck the floor. The next nymph tried throwing more projectiles my way, all of which I ducked or deflected with my blade. When twisting vines burst through the floor to tangle around my feet, I cut through them and kept running. The nymph snarled her frustration and charged, swift enough to evade my swing and drag her nails down my arm, tearing through skin and drawing blood. I kicked her away and followed up with my sword.

The next two nymphs died similarly, unable to counter me, not when adrenaline and iron-willed purpose flowed through my veins. Nothing could keep me from Jalie.

Glancing up from my final kill, I realized there were no longer any enemies between her and me.

"Jalie!" I called, but she couldn't hear me, lost as she was in her vision.

It took all my focus to draw on Elhani's power this time. Every ounce of my energy, until I feared I'd weaken and crumple to the floor. *Not now. Hold on, for Jalie.*

Understanding clarified in my mind, as if Elhani were there, explaining the tie I'd formed with Jalie. The one that had allowed us to see one another across the miles. The one that even now endured, letting me know that this vision she was trapped in couldn't keep me apart from her. Where she went, I could go too.

Our connection was as strong as the love that tethered us. It was born of a tie that had once been a torment to us both, one that had forced me to endure her emotions. But it had transformed into something beautiful and even more powerful after she'd nearly died. Now, it was something I chose. It was a new manifestation of my magic.

Elhani, I prayed, *take me to her. Let me be where she is.*

Jalie

The nestrae never showed themselves, but they never stopped chanting either. Mist wound past like twisting snakes, cool and grey, concealing the Life-Giver-knew-what. With each hissing word from the nestrae in their language, the rune on my cheek sparked with pain, until agony swept through my entire body, and I crumpled to the ground.

Groaning, I fought back tears as my knees struck the earth and a shudder wracked through me. My mouth tasted of dirt and blood, reminding me of the moment I had been plucked from death by Nesrelle's hand. Maybe this was her way of returning me to the place I belonged. Her reminder that I'd cheated death—cheated *her*—and I never should have survived. Not the first time, and certainly not the second, despite Lo's hard work and magic.

When the pain finally abated enough for me to lift my chin and stagger to my feet, the world had changed once more. Now, Inalgoth spread out before me, burning all over again. My people screamed in horror and rage as Alrenians sporting dark scales—soldiers that should have been there to protect them—tormented them with visions or attacked them with fire and blades. Everywhere, innocent citizens were cut down. There was weeping, screaming. Blood and bodies and relentless flame filled the streets. Once-beautiful homes crumbled into ash, stone charred with the sheer strength of the heat raging through the city, and the channels reflected it all until they were as red as blood.

This time, my tears were for my guilt, my part to play in all of this. I'd been foolish to trust Nesrelle.

Bodies appeared all around me…the dead I'd killed with my own hands, like Yaelti and Lady Leanai, and others that were strangers, those who'd died because of my decisions. Sweat trickled down my skin. If it hadn't been for me, my people wouldn't have been slaughtered. My city wouldn't have burned. My palace, my *home*, wouldn't have been destroyed. And maybe…maybe if I'd followed a different path, even the dragons could have been saved from Revaed and his soldiers.

I couldn't stop the tears. This was what Nesrelle wanted—to feed on my misery and grief before she ultimately killed me. Would she set her nestrae on me? Would she send someone else bearing my mother's face? I shivered, covering my eyes to block out the bodies of the dead, staring back at me with their empty gazes. Trying to shut out the searing sight of my ruined city.

This would be a fitting end, I thought.

Revaed

Blood. Chaos. Death. Ash. The city reeked of it, and my heart wouldn't stop pummeling my ribcage and throbbing in my temples.

Defective. Worthless. Pathetic. My father's cutting words spiraled endlessly through my mind, a constant reminder of the way that family betrayed, and those who were meant to love you would hurt you the most. It shouldn't have come as a surprise that Caesiem had done the same and had turned his back on me.

And yet, his words kept ringing in my ears. The way he'd compared me to the High Imperator, the way he'd reminded me of the countless Teramese lives that had been lost.

And his question: *Are you going to kill me?*

My back ached with phantom pains from the lashes I'd taken for him. My vision burned with the searing memory of the mages I'd killed to protect him.

Kill him?

I had to get to him, to talk to him. To explain…

When I finally shoved away yet another attacking Alrenian, adding to the bodies in the courtyard—*meaningless, all of this is meaningless, just more endless death that never solves anything*—I spun to find Caesiem surrounded. He was valiantly fending off three attackers, but another

Teramese man was sneaking up on him.

I charged, every instinct fixated on this one purpose, the one thing I'd spent the last ten years doing. Perhaps the only thing I'd ever done well. Protecting Caesiem.

The flashing steel was faster than me, a sharp punch in the side. But I barely registered it, my adrenaline pounding wildly. As the man reared back with his bloody dagger, I lifted my sword and narrowed my eyes. For one instant, shock and horror registered on his face. His own emperor, the man he'd thought he was defending, had turned against him.

"You will not harm the prince," I snarled, and sliced my sword through his neck.

There was a wet thud as his head rolled away, and another as his body followed, but I didn't stop to notice it. Didn't linger on that disgusting sight and didn't focus on the warmth that was trickling down my forehead from the spraying blood. I whirled to stand side-by-side with Caesiem and fend off his attackers.

At the sight of me, one retreated, but a woman narrowed her eyes in defiance, likely incensed by the fact that I'd taken Caesiem's side. A pity—for her.

Dark spots flashed across my vision when I swung my blade. My mouth was dry. Too dry.

"Revaed," Caesiem said, his voice echoing in my head. Too close and too far away all at once.

He finished off the woman as I staggered back, weakness spilling throughout my limbs.

"Revaed," Caesiem repeated, his voice turning urgent.

I blinked at him, lifting my hand to brush a wayward lock of hair off his forehead.

"You're hurt," he said, sorrow and fear pooling in his eyes. "I'll call for a healer."

It reminded me of how furious he'd been when he'd seen the lashes

I'd taken for him. I reached down, pressing against the bleeding wound in my side, the one that still didn't hurt. There was only numbness, and a spreading cold.

I didn't regret it. Didn't regret a single thing I'd done for Caesiem, the only family I'd ever had. I'd been a fool to think I'd ever choose anything else, to ever lift a sword against him.

Opening my mouth, I tried to speak around the dryness. Tried to blink my eyes against the gathering blackness to better see his face. But it was growing dark, and I was falling.

"Caes, I—"

Caesiem

Mere seconds and terribly long years all passed at once. I was trapped in this moment, the one where the man who'd been my guardian, my teacher, my defender, my *home*, for ten long years collapsed and went still in my arms.

His violet eyes froze on some distant point I couldn't see.

A single tear escaped and trailed down my cheek, the only sign of an emotion beyond the terrible emptiness spreading through my chest.

He'd saved me. He'd died for me.

"I'm so sorry," I choked out, thinking of every angry word I'd said, wishing I had one more minute to take them all back. This final act of his, more than his anger and hurt and betrayal, told me without a doubt that he'd loved me, that he never would have harmed me, just as I never would have hurt him.

Vaguely, I was aware of the chaos around me going quiet. There were more dead bodies surrounding me than living ones, and the living were mostly my allies, or Teramese who'd laid down their weapons at the sight of their fallen emperor.

An emperor who, in the end, had chosen to fight for *me*.

A warm hand settled on my shoulder, and I startled. "Caes." Vander's voice. Vander, who had landed his dragon in the remnants of the garden nearby and joined the fight in the courtyard. "I'll…watch over his body," he said haltingly. "Go to Lo. Make sure Nesrelle is stopped."

His words jolted me back to the present. I glanced toward the jagged crack in the wall of the throne room and stood. Shaking out my hands, coated in blood and aching from how tightly I'd clutched at Revaed's jacket, I picked up my sword.

Lo was all I had left now.

And if Nesrelle had so much as touched her, I didn't care if she was an Immortal or not. There would be hell to pay.

CHAPTER FIFTY-FIVE

Lo

NIA!" I SCREAMED.

For one awful instant, we stared at one another, immobile. Pauni'a knelt before me, one hand pressed to the wound in her chest. Blood poured down her front, slicking her leathers, and her eyes were afraid and pained. She opened her mouth, red bubbling.

Then she fell face first on the floor.

Edi. Naina. Eloiyah.

How many times would I fail to save the ones I loved?

"No!" I screamed, tears of fury spilling down my cheeks. "Not again. Not you. *Nia!*" I pulled her body into my lap, my shaking fingers gently brushing the braids back from her face. Her amber eyes were open and unseeing, a cruel reminder that my best friend, my sister, was no longer here.

Behind me, Nesrelle laughed. "Maybe this is even better." She laid a cold hand on my shoulder. "How does it feel to fail again?" Her voice dipped low, turning into a growl. "But this wasn't my kill—only an accident. The Life-Giver said I can *choose*, and he cannot deny me that."

I couldn't move, too stunned, too horrified, to react to her words. A jolt of pain was my only warning. I glanced down, seeing blood pouring down my chest, reminiscent of the blood that had spilled from my sister. A blade pierced my back, cutting through leathers and skin, tearing into organs. My chest seized, and I was certain Nesrelle had struck a lung.

My vision blurred. But I wasn't afraid. I was angry.

With the last shreds of my strength, I screamed again, but this time, it wasn't full of helplessness. It was one word, full of power and magic and strength.

What once overcame you is exactly what you are capable of overcoming now.

"Elhani!" My voice bounced off the columns, echoed through the vast throne room, and vibrated the very air. It was loud enough to roar through the open ceiling, out into the night. Perhaps loud enough for the entire bloody city to hear.

Fight for your people. Fight for the ones we've lost. The broken, the hurt.

As Elhani's name repeated endlessly, it wasn't just my voice echoing. It gained supernatural strength, until I could hear thousands of voices joined with mine. Every Forwyn, living and dead, who'd wept, who'd suffered, who'd lost and grieved—I heard them. My cry had become every prayer, every plea, every wish, every hope of every one of my people. It was our heartbreak and our dreams. Our need for justice, our longing for mercy.

Elhani.

Hear us. Fight for us.

Nesrelle tore the blade from my back, and her cold grip vanished. I teetered on my knees as hot blood spilled, fast…so fast. It was too much, but I was too enthralled by a new sound, by thunderous approaching footsteps, to even heed my own imminent death.

I had to hang on for a little longer, because he was coming. He was fighting for his people.

World-changer, he'd said. I'd had enough love and determination within me for this one last great act of magic to call upon my god before I passed.

The branches blocking the entry doors shuddered, again and again. With a final quake, they split and broke away, twisting and receding past the broken marble floor and into the earth. The doors flew open, slamming so hard against the walls that the stone cracked ominously.

In the entrance stood a single cloaked figure.

Power, warm and overwhelming and terrifying, sizzled through the room, stronger than the fire that had raged in the city streets. More powerful than the water that had drowned it out.

Awe chilled my skin as Elhani drew back his hood and unsheathed his sword in a deliberate, fluid motion.

Nesrelle hissed.

And then, the two Immortals collided. Steel flashed and the entire room shook as they fought, every movement swift and powerful. It was a breathtaking dance, violent and furious. Despite the numbness flowing through me, I could sense the hairs on my arms prickling as I watched, unable to tear my gaze away. Even the air crackled, as if abuzz with the threat of a lightning strike.

Weakening, I collapsed, curling around Pauni'a's body and cradling her to me, all while my own blood pooled and mingled with hers. But still, I watched Elhani and the Dark Immortal locked in their battle.

Nesrelle's beautiful face had melted into something hideous and deathly. Translucent skin stretched over her skull, while soulless black eyes peered out. Her teeth were like fangs, and it took me a moment to realize she wasn't attacking with her sword anymore. Instead, she was swiping with her arms, clawing at Elhani with fingernails that had turned into long, deadly-sharp weapons.

But the cloaked man, despite his simple appearance and travel-stained clothes, was untouchable. Not a single wound marred his body when he tossed his own blade aside with a clatter and slammed his palm into Nesrelle. It struck her neck, snapping her head back and sending her flying directly into the throne.

A splitting sound rent the air as she hit, the sheer force of her fall cracking the throne, sending half of it spilling to the floor. In a defeated, grotesque heap, she panted and glared at him, her face murderous.

"Send them away," Elhani said in a quiet, rumbling voice. The sheer command in it was so magnetic that it even gave me the urge to stand and do his bidding.

Nesrelle snarled, baring her teeth.

"Call off your army. Send them from here. Retreat to a new shadowy corner of the earth and spread your torment there."

For a long, tense moment, the pair stared at one another. The man stood firm and unyielding, while Nesrelle slowly curled in on herself, cowering. In another blink, she'd vanished.

"Lo!" Caesiem's voice was ragged, like he'd been screaming.

I wanted to sit up, to turn and find him as his footsteps raced to me, but the darkness was closing in. It was so cold.

I love you, I tried to say, as his warm hands cupped my face, as his bright, tear-filled eyes locked on mine. I wasn't sure if my lips even moved. The chill had spread until I couldn't feel my limbs, couldn't tell what my own body was doing. My breaths snagged in my chest with every rise and fall of my struggling lungs.

"Stay with me, Lo. Please. Elhani!" Caesiem was screaming, but the sound was fading.

I didn't want to stop drinking in Caesiem's beautiful face, but my eyelids were heavy. Slowly, I let them close, and sank into blackness.

CHAPTER FIFTY-SIX

JALIE." KOVI'S VOICE WAS AS warm as his arms as they snaked around me, pulling me close, snapping me out of my trance. I choked on a sob, too terrified to open my eyes and look over my shoulder to find that this was another cruel trick. My body trembled, and he held me tighter, until I could feel his solid heartbeat against my back. His breath tickled my ear when he leaned in, strong and grounding. "It's not real. Breathe. In, out."

Swallowing, I focused on his words, letting them wash over me the way they had back when he'd first rescued me from my grief, back when he'd carried me away from an execution. Now, he was saving me from myself. Maybe that's always what he'd done, offering me freedom. Escape.

When I finally opened my eyes, the mist and darkness and visions of death were gone, replaced with a broken throne room full of tangled roots and branches and shattered glass. But the ache remained. I couldn't undo the past or bring back the dead.

"It *is* real," I managed at last, my voice hoarse, my cheeks hot and sticky with tears. Kovi didn't let me go. "All this death, all this destruction, is my fault. That dark place might have been a vision, but everything she showed me…that is a darkness I'll always carry with me."

I faced him, and he brushed back a strand of my hair with such gentle fingers I thought my heart would break. "Then I'll walk through the darkness with you."

Throwing my arms around him, I blinked away the last of my tears, before remembering where I was. In a throne room, with real enemies. I pulled away, scanning the space, but the only nymphs left were corpses. Even the Teramese had vanished, no bodies to be found. The throne itself was cracked, and Nesrelle was gone.

On the other side of the room…Caesiem was crying out, cradling a motionless Lo to his chest. There was blood…so much blood.

I seized Kovi's hand and leapt to my feet, but I didn't need to pull him along. He ran beside me, desperate to reach our friends. Desperate to see that this was just another vision, another trick.

Not the truth.

Caesiem

Kovi and Jalie reached me first, kneeling next to me, their eyes questioning and then turning…sorrowful.

I refused to acknowledge the grief in their expressions. Their mouths moved, but I couldn't make out the words.

Glancing past them, I studied the cloaked man lingering by the broken throne. He approached slowly…so slowly. I wanted to scream at him to run, to hurry. Surely this man that Lo had called upon—Elhani himself, the god she had dedicated her life to—could save her. She had given him so much. Surely he could give her this one thing.

My arms shook as I held her against my chest, ignoring the warm, sticky blood on my hands and leathers, mingling with Revaed's. I couldn't lose another person I loved today. I *wouldn't*.

Lo was too vibrant, too full of life and love. This world needed her. *Don't take the only good thing left in this world,* I thought, unable to find the strength to plead those words aloud. Tears snaked down my cheeks and beaded in Lo's hair, in her frizzy, perfect curls.

"I'm so sorry, Caesiem."

I couldn't lift my head, couldn't meet the eyes of the man standing over me. His voice was deep and rich, yet it was steeped in a sorrow all too familiar. He mourned with me, that I could tell.

But it wasn't enough.

"You have to save her," I ground out. "You can't…" My words trembled, and I cast around helplessly for answers. For a rope that I could grasp, one that could tether me to land before I sank into an endless, raging ocean. One unlike any I'd ever known before—hostile and strange, different from the water that protected me.

Without Lo….

Without her…

I couldn't fathom a future without her in it. There was only darkness, and a yawning, aching void stretching on without end.

"Nesrelle craves death and sees souls into the afterlife, but her power is limited. She has enough to take one life each year on earth, her one chance to send a soul away before their time. Her strike against Pauni'a was an accident. But Lo…she chose her, and that is a kill that cannot be undone. I'm sorry."

His words were meaningless. When I glanced up into those brown eyes, so full of ageless wisdom, I couldn't find comfort. He reached for me, but I shook with repressed sobs. I refused to cry another tear. Not when Lo could be saved. She *had* to be.

"Caesiem…"

"Is there really *nothing* that can be done?" I demanded.

The man's face turned solemn, something flashing in his dark eyes. "Nesrelle." It was a summons, a single word that could not be ignored.

Nesrelle herself appeared in an instant, still clothed in her dragon scale armor. Each one of her red curls was sleek and perfect, not a single one out of place. As if the battle had never happened.

Her grin was wide as she studied me, like she already knew why Elhani had called for her. If I'd had room to feel anything else but loss, I might have been afraid.

But all I could feel now was a devastating emptiness.

Nesrelle

Mortals didn't like to believe my claims. They drowned themselves in absurd denial and false hope. They clung to their goodness or their strength or their sheer stubbornness to fuel the lies they told themselves.

That they could fight against death. That they could be victorious.

But it was all for naught, every time. They might find temporary triumphs, spurning death for a short while and extending their lives a few additional, transient years.

In the end, though, I always won.

I always came for them.

And yet, this time was different. I studied the two bodies on the floor, the way I'd managed to find a loophole in my power's limitations and claim not just one life, but two. The tragic Teramese prince cradled one against him, as if he could bring Lo back to life with his sheer willpower. I sneered.

Still, his determination counted for something. He was prepared to do anything, give up anything, to save the woman he loved.

He'd always been filled with a delicious sort of pain, forever lonely and haunted with questions about his parents' deaths. Even when the Xalenoses had taken him in, he'd been wracked with guilt when he'd killed for them. Darkness lived and breathed within him, an endless, glorious well for me to feed upon. Now, along with the loss of Lo, he was aching with the casualties his people had sustained, with his own guardian's death, and with his fear that he would never be able to save the Teramese from their suffering.

Mortal lives were pathetically short. He would suffer immensely from grief, especially without Lo, but then he would die, and that misery would vanish with him. Or…

Or I could take this chance to feed on his pain forever.

My grin stretched as I lifted my face toward Elhani, the Life-Giver. I couldn't look him directly in the eyes—he radiated *life*, an aura as grating and agonizing to me as pain and despair were intoxicating—but I could see enough of his face to recognize his reservations. He didn't want to let me offer Caesiem this deal, but the very laws of this world demanded that he be fair. He had to let the boy know all his options, which is exactly why he'd called me here.

This was Caesiem's choice to make.

And either way, I won.

Caesiem

"I could undo her death and accept a sacrifice in her place," Nesrelle said, her eyes bright and greedy.

It wasn't a question. I couldn't live without Lo, and the world needed her. "I'll do it."

Elhani lifted a hand. "She doesn't mean that she'll kill you in Lo's place," he explained.

"I mean that Elhani has the power to make you an Immortal," Nesrelle went on proudly, tossing a strand of her hair over one shoulder. "You would be duty-bound to help souls into the afterlife, as I am." Her smile was vicious. "A Prince of Death."

I frowned. "And…Lo would live?"

Sorrow etched lines across Elhani's brow. Kovi and Jalie were frozen, silent, staring at me with horrified eyes. But I ignored the weight of their gazes, refused to let their silent pleading influence me.

"Lo would live," Nesrelle responded begrudgingly. "I will undo my claim on her and use my power to save her life instead."

"But you would endure, long past her lifespan," Elhani interjected. "There is much pain that comes with being an Immortal. Generations will rise and fall, and you will live on. You will be there to comfort the dying in their final moments and usher them into the afterlife, including the ones you love. Yet you would remain here, long after you bid every soul you know goodbye, until the world at last ends and even Immortals must depart. You would endure lifetimes without Lo."

My throat tightened with a new sort of sorrow, but still…

"And your water magic," Elhani continued gently. His eyes lingered on my pendant. "It is tied to your mortal life, and therefore, it would no longer be a part of you."

I swallowed, dread joining the ache building in my chest. "And would I be forced to…*serve* Nesrelle? Like one of her soldiers?"

Elhani shook his head. "You would have your own will, as she has hers. She would have the power to torment you, to wreak havoc on mortals that would break your heart, but you would have the power to defy her. You would be equals, locked in a battle of wills." His mouth twisted in a wistful smile. "There is little joy for you on this path."

And yet, there was no other path for me. Elhani's expression showed me that he knew it too.

I'd pledged myself, every part of my soul, my future, to Lo. I'd never imagined that my future could extend forever, that I could live long past her memory had vanished from this earth. But I wouldn't—couldn't—let this be her end. She had an entire life left to live, whether or not she could spend that life with me.

I'd promised her everything, so everything was exactly what I would give her.

CHAPTER FIFTY-SEVEN

Kovi

A S SOON AS CAESIEM ACCEPTED Nesrelle's deal, Elhani stepped forward, laying a hand on Caesiem's head. There was no visible difference in the young man, aside from his cringe of pain as the change was made. Satisfied, Nesrelle laid her own slender hand on Lo's wound, and everyone froze, watching spellbound as Lo's skin knit back together.

"It may take a while for her to wake," Elhani explained. He nodded toward Karos, who shuffled forward at his silent command. "But she will be safe here." His eyes flicked to Nesrelle, who sneered. The black dragon shifted, the red scales and spikes highlighting his back catching the cold light pouring in from the broken ceiling. He curled up around Lo, settling his head beside hers with a sigh.

"What about…Pauni'a?" Jalie's voice was strained. She didn't know the girl well, but I knew she'd come to respect her in the short while she'd known her.

Elhani studied Jalie regretfully. "I'm sorry, but Pauni'a can't be brought back. It was her time, and once a soul is called to the afterlife, it cannot be undone." His eyes turned to Lo. "Not like others, who are taken before their time."

Tears shimmered in Jalie's eyes, and she leaned her head on my shoulder.

Elhani placed his hand on Pauni'a's small form, and a warm radiance filled the air, like a golden light shimmering and dancing around us, one I couldn't see…only feel. Snatches of that beautiful, magical song I'd come to know so well wafted past. A sense of peace seeped deep into my bones, reassuring me that the nun's soul had entered the Golden After. My heart ached for Lo and the great losses she would wake to, but it rejoiced for her friend, who had found home and rest at last.

"Well," Nesrelle said impatiently, tossing a cruel glance toward Jalie and me, "I think you have a battle to return to." With a smirk, her cold eyes darted to Caesiem, who looked…dazed. Pained. "And you have many dead to tend to."

The Teramese man knelt beside Lo's body, her chest already rising and falling steadily. He pressed a tender kiss to her forehead, a terrible sorrow reflected in his ocean blue eyes. When he glanced up, those eyes met mine for one instant, and I realized all my earlier distrust of him had been ill-founded. A new respect blossomed in me instead, now that I had seen what lengths he would go to protect and care for Lo.

Then he vanished, as swiftly as the Dark Immortal herself disappeared.

Elhani raised his sword, a stern look in his eyes. "To battle," he said, and there was no ignoring the command in those words.

With Nesrelle's army abandoning the fight, the Teramese, even with their greater numbers, couldn't withstand us for long—not with our magic and our dragons. Jalie and I rode astride Ryke, sweeping through the city to defend our army and push back the Teramese. Elhani wound his way through the streets on foot, radiating power and strengthening our magic. Even mine felt restored, fully returned despite Sephrode's efforts to drain me.

Many Teramese, seeing their allies retreating, began to throw down their own weapons. By the time Jalie and I landed Ryke on a street where General Ilowhe was fighting, Jozek landed beside us, with Vander on his back. "Emperor Revaed is dead!" he shouted. "Surrender!"

A large number of soldiers backed away, laying down their weapons in the muddy street and raising their hands in surrender. Without their leader, they seemed lost, purposeless. Perhaps many of them felt that trying to regain control of the capital was futile. Maybe they hoped we would be merciful if they cooperated with us, and that we would send help to their suffering land.

After all, they didn't want to die. They'd come to Alrenor to fight for survival.

Of course, every battle had stubborn soldiers, ones who continued to fight no matter what, and those we faced for long, exhausting hours. With the help of Ryke, Jalie and I made as powerful of a team as we had during the battle for Wynlaen. This time, she fueled us with courage, directing her dragon to plow through enemies while she swung her blade with fierce grace. Thankfully, I didn't need to use my commanding magic, didn't need to taste the deaths of my enemies.

Vander continued to circle through the city, flying low for his shouts to be heard over the chaos of the fighting. "The emperor is dead!"

When a Teramese general approached, surrendering directly to General Ilowhe himself, the number of resisting enemy soldiers dwindled to nothing. As I glanced up at the sky, paling to grey with the approaching dawn, I realized the battle was over. We had won.

With a tired laugh, Jalie twisted in the saddle and threw her arms around my neck. The city was ours.

CHAPTER FIFTY-EIGHT

Caesiem

WHEN ELHANI PLACED HIS HAND on me, making me immortal and rending my human magic from my body, I felt the loss intensely, like my soul had been cloven in two, or my heart had been shredded inside my chest.

The call of death had been immediate too, the burning need to be where the dying were, to tend to their souls. Closing my eyes, the act of traveling elsewhere with a mere thought, the way Nesrelle could, had been instinctual.

Now, I stood in the very courtyard where Revaed had died to save my life, staring at his empty form. I could sense his soul the way I'd once sensed the water. Restless, prepared to leave the motionless husk his body had become and enter the afterlife.

"Lovely, isn't it?" Materializing beside me, Nesrelle sucked in a deep breath, grinning wickedly. "The smell of all this death. The misery that surrounds these lost souls. I wish I could leave them trapped here forever, so I could feed on it always."

I shot her a glare as I stepped toward my guardian's body. "You will not touch him," I snarled. "He's mine to send on."

Nesrelle huffed. "As if I mind. You're more miserable than he is now, and the effort of saying goodbye and letting him go will only cost you more. I'll enjoy this, immensely, just as I'd expected." She waved elegant hands around the courtyard grandly, as if gesturing toward a stage rather than a battlefield of corpses. "An eternity of your heart aching and grieving as you try to comfort the dying, all the while knowing you can't save them. Your job is only to send them on, no matter how sudden or cruel their deaths seem." Her eyes pierced into me. "No matter how *close* you are to the dead or dying, you'll have to say goodbye, and then endure, on and on."

I scowled. "Is that what happened to you? You lost all traces of your humanity and became…*this*…after losing everyone you ever loved?"

Nesrelle laughed. "You say that as if you think I'm diminished. I'm better than I ever was, as a mortal or as an Immortal before I found the freedom in embracing human suffering." She shrugged. "Who knows? Maybe instead of festering in your own tragedy, someday in all these long years, you'll realize this power is better than any mortal love could ever be."

Kneeling beside Revaed, brushing locks of hair away from his face until it was neater, the way he'd preferred it in life, I shook my head. "Nesrelle, for being an Immortal, you're a fool."

She was silent as I concentrated on my new power, letting myself sense Revaed's soul, pulsing with life. Tears burned my throat at this silent reminder that my guardian still existed, still continued on even as he left mortal life behind. Even as I was forced to say goodbye.

It would be the first of countless goodbyes, I knew.

"Caes, I'm so sorry."

If I hadn't sensed Revaed's spirit behind me, hadn't practically felt the heartbreak and regret emanating from him, I might have started. Grateful we had this last chance to speak, I turned away from his body to face his spirit. To my eyes, it appeared much as his body had in life, unwounded and pristine, with every hair in place and each button of his jacket polished just the way he liked it.

His violet eyes were the same too, lined with silver tears.

"I should have listened to you." Revaed hung his head. "I hope you know that…I never would have hurt you."

I blinked back the tears burning my own eyes. "I know."

"I'm so sorry, Caes," he whispered again.

Standing, I approached his soul, setting my hand on his shoulder, finding it…surprisingly solid and warm. Choking back the urge to sob, I threw my arms around him, and he pulled me into a hug, his own body shaking with sorrow.

"I'm sorry too," I managed, burying my face in his jacket. I felt like a boy again, lost and alone and afraid, with only Revaed showing me kindness. He'd become like a father to me, and then a best friend, and finally, a brother. He'd made mistakes, but so had I, our lives darkened with grief and tragedy, pain and regret, twisted choices and manipulative influences. His father had played a role in both our suffering.

But instead of escaping the imperator like we'd hoped, we'd both become like him, terrorizing the citizens of this empire, thinking only of our people's survival.

At last, I pulled back, brushing away my tears and steeling myself. Meeting my guardian's eyes one last time, I drew on the new magic I'd been given, on my power to command Revaed's soul into the afterlife, where I prayed he'd find peace and happiness at last.

"I forgive you, Revaed. You'll always be family."

Closing his eyes, Revaed drew in a deep breath, as if he could feel my forgiveness wash over him. His form faded around the ages, gradually at first, and then swiftly, until I blinked, and he was gone.

Grief and loss punched me in the gut all over again, and I nearly buckled over. "Be at peace, Revaed," I murmured, glancing at the distant stars, wondering just what his welcome into the afterlife was like.

Would he find his mother waiting for him? I hoped so.

Elhani, I thought, *if this new power you've given me means anything, please give him peace.*

Nesrelle snorted, plucking my attention back to her, where she hovered on the courtyard's edge, dismissing souls from other corpses. My stomach roiled as I imagined the manner in which she would do it, scornfully, hatefully. I hoped whatever pain she brought the Teramese man she was leering over quickly abated when his soul found its way into the afterlife.

In a blink, I was standing in front of her, shoving her aside before she could reach for the next Teramese body. "I will send these ones off," I said, my voice a rumbling threat, even if it was still raw from crying.

Nesrelle hissed, more animal-like than human. Then she smiled, the twist of her lips slow and taunting. "Your misery is intoxicating," she mused. "Was it difficult, saying goodbye?"

"You can feed on my sorrow for an eternity," I spat, resting my hand on the next body, "and you can mock me about every mortal I am forced to part with, about the magic and the life that I miss, but I will defy you at every turn. If you want to torment me, so be it. I'll torment you in return."

Nesrelle's eyes flashed, bright and angry. When I was a mere man, my threats had been empty. I couldn't hurt her, couldn't scare her. But now, as I poured every ounce of my hatred in my glare, I saw the moment regret seeped into the Dark Immortal's eyes.

"I may have lost much today, but you have too," I continued, peacefully dismissing the Teramese woman's soul with a thought. "At every turn, I'll be comforting and encouraging the dying and the dead. I'll be taking their misery, weakening you. Every time you plot against mortals, trying to stir up chaos and death, I'll use my power to counter you. I'll be the constant ache in your side, the eternal knife point at your throat."

She swallowed.

"You didn't win, Nesrelle," I said, standing and approaching her until I was a mere breath away.

She flinched but covered it quickly with a smirk that didn't reach her cold eyes.

"You've already done your worst to me," I continued, "but now you'll see the worst I can do to you."

CHAPTER FIFTY-NINE

Kovi

MANY WEARY DAYS FOLLOWED THE battle, full of endless discussions and negotiations with the Teramese, some of whom had agreed to retreat to Teramyl, hoping for mercy from their High Imperator. Upon our invitation, however, many chose to stay, wanting to start a new life in Alrenor. General Ilowhe, the Elha'tonu Elders, and I sat in these discussions with Jalie, drafting an official treaty. Many more hours were spent laying the foundation for a new government, one in which Jalie ruled alongside a council of advisors composed of Alrenians and Forwyn, such as General Ilowhe and Meli.

With much of the city destroyed, camps were constructed, and citizens were assigned to share surviving buildings. We organized teams to rebuild homes and businesses. The palace itself needed repairs too, though there were enough livable spaces for Jalie, her new council, and me to take up residence in the meantime.

All the while, Lo lay recovering in one of the undamaged rooms of the palace, closely tended by healers. General Ilowhe barely left her side, sleeping in a chair by her bed each night to keep vigil over her. Not a day passed without Caesiem slipping in, melting out of the shadows like a thief or a spirit. Always checking on her, always reassuring himself she was safe and recovering. He could never linger long though, not in the wake of so much recent death. Whispers throughout the palace, fueled by those who'd witnessed him on the battlefield with the dying, called him by the name Nesrelle had first bestowed: the Prince of Death. Unlike with the Dark Immortal, though, no fear accompanied those whispers, only wonder and perhaps a measure of pity for those who knew exactly how much the young man had sacrificed.

Though Karos couldn't fit within the palace, we let him sit outside the open window of Lo's rooms often, his golden eyes watching over her. His silent vigils were as regular and faithful as Caesiem's.

Meanwhile, we cleared out the Keep for our dragons and the newly returned hatchlings, and we made plans to send back the Misrothian beasts to our northern allies. Vander insisted that arrangements could be made to bring more eggs from Teramyl to restore our dragon population, claiming there were egg hunters he could contact without dealing with the High Imperator.

Jalie offered Mhel, Huvoki, and Mio'e positions as Dragon Keepers, asking them to work with the hatchlings, and all three gladly accepted. Oru was instated as part of Jalie's personal guard.

With each step toward a new future, toward peace and unity and freedom like my people had never known, the ache in my chest grew. It was a tangle of joy and grief, from the pain of not having Rhi'il and Marukio and so many others here to see our success, and from the wonder of being able to spend each day at Jalie's side. My dreams that had seemed so impossible were becoming reality. The darkness that had haunted Jalie's days was giving way to the new rhythm we'd found, full of bringing our city back to life and setting new precedents and laws. It was a path forward that wouldn't be easy—there were deep prejudices that wouldn't be uprooted overnight—but it was bright and hopeful.

One evening, as the sun painted the sky in shades of scarlet and gold, Jalie and I walked through the grounds after another long day of meetings and work in the city. The garden was a far cry from the vibrant refuge it had once been, but there were some trees and flowers that had miraculously survived, hardy plants that hadn't been in the flames' paths. They added splashes of unexpected color amongst the greys and blacks of the ashy earth.

"She'd probably hate me," Jalie said wistfully, gazing out at the sun sinking beyond the city, dipping into the sparkling Alrenian.

I didn't need to ask who she meant. Her mother.

Pulling Jalie into my arms and relishing her warmth, I kissed the top of her head. "Does that bother you?"

For a long moment, Jalie considered, her gold-flecked eyes distant, the breeze tugging on the loose strands of hair framing her face. I tucked one behind her ear almost absent-mindedly, though I still hadn't quite grown accustomed to the fact that she was mine, that I could casually touch her like this whenever I wanted. Holding her in my arms still felt like a miracle in these simple, quiet moments.

"No," Jalie said at last, meeting my gaze. "It doesn't, not anymore. Not when it means you're here with me." She tangled her fingers in mine. "And you'll really stay here, in the palace, even when the rebuilding is finished, and the world settles into…whatever new normalcy the future holds?"

I pressed a kiss to her scarred cheek. "I'm not going anywhere," I promised.

CHAPTER SIXTY

Lo

I WOKE WITH PEACEFUL, VIBRANT dreams already fading from my mind the moment I opened my eyes. Try as I might, I couldn't hold onto more than snippets—a fragrant garden full of buzzing bees, flittering butterflies, and my mother's carefree, musical laughter. Edi's warm embrace, strong and comforting, as he reminded me how much he loved me. Naina touching the gold ribbon in my braid, a tender smile on her wrinkled face. Eloiyah singing a song about home. Pauni'a, squeezing my hand and telling me to live for her, to live for all of them.

For a few seconds, I was bewildered as I scanned the room. The bed I lay in was soft and vast, and the rooms themselves were cozy and plush. If the carved posts on my bedframe and the simple elegance of the rest of the furniture hadn't given it away, the Alrenian swirling sun insignia decorating the rug would have. I was in the palace, in quarters that hadn't been destroyed. They weren't as grand as some I'd seen, but that made them homier.

Father sat dozing in a chair at my bedside, his expression so peaceful it brought a grin to my face.

A great shadow blocked the golden light spilling in through an open window, and when I turned my head, I found Karos staring back at me, snorting eagerly and pressing his snout against the pane until he fogged up the glass.

Laughing, I sat up, surprised at how energized and refreshed I felt.

The sound jolted my father awake. He sat up, staring at the sight of me sitting up in bed. "Lo!"

He wrapped me in a hug so fierce that tears filled my eyes.

My brain tried to recall the events of the battle—I'd been in a battle, hadn't I? The nymphs, Nesrelle's taunting voice, *pain...*

A door creaked open and two figures emerged from the sitting room, surprise widening their eyes when they found me awake. Jalie and Kovi, the former clothed in a flowing linen dress adorned with green dragon scales that matched Ryke, and the latter in a fresh Aerekni uniform.

Father pulled back from me, clasping my hand instead as he returned to his seat.

"Wh—what happened?" I asked, finding my voice raspy from disuse.

"You've been asleep for days," Jalie said.

"We were worried about you," Father murmured.

"But we won. The city is ours," Kovi interjected, his calm voice reassuring.

I glanced around the room again, sorrow stabbing through me when I noticed the absence of the one person I'd expected to see first. "But...?" My voice trailed off as fear assaulted me.

Grief etched lines in Jalie's brow. She approached my bed, taking my free hand in a surprisingly soft gesture. Together, she and Father told me everything.

When they'd finished and my tears came, I was even more startled to feel her arms sweeping around me, joining my father's as they pulled me into a hug. To feel their bodies tremble as they cried with me.

It was dusk when Caesiem entered my rooms, appearing from the shadows as suddenly as Nesrelle once had. His eyes met mine immediately, and all the angry, hurt words I'd wanted to say melted off my tongue. There was such vast sorrow in his expression, an endless loneliness and loss I couldn't begin to understand, that I realized his sacrifice was far greater than mine would ever be.

"You're awake," he whispered.

Tears burned my eyes as I pulled myself from the armchair I'd been resting in, staring into the fire I'd needed on this chilly autumn night. After spending most of the day in my room, Father, Jalie, and Kovi had finally left me so I could have time alone with Caesiem.

Throwing the book I'd been pretending to read aside, I threw myself into Caesiem's arms.

"How could you?" I choked out between my sobs.

Caesiem's body trembled against mine. "How could I not?" he murmured. He brushed a tear from my cheek and drew back to study my face.

I pressed my forehead to his, basking in his presence, even as I was keenly aware of how fleeting our time was. The dead would always be calling to him. He would be constantly pulled away, never able to linger here for long. And…

"Your magic," I whispered. I'd noticed an absence when I'd woken, my new connection to the water gone, but I hadn't wanted to believe it.

Caesiem grinned, a dimple forming in one cheek. "Immortals have even greater powers," he said with mock arrogance, but it couldn't conceal the brokenness in his eyes. They were the color of the ocean he loved so much and would never be bound to again, not in the way he had been in his mortal life. If even I, who'd only had that water magic for a short while, experienced emptiness at its loss, I couldn't imagine how vast his was.

Another tear spilled down my cheek. "I wanted more for us than this," I confessed. "I wanted a home with you, a life together. A family."

I stifled another sob. "More time to keep you all to myself."

Tugging me against him, Caesiem kissed me fiercely, his mouth passionate and warm and defiant. "I was a thief, remember?" he said. "I'll steal moments like this. Nothing in this world can keep me from you. We'll make time and find home whenever we're together."

Words failed me, so I pulled his face toward mine and kissed him again, relishing in every touch, every moment. I would make the most of every instant we stole.

I knew there would be far too few of them.

EPILOGUE

Lo

Several Months Later

FATHER'S SMILE WAS AS BRIGHT as the spring sunlight filling my rooms with its buttery glow when he stepped through the doorway, taking in my formal attire. For Jalie's coronation this evening, I'd dressed in a sleek black gown, adorned only with a few dragon scales of red and black, scales Karos had shed.

My dark outfit contrasted with the riot of colors woven around my braids—gold for my lost loved ones, black for the pain endured and overcome, white for the woman I had become, violet for the many acts of service I'd completed, as a nun and now as an advisor and councilmember, and orange for my loyalty to my people. Lastly, there was a new color—a vibrant blue the same color as the ocean, the same shade as Caesiem's eyes. It was my constant reminder of my vows to him, my way to keep him close even when he was distant.

O'emia herself had braided and decorated my hair on her visit today, during which she'd updated me on the repairs being made to the abbey, the new sisters that had been recruited, and the different ways in which the nuns had been contributing to the recovery work in the capital.

"You may not be a nun anymore, with your new home and new

life," she'd said as she'd prepared to say goodbye, her dark eyes solemn. "But you'll always be our sister, Lo. *My* sister."

I pulled her into an embrace, thanking her profusely. Her regular visits had become a balm in these lonely months, full of great hope but also deep grief. We'd mourned Naina and our lost sisters together, and I'd told her about my story with Caesiem and his sacrifice. I'd explained how Elhani's mark traced the skin over my heart, forever reminding me that even now, when we were forced to spend more time apart than together, we were bound.

"Thank you, Emi," I'd whispered. "Thank you for being my sister."

She'd laughed and gently pushed me away. "I appreciate the hug, but I don't want to ruin your hair." She brushed a braid over my shoulder. "I'm proud of you." With a wink, she was gone.

Now, Father stood in the entrance to my bedroom, his eyes misty. He was clothed in a pristine Aerekni Academy uniform, medals of honor on his shoulders. He cut the perfect picture of a victorious general.

He echoed the same sentiment that O'emia had. "I'm so proud of you, daughter," he murmured, striding forward to draw me into his embrace.

I relished the comfort of his arms, the familiar sensation of belonging and being home. He'd returned to the academy to train future soldiers, guards, and Dragon Keepers, but as he was also part of the new Alrenian Council, he lived in quarters within the palace, near my own. It meant we'd had plenty of time together even during these busy months, quiet moments to share our stories of Mother and Edi. Moments in which I'd shared more about Caesiem, helping him get to know the man I'd fallen in love with. A man that Father could no longer deny was worthy of me—not when he'd learned all Caesiem had sacrificed.

Stepping back, I grinned. "Don't make me cry now," I teased. "Emi just finished applying enough cosmetics for the empress herself on my face."

Father laughed.

"Speaking of," I added, "I need to help Jalie get ready."

With a smile, Father offered me his arm. "Then let me escort you. I can tell you all about my newest students and you can tell me about the Circle of Serenity's latest work on the way."

Jalie

I stared into my mirror as Lo threaded pearls and Ryke's emerald dragon scales through my hair before weaving it back into a single cascading braid. She left room for the crown that would later be placed upon my head.

Most of Mother's possessions had been ransacked when the Teramese took the palace and likely rested at the bottom of the sea, but I hadn't been upset to discover that her headdress was also missing. With the start of a new government in which the imperial throne worked alongside a full Council, and the beginning of a future in which Forwyn, Alrenian, and even Teramese lived peacefully together, it seemed fitting to wear something different. I'd requested a simple gold crown, light enough to rest upon my head without feeling extravagant.

I didn't need extravagance these days.

Lo's green-flecked eyes met mine in the mirror, her expression thoughtful. Her black dress was understated, but its simplicity only emphasized her natural beauty. When I looked at her now, there wasn't an ounce of hate or anger left in my heart. I didn't see an enemy, or my mother's killer. I only saw a friend, a woman who'd stood by my side fighting fiercely for our people. A woman who wanted what was best for Alrenor…and even for me.

I saw a friend.

Slowly, she withdrew a rich gold ribbon from her pocket and held it up. "I thought maybe you would want to wear this today," she explained. "I could add it to your braid."

I raised my eyebrows. "I thought that was a Forwyn custom."

"Why can't it be an Alrenian custom, for all of us?" she asked gently. "We all lost so much, and I know you're grieving. Gold is a way to respect and remember the dead."

My throat was thick. "So many people died because of me, but they were strangers."

Lo shook her head. "That doesn't take away your pain. Their deaths were Nesrelle's fault, not yours, but you can still honor them."

A smile pulled at my lips, tentative at first. "Yes, I'd like to wear it."

When Lo finished securing it around my braid, the deep gold contrasting with the pale blonde of my hair, she extended her hand to help me off the bench and away from my vanity. My ivory skirts swished around my ankles as I stood, drawing a deep breath.

"You look like an empress," Lo observed with a smirk.

I laughed. "You don't look too bad yourself."

Her expression turned serious. "Are you ready?"

I'd waited years for this day. Dreamt of it. Longed for it. Today, it looked very different from how I'd once imagined it, but that only made it more precious. More perfect.

"Yes."

With a final wish for good luck, Lo left, likely to rejoin her father and accompany him to the ceremony.

I took a few more moments to collect myself, gazing out my windows at the afternoon light slowly fading toward evening. At last, I approached my door, swinging it open to find Kovi already waiting in the hallway. Dressed in an Aerekni uniform, he was as beautiful as ever, his crooked smile my favorite sight. His molten eyes swept over me, making my stomach swoop.

Kovi's grin widened playfully as he leaned in and whispered.

"Fierce and clever and stunning."

He pulled me into his arms, pressing me against the wall, swallowing my gasp as his mouth devoured mine.

Several minutes later, we hurried through the palace grounds, running a little late to my own coronation. Ryke bounded toward us with a contented rumble in his chest, brushing his snout against my extended fingers and then walking alongside me.

"You would take him to Council meetings with you if you could," Kovi teased.

We rounded the final bend in the path toward the arena, the very place where Kovi and I had climbed onto Ryke's back the first time. The one that afforded us a perfect view of Inalgoth, even if the city was broken, the road to rebuilding long and arduous.

The crowd was full of both familiar and strange faces, from Elha'tonu Elders, who had gladly signed a new, formal alliance with Alrenor, to Forwyn and Alrenians and Teramese. My breathing quickened as a thrill swirled through me, mixing with my nerves. Not everyone in this empire loved me, and not everyone agreed with the changes that were occurring. There would be plenty of trials ahead. Plenty of challenging days.

But I was ready.

❧

Kovi

Jalie was radiant as she took her vows and accepted her crown, and she was radiant at the celebratory feast afterward, when I swept her across the pavilion floor in dance after dance. Eventually, though, she pressed a kiss to my cheek and told me she needed to mingle as an empress should, and I'd laughed and reluctantly let her leave my arms.

At one of the side tables, I collected a glass of wine and found General Ilowhe speaking with Lo, Mhel, Oru, and Huvoki.

"So," Huvoki began with a mischievous grin, "when can we begin calling you Emperor Elha'tonu?"

I elbowed him and rolled my eyes. "Jalie and I didn't think now was exactly the appropriate time to busy everyone with wedding plans. There's still so much ongoing work in the city," I said pointedly. "And there's still plenty of time for us to get to know one another, now that we're finally on the same side."

Lo clapped her hands together. "But it *is* happening. I knew it." She shot her father a look, as if they'd had a secret bet going on.

General Ilowhe sipped from his wine glass. "So we can assume it will probably happen within a year or two. Does that really mean you won?"

"Yes," Lo proclaimed proudly. "I've definitely won."

"Well congratulations," Mhel said, winking at me. "You proved us all wrong. She has fought hard for peace, and she truly does make you happy."

The general nodded, his expression solemn. "I never should have doubted you."

"Rhi'il would have been thrilled," Oru murmured. "And Marukio…"

Over the past several months, we'd swapped plenty of stories and relived endless memories of our lost friends. It was our way of comforting one another, of keeping Rhi'il, my cousin, and all the others we'd lost close.

I couldn't help the chuckle that escaped, even if a twinge of pain always accompanied thoughts of my best friend and my cousin. "Marukio would have wanted to be assigned as my personal guard, and Rhi'il would have been planning ways to prank all the councilmembers at the wedding."

We all laughed, even Lo, who had happily listened to us recount our tales. Just as we'd listened to her share stories about the sisters who'd died. Those moments helped brighten the days when grief weighed us down.

As the musicians launched into another song and couples filled the dance floor, swirling past us in colorful gowns and bright vests, I sighed. Relief and contentment flooded me. This was our first real celebration since the battle had ended. Despite the losses we'd sustained, despite the grief and the work ahead of us to rebuild cities throughout Alrenor and to convince the citizens to overcome their prejudice and hatred...we had reason to celebrate. We had a slice of peace and happiness, right here and now.

And somehow, impossibly, Jalie and I had a future.

Caesiem

One last sigh, and the woman fell still. My touch on her forehead was gentle, a comforting presence as her final moments passed and her soul pulled free of her body. I waited until her spirit dissipated, until there was nothing left of this Teramese woman but her empty corpse and the family that would grieve her.

This death was far more peaceful than most I'd witnessed in the past months. There had been so many casualties from the fighting in Alrenor, and then still more from a dragon attack in Teramyl. Others had died from starvation. And then, as the hybrid nymphs had retreated from Alrenor, some had infiltrated the palace in Vicidor and drained multiple mages, leaving them dead in their beds. And lastly, there had been a string of executions ordered by the High Imperator in a rage once soldiers began returning, defeated.

Each one of those deaths had broken me a little more. Elhani had spoken the truth when he'd warned me that there wouldn't be much joy for me in this life. The comfort I could offer the dying in their final moments didn't overcome the pain and guilt I felt for not being able to save them.

And yet...he had also been wrong, in a way. Now I had the constant pleasure of defying and weakening Nesrelle, of knowing the work I did helped the humans I would always care for. I would spend lifetimes protecting and defending them against her, forever enraging her. There was some joy and satisfaction in that.

I sensed death always, calling to me from every corner of the earth, urging me to send souls on their way. Each one that I reached before Nesrelle arrived was a victory—but that victory didn't take away how the constant sorrows and regrets of those souls ate away at me. It didn't assuage my pain over losing Revaed, or my grief in being parted so often from Lo.

And always, always, there was that empty corner of my heart my water magic had once occupied.

I left the dead woman behind, and in a blink, I was standing on the shore of the Terebrys, letting the waves wash over my feet. In my mind, I called to the water, but there was no answer. I lifted my hand, imagining the sparkling element rising to meet me, but nothing happened. The thunder of the waves was a discordant rhythm, no longer matching the beating of my pulse.

Undoing the leather cord around my neck, I lifted the pendant that I'd carried with me for so long, studying it. Though with my loss of water magic, Lo no longer possessed any either, I had a suspicion the pendant might still defend her. Perhaps, if Lo ever found herself tossed into a roaring sea, Sephrode would sense the magic in the pendant and protect her again. I slipped it into my pocket.

With a final breath of briny air to fill my lungs, I thought of Vander, and I left Teramyl behind.

When I blinked, I found myself on a different beach, studying the

Great Sea beneath glistening starlight. Distant strains of music and laughter trailed on the breeze, reminding me that Jalie's coronation had been this evening.

As strongly as the dying souls called to me these days, urging me to them, I felt that same pull toward Lo. Just the knowledge that she was near filled me with an overwhelming need to go to her.

But the sight of my friend standing on the beach held me back, just for a little while. I needed to speak with him.

Vander turned when I took a step closer, spinning to face me. His silver eyes widened, and I wondered what he saw. The same man who had been his friend, or a stranger? A ghost?

"Caesiem," he said, dipping his head, his smile tight and sad. "I didn't want to believe anyone when they told me what happened."

I shoved my hands into my pockets to avoid my old mortal habit of fidgeting. Now, it was easier to be still, but sometimes my body recalled those days and tried to tap out beats to songs I'd played and sang. "Where's Tayla?"

Vander nodded toward the party. "I…had a feeling I might see you around, near the water," he explained. "It's what I hoped for. She understood that I needed a moment to speak with you alone."

"Teramyl is suffering," I said, voice low.

Vander frowned. "Should I return?"

I shook my head. "No, the work you're doing here in helping the Teramese who've stayed settle into Alrenor…it's also important."

"Someday, I'll have to return…no matter the consequences," Vander responded, gazing out at the sea. The wind picked up.

I sighed. "I would like to say the High Imperator wouldn't harm one of his own mages, but I don't know anymore."

"I'll do whatever it takes to help our people and end his reign," Vander promised, his gaze solemn. "After I finish your work of rebuilding here."

"Thank you." I dipped my head. "Thank you for doing what I

cannot." I swallowed, hating the way my voice broke on that last word.

Vander hesitated, sadness glistening in his eyes. "Visit when you can, all right? I've missed you." His gaze flicked over my shoulder, back toward the party. "But I'm sure right now, you want to return to your wife." He smiled in understanding.

My wife. I loved those words, even if they also brought an ache with them, a constant reminder that I'd be forever torn in different directions, never able to settle down with her to a normal, mortal life. And then, the thought of having to endure while I watched time leave its cruel mark on her, whittling away her years, stealing her youth and eventually her life, was almost too much to bear.

More than once, Lo had insisted we'd find a way out of my bargain.

"That would end in you dying all over again," I'd argued, but she was stubborn, certain there was a different solution. I hadn't had the heart to take away her hope by sharing my doubts.

Now, I could sense her presence, leaving the party and entering the courtyard outside her rooms. Pacing. Waiting.

She, like Vander, expected me tonight.

Lo

The party had left me feeling lonely, so I'd given my excuses and slipped away, hoping I'd find Caesiem elsewhere. It'd been a week since I'd last seen him, and I knew that meant there had been a lot of death recently. Death that weighed on him.

Not for the first time, I prayed and pleaded with Elhani. Caesiem had insisted it was in vain, but I had to cling to a thread of hope that maybe my husband's bargain could be undone. That this wasn't our destiny.

For a while, I paced the courtyard restlessly, studying the stars that Caesiem had once pointed out to me. Memories of his warm kiss and his declaration that I was his home made tears pool in my eyes. Frustrated, I blinked them away.

When I glanced up, I saw a familiar figure in the shadows of the courtyard's far corner, and my heart leapt into my throat. My entire body came alive in anticipation. Despite all that was wrong, in these fleeting, perfect moments, everything was right.

My gaze fastened on his bright blue eyes. A smile tugged at his lips, bringing his dimples to life.

He slipped from the darkness like a thief in the night. Like we were still a pair of vigilantes forced to sneak around the city in the shadows. Back then, we'd been forbidden. In a way, it felt like we still were.

I broke into a run, my sandals beating a rhythm on the cobblestones. But this time, I wasn't fleeing anything, wasn't trying to escape my past. I was running toward a future, however imperfect it was. Toward home.

THE END

NOTE FROM THE AUTHOR

Thank you for reading *Empire of Ruins*! If you have a moment, please leave an HONEST review on Amazon.

KEEP READING FOR A SNEAK PEEK AT WHAT RACHEL L. SCHADE HAS COMING NEXT…

ACKNOWLEDGMENTS

For some reason, I'm always intimidated by this part of book writing. I think it's because there will never feel like an adequate number of words to thank all the people in my life for their support and encouragement and assistance in making my dreams come true. And also because I'm always scared of leaving someone out, because there are so many people who contribute in so many ways to the production of a book—let alone an entire series.

To Sheree Whitelock and T.M. Ghent for being my alphas: thank you for reading through my sloppy first draft and enduring all those "[NAME]s" and other obnoxious insertions because I took forever naming some characters and locations. And Drafting Rachel just got lazy. (I was annoyed with her too.) You both have contribute so much to shaping this series, and words cannot express how much that has meant to me.

To Julienne Calhoun and Malcolm Carter, for always being a listening ear as I share and vent about my books and ideas. Your support and belief in me over the years is a treasure.

To my husband, for loving me even though I *did* kill the dragons.

To my betas: Erin, Rai Larsen, and Maren Bivar Letemple: thank you for being my early guinea pigs and for so willingly sharing all your feelings about this book!

To my street team: K.B. Benson, Amanda Chaperon, Erin, T.M. Ghent, Tralyn Hughes, Alex Larsen, Taylor Lust, Alyssa Marie, Courtney Millecam, Leah Salinsky, Sara Smith, Hannah Stansel, and Meaghan Swanson—thanks so much for being my hype team, the ones always cheering me on, sharing about my books, and keeping me motivated and excited through the ups and downs of writing and publishing. This has been such an adventure, and I'm so happy to be able to call you my team and also my friends. Thanks for being along for the ride!

To my readers: thanks for taking a chance on my books and me, whether you stumbled upon them while scrolling on Amazon, discovered me making a fool of myself on social media and decided to also read my books, or a friend recommended my works. Thank you for falling in love with my characters and my world with me. I appreciate it more than you know.

And thank you to God, for gifting me the ability to write and share the stories of my heart.

Prepare to enter a world of Fae, romance, forbidden magic, and ghosts…

Pride and Prejudice meets the Gothic vibes of Jane Eyre and the arranged marriage trope in Schade's next work.

TITLE, COVER ART, AND RELEASE DATE TO COME

Want to stay up to date on all the latest news?
You can visit **www.rachelschadeauthor.com** to sign up for Schade's newsletter, or follow her on Instagram and TikTok:
@rachelschadeauthor

Eager to return to the world of *Cursed Empire*? Check out Schade's other series set in the same world, *Silent Kingdom,* following Halia's adventures, and stay tuned for more news on future works set in this world as well…

ABOUT THE AUTHOR

Rachel L. Schade was born on the first day of summer in a small town in Michigan. She attended The Ohio State University to learn how to write obnoxiously long papers, cite people who use big words, and discuss her passion: books. She has a great love for the color blue, sunshine, chocolate, and not folding her laundry. Currently she lives with her husband and fur babies and surrounds herself with books and coffee on a regular basis.

You can email Rachel at **rachelschade@gmail.com**, or find her on Facebook and Goodreads: Rachel L. Schade, and on Instagram: @rachelschadeauthor.

www.rachelschadeauthor.com